When Fate Isn't Enough

Isabelle Richards

Emilie,
XOXO
Isabelle Richards

Editor: Cassie Cox

Cover Design: Regina Wamba

Cover Models: Max Gust and Hannah Peltier

Books by Isabelle Richards

When Fates Collide

When Fate Isn't Enough

When Fates Align

Hate to Love You

Love to Hate You

Dedication

To my mother,

for always being there

for me through the turbulence

and chaos of my crazy adventures.

Chapter One

I used to think dating the hottest man in the room would be amazing—that I would revel in being the envy of other women. All the mean girls in my life could finally suck it.

During my eight-hour flight to London, I learn that dating the sexiest man on the plane is nothing but trouble. Every time I run to the restroom, I come back to a flight attendant or female passenger batting her overly mascaraed eyes at him or pushing her cleavage in his face. By the third hour, I'm *so* over it. Gavin and I started our relationship under unusual circumstances, so I'm used to it just being the two of us held captive somewhere. That's shielded me from the piranhas in push-up bras.

I can't say I blame them. Gavin Edwards may be one

of the sexiest men to walk the earth. He has dark blond hair and chiseled features. He's kept his body in pristine condition since his days as a model. In fact, his body may actually be better now. But his most striking feature is his eyes. He should have to register those baby blues as weapons. Once I'm caught in those azure pools, I turn to mush and will do anything he asks. Such an unfair advantage.

"Oxford, tell me that it's not always going to be like this," I say when I sink into my seat after a trip to the bathroom.

"Like what?"

His hypnotizing blue eyes make me think for a second that he might not actually know the impact he has on women. But then he flashes me that "you'll be putty in my hands" smile, and I remember that he knows exactly what he's doing.

"Like this," I gesture toward the flight attendant. "Women throwing themselves at you all the time. This trip is supposed to be an escape from stress. If I have to be on hussy-watch every time we go to the grocery store or take the dog to the vet, I may lose my mind."

"I don't have a dog," he retorts.

"But maybe we'll get one, and if we do, clearly we'll need to get a male vet because if we get a woman vet, she may want to play doctor with you instead."

"You're positively adorable when you're jealous."

I snatch the bag of peanuts off of his tray. Oh, honey roasted. I adore first class. "It isn't really jealousy as much as pity. They're so pathetic, and I just don't think I can stand to watch it day in and day out. Take Double D over there. Does she really think that if she undoes one more button, you're going to leave the woman in your lap to go join the Mile High club?"

Gavin laughs and starts to say something, but I interrupt him. "If you're already a member of the Mile High club, I don't want to know."

That only makes him laugh harder. I love to watch him smile.

He twists a lock of my long blonde hair, seductively flashing those eyes at me. "Has it really been that terrible?" he asks.

"Yes. We've lost so much time together. After all I've been through, I think I deserve your undivided attention."

He unbuckles his seatbelt and stands. "Stand up," he orders.

"Why?"

He gently tugs on my elbow. "Stand *up!* Stop being difficult."

I stand and roll my eyes at him. "I'm standing, now what?"

He leans in and gives me the kiss to top all other kisses. The kind of kiss that leaves you dizzy, breathless and desperate for more. I can almost hear jaws dropping and drool forming puddles on the floor.

When he finally breaks away he winks at me. "That

should solve that problem, luv." He sits and resumes working on his laptop, as though he didn't just kiss me stupid. "Oh," he continues. "In case there was ever a doubt, you've always had my undivided attention."

I can feel my face flush as I sink into my chair. "I feel like *I* should be asking you to join the Mile High club."

Gavin returns to his seat and refastens his seat belt. "If it weren't for that pesky heart problem you have, we would have."

I was recently kidnapped by a sociopath trying to find money that my late husband—may he rot in hell—stole from the Morelia Mexican drug cartel. In the end, I kicked the ever-loving crap out of my kidnapper and got away, but my heart did not escape unscathed. I now have to keep things sedate until I get the doctor's go ahead.

"So are you going to kiss me like this everywhere we go to ward off the gaggles of women trying to get in your pants?" I ask.

He brings my hand to his lips, then kisses the top. "If I have to. Lily, if it were up to me, I would retire, buy an island, and do nothing but naughty things to you all day long."

"Why can't we go with that plan? It sounds mighty good to me."

He cocks his head to the side, giving me a knowing glare. "You wanted to find yourself again, re-establish your identity, and be independent. You don't want me taking care of you, because you're perfectly capable of taking care of yourself. Does any of this sound familiar?"

He has me there. There's nothing worse than your own words coming back to bite you in the ass.

I met Gavin about four months ago when my husband and Gavin's wife were in a fatal, head-on collision. Due to my late husband's connection to the drug cartel, Gavin and I were placed in FBI protective custody for a while. I believe we have the worst possible answer to "How did you two meet?"

Gavin wanted to run off into the sunset, but I insisted that I needed time to get my life together and shake off all of the rust that had formed while I wasted away married to Ashton. Gavin had wanted to spoil me rotten and buy me everything my heart desired, and I insisted I needed to do things on my own. My life was a train wreck, but I sorted it out myself. I literally kicked ass and took names. I can walk with a bit more swagger now, and I know there isn't much I can't overcome.

"Well, can we do the whole island thing sometime? I mean, maybe you don't retire and buy the island, but can you rent it for a while?" I ask sheepishly. Normally I would've found some way to twist his words against him and give him a zinger, but all I can think about is him giving me a zinger! One kiss has me completely frazzled.

"Why, Lily Clark, you're positively randy, aren't you?" he says a bit too loudly. "You're blushing. You're just breathtaking when you blush." He kisses me again, but this time he isn't trying to show off. His kiss is soft and tender. "Have I told you how much I've missed you?"

"No, but you can."

He whispers sweet nothings into my ear until I fall asleep.

I'm woken by a hostile drink cart. The attendant's gotten the hint and doesn't hit on my boyfriend when she delivers his scotch, but she's a bit cranky now.

I feel a bit cranky when I hear some persistent giggling coming from a few rows over. I look over at two women pouring through tabloid magazines and looking over at Gavin. He has been on the covers of the gossip rags for weeks now. My kidnapping and rescue became big news, and the media loves putting Gavin's beautiful face in the center of it.

He shares this week's cover with Olivia Philips, Gavin's longtime friend who has been hoping for more. Depending on the cover, she's heartbroken, or they're secretly carrying on while I'm in a coma, or she's pregnant with his child. Where do they come up with this crap?

"Maybe you should go sign an autograph?" I say, nodding toward his fans. "I'd do anything to stop their girly squealing."

Not wanting to encourage them by looking, he continues to work on his laptop. "Just ignore it. I'm not that interesting. It will settle down," he says flatly.

"While we're on the subject, what are we going to do about Olivia? And by 'we,' I mean you."

He stops typing, and faces me. "I fired her. I've cut off all contact. I'm not sure what else needs to be done," he says. “I’m still not sure why she pulled all those stunts, but I don’t care to find out. I’ve cut her out of my life. Problem solved.”

I look down at my nails, which for once are actually manicured thanks to my hospital bed beauty treatments, courtesy of my best friend, Emily. “According to *US Weekly,* she’s having your child.”

“Yes, and John Lennon is alive and well—he was just captured by aliens. They’re looking for a story, and they’re going to print all sorts of things. You just have to learn to ignore it.”

“Hmm, so you say.”

He closes his laptop and returns it to his bag. “Is this a roundabout way to ask me if I slept with her?” he asks pointedly.

“No!” The truth is I’m dying to know more about his relationship with a woman he swears is “like a sister.”

“If you want to know, just ask,” he says as he lays his head back and closes his eyes.

I don’t want to give him the satisfaction of catching me in my passive-aggressive fact-finding scheme, but my curiosity outweighs my stubborn pride. “Okay, you’ve got me. It’s killing me not to know. So spill it.”

He chuckles, and I shoot him a dirty look. “I’m thrilled you find my insecurity so amusing.”

He takes the sleeping mask from my lap. “Insecurity is natural. The fact that you can’t just own up to it is what I find adorable.”

I wait for him to continue, but he goes back to trying to sleep.

After a minute or so, I hit him in the arm. "Out with it!"

He takes the mask off and looks at me. "No, I have never slept with O. Just the thought disturbs me. I've known her all of her life, and I've never seen her that way. She's dated several of my friends, including one of my best friends, and that's a line I won't cross. Moreover, she's a spoiled brat. I overlook it because she's like family, but I could never overlook it enough to be in a relationship with her. I know everyone thinks she pulled this crap because she's interested in me, but I don't buy it. I think there's more going on here."

"Like what?" I ask. "Her actions are pretty textbook for a mean girl who's after a guy."

"I'm not sure, but I don't think that's it. But I have no desire to find out. Like I said, she's out of my life." Clearly he has no understanding of crazy women. Cutting her off is only going to add fuel to the fire.

"So you say, but I don't think this is the last we'll hear from Ms. Philips. What about all of the other women you were spotted with while you were gallivanting around the world? Any of them I have to worry about?"

He scratches the sexy scruff that's filled in the last few days and groans. "Luv, we've been over this. I was on a business trip, not a dirty weekend. As I went to those events unaccompanied, I was often asked to escort the daughter or sister or niece of a client. Most of them were dreadful."

I tap my fingers on the arm rest between us. "You didn't sleep with *any* of them?"

"Bloody hell, woman," he growls. "How many times are we going to go over this?"

I see fury in his eyes, and if we weren't on a plane, I'm guessing he'd be shouting at me. Always the refined British gentleman, he doesn't want to make a scene.

"No," he says through gritted teeth. "I didn't sleep with anyone. I was forced into spending time with them for business, and that is all it was. *I* did not seek out those women, and *I* did not engage them. You have nothing to worry about, no matter how bad it looked in the papers."

I hold my hands up and shrink back in my seat, showing him I'm backing down. "Settle down. Don't get your knickers in a twist," I say. "I trust you. I know you never would've stuck around through all the hospital drama if you didn't truly care for me. But I feel like we need to clear the air so that there're no secrets. I didn't think you would sleep with someone else, but if I don't ask..."

He doesn't veil his hurt. "That's *not* trust. I've been nothing but direct and honest since the moment I met you. Does that count for anything? I won't lie to you, either straightforwardly or by omission. I'm not sure what else I can do to prove that to you."

I wince because he's right. Gavin is the most sincere, forthright person I've ever met. He always says what he means without games. So many of the important people in his life lied to him without hesitation. His parents.

Brooke.

Before I can respond, he says, "It's a whole industry created on embellishing facts and fabricating stories. Thousands of people make their living spinning fiction and calling it news, and it provides entertainment for the masses. It's hard to do, but you have to learn to see it as just that. Fiction."

I lift up the arm rest so I can snuggle close to him. "I'll try. I'm going to warn you, I will mess up. I'm not as strong as you. But I promise to try."

"Hopefully our lives will slip into blissful domestic tedium, and they'll move on to some other poor soul. Someone that does something more exciting than taking the rubbish bags to the skip," he says while gently stroking my hair.

I can't help but purr from how comfortable and safe he makes me feel. "You have no idea how many women would drool over a picture of you taking out the trash. Finding a man that does housework is like finding a leprechaun. Match that with how sexy you must look doing it," I say with a smirk, "and I'd even buy that magazine, and I have the real thing right here. Face it, even when you're boring, you're gorgeous. Our press pals aren't going anywhere."

He sighs. "You're right," he says with disdain. "I promise they'll let up eventually. But, it's going to be a rough go of it until they do. After the last feeding frenzy, once they see me with one woman on a regular basis, you'll be like blood in the water to them."

"I guess we will just have to hide inside," I say with a sigh. I run my hand along his thigh. "I wonder what on earth we'll do to occupy ourselves. Can you think of anything?"

He removes my hand and places it on my lap. "Until the consultant checks you out, I think we'll be watching movies and I'll be kicking your ass at poker."

"Consultant? You won't sleep with me until you have my business plan analyzed? That's not fair." I've read enough English novels to know what he's talking about, but I can't pass up an opportunity to razz him.

"Don't be cheeky." He touches my chin and turns my face toward him. "Someone broke your heart, Lily. It's my job to put it back together. We're following all the rules until we know for certain your heart has healed. It's not up for debate."

I pout and stick my tongue out at him. "You always have to be *so* responsible, don't you?"

He kisses me with a tenderness that reminds me why I'm on this plane. He loves me, and I'd be crazy to pass up another second with him.

The next few hours go by quickly. I read and doze while Gavin goes back to work. I'm woken from a nap by a *ding*.

"We are making our final descent into London, Heathrow Airport," the captain reports.

My heart races. This is a huge risk I'm taking. I hope I'm making the right call.

Gavin grabs my hand and whispers, "Stop worrying. This is going to be smashing. I told you—everything is better in London."

Chapter Two

I'm surprised when I step outside of the airport. I was expecting it to be colder for some reason, but it's warmer than DC. I'm thankful for the overhang because the rain is coming down in buckets. Each time a car drives by, I'm sprinkled with mist kicked up from the tires. I step back closer to the wall, when a limo pulls up and a livery clad driver opens the door. "We didn't need a limo, Gavin," I say as I walk toward the car. "I'd have been fine with a taxi."

The driver tips his hat. "Good evening, Mr. Edwards, Ms. Clark."

Gavin hands him our bags. "Thank you, Martin. How was your daughter's dance recital?"

Martin takes the bags and places them in the trunk.

"Very well, sir. The flowers you sent her were lovely. Thank you." He looks at the ground around us. "Are the rest of your bags still inside, sir?"

"That's all of it. I'm traveling light this trip," Gavin says as he motions for me to slide into the car first.

Martin looks confused. "I don't understand, sir. Surely this can't be it. You pack more for an overnight trip."

I laugh as I hold my hand out. "Hi Martin. I'm Lily. It's nice to meet someone else who finds Gavin's clothing addiction ridiculous."

Martin shakes my hand. "The pleasure is all mine, Miss."

When Gavin slides in the car I ask, "Will there be room for me at your house or will there be clothes everywhere? And do I dare ask if I get any closet space?"

He rolls his eyes. "Very funny. I asked Mason to pop into the flat to prepare for our arrival. There will be plenty of room."

"Who's Mason?" I ask before it occurs to me. "Oh god, is he your butler? You seriously have a butler?"

"Mason's been with my family since I was a child. Growing up he was more of a father to me than my own father was. You'll adore him, I promise. He and his wife, Hazel, live at the country house. We'll take a trip out there in a few weeks so I can introduce you."

I shake my head. "This is going to take some getting used to."

When the limo drives out of the airport traffic and onto what looks like a highway, I look out the window and watch the landscape go by. There are so many things I want to see while I'm here. While Gavin listens to his voice mail, I put together a mental list of places I want to go before I leave.

Before I leave? How can I create a list if I don't know how long I'll be here? I'm here and I have absolutely no plan. What the hell am I thinking? When I got out of the hospital, I went home and declared I was going to London. I didn't think it through. I never even asked Gavin if he wanted me here. I just demanded we go.

When he tucks his phone into his jacket pocket, I tug on his arm. "I know this is a bit late to be asking this, but are you sure you're okay with me being here? I pretty much invited myself."

"No, I invited you—it just took you a while to say yes. I couldn't be happier that you're here. For months, I've wanted nothing more than to see you when I wake up, come home to you at the end of my day, and lie in bed and watch you overindulge on ice cream. Now you're here. It's a wish come true." He kisses my temple. "I couldn't be happier."

"I have no idea how long I'll be here. I don't have a plan," I say.

"You've been through a lot. It isn't necessary to know what you're doing yet. In fact, it's better that you don't have a plan yet. Give yourself some time to heal. No pressure. Just rest, recover, and lie about with me."

"Can you say necessary again?" I just love his English

accent. He could turn me on by reading me the instructions for my DVR.

Martin moves into a right turn lane. He looks over his shoulder and says, "Welcome to London, Ms. Clark. We'll arrive in just a few moments."

Gavin explains that his flat is in Knightsbridge, right across from Hyde Park, which means absolutely nothing to me, since I know nothing about London. Despite the rain, I can tell how beautiful the city is. I can't wait to explore. Martin pulls the limo into the parking garage of a newly built 10-story, red brick building that kind of reminds me of DC. Gavin pats my hand. "Welcome home."

Martin collects our bags and offers to take them up, but Gavin takes the bags from him and sends him home so he can make dinner with his family. When we enter the building, a uniformed doorman greets us. "Mr. Edwards, how was your flight in?"

Gavin shakes the man's extended hand. "Willis, so good to see you. It's my sincere pleasure to introduce you to Lily Clark. Lily, this is Willis. He's the man that makes everything happen around here. He has the patience of a saint, and believe me, I've tested it over the last few months while the flat was being renovated."

"The pleasure's mine. Don't listen to a word he says. He's been a model tenant."

Gavin laughs. "That's only because I haven't lived here yet."

I start to chime in, but a yawn overtakes me. Despite my long nap on the plane, I'm more tired than I thought. I cover my mouth to hide my yawn. "Excuse me!" I say. "It's nice to meet you Willis."

Gavin's hand moves to the small of my back. "That's my cue to get this lovely lady upstairs." He picks up our bags.

"Can I deliver those to your flat, sir?" Willis asks.

Gavin waves him off as he nudges me to the elevator. "You do enough, Willis. Thank you anyway."

"Of course, sir," Willis answers "Have a wonderful evening!"

I whisper in his ear. "It's like people are morally opposed to you lifting a finger for yourself. When you eat, is there someone ready to jump in with a napkin to wipe your chin?"

He pokes me in the ribs. "Don't be cheeky."

"Don't expect me to pick up after you. You're a big boy. You can pick up your own socks." Judging from what I'd seen when we shared a hotel room, it'll be the other way around. He's far more organized than I am.

As we walk to the elevator, I soak in the beautiful lobby with chandeliers, marble floors and tons of crown molding. When we get into the elevator, I ask "Is there where you lived with—"

"Heavens no. For the last several years, Brooke and I lived separately. Her house was in Chelsea and I was staying at the Hampstead house- this ghastly, drafty beast of a house that's been in my family for generations. I bought this flat about two months ago.

Right after I got back from our trip to Boston."

"I'm surprised you never said anything. Or is life just one big game of Monopoly to you? You buy so much it's not worth mentioning?" I sound bitter, but I'm not. I don't resent his wealth, but sometimes I feel as though we live in two different worlds. Gavin's lost in the upper stratosphere of the filthy rich, and I'm on the ground with the rest of the working class. It's not because of anything he says or does. He doesn't flaunt his wealth. He doesn't waste his money on asinine things, or at least if he does he hasn't told me. He's the most charitable person I've ever met. I guess the issue is mine. It seems after Ash, I have an inherent distrust of men with money.

He shrugs. "I wasn't exactly keeping it from you. There just wasn't a good time to bring it up. You had just bought your place, and I didn't want to spoil that. More than I already had."

The elevator car arrives and I step in. "If you have a house in ... where did you say? Hampstead? Why'd you by this place?"

He holds a key fob to a panel on the door and pushes PH. "I wanted a fresh start. Some place that was all mine. Without any ghosts."

He knows I worry about filling the shoes of his late wife. Brooke Livingston was an American actress, and she starred in *Covent Gardens,* one of those teenager shows that became a cult classic. She was strikingly beautiful, and even from the grave, she casts a very large shadow. I used to love that show; now I have to hate it. It's such a shame.

"I've been having the flat decorated since I bought it. Poor Willis had to deal with all the contractors coming and going. They just finished a few days ago," he says as we reach his floor.

"So you haven't seen it yet?"

The doors open and he motions for me to step out. "You and I have a whole flat to break in," he replies with a wink.

We walk in, and the only word I can think of is *magnificent*. The flat is enormous—I lose track of how many bedrooms it has! Each room is painted in soft, clean tones that give the sophisticated, elegant apartment a homey feel. I adore the dramatic floor-to-ceiling windows, and multiple skylights. If the sun ever shines, the whole apartment will be bathed in light. Instead, dense storm clouds cover the horizon, giving the rooms a tempestuous feel that makes me want to climb in bed and make my own storm between the sheets.

Each room has a terrace that overlooks the park and provides spectacular city views. Too bad it's December, or I would spend quite a bit of time out there.

I wander around to get the lay of the land. Each room is more amazing than the last; his decorator has an amazing eye for detail. Each piece of furniture is ornate and unique.

My favorite room is the sitting room right off the kitchen. It's blanketed in white. Overstuffed white sofa. White plush carpet. It just seems so clean and serene, I feel at peace sitting in it. I might even enjoy yoga if I did it in this room, and I hate yoga.

"Gavin, I'm blown away. Your apartment is amazing." I sit down on a very comfortable blue sofa in the living room. "On the ride up here, I was expecting something stuffy and museum-like. But this is a home. A place where you can come kick off your shoes and relax."

He moves the accent pillows to the other sofa so he can sit next to me. "That's possibly the best news I've ever heard." He smiles and leans in to kiss me. "I couldn't be happier. If I'm being honest, I had you in mind when I spoke with the decorator. Before I bought it, the flat was very modern with gray and black and dark wood. Trendy and chic, but not what I wanted. I think my decorator actually cried when we pulled up all the black granite. But I told her, I want it to look like people actually live here, rather than something out of a design magazine."

"You weren't kidding when you said you have a thing for furniture. Your decorators out did themselves. I've never seen such unique pieces. Everything looks one of a kind."

He looks confused for a moment. "Oh, I forgot. You never got my letter."

I trace the seam of the arm of the sofa. I don't know anything about furniture, but even I can tell the stitching is amazing. "What letter?" I ask.

"The letter that went with the desk."

I shrug. "Nope, no letter," I say. "I didn't hear from you for three weeks, thought you'd dropped off the face of the planet. Which made the furniture delivery confusing. A letter would have been extraordinarily helpful."

He puts his arm around me. "Lily, I can't apologize enough about that. I missed you terribly. Every day, I longed to speak to you, but I thought you wanted space. For the rest of my years, I will regret not being there for you. I should have ignored that email and pestered you until you spoke to me. Perhaps if I had..."

I hate how he blames himself. What happened to me was Ash's fault. Not mine, and certainly not Gavin's. "There's nothing you could've done," I say as I thread my fingers through his. "I survived and now we're here together. Let's focus on the positive. Tell me, what did the letter I didn't get say?"

He kisses my hand. "I told you I have a studio. I do some painting, a little photography. You'll see some of my paintings around here, and the shots I sent you when you moved into the flat in Georgetown are mine."

I adore the collection of photos he gave me. They're the most captivating black and white pictures of various places in London. Not the typical touristy places, but places only a local would know and love.

"I also resurrect furniture," he continues.

I roll my eyes. "Dear God, is there no end to your need to save things?" I tease.

He points a finger at me. "Shut it!"

I nudge him with my shoulder. "That's my line! In all seriousness, tell me all about it. How the hell did you get into making furniture?" I shake my head. "So random, Oxford."

"When I was young, Mason, my butler, managed all of my family's properties. He would come across furniture in the attics and spare rooms, and my parents would just want to toss it. Instead, Mason took it and sanded it down and worked with it. He made it into something amazing.

"I spent more time with Mason than I did with my parents, and I loved working with him in his workshop. Manual labor wasn't something my parents thought a proper English gentleman should do, so perhaps I loved it because it pissed them off.

"So sometimes I take an old piece and completely redo it, like the desk I gave you. Other times I make something new. It's a creative outlet. Working with a chainsaw, blow torch, and power sander can be quite a stress reliever," he says with a wink.

I look around the room. "Everything here, you made yourself?"

Gavin nods as he runs his hand over the coffee table, his fingers lingering on the knots in the wood. I notice a sparkle in his eye. He's clearly proud of what he creates. "I only work in wood and metal. The sofas and chairs aren't mine."

"I'll warn you now. I'm not the best at remembering to use a coaster," I say, getting his attention.

"If you leave watermarks on my table, I'll be forced to punish you."

I waggle my eyebrows. "Don't tempt me."

He pulls my legs out from under me and tickles me relentlessly.

"Stop! Stop!" I scream. "I had way too much to drink on the plane. If you want to keep this sofa pristine, enough with the tickles!"

Thankfully he stops and shows me to the bathroom. Even in the bathroom, there's a small cabinet which I'm guessing is one of his pieces.

Gavin feels the need to fix everything he finds broken, but it shows how much hope he has. God, I envy his hope and optimism. I don't think I've had that much faith in anything good since I was a child. But not Gavin. He's always sure he can make things better. I try to wrap my brain around his psyche, but when I think about him sweaty and working with power tools, I get distracted.

I don't often play the Ashton vs. Gavin game, because it's like comparing slugs and unicorns, but sometimes I'm hit upside the head by how different they are. I couldn't get Ash to help me put together IKEA furniture. He'd never gotten his hands dirty a day in his life. Gavin, who was raised with even more privilege, feels an inner need to create. Ash was a parasite who tried to take everything he could out of life, and Gavin wants to make something amazing with his. How can he even be remotely attracted to me after I was with someone like Ash?

Coming out of the bathroom, I find him sitting on the sofa tapping away on his phone. God damn, this man is sexy.

He doesn't look up, allowing me to shamelessly ogle him. A deep growl from my stomach gives me away. I rub my stomach. "You need to feed me."

"I was just thinking the same thing," he replies. "You up for curry? I have yet to find a decent curry spot in DC. I'd been craving it while we were in the states."

I sit down next to him on the sofa. "Well, that would make sense. I've yet to try a curry I like. Maybe I've just been getting it from all the wrong places. Let's give it a whirl. I'm all about trying new things while I'm here. Is it ok if we eat in?"

"Of course." He walks to the entryway where he left our luggage, and pulls out his laptop. "I'll pull up the menu for you."

I lean back and put my feet on the coffee table, expecting him to scold me. "Just order me whatever you think I'll like. I trust you."

He smirks, but doesn't say a word as he takes his phone out of his pocket. I hear him placing the order as he walks out of the room. A few minutes later he returns with a glass of wine. While we wait for the delivery, we cuddle on the sofa. About forty minutes later, Willis brings us an exorbitant amount of food.

"Jesus, Oxford. You feeding an army?"

"I wanted you to try all my favorites." He pokes me in the tummy. "Ordering too much has never really been a problem for us."

I smack him in the arm. "Shut it."

Gavin carries the bags into the kitchen and we set up

the smorgasbord on a rustic table which, again, I assume is one of Gavin's pieces. Dinner's fabulous. I'm now a full-fledged curry lover. As Gavin predicted, I overeat, my pants feel tight, and now I have heartburn. I move to the living room, curl up on the sofa, and moan while he cleans up.

"Gavin!" I call from the living room. "I need yoga pants. Where's my luggage?"

He stands in the hallway with a dishtowel flung over his shoulder. "Tummy ache?" he asks. I can tell he is dying to say "I told you so."

"Nope, just want to be more comfortable," I lie.

He walks to the sofa and kisses my forehead. "Of course, luv. I'll bring the luggage back to the bedroom."

It's clear Gavin's put extra effort into making the master bedroom perfect. The vaulted ceilings and skylights make the room feel huge. With the low cloud cover and the soft grays and slate blues of the decor, the room has a sultry feel. The walk-in closet's the size of my condo in DC, leaving plenty of room for Gavin's gargantuan wardrobe. The best part is the bed. Huge, soft, just begging to be jumped on.

"I haven't showed you the best part." Gavin winks at me and pushes on the molding of the wall next to the bed.

A hidden door opens to show off a secret stainless steel fridge. My mind races with all of the exciting things he could house in a fridge in the bedroom. He opens the door and reveals that it's fully stocked with ice cream—Gavin's one and only vice.

He casually leans on the door of the fridge. "Now, just because there's a freezer full of Chunky Monkey by the bed does not mean you should eat all of the Chunky Monkey."

"Shut it, Oxford."

He grabs my arm and kisses me. I may have heartburn, but my need for Gavin supersedes. I fall backward onto the bed, and our kissing intensifies. His hands roam down my back and over my ass. I caress his amazing rock-hard abs and run my finger along the top of his jeans.

He pushes himself away and jumps off the bed, panting.

"You're a temptress. We're supposed to be avoiding anything that will elevate your heart rate."

I sit up and lean back on my hands. "Well then how the hell am I supposed to stay with you? Just being in the same room with you gets my heart rate elevated."

Gavin locks his fingers behind his head and paces the room. "Okay, why don't you go try out the bathroom? I think the tub will help you get your heart rate down. I'm going to go for a run."

"A run? Now?" I run my finger along the collar of my V-neck sweater and bat my lashes at him, hoping to lure him back. "Wouldn't it be more fun if you joined me in the tub?

He walks into the closet, ignoring my question. Minutes later he returns in running gear. He kisses my forehead. "Take a bath and stop trying to torture me.

I'm going for a run." He closes his eyes and shakes his head while he pushes out a deep breath. "I have some tension to release."

Chapter Three

After a long bath, I hop onto the bed to rest for a moment. The next thing I know, I wake up and the room is pitch black. At first I hear a crackle, then a zap off in the distance. Then I feel the itch of the rope on my wrists and the smell of manure. Then the room begins to spin.

I can't catch my breath. I don't know where I am. Nothing looks familiar. My heart feels like it's going to explode and I feel as if I'm breathing through a straw. The only sound I hear is my gasping for oxygen.

Warm hands gently rub my back. "Shhhh," Gavin whispers. "I'm here. You're safe. Breathe, luv. You need to breathe."

I let my weight collapse into his strong frame while I

try to get a hold of myself. He whispers words of security as I try to get my breathing under control. The vice on my heart loosens. I look over at Gavin. Once my eyes meet his, I feel as though the world is coming back into focus.

He pulls my hair away from my sweat-drenched neck. “Do you want to talk about it?” he asks.

“Can we turn on a light?” I ask. “I’m not loving the dark right now.”

Gavin turns a lamp on, and we both blink excessively as our eyes adjust to the light.

He hands me his glass of water from the nightstand. “Is that better?” he asks.

I try to take a sip, but my hands tremble too severely not to spill, so I hand it back to him. “I’m not really sure what happened. One second I was asleep, and the next second I was a train wreck. I felt like my chest got hit by a train.”

He soothingly runs his hands down my arms. “Was it a nightmare?”

I shake my head. “I can’t remember. But waking up in the dark really freaked me out. I...”

“What?”

“I just haven’t been in the dark very much since it happened,” I say. “At the hospital, there were always lights on. I know it shouldn’t freak me out, but...” I trail off.

“Luv, we can sleep with the lights on if it helps. I’ll do

anything to help you feel safe. I swear." He kisses my temple. "You've been through so much, and it'll take some time for your soul and your spirit to heal. Random things will bother you, but that's just your brain's way of processing what happened. Don't let it upset you. That just feeds the problem."

I nod, knowing that he's right, but I'm still livid I'm so affected by what happened. I should be stronger than this.

"Do you want to tell me what happened?" he asks.

"Not tonight," I reply. "Let's just try to go back to sleep, okay?"

He brushes hair off my forehead. "I understand you're not ready to talk about it. But you have to at some point, luv," he says. "You're going to self-destruct if you keep it bottled up. You need to tell someone."

I pull away from him, and wrap the sheet around my shoulders. "You're wrong. I've had to tell the damn story over and over and over again. I can't do it anymore."

"I know, and I wish I could have shielded you from that." He cocks his head to the side. "But, I know you. I'd wager whatever you told them is only the partial truth, which means you're weighed down not only by what really happened, but by the lies you told as well. You can't live like that."

I shake my head. "I don't want to think about it. I just want to forget it all. Just let me forget," I plead.

Eliminating the distance between us, he scoots closer

to me. "I understand, luv. But it doesn't work that way. The memories will haunt you until you face them. I've seen too many men come back from war and refuse to face the memories of what they lived through. Eventually, their memories swallowed them whole. I won't let that happen to you."

I know he's right, but I'm not ready. I lean my head on his shoulder. "Can you just be here for me? That's all I need you to do. I don't need you to fix it. You can't fix it. Just be here."

He pulls me closer and kisses the top of my head. "I'll be there for you, but first you have to let me in."

I nuzzle his neck. "Gavin, I want to tell you, and I will. But please, I'm begging you, not tonight."

"Of course, luv. What can I do for you tonight? How can I chase the demons away?"

"Just hold me."

Wrapped up in his arms, my body finally relaxes. I can't say the same thing for my brain. Every time I close my eyes, I see Not Charlie's face. I know he's gone, but I swear I can hear his voice in the distance. When I open my eyes, Not Charlie disappears. So, I spend the night watching Gavin sleep. The way his eyelashes flutter. How broad his naked chest looks as he inhales. The way his lips occasionally curl. I spend the night wondering about his dreams so I can evade mine.

Gavin finally stirs around nine. He opens his eyes, which are so brilliantly blue first thing in the morning.

"Hello, gorgeous," I say.

His arms wrap around me like a constrictor, pulling me so close to him that it's hard to breathe. "I'm never letting you leave," he says in a raspy morning voice. "If I could wake up like this every day for the rest of my life, I would die a happy man."

"Even though you can't hit it in the morning for a while?" I tease.

He laughs at my Jay-Z reference. "Yes, luv." He releases me and shifts around a bit, looking uncomfortable. "I need to go for a run," he says after jumping out of bed. "Think about what you want to do today. I'm all yours for the entire day. We can do anything you want."

"That depends. Are you going to have to keep going on run breaks?" I ask.

"Quite possibly," he calls from the closet. "I can't help thinking about sex when I'm with you, so I've got to solve that problem somehow."

"I could help you," I say seductively.

He comes out of the closet tying a pair of track pants. "No, my dear, you can't. Unless you're saying that being with me doesn't get your heart rate up."

"Oh no, just thinking of being with you makes my heart flutter. At least you get to go for a run to ease your ache. If I twiddle my thumbs, you're on my case about my heart rate. Hmm, maybe while you're gone I'll think of a creative use for these thumbs."

He ignores me and goes about getting ready for his

run. I sit up in bed and look out at the amazing view. It's misting out this morning, and the gloomy gray hangs over the trees of the park. I feel Gavin slide behind me. His hand runs gently across my shoulders to toy with the edge of my tank top. As my heart thumps, he pulls my top back slightly and dumps a cup of ice down my back.

"What the hell was that for?" I scream as I jump off the bed and shake the ice out of my clothes.

Gavin rolls on the bed as he laughs. "You have to stop thinking naughty thoughts. Get your mind out of the gutter."

I stick my bottom lip out as I cross my arms. "I like my mind in the gutter."

"We can't live out all those sexy thoughts until your heart heals, and it won't heal if you keep pushing it by thinking about being naughty. So stop thinking about it. Then we can start doing it sooner." He kisses the tip of my nose and stands to start his pre-run stretching. As he reaches up to stretch his lats, his track pants dip low, displaying his perfect body. I can't decide which is sexier: his pecs or his back. His ridiculous eight-pack ends in a perfect V. The V is like a big arrow pointing me to the Promised Land...

I lick my lips. "And how am I supposed to do that when all of this is parading around?" I gesture to his bare torso.

He snatches his sweatshirt from the edge of the bed and quickly throws it over his head. "Fine. No more naked time. I'll only wear sweats around you."

"If only that would work! Have you seen yourself in sweats? They hang low and catch you in just the right places. You make sweats look hot."

He rolls his eyes. "I'll be back. Come up with a plan for the day. Anything you want."

"What if I want—"

He points a finger at me. "Anything *but* that."

He turns to leave and I say, "Hate to see you leave, but I love to watch you go," as he walks away.

He flips me off as he leaves the room. "All this running isn't helping the cause. It's just going to make you sexier," I yell.

While he's gone, I manage to fall asleep and have a few steamy Gavin dreams. Thank god my unconscious self doesn't seem to be impacted by my heart problem.

I wake up and don't see Gavin anywhere. I wander around the massive apartment until I find him in his office working on his laptop. He's showered and changed into a blue cashmere sweater and khakis. He looks like he walked out of a Banana Republic ad.

He jumps up and kisses me. "I was thrilled when I saw you getting some more sleep, but I'm even more thrilled you're up. I've missed you so much over the last few weeks that it's hard to miss one more moment."

He scoops me up and carries me to the sofa. "So what do you want to do today?"

I trace his now scruff-free jaw. "Well, since you have been bragging nonstop about how wonderful London is, I figure you should show me around."

"Smashing idea. What do you want to see?" he asks.

"I'm not in a touristy mood, so show me the best local stuff. Take me to your favorite restaurant and all your favorite places. Let me see Gavin's London."

"You've come at the best time. The Christmas festivities have just started, and London is a wonderful place to be during the holiday. Dress warm."

"Will we be outside much?"

"Of course! I'm not giving you a driving tour. You want to see London, so I'm going to show you London. Now quit whining and get dressed!" He smacks my butt as I scurry out of his office.

Thankfully, Em was smart enough to pack a hat, gloves, and a scarf, allowing me to bundle up for our adventure. He's like a little kid, so excited to show off his hometown. He has so much English pride it's comical. He belongs here. I could tell that from the moment we got off the plane.

We start at his favorite pub,—or one of them. The Lamb and Flag is in Covent Gardens, the name of Brooke's show, and I try very hard not to think about that. From what he tells me, the pub has been around for hundreds of years. Dickens used to drink here. In the US, the popular places are modern and fresh, but here, some of the best places have been the best places for hundreds of years.

The Lamb and Flag is known for their whiskey, so Gavin spends lunch making me try samples of dozens of different whiskeys. I hate them all, and he knows it. I think he just enjoys the face I make when I taste them.

I ask the server what I should order, looking to try something British, and he tells me to get a burger. Who comes to England for a burger? I cannot imagine them being able to make a burger the way I'm used to, so I go for the shepherd's pie, which isn't half bad.

All of the whiskey has me feeling warm and toasty, a blessing as we brave the cold day. The light rain has stopped, so we take a short walk through Covent Gardens. We end up at a palatial building with a giant ice rink in front of it.

As soon as I see it, I skip, dragging him toward the rink. "Gavin, I haven't been ice skating since I was a kid! What a great idea!" I squeal.

He kisses my hand as we get in line. "I'm glad you like it."

"I'm a bit tipsy from you pouring drinks down my throat, so you'd better be ready to catch me." When we get to the front of the line, we give the attendant our skate sizes. I bite my lip. "I hope I can still skate."

Gavin pays for our skates. "It's like riding a bicycle. It'll come back to you."

"Can you skate?" Before he can answer, I hold up my hand and say, "Never mind. You're Gavin. Of course you can skate. In fact, you probably started playing hockey before you could walk and were *this* close to joining an Olympic team, but you didn't because you wanted to pursue something else you're amazing at."

A blush spreads across his cheek as he laughs. “Yes, I can skate. Yes, I played ice hockey, but I was never that good. I played in school, but that’s it.”

I pat his face. “You’re too pretty for hockey.” I kiss him before he can fight back.

He picks up our skates and carries them to the bench so we can lace them up. Getting to go on a normal date with him, like a normal couple, is wonderful. The rink is packed with people, so I pray I can control myself. I’d hate to wipe out and take down a bunch of people with me.

While tying my laces, I turn to him. “So, let me get this straight. Ice skating is okay, but sex isn’t? Explain this to me.”

With a wicked gleam in his eye, Gavin kneels in front of me. He unwraps my scarf from around my neck and places it in my lap. Sliding his hand under the collar of my coat, he runs his finger along my color bone, stopping on the side on my neck. He leans in and whispers, “By watching this spot right here, I can monitor your heartbeat.” His hot breath on my neck sends shivers down my body. “When I slide inside you for the first time and your eyes roll back from the pleasure, I can see you what I do to you. Your breath hitches, your head tips back, exposing your gorgeous neck and this spot tells me how aroused you are. When I thrust deep inside you and hit the sweet spot that makes you moan, I run my tongue along your neck and I can feel the excitement coursing through your body. Your hungry need to come. When you finally come apart beneath me, your pulse races like a jackhammer. Even when you’re one hundred percent healthy, I worry about what I'm doing to you. So whilst I think your heart can handle for a casual skate, I know you're not ready for me. When I finally have you again, taste you again, you'd better be in tip top shape, because you're not going to be able to move for days after I'm through with you."

He wraps the scarf around my neck with an innocent look on his face, as though he didn't just rock my world and drench my panties. "Better keep you bundled up. Can't have you catching a cold." He stands and holds out his hand to me. "Ready to skate?"

I shake my head while taking his hand. "You're evil. Pure evil."

He winks then guides me to the rink.

Of course Gavin glides on the ice as if he does it every day. It takes me about thirty minutes to get my ice legs—or maybe that's how long it takes for the alcohol to burn off. I get confident when my childhood skating skills come back to me, but after a little over an hour, he calls it quits. He doesn't want to push my heart too much.

I hold his hand while we walk away from the rink. "I think my heart had nothing to do with it. I think you just didn't like that I was skating a little better than you by the end."

He smiles. "Not at all. I had a wonderful time watching you."

"I used to be quite the skater when I was a kid."

"Really? I had no idea."

I nod. "There was a lake across the street from the house I grew up in, and I would skate every time it froze over. Which was all stinking winter. Then the boarding school I went to was a big hockey school. Instead of P.E. for two quarters a year, we would go to the rink. The boys would play hockey, and the girls would figure skate."

He pulls me in for a kiss. "You were impressive. We'll have to come back so you can show me up!"

When we're walking again, he says, "Lake skating is very dangerous, you know. I almost fell through the ice once at our country house."

"My best friend's grandfather was the fire chief," I say. "He went out and checked the lake every day and put out cones to mark when it was safe. That was one of the great things about growing up in such a small town. There were lots of little things like that."

"Tell me about it," He says while motioning that we need to cross the street. I have no idea where we are, but it's relatively quiet.

"When I lived there, Ashfield had less than a thousand people in it. It's a one-stop-light town, and that stop light is always blinking. Everyone knew everyone, which had its pros and cons. There were thirty-two kids in my grade, and we all knew each other from kindergarten, and our parents knew each other from kindergarten. It's a different way of life."

He gently tugs on my arm, helping me avoid a mud puddle. "Do you miss it?" he asks.

"I try not to think about it. The girl I was then died in

the fire with my parents. I had to grow up so fast. When the church took me in and sent me to boarding school, I was surrounded by rich kids, and I knew nothing of their world or how to fit in. After some trial and error, I learned to adapt, and when I did, I was never the same person again."

He doesn't say anything, we just keep walking. The only sound between us is the squishing noise my wellies make when I walk on the damp ground. Uncomfortable with silence, I say, "I haven't been back since I was thirteen."

"I think this is the first time you've spoken of your childhood," he says.

I think about it. "It isn't something I talk about often." He doesn't say anything, which feels like a silent prodding to talk. "They aren't fun memories, Gavin."

"There aren't any good memories? Even from before?" he asks.

"No, I have wonderful memories from before my parents died. I just don't allow myself to think about them. I never wanted people to know I was a poor orphan girl, so I keep that part tucked away. It's like she never existed."

He pulls me to him and kisses me. "Well, I love the poor orphaned girl. All of her."

We arrive at the Covent Garden Market just in time for me to escape continuing this conversation. The market reminds me of the Eastern Market in DC, but it's bigger and completely decked out for Christmas. The market has two stories full of fresh produce, bakeries, and flower shops. I'm in love with it. We wander around and pick up things for the flat. I try not to go overboard, but everything looks so fabulous. Gavin, of course, knows half the shop owners and chats them up as though they're his long-lost pals. After about two hours of wandering—and me eating too much—we decide we have more stuff than we can carry, and we take a taxi home.

I snuggle in next to him. "Thank you for today. It was wonderful. It was a normal date with no drug dealers or boogey men. I didn't look over my shoulder once. I can't tell you how much I needed that."

He looks down and away. "Well, not exactly. You did meet my hook up."

No way! There's no way Gavin's a junkie! I'd have seen the signs. "What?" I spit.

"My Chelsea unwinder connection. Hugh? You met him."

I scoot to the other side of the cab. "What the hell is that? Some new kind of designer drug? I can't believe you! You let me fly across the ocean –"

He tips his head back and laughs. "Cinnamon buns, luv. Hugh's the baker that makes those fabulous buns. You ate three of them whilst we were strolling the market. Don't get heated up, I was just having a laugh. Too soon for junkie jokes?"

"Bastard," I say as I poke him in the ribs. "Yes, it's too damn soon."

He kisses behind my ear. "I'm sure you can find a way

to forgive me."

His lips brush the spot on my collarbone that makes my whole body melt. "Yeah, I guess I'll find a way."

My muscles relax into him. "Other than your silly joke, it was the perfect day."

"So you've figured it out then?" he asks, threading my fingers through his.

"What?"

He brings my hand to his lips, and looks at me over my knuckles with those hypnotic eyes. With a voice as smooth as melted chocolate he says, "Everything's better in London."

I lean my head against his shoulder and smile "Shut it, Oxford."

Chapter Four

Jet lag and excessive snacking knock me out until the next morning. After my night terror the night before, I'm thrilled I'm able to sleep through the night.

In the morning, my foot crosses the barrier, searching for Gavin's warmth, but the sheets are cold. I open my eyes to an empty bedroom. I call out to Gavin, but he doesn't respond. Reluctantly, I climb out of bed to search for him. The layout of his apartment is a bit confusing. Random sets of stairs go up or down a half flight to various rooms. Eventually I make it to the kitchen, which I find empty. No note.

I haven't seen my cell phone since before I was kidnapped, or the "incident" as I'm calling it. I have no idea where it is. It could be in my condo, or in pieces on the sidewalk on Q Street where I fought with Charlie. I've searched the house and Gavin doesn't seem to have a landline. Even if he did, I have no idea what his cell number is. With no way to track down Gavin, I head for the shower. I set the shower to the rainfall function with steam, and I'm transported to heaven.

While I'm in here, I don't have to think. I don't need a plan. There are no expectations. Just hot water beating down on my aching muscles. It's been over a week since my run-in with Charlie, but the cuts and bruises remain. One touch on the wrong spot transports me back to the barn. I need my wounds to heal so that the portal to those memories can be sealed forever. I turn the water temperature up, hoping it will scald the thoughts away. By the time the air in the shower is so thick with steam I can barely see, the tension in my body and soul finally starts to break down, disappearing down the drain with the water.

The steam clears, and I feel cold hands on my stomach and hot, soft kisses on my shoulder. Gavin's arms envelope me, drawing me into his body. The backs of my thighs stick to his drenched track pants. His fingers dig into my hips, pulling me closer, so that his growing excitement nestles into the crack of my ass. Gavin's kisses on my neck are no longer tender, but rather a passionate assault, intense and almost painful from his desire-fueled aggression. Typically Gavin's all about slow seduction, but today his exploration is deliciously raw, teetering on the fine line between pleasure and pain. He molds my body against his with a powerful command that makes my knees weak. He pushes me against the cold marble wall, positioning my hips just where he wants them. And then... nothing but cold air.

Goosebumps spread across my skin from the absence of his body pressed against mine. I turn and see the shower door is open, allowing all the hot air to escape, leaving me shivering, confused, and painfully disappointed.

After wrapping myself in a towel, I follow the trail of wet sneaker prints on the hardwood floor. I find him in his study, dripping wet and drinking scotch. If I weren't freezing and feeling rejected, I'd find the dark brooding look on his face as he sips his scotch sexy.

"You're ruining your lovely leather couch," I say.

He downs the rest of his drink but doesn't say a word.

I lean against the wall, not caring that my sopping wet hair is leaving a mark on his beautifully textured wall. "A bit early for scotch, don't you think?"

"Could you go get dressed please?" he says, looking into his empty glass.

Feeling naked, I tighten the towel around me, then cross my arms over my chest. "Wow. Really? That's all I get? There isn't anything else you want to say to me?"

He stands, walks to the bar, and pours another drink.

"Gavin! What the *hell*?"

Gavin turns his back to me, now facing the window.

"Lily. Go. Get. Dressed."

I've never seen him this way, and it makes my blood boil. I want to strangle him, but instead, I throw at him the only thing I have—my towel.

"Fine. Fuck you and your bad mood!"

I storm down the stairs. As I stomp back down the hallway, I hear a crash and glass shattering. I'm preparing myself for how loudly I'm going to slam the bedroom door when I'm scooped off the floor. His wide frame completely envelopes me as he carries me to the bed.

When he places me down gently, he kisses me. He tastes of scotch, which does not mix well with my freshly brushed teeth, but I'm not complaining. The voice in my head nags me to stop and find out what is going on, but I'm not in the mood to listen. I attempt to deepen the kiss, but he pulls back. He sighs, kisses my forehead, and covers me with a sheet.

Despite the fact that he's covered me, I feel naked. Being turned away twice in a matter of minutes, I feel exposed, vulnerable, and rejected. "You want to tell me what the hell is going on?" I try to sound angry, but I know all that's coming through is the hurt.

He hangs his head. "I woke up this morning... and I went for a run. When I came back, you were in the shower. No matter how much I knew I should leave you alone, I just couldn't. I had to see you. Touch you. I know you can't be put in that position, and I endangered you because I let my todger take over. I was completely out of line and out of control. I'm so sorry, luv."

A deep sigh of relief escapes as I run my fingers through my still tangled hair. "Jesus, Gavin! You had me really worried. Do you seriously think you're the only one having trouble controlling themselves? You think you have the market cornered on that pity party? I've gone just as long without getting any as you have. I want nothing more than to be swept up into your arms and feel connected with you. I'm just as frustrated as you are."

He drops his head on my shoulder. "I'm furious with myself for being so careless."

"You have nothing to be upset about. But if you're going to beat yourself up, leave me out of it. Really, emotional stress is far harder on the heart than a little bit of sexual tension."

"I know," he says softly, avoiding my gaze. "I promise, it won't happen again."

"I sure hope the whole shower thing happens again," I say, stroking his cheek and trying to get him to look me in the eye. "Only with a better ending. I'm not going to be on the DL forever."

"DL?"

I roll my eyes. "There's no DL in cricket?" He shakes his head. "DL is the disabled list in baseball," I explain. "Speaking of which, we need to find a cardiologist."

"I have just the man. Alexander Baker. We were at Oxford together, and he did a tour with me in Afghanistan. He's become a brilliant cardiologist. I can't think of anyone I would trust more."

I pat his leg. "Set it up! The sooner we get this whole heart problem signed off, the happier we'll both be," I say.

He walks to the bathroom and grabs a towel. When he returns to the bed, he gently dries my hair. "I just want you healthy and safe. I don't care about anything else. I'd be celibate for eternity if it meant you were safe."

I look at him as if he has twelve heads. "Bite your tongue! Let's hope no one has to be celibate! I really feel fine. I'm sure all of this worry is over nothing."

He gives me a chaste kiss. "I hope you're right, luv. Now, really. Please get dressed before my libido takes over again. I'm going to go clean up the mess I made."

"Oh, Gavin?" I call out to him before he leaves the room.

He stops and looks over his shoulder. "Yes, luv?"

"No more drinking before nine in the morning. Unless I'm a part of it, okay?"

"I needed something to calm me down. That's just the effect you have on me," he says as he leaves the room.

I throw on a sweater and yoga pants, and my stomach growls. I skip hair and makeup to head down to the kitchen. Gavin's still cleaning up his mess.

He walks into the kitchen to see me inhaling some of the fruit we bought yesterday. "Oh, I brought you breakfast."

"You did?" I ask with my mouth full.

"Yes, but when I got side-tracked, I completely forgot about it." He grabs a paper bag on the counter and hands it to me. "I ran down to Muffinski's and grabbed a bunch of muffins. I know how much you love blueberry. Would you like some juice?

"Yes, please," I reply as I walk to the cabinet to look for plates. Gavin and I start on opposite ends of the kitchen looking for plates and glasses. After opening and closing a few, I find the glasses and he finds the plates. The kitchen is organized in the worst way, but I suppose that's what happens when someone else sets up the house. Things aren't always in the most practical places. I kiss him on the cheek and hand him a plate as I sit at the table.

The most heavenly scent hits me when I open the bag. The muffins are still a little warm when I place one on each of our plates. "Now *that* is so much sweeter than sexually tormenting me and then giving me the cold shoulder. Next time, open with that."

He places our juice glasses on the table. "Lil, I've apologized. It won't happen again. Call it temporary insanity. Can you please let it go?"

"I'm relentless. It's why you love me." I take a bite of my muffin. "Oh. My. God. This is amazing." This muffin may be worth the cranky Gavin I endured, but I won't tell him that. I tilt my head back and moan as I savor the blueberry explosion going on in my mouth.

Gavin storms out of the room.

My bliss interrupted, I swallow. "What?" I call after him.

"I'm leaving until you finish your foodgasm."

"Okay, okay. I'll stop moaning. Come back!" I plead.

He comes back after I've finished. He collects my plate and glass and takes it to the sink. "Word's gotten around that I'm back in town. Liam, my best mate, texted this morning to see if we wanted to meet up later."

"What do you mean 'word has gotten around'?" I shout over the running water.

He places the rinsed plates in the dishwasher. "My friends find it hilarious to subscribe to those celebrity stalker apps that tell you where people have been spotted."

Not wanting to make him do all the clean-up, I wipe the crumbs off the table and into a napkin. "Trash can?" I ask.

He points to a cabinet at the end of the center island. "The *bin* is over there."

I roll my eyes. "So you were saying? You've already been spotted?"

He closes the dishwasher and looks at me. "Luv, I was spotted the second we got off the plane."

I let out a whimper. Gavin's pseudo-celebrity status is my least favorite part about being with him.

He gently rubs my shoulders. "I know. It takes some getting used to. I'm sorry."

"It's part of your package, I know..."

His brows furrow. "What?"

I lean against the center island. "That's what Max told

me. That the three-ring circus is part of your package. If I want you, that's what I am signing up for. I either love the whole thing or walk away."

"I guess I'm lucky you didn't walk away!" he says. "Remind me to strangle Max for giving you such a lovely ultimatum."

"You should thank him. I'm here, aren't I? I would love to meet your friends, but before then, can we run to the store? I need to get some toiletries. I love it when I have your smell on me, but it isn't quite the same when I use your shampoo. Now I just smell like a guy."

He chuckles. "Yes, I much prefer it when you smell like you."

After we eat, we head out to shop for a bit. The weather isn't too chilly, so we decide to walk. Gavin takes me to a beauty and bath store that's every woman's dream. Lotions, shower gels and bath salts in decadent scents. A small square of soap costs more than my beauty budget for three months, but the smells are so heavenly I give in and let him spoil me. I'm stubborn, but even I have my limits.

On our walk, I see a coffee shop that looks familiar. I can't figure out why I would recognize a coffee shop in London until we get closer and see a standing tribute to Brooke Livingston. It's Monmouth Coffee, frequent hang out of Brooke's character on *Covent Gardens*. A picture of her hangs in the window with the tag line *Gone But Not Forgotten*. I get chills seeing her picture.

"Sorry. I usually know better than to come this way," he says after we're a safe distance away. "I try to avoid going by there."

I don't say anything, but my mind races. Does he not want to be reminded of her? Is it too painful? Of course it would be painful. She *was* his wife! If it didn't bother him, he wouldn't be the caring, sensitive guy I've fallen for. It's such a shame that for me to get the wonderful man he is, I'll have to share part of him with her ghost.

By the time we get back to Gavin's, I'm drowning in insecurity. Gavin says he needs to check in at work, and I'm relieved. We have about an hour before we need to leave to meet Gavin's friends, which is just enough time for me to lie down and try to get my head straight.

As excited as I was to meet them, I suddenly just want to crawl back into bed. Searching through my luggage, I find I have nothing appropriate to wear. Gavin will be dressed impeccably as always, and everything I have is just so pedestrian. Desperate, I call Em.

"How could you not pack me anything cute?" I ask before she even has a chance to say hello.

"Um, I packed you perfectly. Why don't you tell me why you're throwing a hissy fit?"

"We're going to meet some of Gavin's friends, and I don't have anything to wear. Not one damn thing."

"Why are you worried about what you're wearing to meet his friends? All guys love you. Even Ash's friends liked you better than him."

I hold up a pink sweater and look at myself in the mirror before throwing it in the discard pile. "That isn't saying much," I retort.

"You were practically an honorary member of his fraternity. You become everyone's little sister. Personally, I couldn't stand it if guys treated me that way, but you thrive on it. So why are you worried? This is your bailiwick, kid."

"Maybe not anymore. Things are different."

Em is quiet for a minute, while I sift through my reject pile again. "Ahhhhh. I know what this is about."

"What?"

"It's the ghost, right? You're worried about the ghost."

"I don't know what you're talking about," I lie.

"Drop the act. We both know you're intimidated by Brooke," she says.

I sit down with a pair of jeans in my hand. "Can you blame me?"

"One, I hated that show. I never saw what everybody was so nuts about. Two, you're a fucking rock star. If his friends can't see it, then fuck 'em. I didn't know the chick, but I do know that she died because she was a cracked out junkie. Maybe she was great once, but my guess is she had a long fall from grace. You're not in competition with her. She's dead, and her role in his life has nothing to do with you. So put on your big girl panties and suck it up."

I fiddle with my cross necklace while I process what she's said. I know she's right, but my insecurities are screaming louder than she is.

"I take your silence to mean you're letting that soak in.

Now, tell me where you're going."

"A bar," I say. "I'm guessing it'll be casual. But you know how Gavin dresses. Dating a super model sucks!"

"Yeah, boo-hoo. He isn't a super model, he just looks like one."

"Help me, Em!"

"I am, I am. Okay, wear the skinny faded jeans, the white V-neck top, and that red vest that I got from that Goop event I went to."

I find the vest at the bottom of the suitcase. "Oh, I like that."

"Hence why I gave it to you. Like I would wear a down vest. I don't do rugged casual. But you, my dear, you pull it off well. Wear those tall brown boots, and you'll be golden."

"Have I told you how much I love you?" I say as I find the boots.

"Not nearly often enough."

As I hang up with Em, Gavin walks in looking surprised. I look around and see the entire contents of my suitcases thrown all over the room. I hadn't realized how frantically I'd been searching for something to wear.

He clears off a space on the bed and sits. "You okay?" he asks. "You've been quiet since our walk."

Embarrassed by the mess I've made of his room, I pick up my clothes. "I'm okay. I was a bit off earlier, but

Em helped."

"I meant what I said. I'm sorry we walked that way. I'm sure it's weird for you. I know it's weird for me."

Not wanting to look at him, I focus on folding the clothes in front of me. "I'm not going to lie. I get a bit intimidated by her. She's not just anyone, she's Brooke freaking Livingston! She was the face of the lipstick that I wear, for crying out loud. Well, used to wear anyway." Note to self, throw away Wanted Red lipstick. The last thing I need is to think about how much better she looked in the shade than I do.

He moves from the bed to the floor in front of me. "Oh, Lil. You have nothing—"

I hold my hand up and shake my head. "Em gave me the 'Lily is wonderful' speech. You don't have to go there. I'm fine, really."

He takes the sweater from my hands, causing me to look at him. "You're not, I can tell," he says. "You're wonderful. Never in my life have I been as happy as I am when I'm with you. Never."

He leans down to kiss me, but he pulls away before we get carried away. "You'll be in good company tonight. Liam and James never made it a secret that they disliked Brooke, and they're very excited to meet you."

Suddenly, the evening's looking up.

Chapter Five

We catch a cab to the pub to meet Liam and James. The cab is a stick shift! I've never seen that before. Sticks are virtually obsolete in the US, but Gavin says almost every car in the UK is a stick.

Gavin's about to tell me how he met Liam and James when Max calls Gavin's phone and asks for me.

"Max!" It's so good to hear his voice. I've only been gone a few days, but I miss him. We'd grown so close in the short time we lived together.

"Hey, Slugger. How's it hanging?"

I fiddle with my cross necklace. "Well, no one has tried to kill me since I've gotten here. So I'd say that is a plus."

"Give 'em time. I'm sure you'll end up knee deep in some shit soon enough," he says with a laugh.

"That is why I love you, Max. You're a beacon of positivity and optimism." The cab enters a roundabout and my life flashes before my eyes. It appears yielding is a US concept. I almost drop the phone when I grab the door handle.

"I only have a few minutes," he says bringing me back to our conversation. "I wanted to call because I'm going out on assignment, and I wanted to let you know you won't be able to reach me. Not sure how long I'll be out of pocket."

"Oh..." Max is a great FBI agent, but I wish he didn't do undercover work. Because he's exceptional at his job, he lands the big cases. "Big" being the nice way of saying dangerous.

"Stop that right now," he shouts at me. "No worrying. I'll be perfectly fine. Got it?"

"I know. Promise you'll be safe?"

The voices in the background on his end get louder. "I'm always safe, slugger. They're calling me in, I've got to run. I'll call you when I get back. Greene'll check on the condo and water the plants. Hugs and sloppy kisses!"

He's gone before I get a chance to say good-bye. I turn to tell Gavin what's going on.

He scoots closer to me in the cab and puts his arm around me. "I heard. You okay?"

I swallow down the lump forming in my throat. "Yeah," I say with a nod. "I just worry. I hate that I can't know where he's going or even check in with him. Radio silence is the worst." I stare at the phone in my hands, hoping it will ring again.

Gavin takes his phone back and caresses my fingers. "He's very good at what he does. You know Max, he can talk his way out of anything. If he ever got in a jam, he'd find a way out. He comes off like a slacker, but he's careful and methodical."

The taxi pulls up to the pub, saving me from having to come up with something to say.

The bar is called the Cheshire Cheese. I love the names of places in London. Unlike the Lamb and Flag, the Cheshire Cheese is modern but still uniquely British. While it can't brag that it has been slinging drinks for hundreds of years, it's a pretty great place to play darts, or arrows as they call it here.

Gavin steers us through the crowd, looking for his friends. Out of nowhere, a giant man punches Gavin in the gut.

"Gotcha," the giant yells.

Gavin stumbles. I stand there in complete shock. At first I think Gavin is crying because he's so red and tears are coming down his face. As he stands up straight, I see that he is laughing.

Gavin points at the giant. "You bastard!" he shouts. "You got me. I didn't see that coming. You're lucky I didn't ralph all over you." He gives the man a hug as he catches his breath. "Lily, this is my best mate, Liam

Moynihan. Liam, this is Lily."

I put my hand out to shake his, but Liam throws me over his shoulder and spins me around a few times. I get a hard slap to my backside

"Hey now," Gavin says. "Hands to yourself, Moynihan."

"All in good fun." Liam sets me back down. "Lily, it's good to meet you."

"It's nice to meet you too," I reply as I straighten my vest "Although you've just smacked my ass, so I feel like we know each other so well already. For the record, I prefer the spinning/ass slap combo to the sock in the gut."

"Oh, Gavin here had that coming," Liam says with a laugh.

I raise my eyebrow and motion for him to continue. "You can't just leave it at that. Come on, details!"

"You see, it all started back when we were eleven," Liam says as he slings his arm around my shoulders. "We were fishing, and I bet Gavin he couldn't eat a whole jar full of worms. If he did, he got to sock me in the gut, and if he didn't, I got to sock him. We've never been able to agree if he finished the whole jar or not. Since then, we've been throwing punches back and forth. The goal is to get him when he doesn't know it's coming."

I stare at Gavin for a minute. "So you agreed to eat a whole jar of worms so you could punch Liam in the stomach? Knowing that if you missed even one worm, you would have a belly full of worms and still get punched?"

"We were eleven. That's what lads do when they're eleven," Gavin says, defending his honor.

"And this has continued for - eighteen years?" I shake my head at them. "Boys are dumb. If you're going to eat worms, you at least have to get some cash out of it. I once ate a grasshopper for five bucks, a pack of gum, and the right to cut in line at the diving board for a whole summer. Who would have thought that between moneybags and me, I would be the more enterprising one?" I nod my head in the direction of the bar. "Come on, Liam. Buy me a drink while Gavin pulls himself together. He still looks a little green."

Liam turns toward Gavin and says, "Oh, I like this one. She's feisty!"

Gavin yells back, "You haven't seen anything yet. Wait till she gets some tequila in her."

On the way to the bar, I get slapped on the ass again while Gavin is talking to someone, so I know it isn't him. I catch the guy's hand and twist his arm up behind his back. *Thank you, Max.*

"Uncle! Uncle! I'm sorry. I'm James, Gavin's friend. I didn't mean anything. I was just trying to wind him up."

James is about six feet tall, and he has light brown hair and coffee-colored eyes. But he looks like a deer in headlights right now.

I give him the evil eye and let him go. "I was under the

impression you Brits were supposed to be gentlemen."

"Who gave you that idea?" Liam asks, barely able to get the words out because he's laughing so hard.

"Well, James, Gavin missed the whole thing. So your mission crashed and burned." I glare at him.

He smirks. "I got to slap your ass, so I'm not really sure I agree with you."

I try not to laugh. "Quick. He's looking this way. Dip me and plant a big kiss right on my cheek."

Before I know it, I'm dipped back, and he looks as if he's going kiss me for real.

He leans in and whispers, "Three, two, one."

Gavin comes up behind James, grabs him by the scruff of the neck, and says "Wallace, don't even think about it."

James, Liam, and I crack up. As James places me back on my feet, Gavin realizes what's going on. He throws his hands up and storms back to our table. He has a big smile though, so I know he's taking it in jest.

Liam and I get drinks for us and head to the table. He somehow talks me into doing an Irish Car Bomb.

Gavin orders some fish and chips for me. "We need to get some grease in this one, or we'll be carrying her out of here."

"Oh no, boys," I reply. "I plan to beat the pants off you all at darts. I won't be getting carried away tonight!"

"That sounds like a challenge," Liam says.

I adore James and Liam. They're pranksters, and hanging out with them is a laugh a minute. The best part is seeing Gavin with them. He's always so composed and mature, but the three of them act like teenagers together. Apparently, Gavin is human after all.

The three men couldn't be more different. Liam is a professional rugby player, which suits him to a T. James is an energy trader, which I don't entirely understand. But he's clearly crazy smart. Gavin runs the family business, a defense technology company. The three met in boarding school when they were six years old and have been the best of friends since.

I keep my promise and cream Liam and James at darts. Gavin and I are neck and neck the whole night. I keep hoping that if he drinks enough, I'll gain an advantage, but unfortunately he does better a few shots in.

Right before the tie-breaking game, I ask,

"What are we playing for, Oxford?"

"*Oxford*?" James and Liam repeat in unison.

Gavin ignores them. "What do you want?"

I raise my eyebrows. "You know what I want."

He glares at me. "Don't go there, Lil."

Liam jumps up and down, like a toddler. "Oh! Oh! What does she want?"

I stick my bottom lip out and pout. "Fine." I stomp my foot like a spoiled teenager. I look at Liam. "Your friend can be such a stick in the mud."

"I know," Liam says with a sympathetic look. He puts his arm around my shoulders. "You need to ditch the blighter and find yourself a real man." He touches my chin, directing me to face him. "Oh, look at that. You found one."

Gavin kicks the back of Liam's knee, causing his knee to buckle. With a few Irish Car Bombs in him, Liam loses his balance and falls on his ass, almost taking me down with him. "I said hands to yourself, Moynihan."

James helps Liam to his feet. "You might want to listen to him, mate. He's sensitive about this one."

Liam holds his hand out to Gavin. "Good ol' Gavin knows I'm just having a laugh. Right, mate?"

Gavin moves to shake Liam's hand and Liam punches him in the gut. "That's two!" Gavin falls into James and somehow the three end up on the floor laughing.

"Boys!" I shout, getting their attention. "I believe I was making a bet."

"What's your flutter?" James asks.

"My what?"

"Your wager?" he replies.

I put my hands on my hips. "If I win, nothing but embarrassing Gavin stories for the rest of the night."

Gavin gets to his feet, then helps James up. "What do

I get when I win? We both know I'm going to win," he boasts.

"Oh, the arrogance! Has he always been such a cocky bastard?" I ask Liam and James. They're both laughing hysterically.

"If I win, you have to promise to stop being naughty," Gavin says.

Liam elbows Gavin in the ribs. "I think you've got it backward there, mate. You're supposed to *try* to get her to be naughty."

"She knows what I'm talking about," he says, glaring at me.

I put my hands on my hips and glare back. "Oh, it's on. Let's play."

We have a heated match with intense trash talking going back and forth. I end up winning, but barely.

"Gavin, I think you've finally met your match. She's more competitive than you. I didn't think that was possible," James says as he and Liam laugh at us.

I order another round of drinks. "All right, boys. Spill it. I want to hear every embarrassing story."

"Oh, I've got one," Liam says. "When we were twelve or thirteen, we were meeting some girls at the pond near my house. Gavin decided to be clever and take out his parents' car. A Rolls Royce, of course. Gavin wasn't even tall enough to see over the steering wheel. Well, he forgot to put the car in park, and it rolled right into the pond."

My hand covers my mouth. "Gavin! Oh my god! Your parents must have been furious."

"Mason got it all cleaned up before they got back from holiday. They never knew," James explains.

"So were the girls impressed?" I ask.

Liam rolls his eyes. "Of course they were. It's Gavin. He could trip and fall, and bust up his mug, and girls would rush over to kiss his boo-boo. He's always been a snatch magnet."

I shake my head. "Why doesn't that surprise me?" I respond.

"This one is better," James says. "Right around that same time, we got into my parents' liquor cabinet. We were all legless, and Gavin had a huge football match the next morning. He showed up, still pissed I think, and threw up on two players from the other team. The bastard still scored three goals!"

I motion for the bartender to send over another round. "Guys, no more 'Gavin can do no wrong' stories. Only embarrassing ones! I know he can walk on water, and quite frankly, I'm sick of hearing about it."

James tilts his beer bottle toward me. "Try growing up with it."

"I can't imagine. I'm impressed you're all still friends. The golden boy thing gets so old, doesn't it?"

Gavin just sits back, drinking his scotch, his lip slightly curled. I can't tell if he's slightly amused or slightly annoyed. Maybe a little of both.

Liam does a short drum roll on the table. "Got it! What about the time Gavin and O—"

James slams his drink on the table, causing me to jump. "No," he says firmly. "You know not to mention her name in my presence. I'm hitting the head." He gets up and sulks away.

"What was that about?" I ask.

"James and O were sweethearts," Liam explains. "She broke his heart. She still does on occasion. We used to call her 'she who shall not be named' before those wizard books came out. Now everyone says it, so it isn't so clever anymore. What's up with her, Gavin? Tell me quick before James gets back."

My ears perk up, anxious to see what he has to say about this. "O and I are done," Gavin says coldly.

"She finally pushed you too far, huh? It was bound to happen. That woman is pure poison. I just wish James could get her out of his system."

Liam tips back his beer.

James heads toward our table, and Liam changes the subject. "We need one last drink to our reigning darts champion. I'll go get another round. No wimping out, lass. It's another car bomb for you."

We do one more shot and head out to find a taxi.

"Damn, it's brass monkeys," Liam says as he rubs his hands together.

I slip my gloves on. "*Brass monkey*? As in the Beastie Boys song?" I ask.

"No, as in it's cold enough to freeze the balls off a brass monkey," he replies. Before I can respond he throws me over his shoulder again. "Lily and I are headed home. You two have a good night. What? Don't look at me like that. I'm carrying her like a caveman, and I've slapped her ass. Oops, did it again," he quips as he slaps my ass. "In some cultures, we're married now."

"Liam. Enough," Gavin says. He isn't messing around.

"Nope, Gavin, I like this one. I'm keeping her to myself."

"I'll call your mum," Gavin responds.

Liam promptly puts me down and kisses my hand. "Looks like we're divorced. Gavin played the mum card. She thinks I'm in Australia for the month, and that's how I'd like it to stay. It was nice while it lasted, Lily."

"What'd you do to piss off your mum?" James asks.

A sinister grin creeps across Liam's face. "I did a bang and dash with one of the nurses on Da's staff. From what my sister tells me, the girl comes in crying about her broken heart every day. Mum's cheesed off."

"You wanker," Gavin says. "Didn't anyone ever tell you not to dip your pen in the company ink?"

A cab pulls up and Liam walks toward it. "It's Da's office, not mine. And my pen was in dire need of ink at the time. Mum'll get over it in time. Get home safe!" He hops in a cab and drives off.

"He's like a tornado," I say. "He blows in, upturns

everything, and leaves you wondering what the hell just happened."

"That's Liam." James chuckles as another taxi pulls up. "Lily, it was great meeting you. I'm giddy this bloke has someone to put him in his place for a change. Hope to see you both soon. Cheers."

Gavin and I hop in the next cab. I'm ready to be off my feet. While I look fantastic, these boots are killing me.

Leaning my head on Gavin's shoulder, I say, "They're so much fun. I can see how you've stayed friends for so long."

"You passed all their tests with flying colors."

"What tests?" I ask.

"Oh, they were pushing you to see if you'd snap, and you handled them beautifully. You gave it as good as you got. I knew they would love you."

I smirk. "I can hold my own." I'm not proud, but I can't help but wonder how Brooke faired with their tests.

We're quiet for the rest of the ride. We're still jet lagged, and we probably drank a little too much. By the time we get back to Gavin's, I'm barely conscious and I just want to sleep. I strip down and get right into bed.

"Lily, you can't do that."

"Hmmm?" I groan, half asleep.

"Lil, I cannot sleep next to you naked. I won't get any sleep and will probably maul you. You're testing what little resolve I have."

I know I should get up and put clothes on, but exhaustion has taken over. The warm soft bed has captured me and I have no desire to move.

"*Lily!*"

I continue to ignore him, assuming he'll give up and get into bed. After a few minutes, I hear him walk away and slam the door.

Chapter Six

I wake up screaming and drenched in sweat. I'm back in the barn. The smell of hay is so powerful, I can feel hives forming on my skin. Knowing Not-Charlie could strike at any moment, I search for a hiding spot. I find a corner, slink to the floor and pull my knees to my chest. Seconds later, the lights come on and I find I'm in Gavin's bedroom, stuck between the dresser and the wall. Gavin rushes to me, and picks me up off the floor and carries me to the bed. I collapse into his arms, weeping. Whispering soothing words, he strokes my hair as I cry. When the sobs finally subside, he whispers, "Are you ready to talk about it yet?"

I can't keep doing this. To either of us. The nightmares aren't going away, and he deserves to know about the craziness on the other side of the bed. I wipe the tears from my eyes and tell him the whole story. Lorenzo's warnings, Not-Charlie attacking me and later kidnapping me. I go into detail about what happened in the barn, bawling as I replay it in my head. He holds me tighter when I describe Not-Charlie's brutality. He's trying to be supportive but he can't hide the anguish on his face.

"Gavin, I made it out," I say, seeing how he is affected by the story. "You couldn't have done anything to protect me. This insane sequence of events was set in motion when Ash died. Before that. When Ash got in bed with fucking drug dealers. Even if you had been there every second, something would have happened. At least it's over now. I'm finally free of the curse that was Ashton Preston."

He lets out a frustrated sigh. "I'm so proud of your bravery and courage. You're a survivor, and I'm in awe of your strength. But you were alone. If I had been there with you, we could have faced this together, and I promise you I never would have let anyone lay their hands on you. But I was thousands of kilometers away. I left you vulnerable."

Knowing that nothing I can say will change how he feels, I continue with the story. For the first time, I tell the whole truth about Lorenzo, finding the money, and my meeting with Carlos.

"You sat down with a guy from the Mexican drug cartel? By yourself?" he asks.

I rub my cross between my finger and thumb. "It was the only way this would be over. I couldn't keep looking over my shoulder."

His body tightens around me. His soft, cradling embrace turns into a constricting squeeze. "You are the most daring, mad woman I've ever met. I'm afraid to ever let you out of my sight. You're going to run off to try to slay dragons or something."

"Dragons may be less intimidating," I say. "I may have looked calm and collected, but I was scared shitless."

"Lily, I don't think you know what it means to be scared shitless." He kisses my neck a few times. He shifts under me and clears his throat, making me giggle.

He moves my hair so it covers my neck, shielding him from temptation, then rests his chin on the top of my head. "All it took was my sexual torment to get you to smile."

I gently elbow his stomach and wiggle my ass into his lap. "You're not the only one tormented here, buddy. When can I go see your doctor friend?"

"Stop that," he says as he slaps my butt. "You have an appointment next week. We can behave until then."

"That's so far away," I whine.

He reaches between us and adjusts himself, making me snicker. "Subject change," he says. "Thank you for sharing with me. Do you feel better?"

"Yes, I do. I'm just not sure why I keep having these terrors. I'm finally free from it all. From Ashton, from the drama, from that life. I don't understand why I'm still having nightmares. My subconscious should be throwing a party, not freaking out."

"You won the war, but what you went through was still traumatic. It takes some time to get over that. Even after all these years, I still struggle with what I witnessed in Afghanistan."

I lay back on the bed. "You don't talk about it much."

He pulls the blanket from the end of the bed to cover me and then leans against the headboard. "No, I don't. I've been through a lot of therapy, but it doesn't make it less painful. I host a group of fundraisers in January for veteran's causes. It's probably the toughest time year for me because ... I immerse myself in it for the cause and it ends up swallowing me whole. The rest of the year, I try to keep it tucked away."

I nod. I know there aren't really any right words to say.

He draws figure eights on my bicep. "Do you think it would be helpful for you to see someone? My parents died at the same time I came back from Afghanistan. I thought I was right as rain, but I wasn't. Mason dragged me kicking and screaming. I hated it at first, but in time I learned to appreciate it. My time with Dr. Sparks changed my life. Helped me come to terms with some issues I just couldn't let go of."

I shrug. "I'll think about it. I'm not opposed to therapy, but I also think I may just need a little time." I look up at him.

"Where were you tonight? Why weren't you in here?"

"There's no way I could sleep in this bed with you naked and be able to control myself. I'm a gentleman, but dear God, woman. You test me."

I smile, loving every second of it.

"So are you going to get dressed, or do I have to go back in the guest room?" he demands.

"Fine. I'll get dressed if you get some ice cream." I do my best to mask my big smile. While I don't want him to be tortured, I love that he's pining for me.

Em didn't pack chaste pajamas. Everything is lace and satin and designed for minimal coverage. I take a pair of boxers and sweatshirt from Gavin's drawers. We climb back into bed and eat ice cream while he tells me embarrassing stories about Liam and James. As usual, he makes me laugh so hard, I'm distracted and don't realize how much I've eaten until I'm about to explode. This is my favorite part of us.

We sleep past noon and then lie in bed and read. He reads *The Economist* and *The London Times*, while I read a trashy romance. He pokes fun at my choice of reading material, but every once in a while I catch him reading over my shoulder.

It's Sunday, and tomorrow Gavin has to go back to work. I want to relax and enjoy him before we have to return to the real world fraught with demands and deadlines. By two, my stomach is growling so loudly that neither one of us can ignore it. I'm craving pizza, so we decide to get dressed and venture out. I'm eager to take the Tube, but Gavin wants his car for work, so we take a taxi to the garage he was storing it in while he was gone.

"A Range Rover?" I say when he pulls the car of its parking spot. "This is not at all what I expected. I figured you had a sports car. Something flashy and not practical."

"I have a sports car. Several, in fact, but having a sports car in the city is silly. Too much traffic. Too many bad drivers. It's brutal on the transmission. What's wrong with a Range Rover?" He sounds a little offended.

"Nothing. You've just surprised me, that's all."

He turns on the MP3player, and Phish blares through the speakers. This also takes me by surprise. Phish is stoner music, and Gavin hasn't shown any signs of being a stoner. Granted, I like Phish and I'm not a stoner, but I'm the exception, not the rule. Is there a side of him I don't know? It gnaws at me a little. We know so much about each other, but there's so much that's still a mystery. I feel the whirlpool of doubt starting, and I do my best to shake it off.

He turns the volume down. "Sorry about that. I find listening to Phish keeps me calm during traffic. Otherwise, I go insane and have the urge to smash things with my Rover."

We arrive at Saporitalia, a quaint restaurant with wood-fired pizza that smells to die for. The host seats us, and I look over the menu. I feel Gavin watching me, but I pretend not to notice.

When the server comes to take our order, Gavin hands her his menu, then looks at me. "You order, and we'll split it."

My hands cover my stomach. "Gavin, I'm not very good at splitting. I end up eating it all."

"Just order whatever you fancy. Whatever you don't eat, we'll have for later."

Easy for him to say. His pants will fit fine tomorrow. I order a four cheese pizza, a pasta Bolognese, and fried eggplant.

"Could we get that for take-away, please?" Gavin requests.

The server nods and leaves.

"You don't want to stay?" I'm surprised. I thought he wanted to go out.

He pulls out his phone and scrolls through his messages. "I think I need to take you home."

I cock my head. "Why?" I ask, totally confused.

His focus remains on his phone. He never looks at me. "I'm not sure. But when you're ready to tell me, you will."

I don't take his bait. I'm not even sure what I could say that wouldn't make me sound like a psycho. We're quiet as we wait for the waiter to return.

After Gavin pays the check, the server hands us two bags filled with Styrofoam containers and we go back to Gavin's flat. Once inside, he pours some wine and starts a fire in the living room.

He lays a blanket on the floor and sets up a fireside picnic. He pats the place on the blanket next to him. "Come sit. Eat. Relax. Maybe after a glass of wine, you'll want to tell me what's going on in that pretty head of yours?"

He serves me, tapas style. He brings out a dozen appetizer size plates and gives me a little bite of everything. Just like I like it. When he's done, he turns on some music that I can't quite place. It's an orchestra, but it doesn't sound classical. I ignore the food as I focus on sounds and look out the window. We have a great view of the park all lit up for the Winter Wonderland festival. That gives me something to look at when I'm avoiding Gavin's gaze.

His fork clangs when it hits his plate. "Okay, now I know something is wrong. You're not eating," he states.

"What are we listening to? It sounds like Led Zeppelin mixed with an orchestra."

"That's what it is. The London Philharmonic plays Zeppelin. It's one of my favorites. Perfect dinner music."

"I never would have guessed you're a Zeppelin fan." I pick up a slice of pizza but put it down before taking a bite.

"There's a lot you don't know about me. For the record, that isn't a bad thing. I'm excited to learn all there is to know about you." He takes a sip of his wine.

"Isn't it weird?" I fiddle with a fork as I keep avoiding Gavin's eyes. "We're so close in some ways, but not at all in others. I mean, sure, we've proven we can handle tragedy well. But are we a good match for just a typical Tuesday night?"

He sets his wine glass down. "Where is this coming from? I think you know me better than some of my best mates. No, we haven't had a typical dating experience but we were trapped together in a flat for five bloody days. I think we've learned more about each other than most people learn in a year of dating. Truly, Lily, I respect your feelings but I just don't follow this at all."

I twirl a string of pasta around my fork. "I'm sorry. This is out of left field..."

"Luv, we have a level of trust that is beyond compare. At least that's how I feel. That's how good relationships are built. Don't spoil that because you don't know my shoe size."

"Which is?" I ask. I'm not sure why I need to know. It's not like I'm going to buy him shoes or anything but knowing is important to me.

"Twelve and a half... Do you feel better now?" He smirks. "You need to get out of your head."

I don't know how to respond. The rest of the meal is tense because my head is still somewhere else. He doesn't push me further, and I'm thankful.

After we clean up dinner, Gavin goes for a run. I'm not sure why I feel so unsettled. He hasn't done anything wrong. Quite the opposite. My time with him has been a dream. So why am I full of doubt?

I'm four thousand miles from home and staying with someone I know intimately on many levels, yet he's still a complete stranger. What if this completely backfires? What if we can't stand each other once we spend time together? Real-life time where we have to negotiate, compromise, and empty the dishwasher. What if he doesn't separate his whites from colors? Hell, he probably doesn't even know how to do laundry. What if he doesn't cover his dish before putting it in the microwave and then leaves the splatter to get crusty and gross? What if I want to kill him after a week?

I call Em for support. As I dial, I walk to the window and notice it's finally stopped raining.

"Hey there, Schmexy girl. How's London?" she says.

Grabbing a throw blanket I find draped on the sofa, I wrap myself up and go onto the terrace. Sitting on the chaise lounge, I pull the blanket tight around me. "Em—"

"Oh. This isn't a check-in call. This is a panic-attack call. Shoot. What's the crisis?"

"Why the hell did I come all the way to London with someone I barely know? Yeah, we've been through a lot but do I know him well enough to stay here with no return ticket? How nuts is this?"

"Wow! Estrogen overload," Em declares. "First of all, you *do* know him. Hell, even I know him well enough to know you two are perfect for each other. He's the exact opposite of Ash and one hundred percent what you need. You've got your panties in a bunch over nothing. Stop being such a chick. The man read you Jane Austen while you were in a coma, for Christ's sake. *Jane fucking Austen*. When he read Mr. Darcy, I swooned, and I hate Austen. That man loves you and would do anything for you."

The wind picks up and I pull the blanket up to my chin. "What if we aren't compatible?"

"You really think you'd have a better idea if you were

compatible if you met under normal circumstances? Kind of like you and Ash? Remember, I introduced you at a party. He used to walk you to class, take you to dinner and tailgating before Cats games. You two had the quintessential college dating experience, and look how that turned out. Pull your head out of your ass! There's no magic formula that'll guarantee your relationship will work. All you can do is have faith. Which it seems you're completely lacking. You're looking for trouble, for flaws that aren't there. If you keep this up, it'll end in total and complete self-destruction. Stop sabotaging a good thing."

Damn, she's right.

"I'll take the silence to mean you're seeing the error of your ways," she says smugly.

"You just love being right." A gust of wind blows through, almost taking my blanket with it. I pull it tight around me, and take the phone inside, thinking I'll get ready for a hot bath.

"Damn straight. Now listen and listen good. Gavin's amazing. You deserve some fucking happiness for a change, so go be happy together. You have every reason to trust him. Enough with this bullshit. Call me tomorrow after you get your hormones in check."

"Love you, Em."

"One more thing. Gavin is not Ash. I know your asshole detector is busted and you can't trust your judgment any more but you can trust mine. I can spot them a mile away and I know Gavin's one of the good ones. You let Ash wreck you once. He doesn't have the right to do it again. So don't let the scars he gave you ruin your chance at happiness."

After she hangs up, I turn the hot water on and digest what she said. Em's always been the voice in my head that I wish I could ignore. A very foul-mouthed Jiminy Cricket. She doesn't pull punches, especially when I'm screwing up. The last thing I want is to sabotage things with Gavin.

I thought I knew what I was getting into with Ash, but it turned out much worse than I expected. Even after four years together, I didn't foresee how Ash would change. He was a narcissistic bastard the whole time we were dating, but he was fun, and he fawned over me because I was his shiny toy.

After we got married, I grew up and had to take care of his father. By that point, there was no room in my life for parties. My days were filled with physical therapy appointments, adult diaper changes and housekeeping. The playboy lifestyle got old. I needed more substance and less substance abuse. We were no longer operating on the same plane and it all went downhill from there.

I mull it over in a long bath and climb into bed. I wake up an hour later when I hear Gavin turn on the shower. He left the bathroom door open a crack, just enough that I can see him undress. Damn, the man is sexy. Celibacy running has made his ass look even better than before. Maybe all the hormonal fretting is just me really, really, *really* needing to get laid?

Gavin catches me watching him. "Keep staring and I'm going to charge you admission."

I fold my arms across my chest. "I can't touch, and you're seriously going to deprive me of looking? That's just cruel."

He uses a second towel to dry his hair. "Doesn't that just make it harder? To look and not touch?"

"I don't know, Gavin. Does it make it harder?" I ask with a smirk.

He hangs up the towel and walks toward the closet. "Don't put those thoughts in my head. I don't want to have to go run another thirty kilometers."

"Damn!" I quickly try to do the math in my head and fail. "How many miles is that?"

He rolls his eyes. "Don't they teach Americans conversions when you learn math? Almost twenty miles."

I give a low whistle. "Okay, I repeat, damn! You must've had all sorts of thoughts stuck in that handsome head of yours."

"I did. I ran them off, and I'd like to keep it that way. It's the only way I'll make it at least another week without being able to touch you. Of course, seeing the way your eyes light up when you smile is doing a number on me."

"I'm sorry my heart problem has become your problem."

Gavin walks out of the closet, pajama pants slung low over his hips. "Lily, I want all of your problems to be my problems. I never want you to have to face anything alone again. I would gladly give up sex forever to know that you are safe."

I lean over and kiss him, but my sweet kiss turns heated. I can actually feel sparks generated by our passion. My hands move from Gavin's neck to his stellar abs. I run my finger along the top of his pajama bottoms.

He pulls away. "We're getting a bit carried away. Are you okay, luv?"

"No, I'm not. Start kissing me again and I'll be all better."

"Damn it, what am I going to do with you? Kisses like that can't be good for your heart. My heart feels like it's going to explode!" He pulls back and closes his eyes. He rests his head against the headboard and takes slow, deep breaths. "I think I need to take up yoga."

Chapter Seven

Back to reality. Gavin returns to work today, which makes it a big day for me. Either I find a way to put my own stamp on London, or I go home. I don't expect to have my life worked out in one day, but I need to start. I'll be miserable if I just sit home and watch British soap operas all day. Do they even have soap operas anymore?

Lounging in bed, reading a romance on my Kindle, I catch a peak of Gavin getting ready. My Kindle slips through my fingers and bounces on the bed. "Good God, you're going to go to work like that?"

Oxford in a suit... hot damn. It's obviously a custom job because it fits him perfectly, showing off his broad shoulders and tight, toned torso. The allure of the suit is more than just the way it highlights his ridiculous body. His commanding presence while wearing it, the air of confidence that surrounds him. Everything about him screams "power". Or more accurately it screams, "Don't fuck with me or I'll destroy you." I may not give a shit about his money but power seems to be a bigger turn on than I would have expected.

"What? What's wrong?" He looks in the mirror, trying to figure out what isn't working.

"Your ass in those pants! I can hardly contain myself. How does anyone get any work done? All your female employees must just swoon with you strutting around like that. I bet you actually stop traffic. You do, don't you?"

A sexy smirk spreads across his face. "Trousers, Lily. They're called trousers. I can assure you I'm a slave driver. My employees are too busy to notice me." He straightens his tie and looks back at me. "And only occasionally."

"Occasionally what?"

He winks. "Occasionally I stop traffic."

I throw a pillow at him. "You're an arrogant bastard, you know that?"

He sits on the edge of the bed and slips his shoes on. "Hey, you asked! Don't ask a question unless you can handle the answer."

I scoot down on the bed and wrap my arms around his stomach. I rest my chin on his shoulder and say, "You're just lucky I'm prohibited from attacking you, or there's no way in hell you would be leaving this bedroom. Not for a good long while anyway."

He peels my arms off of him, stands, and then kisses each of my hands. "I'm going to hold you to that after the doctor clears you." He walks to his dresser and puts his watch on.

I smirk. "Oh, you'll be holding something to me all right."

Gavin closes his eyes and leans against the wall. "You'll be the death of me, woman. Can't you talk about football or skiing or carpentry? Anything other than... this?"

"You want to show me what you can do with a hammer, Gavin?" I bat my eyes at him.

He glares at me.

I cock my head and flash him a coy smile. "What? You said carpentry," I say innocently. "Fine, soccer? You want to come over here so I can show you how to score? I'm sure you're amazing at getting it in the goal! No? Not better?" I explode into laughter as he storms out of the room.

"Goodbye, Lily," he yells from the hallway.

I don't know what he's so pissy about. I'm just as sex starved as he is! I lie down and close my eyes for a few moments, mentally calming my libido. Suddenly, I feel his weight on me, and he kisses me with a passion that literally takes my breath away. I feel my heart pounding as if it's going to fly out of my chest.

I pull back. "You change your mind about staying in bed with me all day?"

"If only, Lily. If only. I couldn't leave without a proper goodbye."

"Well that was one hell of a sendoff. You'd better go. Don't want to be late. I hear your boss is a real bastard."

He kisses my forehead and walks out the door. Damn, that man knows how to make an exit.

It takes me about an hour to unravel from the sexual tension spurred by that kiss. I flip open my laptop and investigate places to go on my day of exploration.

While I'm trying to decipher the Tube map, the intercom buzzes. Since I'm wearing fuzzy socks, I slide across the hardwood floors to get to the intercom phone. "Good morning, Willis. What can I do for you?"

"Ms. Clark, I have a package for you. May I deliver it now?"

"Yes, please!" I look down and realize I'm only wearing Gavin's shirt, white panties and socks. If only I had a pair of sunglasses, I could slide across the wood floor and lip sync to eighties music. Regardless, it's not appropriate attire for company. I rush back to the bedroom and throw on yoga pants.

A few moments later, Willis is at the door with a big white box with a deep purple ribbon. I open the box to find two dozen long-stemmed lavender roses, a small box wrapped in violet paper, a large purple envelope, and a small white envelope. I open the small first, revealing a cream card embossed with GE.

My dearest Lily,

Circumstances have prevented me from courting you in the manner you deserve. A woman as spectacular as you deserves to be wooed. Please do me the honor of joining me this evening for a proper date. More details to follow.

In preparation for a lovely evening out, you deserve to be pampered. As I am not able to properly fill that role at this time, I hope that this will be an acceptable proxy.

Counting the moments until I see you,

G

I'm moved that even though I horrifically overreacted yesterday, he still listened.

I open the second envelope. It's a spa package at the Four Seasons—where else? A full day of soaking, massaging, scrubbing, and primping, set to start in an hour. I guess my first day of London vs. Lily will have to be postponed.

Finally I open the small box. It's a new iPhone and a note. *Can't have you wandering the city without a mobile!*

He's pulling out all the stops!

I text him:

Sweetest boyfriend ever!

Gavin: Does that mean you've accepted my invitation?

Lily: How could I not? Where are we going? What

should I wear?

Gavin: Did you not read the card? It says details to follow. Have some patience!

Lily: Bring sexy, seductive Gavin back. Cranky Gavin isn't as fun!

Gavin: You'd best chivvy if you want to make your appointment.

Lily: I'd best what? I hate it when autocorrect makes you say silly things.

Gavin: That isn't an autocorrect problem, that's just a sign I need to get you a British English to American English translator. Chivvy, it means get moving.

Lily: Huh, learn something new every day. Vocab lesson aside, thank you. This was really too sweet.

Gavin: This is just the tip of the iceberg.

Lily: Curious...

He doesn't reply, which is the kick in the pants I need to get myself together. I search the kitchen for a vase but come up empty. I guess Gavin's designers didn't think of everything! I find a pitcher that'll make do then bolt out the door. Willis gives me directions to the hotel, which is only a few blocks from the flat.

When I arrive at the spa, I'm asked to change into a robe and wait in the relaxation area. A woman named Nicole comes in and checks me out. She says she needs to examine my skin tone and body type to make sure they use the right products during my treatments. Something feels off about it and creeps me out. But by the time I'm in my seaweed and eucalyptus scrub, I've completely forgotten about her.

Eighty minutes later, I'm back in the relaxation room with a bottle of water and waiting for my hot stone massage. A messenger delivers me another big white box with a purple bow and ribbon. This time, the card is on the outside.

My dearest Lily,

Please join me for dinner followed by an evening at the London Philharmonic. A car will pick you up from the spa at 6:00.

Counting the moments,

G

I open the box and find a stunning Versace gown. It's strapless and black along the bust. Down the floor-length straight skirt, it transitions into the most spectacular shade of deep purple. This is the most unique and stunning dress I've ever seen. Moments later, a box arrives with a pair of Giuseppe Zanotti's four-inch heels. The ensemble is show-stopping, and a woman needs balls to pull off an outfit like this. Otherwise, she'll look like a little girl playing dress up. I never would've had the courage to choose this for myself. How the hell am I going to pull it off?

Before I have too much time to feel insecure, my masseuse calls me back. Another note is waiting for me in the treatment room.

Get out of your head so you can enjoy the massage!

The man knows me well, that's for sure.

Gavin's advice is sound. If I sit and stew, I'm completely wasting this experience. I do my best to turn off my brain and live in the moment. The massage is spectacular, almost ethereal. I return to the relaxation room, curious if there's any more surprises coming my way.

I'm called back for my facial, which I hope won't leave my skin too raw for the evening. The esthetician assures me I'll be in tip-top shape and the makeup artist will help me get ready. Gavin has done the full spa day thing for me before, but this level of extravagance is intense. After the facial, I'm swept away to another room where someone starts on my hair, makeup, and nails.

After I'm primped and pampered, my gown is brought into the room, along with a thin square white box with purple ribbon. In the box is the most delicate diamond tennis necklace. *Holy crap! This is too much!* I see why he's giving me the necklace by proxy. If he were here, I'd never accept it. But what am I going to do, leave it at the spa? Melanie, the makeup artist, puts the strand of sparkle on me and turns me to face the mirror.

I want to hate it. I want to think it's too much money and Gavin has gone overboard with all of this. But I can't. It is *so* pretty, and it lies on my neck as if it were meant to be there. All of my strong, feminist, independent pride melts away, and I'm transformed into a little girl who feels like a princess.

I'm giddy beyond words. This isn't my first black tie affair. Ash and I used to attend functions like this all the time back before Franklin's accident. But this feels different. Like that was playing dress up and this is the real deal.

Melanie helps me get into my dress and makes a few last-minute touch ups. Nicole returns to the room and asks, "How does it fit?"

"Perfectly," I respond.

"I thought it might," she grins. "I'm one of Mr. Edwards' personal shoppers. Sorry if I seemed like an odd duck earlier. Mr. Edwards mentioned that this was all a surprise, so I was trying my hardest not to give anything away."

"Mission accomplished. I was completely surprised!"

"Well, let's look at you." I slowly turn around so she can see her handiwork. "My word, you're gorgeous. That dress didn't need a stitch of alteration."

When I look in the mirror, I can't believe it's me. I forgot that I could actually look like this. For the past five years, my wardrobe has consisted of yoga pants, tank tops, and flip flops. With each different perfume I'd smell on Ash's laundry, my self-esteem diminished. I didn't see the point in trying.

When I was in college, I used to strut into events like I owned the place, confidence oozing from my pores. Hell, that was why Ash fell in love with me. But that light burnt out of me. My marriage, taking care of Franklin, ignoring myself. They suffocated me. When I look in the mirror now, I see glimmers of the woman I used to be.

Gavin is very good at the woo. I take a quick picture of myself and send it to Em, then make my way to the lobby. The concierge directs me to Lucas, my driver for the evening. He leads me to a black Mercedes, and we're on our way.

Em texts me back: *There's the girl I know and love. Can't wait to hear the story behind this. I owe Gavin one for getting you out there. Welcome back to the land of the living. Your throne has been waiting for you.*

Her reference to my throne cracks me up. My sorority sisters used to joke that Ash and I always "held court" like a king and queen. I never thought it was quite that bad, but I've seen enough pictures to know there was some truth in it. Part of why Em and I lost touch after I married Ash was because she couldn't stand to see the queen bee reduced to a mousey maid.

Lucas informs me when we arrive at the Royal Festival Hall. Before I have a chance to wonder where I'm going to meet Gavin, my door opens to heaven in a tux. Tux Gavin is a sight to be seen. I'm frozen in my seat, breathless.

"Are you getting out, or shall I come in there to get you?" he jokes.

I will my legs to move. "Good evening, Mr. Edwards. I must say this whole day has been quite the surprise." I give him a chaste kiss, then wipe away the lipstick mark. "I cannot thank you enough."

Gavin stares at me as if he's in pain and swallows hard. "Lily, one of my hopes was that this would give us an activity that would prevent me from thinking about sex. I've failed miserably. You look devastatingly gorgeous. I don't think a woman has ever looked so beautiful. Let's get you inside before I lose all self-control and ravish you." He puts his hand on the small of my back and guides me toward the building.

"How did you orchestrate all of this?" I ask. "I feel like this was a Cinderella day for me."

"After last night, I realized you were in dire need of pampering and romance. After some googling, I pulled it all together. Get used to it. You'd best be prepared to be wooed."

"Bring it, Oxford." I beam.

He kisses my neck, which makes me giggle. "Thank you for not fighting me on the necklace. It's stunning, and highlights one of my favorite parts of you."

"Oh, yeah? Which part is that?"

He runs his tongue along my collarbone and up my neck and whispers, "This part."

If only I'd brought a change of panties.

I link my elbow through his and we walk through a small collection of reporters before entering the building. Gavin handles it all without flinching, but I'm blinded by all the flashes. Apparently if you are born into money, you're also born with pupils that avoid dilation when necessary. I was squinting and crinkling my nose, trying to block out the light. From the face I was making, I'm guessing there's now a bunch of photos that look like I was about to sneeze. Perfect.

Gavin guides me through the lobby. As we climb the stairs, he whispers, "Every bloke in this building is painfully jealous of me. I'd best be on guard tonight. Several look like they're ready to pounce on you."

I pat his arm. "It's hardly me people are looking at. You really know how to work that tux, Oxford."

"They're used to me, luv. Take a look around. You're the one causing the commotion."

When we reach the top of the staircase, I causally look around and notice that we do seem to be a focal point. I look down to avoid the stares and let out a slow breath. Em's words come back to me, making me silently laugh. I stop looking down and strut through the crowd. It's nice to feel some swagger back.

Gavin directs us to a balcony with a spectacular view of the stage. I never even asked what we're hearing tonight, and I honestly don't care. I'm sure whatever it is will be amazing, and I'm enjoying living in the moment.

The house lights go down, and the performance is powerful and entrancing. I become lost in the music. My pulse races with the crescendo, luring me into a seductive trance. I'm only pulled out of the allure of the music by Gavin's gentle touch. He draws patterns on my arm with his fingertips, while whispering sweet nothings in my ear. He's pulling out all the stops.

After the show, we go to the most intimate, romantic restaurant I've ever seen. The restaurant only has a handful of tables. Parties of two only. The roaring fireplace, candle light, and exquisite food perfectly set the mood for seduction. Clos Maggiore could rename itself Gonna Get Laid. That is, of course, if one part of the couple doesn't have a pesky heart problem. The fact Gavin's trying so hard to court me while knowing there's only a PG ending to his evening makes it all the more sweet and genuine.

We take the long way back to Gavin's flat, and he points out various places that have significance to him. Where he fell and broke his arm when he was nine. The dive bar he and his friends would sneak to when they were fourteen. The bakery he and his grandfather went to every Sunday for fresh bread for family dinner. Each story is lovely and always told with humor. I laugh the whole way home. More than anything, I'm touched by his effort. He heard my concerns yesterday and did everything imaginable to soothe my anxiety.

A man who actually listens... He is a freaking unicorn.

All the distance and drama allowed me to forget why I fell in love with him in the first place. My feelings for him developed during the quiet time we spent together. Spending this night with him brings it all back and reminds me why I came to London.

By the time we return to Gavin's, I'm floating on air. I feel as though I've spent the day in a fairy tale. While Gavin showers, I throw on a pair of sweats, grab a glass of wine and a heavy blanket, and go onto the terrace. It's cold but peaceful. I feel serene for the first time I can remember. I want to hold onto this feeling and never let it go.

Chapter Eight

I wake up the next morning in an empty bed. I don't remember coming back inside last night, so Gavin must have carried me to bed. There's a box and a card on the pillow.

Lily,

Had an early meeting. Sorry you're waking up to an empty bed, but it's better than waking up on a cold terrace! Silly girl!

I'll be thinking of you all day. Call if you need anything.

Love,

G

P.S. Special plans for today. More details to follow!

Inside the box is a book: *Bum Bag and Fanny Packs: A British- American Dictionary.*

I grab my phone from the nightstand and send him a text.

Lily: Hate waking up alone, but love to get your notes. The book's great, but I live to tease you about your British nonsensical words! Anxiously waiting for details about my special plans.

Gavin: You Americans and your need for instant gratification. Patience, luv! Pleasure is built by anticipation.

Lily: Is this a promise of pleasure? Because I'll be as patient as you want if there's a happy ending involved. You're so good at delivering instant gratification.

Gavin: I have to give a presentation now and all I can think of is happy endings. Thank you for that. I'll have to sit for my presentation until things... settle down.

Lily: Happy to help!

This man sure does know how to keep a girl on her toes! While I wait for more information on today's adventure, I attend to my ever-growing to-do list. I plot some blog ideas and start writing.

Around ten, I head out to learn my way around London. I take the Tube to Piccadilly Circus, which wasn't what I was expecting. No elephants. No big top. Not a clown in sight. Just billboards and buildings. I walk a few blocks to the London Library, which is by far the largest, most impressive library I've ever been to. I meant to just learn my way there, but I get lost exploring it. I'd been worried I wouldn't be able to do the research I need for my writing, but clearly I was mistaken. For a research junkie, this place is like Disneyland to me.

After the library, I wander the streets for a bit. I've always found that the best way to learn a new place is to get lost and find my way home. I wander and find Buckingham Palace, which is spectacular. I watch the Changing of the Guard like the other tourists. After two hours of walking, I'm exhausted and frozen. I grab my phone to look for the nearest Tube station, and see that I'm not far from Gavin's. It's cold and windy, but I decide to walk the rest of the way.

My fingers and toes are numb by the time I get to Gavin's. The tub calls to me the moment I walk in the door. I overdid it a bit today, but it was worth it. My cell rings, snapping me out of my bath coma. It's Greene.

Feeling weird about being naked in the tub talking to Greene, I hop out and dry off.

"Hey, Greene! How's it going? I'm amazed you have this number."

"I just called Gavin and he gave it to me. Look, Lil, I wish I was calling just to check in. I have to talk to you about something." He sounds somber.

I sit down on the edge of the tub and ring out my hair. "Jesus, I thought all of the doom and gloom was behind me."

He sighs. "Max's gone dark. I'm worried about him. I

didn't think he should take this assignment, but he did, and now you may be in danger."

Panic swells inside me. "Greene, you aren't making sense. Start from the beginning."

"Max went undercover with a FBI/DEA taskforce, going after the cartel. He believed that they were more involved in your capture than you thought. He's too damn close to this case and had no business getting involved, but he has some good contacts and the DEA jumped at the chance to bring him in. Since he went in, he's missed every check in with his handler."

I gasp. Suddenly, it's freezing in here. I quickly pad to the closet and shrug into Gavin's cashmere robe. It's huge, but warm. "What was Max thinking? I can't believe he did this. If he gets out of this alive, I'm going to kill him. Everything was wrapped up. Why the hell did he need to stir things up? Not- Charlie wasn't connected to the cartel!" The lie flows so easily, I almost believe it myself.

"A few reasons," he replies. "But mostly guilt. He feels like he let you down and needs to avenge you by going after them. "

"That's bullshit! Dammit, Greene, this shit was behind me. I was moving on!"

"I know. I tried to talk him out of it, but he couldn't let it go. He was obsessed. The deeper he got into the investigation, the more he learned just how nasty these guys are. The things they've done, Lil... It's enough to make your hair turn white. I'm not sure if I'm more worried that his cover's been blown or if he's going rogue and is trying to take down a bigger fish than his assignment entails. This is too personal for him to stay objective."

Yelling at Greene isn't going to solve anything, so I try to regain some composure. I sit on the edge of the bed and take a few deep breaths. "What happens now? How will you know if he's in trouble or not?"

"Everyone is reaching out to contacts to see what they can find out. I want you to be on your toes, though. I seriously doubt this is going to come back to you, but with Max gone dark, it'll make me feel better if you're on high alert."

"I'm not just worried about me. What about Max? He could be in way over his head. We need to pull him out." And if they figure out that my roommate has infiltrated them, my head's on the chopping block.

I hear him shuffling papers. Looking at the time, he's probably off to the daily staff meeting. After living with an FBI agent, I learned it's nowhere near as sexy of a job as it sounds. They spend more time in meetings and doing paperwork than they do in the field. "Look, don't worry too much yet. This call may be premature; he may be fine. Just promise me you'll be smart and stay aware of your surroundings, okay?"

"I will. Please keep me posted when you can," I say.

"Will do. Try not to worry," he says before he hangs up.

Fat chance of that! I cannot believe Max would do something so stupid. He couldn't just let sleeping dogs lie. I wish I could speak to Lorenzo or Carlos and find out what the hell is going on. Damn them and their no-communication rules! I have no choice but to sit and wait.

Too frustrated to stay in the condo, I decide to go get some fresh air. I blow dry my hair quickly, then throw on a pair of jeans and a sweater. As I walk out of the building, I look at the map on my phone and walk straight into someone. My phone and her purse fall to the sidewalk.

"Oh, my goodness, I'm so sorry! What a klutz I am!" I say as I reach down to pick up her purse.

As I hold her Gucci bag out to her, I catch a glimpse of her face. She looks so familiar, but I can't place where I've seen her.

She snatches the purse from my hands and scowls at me. "Can't you watch where you are going? Damn Americans!" She inspects the bag closely. "This is alligator! Do you have any idea how much it's worth?"

Something clicks in my brain.

"Olivia?"

She scoffs. "I see you aren't dead. I told him all the theatrics were for nothing."

Trying to look as casual as possible, I dust my phone off and look for scratches. I don't want to give her the satisfaction of knowing how much she bothers me. "Nope, alive and well. What are you doing here?"

She's more beautiful in person. The pictures hardly do her justice. Her raven hair is so shiny, it looks wet. Her flawless alabaster skin makes me wonder if she's ever needed make up a day in her life. Not a pore in sight.

She's disgustingly perfect. Until she speaks, that is. "I came to see Gavin. I heard he was back. I just didn't realize you were here as well." Her voice is filled with disdain.

I've dealt with plenty of her type before and she doesn't intimidate me in the least. Women like her only have power over you if you let them. So the more she looks at me like I'm a piece of gum stuck on her shoe, the more I show her I don't give a shit. "It's the middle of the afternoon, Olivia. He's at his office. If you want to see him, you should call and make an appointment."

She tries to put her hand on my shoulder, but I dodge her move by shifting my weight onto my back hip and looking down at my phone. My incoming text is far more important than whatever she has to say. And yet, she keeps on talking. "You, Lily, are a passing fling. I don't need a lecture on Gavin from you. I was here long before you and I'll be here long after he loses interest in you. You're no longer in crisis and he'll tire of you. Quickly. Avoid the flight of shame and just go home now while you still have some dignity."

After tucking my phone in my back pocket, I sniff the air dramatically. "The stench of your desperation is suffocating, like cheap perfume. If you think Gavin is so in love with you, go talk to him. Try acting like a grown up instead of a high school tramp."

I notice a cab turning a corner and I walk to the curb with my hand up. I'd give anything to turn around and see the look on her face but looking back will lessen the impact of my exit. I give the driver Gavin's office address, which may be a mistake. I've never been there before and I haven't specifically been invited but between Greene's call and Olivia's tirade, I need to talk to him soon or I'll explode.

When the cab pulls up to Gavin's building, I chicken out. I'm not dressed for an office, and the last thing I want to do is storm in like some clingy bimbo. His office is in Canary Wharf, an area of London I haven't seen yet, so I wander around the docks and take in the scenery. It is a very cool area that sort of reminds me of the Boston Harbor. The Thames is beautiful and being outside is calming my nerves. Even though I'm freezing my ass off, I enjoy myself. I can see why Gavin loves it here so much.

At five, I'm still popping in and out of the shops on the wharf when Gavin texts.

About to leave my office. Be home soon! Counting the minutes…

Lily: Great, can I catch a lift?

Gavin: Where are you?

Lily: In front of your building.

I sit on the steps of his building to wait for a response. After about five minutes, my hands are frozen, and I'm ready to head down to the Tube. Maybe he didn't get my message. Looking at the map on my phone, I stop paying attention to what's around me and I'm grabbed from behind. I lash out. I look down and see my attacker is off balance, so I elbow him in the gut and pivot. As I turn, I kick and knock his legs out. He lands on his ass.

I look into his face, instantly feeling guilty.

I crouch down to see if he's okay. "Gavin! Oh, my God, I'm so sorry! Did I hurt you?"

His eyes are wide, and he looks shaken. "That was so foolish of me. I'm sorry. Are you okay?"

"I'm just glad I didn't hurt you. " I put my hand over my heart as he stands.

He dusts off his backside. "I received your text and was so excited you were here, I ran down straightaway. I was about to scoop you up but I should have known better."

Hearing him make me sound like a victim makes me cringe. I'm a survivor. I kicked ass and got out alive. Why I am still so jumpy?

As if he can read my mind, he hugs me. "Just because you're still processing what happened doesn't make you a victim. Allow yourself time to heal. If you promise to do that, I promise not to sneak up on you again."

I gently punch his shoulder. "Get out of my head," I say teasingly.

"Oh what I wouldn't do to see what goes on in that head of yours," he says, then kisses my forehead. "I'll have to commend Max. He certainly taught you well," Gavin says with a smile.

"Ugh, about Max. I have so much to tell you." I groan.

He holds his finger up. "I want to hear all about it, but first, let me tell you about our plans for tonight," he says, waggling his eyebrows. He takes my hand and leads me to his car.

"I completely forgot. Do tell!"

He pushes the button on the elevator to the parking garage. "First we grab a quick dinner, and then we're off to the Royal Observatory. I have an astronomer friend there who's going to give us a special tour of the universe."

I'm completely blown away. "That's so cool. Like, best date ever cool. It pays to have friends in strange places, huh?"

The elevator arrives and he motions for me to get on. The elevator car fills up quickly, so he puts our conversation on pause until we get out three floors down. "When we were at the hospital, Em shared many Lily stories, and—"

I bury my head in my hands. "Urg, I can only imagine what she said."

He unlocks his Range Rover with the remote and opens the door for me. Once I'm in, he closes the door and then circles around to the driver's side. "It was all wonderful and just made me love you more. Anyroad, she said that one of your favorite classes at university was astronomy. Something about how Tucson has a big observatory and going there was one of your favorite projects. Then something went sour and you couldn't go back?"

"Yeah, she slept with the professor. The married professor. I went from being able to go whenever I wanted to being banned from the premises."

He looks over his shoulder as he backs out of the space. "That's bollocks! Why would you carry the can because she bunked up with the professor?"

I raise an eyebrow. "You went all British on me. Who's carrying a can?" I think I get the gist, but I like to break his balls a little. Or his bollocks, I should say.

He rolls his eyes. "It means take the blame. Why'd you lose privileges because Em couldn't keep her legs together?"

"Technically, only grad students were allowed to go there with any sort of regularity. Undergrads got one field trip there, and that's it. Unless you are boinking the teacher. Once his wife found out about them, I was taken off the VIP list."

"Well, you're in luck. Em has not slept with Gordon, so tonight you get an all-access pass."

Looking down at my jeans and V-neck sweater, I say, "I'm not really dressed for anything fancy."

He gently squeezes my thigh. "Don't worry, luv. You're perfect as you are."

After fighting nasty traffic, Gavin takes me to a small restaurant that he claims has the best bangers and mash in the city. I wasn't crazy about the sausages, but the mashed potatoes were out of this world. Like many pubs in London, they have cider on tap, which thrills me.

After dinner, we fight even heavier traffic to the Observatory. While we inch along through gridlock, Gavin tells me about his day. So much of what he does is classified or top secret as they say here, but he shares as much as he can. The office politics are highly entertaining. Everything from fighting over food in the fridge to some serious cutthroat competitive behavior. It seems jobs at Edwards are highly sought after, and people do the damnedest things to try to impress Gavin. If they only knew he sees right through their antics.

I should tell him about O and Greene, but I'm not ready to darken the mood. I'll tell him later. For now, I just want to enjoy the casual banter of two normal people, with normal lives.

It takes us almost an hour to go the few miles to the Observatory. We park in the back and enter through an employee entrance, where Gordon is waiting for us. He's five foot four, if he's lucky. If his hair were blond instead of light brown, I would say he's an older Elroy Jetson.

I walk up to him and hug him. "Gordon, it's so nice to meet you. I can't tell you how excited I am." I notice that he doesn't hug me back, and when I pull back, I see that he's beet red. I cringe. "Sorry! We Americans can be a bit forward. Big huggers over in the States." The more I talk, the redder he gets, so I shut up.

Gavin bursts out laughing, and Gordon punches him in the shoulder. "Lily, it's a pleasure to meet you. I hear you love looking up at the stars. I owe this Neanderthal a favor or two, and you're in luck. The rest of the crew is out at a conference, so I can show you around."

He takes us to the Observatory. Gordon gives us a bit of a lecture, most of which flies right over my head. His current project is galactic evolution, which sounds like the name of a soccer team to me. The pictures he shows me are amazing. My favorites are the star formations. So beautiful.

Once he's been around me a bit longer, Gordon stops blushing every time I ask him a question or look in his direction. I often touch people when I talk to them which clearly makes him uncomfortable, so I try to rein it in. When we get to the telescope, we end up standing very close to each other, and he jumps back.

Gavin whispers in my ear, "Stop flirting with him. You're making him nervous, luv."

I elbow him in the ribs and give him a death stare.

After an hour of looking at stars and planets, Gordon says, "Time's up. I've got to run off to dinner with my mum. Gavin, the other room is all set for you." He picks up his briefcase and directs us back to the lobby. "We're the last ones here. I trust you'll clean up after yourselves and close up when you leave."

Gavin pats him on the back. "Of course. Thank you for this. Say hello to your mum for me." Gordon nods and leaves with a wave.

After I hear the door click closed, I say, "What a strange little man."

"He's quirky, that's for sure. Positively brilliant, but he gets a bit uncomfortable in social settings."

I lean against the wall. "How did you two meet?"

"His twin brother, Graham, has been one of my closest mates since Oxford. We were both Full Blue in crew—"

I raise an eyebrow. "Come again?"

He rolls his eyes. "Full Blue is first team. Or, I suppose maybe you'd say varsity in the US." He takes my hand and leads me through a set of double doors.

"Anyroad," he continues. "The guys are twins, but polar opposites. You've met Gordon. He's never been social, but he's getting better. Five years ago, he probably would have fainted when you hugged him. Graham, on the other hand, is a social butterfly. He's trying to be an actor down in Australia, otherwise I'm sure you would have met him. He's tall, couldn't pass a science course if his life depended on it, and he's a big hit with the ladies."

I gently slap his arm. "You should have warned me Gordon's so shy, you dork! I feel awful. He was so kind to let us come."

"I just helped him get a grant that will fund his research for the next ten years. This is the least he can do."

I follow him through several sets of doors and down several corridors. "Where are we going?" I ask.

He opens another door and motions for me to go before him. "We're starting the next part of our date. In through here, my darling."

I step into the domed room, and I'm surrounded by stars. I stare up at the sky as Gavin leads me to a blanket with a picnic basket. He sits, pours two glasses of champagne, and pulls out a platter of strawberries.

He sits me down in front of him and rubs my back.

"Now tell me what happened that had you so stressed earlier."

I moan. His hands are so amazing. "I don't want to ruin this perfect moment with stressful talk."

He kisses my neck, and I get lost in the moment. He massages my lower back, and his hands creep farther down. Every muscle in my back and neck relaxes as his kisses become more passionate. He caresses my hips and runs his hands over my hip bones toward my center. I crave his touch. Each time he runs his strong hands over my pelvis, I quiver. He grazes me, and I whimper. I push into his hand, encouraging more.

He whispers, "I think we should stop," in the most seductive voice.

"Fuck stopping," I whisper back. "If I have a heart attack, call 911. It would totally be worth it."

He doesn't stop kissing my neck, but his hands move from my hips up my stomach. His fingers run along the underwire of my bra. He traces the deep V of my sweater, brushing the swell of my breasts.

"Seriously, Gavin," I say breathlessly. "Touching me everywhere but where I so desperately need it is so much worse than just going for it. All this torment is killing me. Please! I promise it'll be okay. Don't stop."

He plants a chaste kiss on my lips, then moves to the other side of the blanket to fill our glasses. He drops a strawberry in my glass and hands it to me. "We need to stop."

I know he isn't messing around now. Playtime's over.

Always the fucking Boy Scout.

He hands me a glass of champagne. "Don't pout. Let's enjoy the rest of the evening," he says.

This is probably the most romantic date I've ever been on, so I won't ruin it by sulking. My girly parts will have to remain neglected for a bit longer. Curse you, McDreamy, and your Sex Embargo. "Fine. But you'd better bring me back here after... you know."

"I promise," he says. He kisses my hand then pulls me close so I can lean into him. "Now tell me about your day."

I take a quick sip from my glass. "Well since I'm tense now, I might as well tell you all the stressful stuff." I sigh. "Greene called. Max has gone MIA. His handler hasn't heard from him. Max hasn't been under for very long, but Greene's spooked. He said Max was convinced the cartel was behind my kidnapping and he's out for blood. Obviously this is bad news because Max is in great danger and my deal with the cartel hinged on me making the FBI lose interest. If Max is going after them, my deal is void and I'm back in the crosshairs."

Gavin slams his fist into the ground. "Bloody hell! This is why you should have told them! Keeping secrets gets people killed."

"Don't you think I know that?" I snap. "I feel awful. You yelling at me doesn't help matters." No sex and a lecture? I don't think so!

He releases a deep sigh, and rubs my arm. "Sorry, luv. You're right. I'm just worried."

I run my cross back and forth across the chain. "I have no idea what to do. I wish I could talk to Lorenzo."

Gavin scoots me around so that I'm facing him. "Lily, you should tell someone at the FBI. Or, I have contacts at Interpol and MI-5. This is getting serious and we need professional advice. It's your life we're talking about, we have to be smart about it."

"How can I do that without bringing Lorenzo into it?" I ask. "I can't sell him out after all he has done to protect me."

Gavin feeds me a chocolate covered strawberry. "I think you should talk to Greene or Sully. They care about you, and they'll be able to keep a few details to themselves. Especially if it means protecting Max."

I savor the strawberry in my mouth as I consider his point. "You're probably right. The question is which one?" I ask. "Greene's softer but more by the book. Sully's hard core but not afraid to bend the rules."

"I think Greene. He'll put you first," Gavin responds.

I think for a minute and nod. "All right, I'll call him tomorrow."

He refills both our glasses. "Is that all the stressful news?" he asks.

I crinkle my nose. "Urg. No."

He turns me around again and resumes rubbing my shoulders. "Okay, tell me the rest."

I take a long sip of champagne. "Olivia stopped by your building today to inform me, again, that I'm just a temporary resting place for your penis and I shouldn't get too comfortable as you'll surely kick me to the curb any moment now. I told her to take it up with you."

"For the life of me, I cannot figure out where this is coming from." Gavin groans and drops his head onto my shoulder.

I set my glass down. "She wants to be your new penis warmer. That's where it's coming from," I say, highly annoyed. "I'm not sure how you don't see it."

He brushes my hair off of my shoulder, exposing my neck. "I'm not doubting you. It's just catching me so off guard. I've known her forever, and she has never shown any interest in me. She's never even looked at me like that. Plus, she's a bit of a slapper."

"A what?"

"A slapper. A slut," he answers.

I dip a strawberry into my champagne and nibble on it. "That's a real charming term," I reply.

Gavin rolls his eyes. "O's never been one to sleep alone. On our bloody business trip, men were constantly doing the walk of shame out of her hotel room. If she really wanted me, wouldn't she have made a move then?"

I turn toward him. "She hacked into my email and sent you an email saying I never wanted to talk to you again. People don't do that for 'brothers.' I may not know her, but I know women. She wants you. She probably put all those boys on parade to try to make you jealous. Whichever way to slice it, this is going to get messy."

"What would you like me to do?" he asks.

"My advice is to ignore her. She wants attention and anything you do will just provoke her. If you ignore her, more likely than not, she'll move on to some other poor schmuck."

"You're fine if I do nothing?" He looks at me as though he doesn't believe me.

I shrug. "I don't think there's another option. I'm not threatened by her. If you leave me for crazy cakes, well, you've got bigger issues to deal with than me and I'll have dodged a bullet."

"I'm *not* leaving you. But I'm uncomfortable being passive. I fear if I do nothing at all, she'll become combative."

I take a sip of my champagne. "The train's already left the station on that one. Just from my one encounter with her, I can tell she's come to play. You can react and play right into her hand or do nothing and watch her self-destruct."

He kisses me. "I've had enough talk of stressful things."

He pulls me down so my head is resting on his chest. We can look at the starry ceiling.

I loved looking at constellations as a kid but Gavin never did. I point out where they all are and tell him the stories behind them. He corrects me when I identify the Big Dipper. Apparently it is The Plough over here. Of course Gavin knows nothing but still knows enough to correct me! Smartass. After a while, I get sleepy and we pack up to head home. It was the perfect date.

Chapter Nine

I dread calling Greene. I wish I could break the news in person but I don't have any choice at the moment.

"Lily! How's it going, sweetheart?" Greene says.

"Greene, we need to talk and you're not going to like what I have to say. But I have to tell you. I need to know that we're on a secure line." I'm not exactly sure what a secure line gets me. He's in a government building. If Big Brother wants to listen, he's going to listen. People always say it in spy shows, so it seems appropriate.

"I'll call you back," he says flatly.

Ten minutes later, the phone rings, and the caller ID is unavailable.

"You know it's never good to start a conversation by telling someone they aren't going to like what they hear," he starts.

"I just wanted to prepare you," I reply. I take a deep breath and pray he takes this well. "The situation's complicated. I can't tell you everything, so you just have to trust me."

"Out with it, Lily," he orders

"Max needs to get out of ... wherever he is. He has to stop investigating the Morelia cartel. He's putting himself and me in grave danger."

"I'm going to need more than that."

Nervous, I twirl a lock of hair as I pace the room. "I found Ash's money and gave it back to the cartel. They weren't behind my kidnapping but they were pissed off that everyone thought it was them. They didn't kill me because I promised I would convince the FBI they had nothing to do with it. Max being in there breaks that promise. He's going to get me killed."

"God damn, Lily," he shouts so loud I have to pull the phone away from my ear. "I don't even know where to start with you."

"Start by getting Max out. Now."

"I'll do my best. I have to say, I'm hurt that you've been keeping secrets after everything we've been through."

It kills me that he feels betrayed. I never wanted anyone to get hurt but I also didn't know what else to do. I was stuck between a rock and a hard place and I made the best of it. "Greene, I'm grateful for everything you've done for me. I adore you. But as you know, there's a pretty ugly cast of characters in this drama I've been thrown into. Being buddies with the FBI has protected me at times and almost sealed my fate at others. I've never kept anything from you unless it would put me, you, or someone else in danger."

I hold my breath while he quietly takes in what I've told him.. "I expect when I retire, you'll tell me the full story."

Hearing his voice soften has me breathing again. "Yes, I will tell you everything once it's safe and you no longer carry a badge," I promise.

"Fine. I'll push harder to get Max out. On a different note, a nurse from the hospital leaked your story. It'll be all over the news tomorrow. Based on what you just told me, this could really put you in the hot seat."

Son of a bitch. "Thanks for the heads up. I appreciate it."

"Anytime, kid."

I sit down on the sofa. "Greene, we okay?" I ask. I need for this not to come between us. Not only because I know we'll need to work together but because I love him. He, Sully and Max, they've become part of my family and I've lost enough family already. I can't lose anyone else.

"Yeah, kid. We're okay. I've got to go and pull your roommate out of the fire, though. I'll talk to you soon. Try not to get in any trouble." He hangs up.

Well, that could've gone far worse. I didn't reveal too many secrets and I think Greene understands the urgency. Now we just need to get Max out before I have another bounty on my head.

****

The next day, my story hits the news. The nurse knew everything and revealed every detail. All the way down to the group of photos they found in Not-Charlie's apartment or how Max refers to it, the "cum collection." I still get nauseated thinking about Not-Charlie getting off on pictures of me. And saving them after! So wrong!

But the news story stays true to the version I told the FBI. Not-Charlie was obsessed and took me on his own volition. Nothing about drugs or cartels or ex-husband's debts. If they're getting wind that the FBI is still looking into them, all of this press may help soften that blow.

So far, the coverage is complimentary. They don't make me seem weak at all. *The Today Show*, which only a few months ago vilified me as a home-wrecking slut, is saying I'm a role model for women. I refused to be the victim and I was my own super hero. That's quite the turnaround. Not that I'm complaining but it boggles my mind that journalists can flip their position so easily without the least bit of remorse.

My phone rings nonstop. Reporters, publishers, bloggers. How the hell they got my number is beyond me. For three days straight, the calls, emails and texts come constantly. I was about to throw my phone out the window when Gavin got me another new phone. It's a pain in the ass getting people my new number but worth it. I send out an email with my new contact information to all my work contacts and the few friends I'm confident won't sell my number to the press.

Thankfully, the media hasn't realized I'm in London yet. I've been seen with Gavin but no one knows who I am. The story hasn't gotten international attention but as soon as it catches over here, I have a feeling my life will be pandemonium.

So Gavin and I do our best to stay inside. We're still under the radar but there's no reason to tempt fate. We eat carry-out, specifically a lot of curry. I'm obsessed! He gives me an amazing massage and goes for a twenty-mile run. With the exception of the kibosh on sex, it's domestic bliss.

Hopefully, all that will change today. I see Dr. Baker at twelve thirty and the appointment can't come soon enough.

Gavin's up and off to work before I stir, as usual. He says he's swamped with work but I'm fairly certain he's just avoiding temptation. I wake up from a sexy Gavin dream frustrated and wound so tightly I might explode. In just a few short hours, this will hopefully all be over.

Gavin said he would pick me up at eleven thirty, which gives me a few hours to get ready. I head back to the Four Seasons Spa for a waxing and exfoliation scrub. If all goes well today at the doctor, I want to be smooth, soft, and addictively touchable.

By eleven, my mission is accomplished. I walk by a news stand and see myself on the cover of half the tabloids. The picture is of me the night we went to the Philharmonic. Typically I hate pictures of myself but I actually look decent. *American Heroine Living it up in London!* My favorite is a picture of me and Gavin laughing. It says *Finding Love in London!*

I buy a few of them and look through them when I get back to Gavin's flat. I'm pleasantly surprised to find I'm not called a whore once! They paint me as a strong woman who won't be held down by the evil in the world. I fought for my freedom and am now taking some time for me in jolly old England. According to the rags, England's happy to have me. It must be true, right? Tabloids don't lie or anything! The whole situation makes me laugh. I've been a whore and a hero. I wonder what they'll come up with tomorrow.

While I'm getting dressed, Gavin calls to tell me he can't make it to the appointment. He has some work crisis. The price you pay for having your name on the building, I suppose. I'm disappointed I have to go alone. I'm not entirely sure what will happen today. I'm hoping the doctor will give a listen and tell me I'm good to go. He may require tests, which could take weeks! From my understanding, the health care system here moves slowly. If that is the case, it won't be a problem if Gavin isn't there. In fact, it would be a gigantic waste of his time. However, if the doctor is able to do an exam and does find something wrong, I'll be a wreck without Gavin. But I don't see that in the cards today.

I hail a cab to Dr. Baker's, and despite getting to the building with plenty of time to spare, I'm almost late to the appointment. I wrote the suite number down wrong and end up at the wrong doctor. I get as far as filling out the forms before I figure it out. So embarrassing! Once I realize my mistake, I sprint up three flights of stairs and rush into the office, sweaty and flustered. The secretary hands me a stack of paperwork to fill out while I wait in the exam room.

"Lily, it's nice to meet you. I'm Mr. Baker," he says holding out his hand. It's so funny how they don't refer to themselves as doctors here. Dr. Baker is gorgeous, like all of Gavin's friends. I don't know what they put in the water here, but damn!

"Thanks for squeezing me in. I know you have a packed schedule."

He closes the door, and drops the file on the counter. "Well, Gavin and I go way back. I owe him a few favors, so this is the least I can do."

"You were in med school together, right?" I ask.

Dr. Baker leans against the counter in the exam room. "Yes, and I served with him for a bit. We went through a lot together, both in and out of uniform. It's too bad he didn't finish school. When we were out there, he was always the better doctor. Never met a smarter bastard."

"Annoying, isn't it?" I joke.

"Except when you need him." Dr. Baker smiles. "There's no one else I would want by my side in a crisis, I can tell you that."

He turns around and grabs a frame off of his shelf and hands it to me. The picture is of him and Gavin in uniform. From the background, it looks as though they were at a field hospital in the desert.

I'm overcome with pride but I'm also shocked. Military Gavin is even hotter than Tux Gavin. I shift in my seat and cross my legs. A throbbing between my thighs reminds me it's time to get this show on the road.

"Speaking of Gavin, he stormed in here not too long ago," Dr. Baker says when I hand back the frame.

I sit up ramrod straight. "What do you mean 'he stormed in'?" Dear God, what did he do?

He waves me off. "Nothing really. He just threatened my life and the lives of my future children if I didn't take topnotch care of you. As if I wouldn't!"

I feel my cheeks getting hot with my embarrassment. "He does like to make a scene, doesn't he?"

"He clearly cares for you. So my dear, in the best interest of my future children, let's get started. I need to do an echocardiogram and a stress test. When you're done, we'll meet back up in a few hours to take a look at the results."

"All today? That's fabulous!" I'm even more grateful I decided to visit the spa before my visit. I don't want to waste any time after he gives me my good news!

"Let's just say you're on the fast track." He smirks.

I'm ushered from test to test. For the stress test, I'm put on a treadmill. Even when they crank up the speed, I feel fine. A bit out of shape, but fine.

After I've completed everything, the nurse calls me

back into Dr. Baker's office. I watch him at his desk. He taps his thumbs on the desk, and I see his knee bouncing. He looks stressed.

I brace myself for bad news.

I lean against the doorway. "Lay it on me, doc. No beating around the bush. Just hit me with it."

He stands and motions to the chair in front of his desk. "Lily, please sit."

I comply. Dr. Baker looks green, which makes me all the more nervous.

He pulls a file from the pile on his desk and opens it. "Based on what you endured and what your tests looked like just a few weeks ago, I expected to find severe damage to your heart," he says. "I've been looking at today's results over and over and I have to say..."

I flinch, waiting for the bad news.

"Your heart looks pretty good," he concludes.

I'm astonished. "Say that again? I thought you said my heart is in good shape but the look on your face says I'm dying."

"I'm sorry. I need to work on my poker face, I suppose. Before you walked in, I got a call that a patient just passed. It has me a little out of sorts."

I cover my mouth with my hand. "That's awful."

He shrugs. "It's the nature of the business, sadly." He offers me a weak smile but from the look in his eyes, I can see how hard he's taking this. He taps his pen on a file. "So, on to you. Looking at these tests, I'd never have guessed the trauma you've been through. You have a bit of thickening on the wall of your heart and when your heart pumps the third ventricle doesn't always get as much blood as it should. These are things we should watch but they may never impact you. I'm not worried about anything I've seen here."

I let out a huge sigh of relief. "Yeah, doc, you've got to work on that poker face. You'll give a girl a heart attack."

"I'm sorry. I let my guard down around you. Even though we just met, I feel like I know you through Gavin. He talks about you all the time."

I grimace. "Sorry about that."

"Not at all. It's nice to see him so happy. It's been years since I've seen him chuffed. I can't even remember the last time he didn't look gray and hollowed out. You must be good for him."

"Dr. Baker, that warms my heart. He's done well for me too." I relax into my chair.

Dr. Baker sets my tests aside.

"With how your heart has healed, I would say he has. And please, call me Alex. So do you have any questions?"

"I've been on restricted exercise and activity. Do I have to keep restricting or can I go back to my normal routine?" I ask, hoping I don't sound too desperate.

A grin crosses his face, and he laughs. "Ah, Gavin's

tirade makes so much more sense now. I'll have to cut him some slack."

My face burns up with embarrassment. I must look crimson!

"Oh, I've embarrassed you. I'm sorry. I feel for my friend. The answer is yes, Lily. You can resume normal activity. Don't start running any marathons tomorrow but you can go back to your typical routine."

Sweeter words have never been spoken!

Alex chats for a bit longer but I have checked out. A nurse comes in to remind him of his next appointment and I get up to leave. I take the Tube, which I'm becoming quite comfortable with, to Oxford Circus to the flagship Victoria's Secret store. The lingerie store is bigger than some department stores! It takes me a while to wade through the bath and body products, functional bras and panties before I get to the good stuff. Lace, garters, stockings. I pick up an array of bras, thongs, bustiers and teddies, putting a small fortune on my credit card. I know no matter what I wear, I won't be in it for long but I have fun adding to the excitement.

I wander around the other shops looking for inspiration and I spot a Burberry store. I make a quick, expensive purchase and head back to Gavin's. After a quick shower, I get dressed. Soft curls and light make up complete the look. After finding a bottle of Vodka in the freezer, I slam back a shot, lock up and make my way downstairs to my waiting cab. Going to his office in the middle of the afternoon without checking with him first is a risk but some risks are worth taking.

When my cab arrives at Gavin's building, I just about lose my nerve. The very horny voice inside my head nudges me out of the taxi.

The building is bustling with hundreds of people going about their days, looking very professional. I'm wearing a black trench coat, fuck-me heels, and smoking hot lingerie. Gloating in my naughtiness, a smirk crosses my face and I feel a sway in my hips and swagger in my step.

When I arrive at Gavin's office, I spot Snooty Smythe, Gavin's assistant. She looks exactly like I expected her to—plump, silver hair, and tough as nails. If my plan's going to fail, it'll fail here.

"Good afternoon, Mrs. Smythe. I stopped in to surprise Gavin. Is he in?" I ask.

She stares at me blankly. "And you would be...?"

How many American women stop in to surprise him? Wait, I don't want to know the answer to that question.

"Lily Clark. We've spoken on the phone."

"Oh, yes. Ms. Clark, he has a very tight schedule. I'm not sure he has time for an unauthorized visit. Perhaps if you'd rung and made an appointment, I could have saved you the trip."

Listen, bitch, I came here for something, and I'm not leaving till I get it and get it good.

Deep breath and sugar sweet smile. "Could you possibly check with him to see if he could spare a few minutes? He had to miss an important appointment today and I'm sure he wants to hear all about it."

"Certainly. If you have a seat, I'll check. Shall I take your coat?"

"No!" *Get it together, Lily.* "I mean, no, thank you. I'm a bit chilly."

I notice she doesn't call Gavin to see if he's free, so I take matters into my own hands and text him.

I left a package for you with Mrs. Smythe. If you have a minute, you should go get it.

Gavin: I've been going mad waiting to hear about your appointment with Alex. He wouldn't tell me a bloody thing. I'm finishing a meeting. I'll get it in a moment. What did Alex say?

I decide not to answer and let him stew a bit. Ten minutes later, Gavin and a group of suits exit his office. The groups clamors around him, like puppies following their master. Each person hanging on his every word. His suit jacket is off, his sleeves are rolled up and his tie is loose. His hair looks as if he's been running his fingers through it all day. The whole look is slightly disheveled but so hot.

"Mrs. Smythe, did Lily drop something by for me?" he snaps.

She lets out a huff and glares at me. "Ms. Clark is here, Mr. Edwards. The remainder of your day is booked solid. You have less than ten minutes to speak with her before your next appointment."

Ten minutes. I can work with that.

He gives me a curious look. I walk over to him and he

kisses my cheek while pulling me into his office.

"I thought you said you left a package," he says as he closes the office door. His phone dings and he looks at it while walking to his desk. "Sorry, I'm a bit distracted, luv. Crazy, crazy day. Major crisis here. Are you going to tell me what Alex said or do I have to guess?"

While he searches his desk for god knows what, I let the trench coat fall to the floor. I don't say a word, waiting to see how long it'll take him to notice. I can feel Snooty Smythe's clock ticking down and my opportunity slipping away. He looks tense, stressed and still a bit angry. I seem to have chosen a horrible time for an afternoon delight. By the time I'm standing in front of him, he still hasn't looked up at me.

"Gavin, do I need to get on your desk to get you to look at me?"

"What's that, luv?" He looks up, and his jaw drops. Papers fly everywhere when he drops a stack of file folders.

"Mrs. Smythe said you have ten minutes. You've wasted three. What can we do in seven minutes, Gavin? Any thoughts?"

I've rendered him speechless. Thankfully, the stun wears off and Gavin jumps into action. "You minx." He crashes into me with a desperate kiss.

His hands roam my body as of his is on fire and touching me is the only thing to calm the flames. My hands go directly for his belt. Foreplay is all well and good, but we're on a clock and I'm not letting this opportunity pass me by.

When I get his belt undone, he stops kissing me. "The door. I've got to—"

"Took care of it when we walked in. We've got five minutes." Buttons go flying when I pull his shirt apart. He groans as I attack his neck with kisses.

"Fuck that." He pushes a button on his intercom. He clears his throat, then says, "Mrs. Smythe, something has come up. I need you to push my next meeting." He pulls his arm back, and in one sweeping motion, he clears everything off his desk and lays me down on top of it.

Holy hell. That was hot.

"You look so fucking sexy. I can't decide if I want to tear this off of you and fuck you or just stare at you," he whispers.

I push him back onto his chair. "I can always put this back on later. Right now is *not* the time for staring."

I kick off my heels and place my foot between his legs. My toes gently rub against his growing bulge. His breath hitches as he watches me unhook the garters, and slowly roll down my stockings. Once both stockings are off, I remove my bra and toss it aside.

His intercom keeps buzzing but he makes no move to answer it. He kisses my leg from my ankle up toward my knee. The damn buzzer keeps going, distracting me and killing the mood.

I slap my hand on the desk. "Gavin, you've got to answer that."

"What!" he says through gritted teeth after he presses the button.

"Mr. Edwards. I heard a crash. Is everything all right?" Snooty asks.

"Everything's fine. Something fell off my desk. No interruptions for the next hour. Understood?"

He tosses the intercom on the pile on the floor. He lays me down and toys with the small fabric of my g-string. He kisses my hips along the strings of the tiny underwear before pulling it down. After tossing it aside, Gavin runs his tongue from my calf to my core. He teases me by kissing me everywhere but where I want him to.

I just can't take it.

I squeeze his head between my thighs. "Gavin, we have had weeks of foreplay. I can't stand one more second. Either make me come or I'll do it my damn self."

He smiles and says, "Yes, milady."

My head falls back as he devours me. I had forgotten how masterful he is with his tongue. In moments, I feel the heat build and the wave takes over. I hold my hand over my mouth to muffle my screams when I come. Normally he would stop and plow inside me but he keeps going. Every nerve ending feels raw and exposed. He laves my clit and I feel electrified. The intensity is too much, I don't think I can take it. I pull my hips back.

"Get back here," he growls and pulls my hips back

toward him.

He attacks me. His assault teeters on the razor sharp edge of pain but Gavin won't relent. Pain turns into pleasure as another orgasm builds. I come so hard my whole body quakes. Electrical pulses run through me as he keeps going.

"I want you inside me. Please," I beg.

He leaves a trail of kisses up my stomach. Stopping at my breasts, he lavs and sucks my nipples. It drives me crazy but doesn't fill the void I'm feeling.

"Gavin, please. I need you. *Now*."

He kisses up my neck to my ear and whispers, "Gentle or hard?"

Lost in a post-orgasmic haze and filled with too much wanting to decipher what he is asking, I say, "What? What are you talking about? Please. Now."

"Do you want me to fuck you gentle or hard?" he whispers again.

"Hard. Now," I demand.

He flips me over, bending me over his desk. As he pushes into me, I dig my nails into his desk. I'm tight from weeks of abstinence but I'm so aroused he slides right in. I feel his body shudder as he enters me.

He releases a deep, slow sigh. "Fuck, I forgot how good you feel."

He drives into me and it's glorious. Not wanting to scream but unable to contain myself, I bite my lip. Each time he slams deeper into me, my nails dig deeper into his desk. When he pulls my hips to reach his, I leave claw marks in the wood. He hits me in just the right spot and I feel another orgasm building.

I contract around him. He pushes deep into me and stops thrusting. When my body stops pulsating, he starts back up harder and faster.

I'm lost in the whirlwind of pleasure. Gavin reaches between my thighs and rubs my clit.

"No, I can't." I can't possibly have another orgasm in me. I try to push his hand away but he holds firm.

"Trust me," he moans.

He massages me while he thrusts into me. In a few moments, I'm building again. Gavin speeds up.

I'm pushed over the edge just as he screams, "Fuck!"

We collapse onto the floor, panting and breathless. He pulls me on top of him and kisses me. "I never want to go that long without having you ever again."

"If that's what it's like after weeks of abstinence, it might be worth it. That was pretty..... There aren't words for what that was." I'm still trying to catch my breath.

He brushes a stray piece of hair out of my eyes. "Luv, we're always bloody spectacular together. It has nothing to do with the time apart."

Consumed in the afterglow, we lose track of time. The intercom buzzes again, forcing us back to reality.

"Bloody hell," Gavin yells as he smashes his fist on the floor. He drags his fingers through his hair. "Some days I hate my job. There's nothing I would rather do than continue to lie here with you and maybe go for another round. Unfortunately, someone in my company seriously buggered up a program and we've been spending all day trying to figure out if it can be fixed. Millions of pounds are at risk. I have to get back to work."

I pat his chest lightly. "Gavin, I still can't feel my legs. Go back to work if you have to, but you can't do it here. Don't you have a conference room you can use or something?"

He kisses my neck. "Lily, I can't leave you like this."

"You got all caveman and needed to try to break the orgasm record. Well, this is what happens afterward. Go do whatever it is that you do and leave me to my post-orgasm bliss." I close my eyes. "All your tension is killing my buzz."

He picks up his shirt from across the room, then slides it over my shoulders. "If I don't cover you up, I'm likely to try to go back for more."

I shoo him away.

He calls Snooty and tells her to have the team meet him in another office. I fade out of consciousness until he brings me back with a deep kiss. Opening my eyes, I see he has showered and put on a fresh shirt. No one would guess he just spent an hour fucking my brains out. Unless they heard us, that is. Just the thought of being heard by his stuck up secretary makes me tuck my head and blush.

He crouches lifts my chin and kisses me. "I don't want to leave you."

I smile. "You have a company to run."

He leans his forehead against mine. "Luv, I don't know when I'll be done today," he says. "I may be working well past midnight."

"Gavin, I'm a big girl. I got here by myself; I can leave by myself."

"I feel awkward. I don't want you to feel..."

"Tawdry? Please, I came here for one thing and I got it. Don't feel guilty. I sure as hell don't. We can cuddle and play kissy face later." I slap his ass. "Now get out of here and play CEO. It's kinda hot."

He kisses me and laughs until the door closes behind him.

When I come down from my high, I collect my lingerie and try to put myself together. Gavin strolled out of here looking perfect but when I look in the mirror I see I'm a wreck. My lips are swollen and my makeup is smeared. I clean up as much as I can but I still make a beeline for the elevator when I sneak out of his office. Snooty says something, but I ignore her.

When I get in a cab, I text Gavin. *That was my first walk of shame. Totally worth it. See you at home.*

Gavin: *That breaks my heart. What we did was too amazing to have shame attached to it. Plus, I own the building. If I want to shag in the middle of the day, I will. Everyone else can piss off!*

Gavin: *I'm thrilled you called the flat home* ☺

Chapter Ten

Gavin doesn't get in until after one in the morning. I'd been dressed in another sexy outfit and hoping for round two, but I fell asleep reading my latest book long before that.

The next week is full of marathon days for Gavin. He wakes up early to roll around in the sheets with me and then works for fourteen hours. I'm still not entirely sure what went wrong, but it sounds catastrophic. I wish we could spend more time together, but he's needed there.

The little time we do get together is frantic. The press is the third wheel in our relationship. Everywhere we go, they're there. Fortunately, their coverage has been kind. I'm doing my best not to fight them because I know if I do, they'll turn ugly real fast.

Greene and I touch base every other day. He still hasn't gotten word from Max. With each passing day, my nerves flare and my heart shatters a little bit more. If they know who he is, they'll torture him and then kill him. Once they're done with him, I'll be next. Green swears the FBI is doing everything they can, but it doesn't set my mind at ease.

Greene calls me early Tuesday morning, which makes it middle of the night for him. When I see his number on the caller ID, I panic. He'd only call at this time if something bad has happened. "What happened?"

"We've heard from Max. I can't go into it, but he's safe."

I jerk upright in bed, knocking my Kindle on the floor. "You have to get him out of there." I reach down to pick it up, and bump my head on the nightstand on my way back up, spilling my water in the process. Rubbing the egg forming on the back of my head, I walk to the bathroom to get a towel.

I look through the cabinets under the sink, looking for paper towels. "Lily, he's refusing to come out," Greene replies.

This stops me in my tracks. *He's what?* Why the hell won't he come out? Shocked, I sit up and bump my head on the edge of the granite countertop. Fabulous, now I have two lumps on the back of my head. "Did you explain everything? He's signing my death warrant if he stays in."

Greene sighs. I can hear exhaustion in his voice. It

must be around two in the morning his time, and I know he's as worried about Max as I am. "I didn't talk to him." He clucks his tongue. "I don't think his handler explained the whole situation. They want to make their case, and they aren't going to worry about you because what you told me was off the record. If you came clean, maybe I could do something. My hands are tied right now."

"Damn it, there must be something you can do." Between the stress and the bump, my head is pounding. I dig through my makeup bag for a bottle of Advil.

"You chose to keep secrets. This is what happens!"

Startled, I drop the bottle of Advil, the little brown pills scattering across the marble floor. In all of our time together, Greene has never raised his voice at me. I slide down the wall, pulling my knees to my chest as I hit the ground.

"We can only protect you when we know everything," he says, his voice still curt. "You kept crucial information from us, and now we all have to deal with the consequences. I still can't believe you didn't trust us. I can't believe you didn't trust me."

"I'm sorry, I really am. I screwed up. I never should've kept it from you," I lie. I'm sorry he's hurt and I'm sorry Max and I are in hot water, but I don't regret what I did. It was my best option at the time and I took it.

"What's done is done. We can't undo it, so now we have to wait to see how it plays out."

Easy for him to say. We talk for another few minutes and hang up. Greene's icy tone melts a little, but I know the tension remains.

What if he's right? What if my renegade actions were a short-term solution for a long-term problem? What if I get Max killed? I wish I could talk to Lorenzo. Damn him and his secrecy.

When the throbbing gets the better of me, I finally get off the bathroom floor and make my way to the kitchen. I tear through the cabinets looking for Ziploc bags to make an ice pack, but come up empty. Grabbing a handful of ice, I throw some in a dishtowel and some in a glass. I put the ice to the back of my head with one hand and pour vodka with the other. I add a splash of orange juice. That makes it breakfasty, right?

I had a laundry list of things to do today- work on my blog, figure out how to transfer my birth control prescription from the US, answer a million emails. None of those things happen. The jackhammer in my head is relentless, and I'm worthless. The vodka knocks me out until Gavin gets home. Sadly, the headache is still there. Gavin's trying his best, but I'm cranky and irritable. We talk in circles about what I should do.

"Luv, I'm not sure there's much more you can do. Max isn't coming out until he has a resolution. When he gets out, I think we should talk to him and tell him everything. All of us can work together to figure it out." He cups my face. "I won't let anything happen to you. Ever."

I let my head fall to his shoulder. "But what about Lorenzo? I can't out him."

He puts his hands on my shoulders and guides me

back so he can look in my eyes. "Lily, it's your life or his. They aren't going to arrest him for helping you, so what if they know who he is? They probably already know who he is. You have to think about your safety."

Tears well up in my eyes when I think about Max. "Gavin, I'll never be able to live with myself if he dies because I went off book."

He runs his thumb along my cheek. "Max is very good at what he does. You have to have faith he'll get out of this."

Faith? How can I have faith when everything ends in heartache?

******

On Thursday, I'm working on an article when I get a frantic call from Gavin.

"Luv, is there something you want to tell me?"

I stop typing and think. "We're out of milk?"

"Anything else?" he growls.

I close my laptop. "Clearly you think I should be telling you something, so why don't we cut to the chase, and you tell me what you're thinking."

"Are you pregnant?"

"*What*? Where the hell did that come from?"

"You were seen in an obstetrician's office earlier this week."

I laugh hysterically. So hard I can't get any words out.

"Luv, I'm not sure why this is so funny. The tabloids have pictures of you filling out paperwork in an obstetrician's office. At first I thought maybe it could be routine, but I called, that doctor only handles obstetrics. I don't often buy into this bilge, but this is hard to dispute."

"Gavin," I squeak out in between laughs. "I'm not pregnant. When I went to see Alex, I forgot the suite number. I looked at the directory, then went to Dr. Baker's suite. As it turns out, there are two Dr. Bakers in his building, and I went into the wrong one. Filled out paper work and even paid, before I figured out the mix up."

He lets out a long sigh. "Thank heavens."

"Relieved?" I ask, the humor now gone from my voice. I'm sure it must have been a shock, but does he have to sound *so* alleviated?

"Thank you for explaining. I have to get back to work."

I drop my hand on the sofa. "You're seriously going to drop that bomb and run?"

"Lily, I'm underwater here. My publicist called, and I needed to call you and get this sorted. Now that there isn't anything to talk about, I have to get back to work. I love you. Hopefully I'll see you later, luv."

Too frustrated to work, I get dressed and head out for

my day of errands. I walk by a newsstand on the way to the Tube. My picture is splattered over the front pages. *A Baby for Lily!* Where do they come up with this crap? *Bump Watch?* That means there's no end in sight. They're going to stalk me for nine months.

The press has multiplied overnight. Where we had just a handful, there seems to be an army. They shout at me so constantly, I almost miss my cell ringing.

"Bitch. You got knocked up, and I had to find out online?"

"Good morning, Em. No, I'm not knocked up. You should know better than to buy in to that. When have the tabloids ever been right?" I intentionally shout this loud enough for the reporters to hear. They're not deterred, so I sneak into a coffee shop and grab a table.

"Okay, you're forgiven. I'm not ready to be an aunt, that's for damn sure. I'm coming into town next week, and the thought of going baby-shit shopping made me violently ill."

"Em! That's the best news. I can't wait to see you. Do you want to stay at Gavin's?" The women behind the counter glare at me with an evil eye. Perhaps because I'm talking too loud. Or maybe because there's a herd of photographers blocking the door, preventing customers from coming in.

"The only time I don't stay in a hotel is when you're in desperate need of my supervision. Do you need me?"

"Hold on, let me order." I put the phone down and order a hot chocolate from the waitress. Maybe if I order something and leave a big tip, they'll stop giving me the hairy eyeball. "No," I say back to Em. "I'm pretty good. Since I'm not pregnant and all."

"Then I have no desire to listen to you and Brit Boy romping in the sheets all night."

I shrug out of my jacket and hang it on the back of the chair. "Gavin's place is enormous. I could have an orgy, and you wouldn't hear it."

"I'll think about it. Hey, have you heard from Boston?"

"Max? He's on assignment. We won't hear from him till he's out, which could be months." I wish I could tell her the truth, but it wouldn't do Max any good and it'll just stress her out. "Why, do you miss him?" I know she'll never admit it, but there is something between those two.

"Hardly. I don't miss boys. He hasn't stalked me for a while, so I wanted to make sure he hadn't fallen off the face of the earth. I was worried for your sake."

My hot chocolate arrives and I thank the waitress while Em tries to convince me she doesn't care. "Sure, Em, you keep telling yourself that. If I were a betting girl, oh wait, I am, I'd bet a hundred dollars Max calls you the day he comes out."

"If I cared, which I don't, I'd take that bet. But I don't, so I won't. I've got to jet. I'll see you on Tuesday, and I have crazy fun plans for us. Be ready."

I love that girl.

The weekend comes and goes. I only see Gavin in passing until late Sunday afternoon when he collapses on the bed.

I run my fingers through his hair. "Gavin, you can't keep up this pace. You need to slow down."

"Are you doubting my stamina?" He flips me over so that I'm lying on my back underneath him. "Because I'll show you right now what kind of pace I can keep up with."

He tears his shirt off and kisses my neck. His hands find the back of my thighs and slowly slide up until he's gripping my ass.

I trace his jaw with my finger, enjoying the abrasive feel of the scruff he's sporting. "Gavin, I'd never question your stamina. But you can't keep this up forever. Is there any sign of things slowing down?"

He unties my wrap-around sweater and notices I'm not wearing a bra. "Do you really want to talk about this now?" He softly kisses the valley between my breasts. "This is the last thing in the world I want to talk about. In fact, I have no desire to talk at all. I can think of far better things to do with my mouth."

I hadn't even been thinking about sex before he got home. Now my body is on fire craving him. I've gone from zero to desperate in seconds. What this man does to me...

He takes my nipple into his mouth and sucks on it while his hands pull off my pants. He strokes the sensitive spot behind my knee. Greedy for him, I use my legs to nudge his hand to my core. A moan escapes me when he touches my folds.

I can tell by the way he's touching me that he's trying to draw this out, but soft and slow isn't what I need right now. "Gavin, please."

"Please what, luv? Tell me what you want."

The throbbing need between my legs is so intense I can barely think straight, let alone form words. "Gavin, I need to come. Now. Please."

I've never been one to believe in the instant orgasm. I've read about it, heard men brag about being able to do it, but I've never believed it. It's a myth. The sexual equivalent of an urban legend. I'm now reconsidering my stance.

Gavin slides down the bed, pulls my hips to his face, and devours me as though he's been wandering through the desert and I'm his oasis. His tongue twists and twirls around my clit, driving me straight to the edge in mere seconds. I'm not sure if I'm that turned on or if he's just that good.

It wasn't orgasm on demand, but pretty fucking close.

Before my body has a chance to recover, Gavin's inside me. As fast and intense as my orgasm was, he's slow and deliberate. I think he's on a mission to prove the length and breadth of his stamina. He takes his time, moving me in positions I don't even think are in the *Kama Sutra*. Each position seems to find a new way to get him deeper inside me, hitting that magic spot that makes me see stars.

An hour and four orgasms later, he finally comes, and we collapse into a sweaty, breathless heap.

It takes me a while to catch my breath and come out of my post-orgasm coma. When I look at Gavin, I don't see him moving.

"You alive over there?" I ask.

He doesn't answer, so I nudge him.

"That was so bloody incredible. I've heard about the whole tantric sex thing, but never really bought into it. Holy fuck, was I wrong. I've never come that hard."

I turn toward him, resting my hand on his chest. "Is that what you were shooting for?"

"Well, it started off because I had something to prove—"

I scoff. "You're so damn competitive."

"Yes, I am, and you love me for it. After I felt like I'd given a sound demonstration of my stamina, then I just wanted to see how long I could go. It was unbelievable."

"That good, huh?" I ask with a raised eyebrow.

He leans over to kiss me, then, too tired to hold himself up, he falls back on the bed. "You'd better get used to it, because we are doing that again."

Before I have a chance to respond, he quietly snores. I pull the blankets over us, then nestle into his side.

When the alarm goes off the next morning, Gavin yanks the clock out of the wall and throws it across the room.

"Not ready to wake up, Oxford?" I ask.

He's typically a morning person, so this grumpy side catches me off guard.

"I just don't want to go in today," he says with his face still in his pillow. "I've been there every day for over a week, and we're no closer to solving the problem. I'm exhausted, I miss you terribly, and I've spent so much time with my staff they're all driving me mad."

I slide over to him and drape my arm across his stomach. "What's going on? You've never really explained it."

He places his arm over mine. "The new system we created has a glitch, and we can't figure out what the cause of it is. It's crucial we solve this problem. If the product fails, it could cripple the company."

"No wonder you've been working so hard. Why don't you go back to sleep and go in late? You'll be more productive if you're res—"

His phone cuts me off.

He crawls out of bed to answer and immediately starts fighting. Guess he won't be coming back to bed. He leaves the room because he paces when he's stressed and he knows it makes me crazy. I climb back into bed. A loud crash jerks me up and out of bed five minutes later.

He storms back into the bedroom, seething mad. Gavin is always so collected and calm, and seeing him this angry is like seeing a fish out of water. Something horrific must have happened for him to lose his cool like this. Not wanting to push him, I don't ask any questions. I look him in the eyes, trying to show him that I'm here for him.

"Olivia," he says through gritted teeth while he paces around the room. "IT just figured it out. She embedded code into the program so that it would report like it was failing. I can't legally prove it, but they're confident she's behind what's going on."

I sit up and wrap the blankets around me. "I thought she was your assistant. What was she doing writing code?"

"She was my assistant on the trip. I was trying to bring her over to the executive side, but she'd been working on the tech side for the past three years. From what I hear, she's very good at what she does, but she's bored by it. Hence why she wanted to move."

I bring my knees to my chest. "I don't know her, but it seems crazy that she would do that intentionally. Maybe she just wrote bad code?" I ask.

"The IT guys tell me this is deeply imbedded into the code, and quite intentional. George only found it on accident. He called it 'masterful'. He suspects she did this right as she was leaving. The program worked fine whilst she was here. As soon as she leaves, it falls apart, making it look like the rest of the team botched the whole thing. They think she concocted this plan, so I would have to ask for her help. She'd come in and with a few keystrokes, she'd fix it all, and I'd no choice but to hire her back."

"What a twatwaffle. I'm sure she thought she'd save the day and you'd run right into her arms. She's watched too many bad soap operas."

"I still don't think she has feelings for me. Something else is going on," Gavin insists. He sits down on the edge of the bed and fidgets with the edge of the duvet.

How can someone so smart be so oblivious? "Regardless of her motivation, she's a manipulative bitch. You need her out of your life and out of your company," I say as scoot closer to him "Can they undo whatever she's done?"

"Yes. Now that they've found it, they say it's an easy fix," he says.

I wrap my arms around his stomach, tracing the contours of his abs with my fingertip. "What're you going to do?"

He sighs, and his body goes slack. His chin falls to his chest and his shoulders slump. This is eating him up. "I think I need to talk to her."

"You need to stay the hell away from her." Up until this point, I've been calm about her. I thought she was an annoying gnat that wasn't worth the energy to swat away. Now I think she needs to be squashed.

"She's a longtime family friend. We have history. I have to trust that I can resolve this," he says.

I may not have known her my whole life, but I know for certain that girl is as trustworthy as a viper.

Chapter Eleven

Em arrives tomorrow, and I can barely contain my excitement. I'm enjoying London, but it's been lonely. I'm getting a lot of writing done, but this trip is supposed to be a way to test the waters to see if I could live here. I haven't made friends of my own yet, but I haven't put myself in a position to either. That's a problem for another day.

Between the few days Em will be in town and the time I'll need to recover afterward, I know I won't be working for at least a week, so I spend the day writing. At twelve thirty, I get a call from downstairs about a package. I was writing in my tank top and boy shorts, so I throw on some clothes and head downstairs. Willis isn't at his post, which is strange.

A teenage boy, probably about sixteen, steps out from

behind a corner.

"Lily Clark?" he asks.

I bet this is some damn trick by the press. I haven't run a comb through my hair, and the only makeup I have on is whatever's leftover from yesterday. I put my hands on my hips, and glare at him. "Yes?"

He hands me a manila envelope and walks out the door.

Before I lived with Max, I just would have torn into the envelope. Having some experience with this now, I do my best to touch the envelope as little as possible. I open it using a pair of tongs and a boning knife. I feel ridiculous while I'm doing it, but I know my friends at the FBI would be proud.

Inside is one piece of paper.

St Etheldreda's Church

Two hours.

Try to ditch the parasites.

LG

Lorenzo, my knight in polyester pants with a sense of humor.

Not knowing how far away the church is, I grab my coat and run out the door. The press swarms me the second I step out of the building. Even with blustery wind and torrential rain, they never let up.

Thankfully, a cab drives by as soon as I reach the curb. When I get in, the driver looks at the swarm of press and says, "You all right, dear? That's quite the mob."

I shake the water out of my hair. "They can be a bit much sometimes. Think you can lose them?"

He grins. "This is the most exciting thing to happen in this cab all year!"

Lionel, my driver, hauls ass. He takes the long way, adding random twists and turns. There were several cars on our tail, but he seems to have lost them.

The church is across the city, which I'm guessing was intentional. Two solid hours of battling traffic gives me plenty of time to wonder what he's going to say. I usually hate the traffic here, but today, I'm thankful for the time.

When we arrive at the church, Lionel gives me his number and tells me to call him if I ever need another getaway driver. A real Jason Statham!

I pull my jacket over my head to protect me from the rain. It'll be the last time I leave without an umbrella.

The church doesn't catch me from the outside, but when I walk in, I stop dead in my tracks. I stare at the breathtaking stained glass. It's hard to imagine now with the storm, but I bet on the rare sunny day, the light through the glass is magnificent.

Lorenzo's in a pew toward the altar. While I trust Lorenzo, I know he comes from a different world. He may like me, but that doesn't mean I'm not expendable. As I approach him, I see he is deep in prayer and holding the rosary. I never would have guessed he was a religious man. It's like a scientist who doesn't buy into evolution.

I stop at his pew and he clears his throat. "Sit in the pew in front of me," he whispers.

After I sit and slide down the pew so I'm sitting in front of him, he unfolds the kneeling rail and kneels, so that he can speak into my ear. "Your FBI friend is putting you at grave risk. He's going to the mattresses with the cartel."

I move my chin to my shoulder and whisper. "Lorenzo, did you just quote *The Godfather*? Really?" I tease. "Your Brando needs some work though."

"Where do you think they got that line from?" he asks. "You ever think it's Brando that needs the work?"

I turn around and raise an eyebrow. He smirks but motions for me to face forward. "Back to what I was saying, he's lost perspective, and his cover has been blown."

The back door to the church blows open, presumably from the storm. A staff member rushes to close it. The draft sends chills up my body, and I pull my jacket close to me. "I tried to get the FBI to pull him out, but they wouldn't listen," I explain.

"It's in everyone's best interest for him to return to Washington. I've spoken to Carlos, and we're working together to come up with a plan to get him out alive."

I wish I could hug him. "Thank you, Lorenzo. I would crumble if something happened to Max. Especially in a misguided attempt to defend me."

"Lily, this is only one small part of your problem. A faction within the cartel is looking to gain clout. They want to push Carlos out. If he goes, so does your security. From what I understand, his deal with you is a sore subject. They do not like loose ends, and you're a giant one. Between him letting you go and an FBI agent in their midst, his enemies are building a case against him."

I want to shout "Jesus Christ!" but I refrain. My mother would roll over in her grave if I was kicked out of church. "Lorenzo, how did I become responsible for the fates of so many? Carlos, Max, Gavin. Somehow their lives have all been tied to mine. If I don't make the right choices, they all could end up..." I can't even finish the sentence. "I didn't ask for this, Zo."

"Maybe not, but this is how it is. This is not a business for the faint-hearted."

A lump forms in my throat. "I didn't choose this business."

"No, but you're in it. You live or die by the rules. Until we know what happens with Agent McCarthy, you need to be on high alert. If I were your boyfriend—"

"You applying for the job?" I sass him. I can almost feel him roll his eyes.

"You'll need a security detail, limited exposure. Your home system must be upgraded."

I move my purse to my lap, as though this Michael Kors knock off could protect me. I'm in a church. It should be the safest place on Earth, and yet I feel the evil encroaching from all sides. "I'm sure when I explain this all to Gavin, he'll freak out and lock me in the basement."

"Don't be stubborn. Please. I don't want to have to go to war."

I shudder. "War?"

"Yes, Lily. If I have to fight for you, I will, and if it comes to that, everyone's lives are at stake. Remember that as you make your choices."

His statement weighs heavily on me. For him to save me, he would have to fight the Mexicans and start a gang war. All that damage and destruction because of little ole me.

"Zo, would all of this with Max have been avoided if I'd told them the truth from the beginning? The FBI wouldn't have come after you. I know they wouldn't. Max wouldn't have gone after the cartel if he knew."

"Good law enforcement has a very hard time turning a blind eye, even for those they love. Carlos has eyes on you everywhere, even inside the FBI. The only reason you're still alive is that he has good cause to believe you have kept your word. This isn't the movies. The story doesn't get wrapped up in a pretty package where the bad guys go to jail and the good guys ride off into the sunset. Real life is messy. People get killed. Lives are destroyed."

Bile rises up in my throat. I want to run and hide. I move my hand to my throat, as though that will help keep me from throwing up. "I don't have the stomach for this."

"You're stronger than you think, little girl." He lets out a quiet laugh. "I'd take you over some of the recruits I've seen lately."

"How do I get out of this? I don't have anything to offer them this time. I have no leverage."

I hear him shift the rosary beads between his fingers. "Carlos and I are working on that. In the meantime, keep your head down."

I scoff. "I've got the paparazzi attached to me like an extra appendage. There is no keeping my head down."

"Be aware of your surroundings. Get a bodyguard. Don't do anything reckless."

A light bulb goes off in my head. "Zo, can I go to him? Carlos knows where Max is, right? I could go and get him out. Clearly the FBI isn't going to pull him, but I know I can convince him to get out."

His rosary falls to the floor. I hear him shift around as he picks it up. "That's playing with fire. You could get both of you killed."

"Haven't you learned by now, playing with fire is my specialty. Please, ask Carlos."

"I'll think about it, and I'll be in touch."

"Please give me a way to contact you. Please, Zo. This is nuts," I say.

"I'm eighty four. I've stayed under the radar and alive by following my rules. I'm not changing now." He stands, walks to the altar, does the sign of the cross, and leaves.

The weight of the conversation smothers me. Hoping for a long walk, I exit the church only to be attacked by the press. Damn, these guys can find me anywhere. I cover my head with my purse and look for a cab.

“Will the baby be raised Catholic, Lily?” a reporter screams.

Oh, hell. I hope I didn’t just step on a religious landmine. The British press likes me today, but if my hypothetical future royal baby—who doesn’t stand a chance of being in line for the throne—might be raised Catholic, our amicable relationship could be short lived. I seriously have to get Gavin’s family tree published, so maybe all of this royal connection crap can finally be laid to rest.

“Now, now, boys, let’s not get carried away! I was told by a friend that this church is one of England’s secret treasures. The stained glass is simply breathtaking. You guys should really take a look in there. Be sure to take lots of pictures. Good for tourism!” I smile, hoping I’ve derailed the conversation.

Note to self: visit other churches. Protestant Ones. Maybe this would be a good series to write on?

“Thought you might need to make a quick getaway,” Lionel calls from across the street. “Come on, get in.”

Oh thank God! I run across the street and jump in the cab. “I can’t thank you enough for waiting. If I would have had to wait for a cab those vultures would have eaten me alive.”

“Happy to help, my dear. Just tell me where we’re off to next.”

I give him the address to Gavin's building. I need Gavin to help me sort through all of this. Lionel weaves around town, losing my tagalongs, but it's only a temporary reprieve. There's a gaggle of camera men outside of Gavin's office. What a sad reflection of the world that someone thinks our relationship is worthy of so much attention. They don't even know the most interesting part! The press was so focused on the imaginary baby, they completely missed my meeting with a mob boss. Ah, irony!

As I step out of the cab, I'm relieved the rain has finally let up. Walking toward the building, I see Gavin across the courtyard, talking to James. God damn, he's sexy beyond words. Even from fifty yards away, I'm drawn to him. The lines of his navy suit highlight his toned body. I can tell he's in a serious conversation by the way his brow is furrowed, but every once in a while, he flashes that smile that melts me.

He doesn't see me as I stalk over to him, allowing me to soak up his gorgeous glory. I cannot believe that this Adonis comes home to me every night. I get to see him naked. Often. It feels surreal. Of all of the women who throw themselves at him, he chose me. It's still hard to wrap my head around.

I toss my hair back and do my best to strut with command. I'm still rain drenched, so I can only imagine how bad I look, but it's not about looks. It's about confidence. When I reach him, I wrap my arms around him for a kiss. Without hesitating, he scoops me up and takes the kiss deeper. His arms pull me so close I can hardly breathe. Caught up in the moment, I forget we're in front of his office and that we have an audience. I run my hands through his hair and moan. If I weren't wearing a skirt, I would wrap my legs around him. James clears his throat and snaps us out of our tongue-tangled bliss.

"Sorry, James," I say. "I was in the neighborhood and thought I'd say hello."

"Oh, in that case." James picks me up and spins me around, planting soft kisses on my neck until I giggle. When he sets me down, Gavin glares at him. "What? I was just getting my hello. You aren't the only one who gets Lily love," James says playfully.

Gavin growls, "Yes, as a matter of fact, I am the only one who gets Lily love. Touch my girlfriend again and we'll have serious problems, mate."

The two boys glare at each other as if they're about to throw down.

"You can't handle a bit of healthy competition, *mate*?" James throws back at him.

I don't know their relationship well enough to know how seriously Gavin's taking this. Wanting to avoid major conflict between these two lifetime friends, I step in. "Settle down, Gavin. Can't you see he's just trying to rattle you?"

Gavin steps toward James until they're almost toe to toe. He clutches his fist, and I'm sure he's about to throw a punch. James rolls his eyes, and he and Gavin laugh.

"You brats!" I punch them both in the arm. "I hate you both."

"We're just having a laugh, Lil. Don't get your knickers in a twist," James chokes out in between laughs. "We wouldn't have a barney right in front of Gavin's office."

"With this crew, you can't be so gullible." Gavin kisses the top of my head. He leans in and whispers, "James wouldn't tease you if he didn't adore you. Take it as a compliment."

"Oh, I do," I reply. "Boys never really evolve past kindergarten. They pull your hair because they like you. Just be ready, James. I give it as good as I get."

"Oh, Gavin, I like this one," James says with a smirk.

Gavin puts his arm around me. "Yes, yes. Just remember she's taken. Lily, to what do I owe the pleasure of getting to see you in the middle of the afternoon?"

"Had some news to share. Nothing that can't wait though." I don't want to even hint about it with James around.

"Let me guess, we are having twins," Gavin teases.

I look around to see if anyone is in ear shot. "Shhh! Don't say that too loud. The last thing we need is to add fuel to this fire."

"What? Triplets, you say?" James shouts.

"Bastard!"

"That's two, Lily. You'd better catch up," he says smugly.

Gavin chuckles. "As much as I would love to hang out

with you two all afternoon, I have a meeting I must attend. Lily, dear, dinner tonight? Say seven?"

"You're getting home before midnight? I love it!" I kiss him.

"Get out of here so I can make passes at your girl," James says, pulling my arm.

"Behave, James," Gavin calls as he heads toward the building.

"So, lovely Lily, fancy a drink? I have the rest of the afternoon off and would love to torment Gavin with pictures of the two of us getting sozzeled . There's a local down the street."

"I'd love a drink. Let's go."

We walk down to the Cat and the Canary. After bypassing the bar, we find two leather armchairs with a bistro table in a side room in the back.

"Shots?" he asks with a look that says nothing but trouble.

I wave him off. "Dear God, no. Not for me anyway. Don't let me stop you."

His eyes narrow. "Here I thought you were up for anything. Maybe you really are up the duff."

I stand to take off my coat. James jumps up to help me out of it. "I'm *not* pregnant. I have a date later, or didn't you catch that? What kind of lady shows up for a date already sauced?"

"My kind of lady, that's for sure." He winks, before

hanging our coats on the coat rack.

"James, you are incorrigible! And here I was thinking Liam's the bigger flirt."

"I think between the three of us, we're always fighting for top spot. Of course, Gavin has dropped out of the game. For the first time ever, I must say." He leans in closer to me and says, "You really have him smitten."

"Oh, come now. Don't exaggerate for my benefit," I say, pushing him away.

"I'm quite serious. It's like you have consumed him. You're all he thinks about, talks about, and cares about. I've never seen him like this. Even when he was with Bitch, I mean Brooke, he wasn't like he is with you. Can't even compare. He cared for her, sure. At one point, he thought he loved her. I always thought he loved the idea of her more than the real thing though, but what do I know?"

The waiter stops by and takes our drink order. James tries to push for shots, but I'm firm with my resolve. Wine for me and whiskey for James.

When the server leaves, I say, "You really didn't get along with her, huh?"

He leans back into his arm chair and says, "She was into Gavin for the same reasons all the others were. Bitch just did a better job of hiding it. Gavin was ready to settle down, and she wrapped herself in the perfect marriage package. Then she learned he has a weak spot for the damsel in distress, and she played that card every chance she got. Gavin's loyal to a fault, so even when he figured out her game, he stood by her." He leans forward and says, “I’m sick of talking about crazy bitches. Tell me about you, my lovely Lily.” He takes my hand and runs his fingers along my palm like he is studying me.

The server delivers our drinks, but James pays them no mind. His gaze is locked on me.

“What do you want to know?” I ask.

He runs his finger along my life line. “Favorite band?”

“Depends on the mood. I have eclectic taste.”

“That’s a non-answer, but I’ll let it slide. First concert?”

“Bruce Springsteen, in Boston. My parents took me when I was twelve.”

“How old were you when you lost your virginity?”

I pull my hand away and look at him through slanted eyes. “Are we playing twenty questions? When is it my turn?”

“Just answer.”

I pick up my wine and take a sip. “I was seventeen.”

“Spit or swallow?”

“Did you really just ask me that?” Damn, the balls on this man!

“Are you going to break his heart?” His tone is no longer playful and his posture is tense and a little intimidating. This switched from a game to an interrogation.

I look at him over the rim of my wine glass. "No beating around the bush with you, is there?"

He shrugs. "Why waste my time?"

I put my wine glass down, and fold my arms over my chest. "James, I have no intention of breaking his heart. Do I pass?"

His body relaxes and his smile returns. "You passed the first time we met. I just wanted to see how far I could go before you decked me."

I punch his arm. "Bastard. My turn. What's the deal with O? I remember hearing you two used to be a thing."

He claps his hands and rubs them together. "It must be my lucky day. Two conversations about the woman who'll drive me to an early grave. I'm going to need more to drink if I'm going to talk about her again." He flags the waiter, letting him know we are ready for another round.

"What do you mean 'again'?" I ask.

"Gavin asked me to lunch to ask the same question."

"Good, so you know what's going on. So what's her deal? Gavin is convinced this isn't about him. But her actions scream psycho, obsessed stalker."

He sighs and takes a sip. "O has always been a little bit batty, but she usually keeps it in check. I've never seen her like this. If she were ever going to be pushed over the edge, Gavin would be the one to do it."

"I don't understand. I thought you two had a thing."

He shifts in his seat, then places his glass on the table. "Oh, we did. We do. Off and on since we were fourteen. We spend time together, everything goes great. As soon as it gets real, she backs off. She'll whore around and then come back."

I cross my legs, then lean forward, with my elbow on my knee and my chin resting on my hand. "Why do you keep taking her back?" James is such a good-looking, successful guy with a killer sense of humor. Why would he go back to that tramp?

He takes another sip and lets out a quiet laugh. "Isn't that the burning question? If I knew the answer, my dear, I'd be in a far different place than I am now. She's in my blood, and I can't seem to shake her no matter how much I want to. I hate her because I can't stop loving her."

"Damn, James. I guess first loves will do that to you."

"Each time she comes back, I hope it'll be different, but deep down, I know it won't. She'll always leave. Despite how much I love her, it'll never matter. I'm her in-between man. I'm not her final destination." He downs the rest of his drink, but keeps looking at the glass like it holds the answer he's looking for.

"What does that mean?"

"She wants Gavin. She's always wanted Gavin. She doesn't love him—well, not like that anyway. Her mother set Gavin as the high prize, so he has always been her goal. For years I ignored it because she didn't love him. She wants to make her mother happy. I thought she loved me, and in time, she would tell her parents to bugger off." He sighs and runs his fingers through his hair. "It's never going to happen. I don't know what's going through her mind with the crap she's pulling now, though."

The waiter drops off another round for James even though we hadn't ordered it. I wonder if James told him to keep them coming. "So this stunt she pulled at Edwards is out of character for her?" I ask.

"O's always been venomous—Gavin's just never seen that side of her. She thrives on capturing people and slowly going in for the kill. O has the worst daddy issues, and her mother is the most wretched woman to walk the face of the planet. O's whole life has been about trying to get their attention, and it only happens when she scores big. So no, what she's doing isn't really out of character. If I had to guess, she's just getting started. I think the way she sees it, she waited patiently for Brooke to disappear, and now it's her turn with Gavin."

I swirl my wine in my glass as I take in what he's saying. "She sounds like pure evil. I don't get it. You're such a great guy. How can you be drawn to her?"

He shrugs. "Like you said, Lily. You never really get over your first love. I know who she is, and I love her anyway. I always thought that would make the difference. But it won't. I'm just another pawn to her. I've tried moving on, but she always comes back and turns everything to shite." He drinks his whole drink in one swallow.

"I know I'll sound daft, but it really isn't her fault. She was born into a vipers' nest. Her family is void of any moral compass, and their priorities are so out of whack, I'm amazed they've functioned this long. We all had hoped after her sister Daphney died that they would have woken up and changed their ways, so to speak." He sighs and shakes his head. "But no. I think they only got worse. When you're raised like that... let's just say, it was always in the cards for her to be a bitch, but that doesn't make it her fault."

"I think I follow that all," I say. "What I don't understand is how you kept this from coming between you and Gavin?"

"Gavin never knew. Hell, I'm still not sure he sees it. He's so worried about saving her that he's never seen her as anything other than a little sister. After Daphney died, he swooped in and she became his sidekick of sorts. He's never had eyes for her, and it's not like she ever left me for him. She left me to sleep with half of London, but never Gavin. Since she never really loved him, I never saw him as a threat. I still can't believe she's going after him, but it seems she is."

Dear God, he loves her. My head is spinning. I know his isn't a unique story—beautiful mean girl entraps handsome nice guy and breaks his heart over and over. And for some foolish reason, he keeps going back for more. If he wasn't British, I'd say he's a living, breathing country song. All he needs is a broken-down truck and for his barn to burn down.

"I didn't know she had a sister," I reply.

"We don't talk about her much." He taps his fingers on the table. "She died way too young, taking with her O's only chance at being sane. She's a story for another day."

He pulls out his phone and types out a few messages, effectively telling me this conversation is closed. Quite the cliffhanger, but I'm not going to push him any more than I already have.

I reach out and squeeze his hand.

"You've got to break this cycle, my friend. My new mission is to find you an awesome chick that will help you forget Skanky McCumbucket."

He looks up from his phone. "Skanky McCumbucket?"

"Yeah, I just made that up. It's fitting, don't you think? I may not know anyone in London yet, but now I have motivation." I point at him. "I'm going to find you the perfect lady."

He puts his phone on the table and waggles his eyebrows. "I hear your friend Em is coming into town tomorrow."

I shake my head. "Oh James, Em would be the worst thing for you. Trust me. Em is her own version of an evil villainess. She takes what she wants and doesn't care who gets hurt in the process. The difference is Em isn't manipulative. She'll tell you up front that she's going to fuck you, you'll fall in love with her, and she'll leave you in the dust."

He holds his hands up. "Okay, no Em. No more praying mantises for me. Find me a fitty, a girl-next-door type who secretly enjoys a healthy side of kink."

"How would one define that exactly?" I hold up my hand to stop him. "Wait, no. Never mind. Answer me this, though. What's with Gavin's whole hero thing? Why does he need to always charge in on the white horse?"

"Ah, the Prince Charming complex. Gavin's always needed to be the savior. He's seen some horrific things, but I can tell you that growing up with the knowledge of what his family's company did messed him up. He was disgusted by the deaths their weapons caused. They got death threats and hate mail. It was too much pressure for a child.

He was always saving things. One time, his father hit a dog while driving home. Refused to stop to check on it or anything. His dad was a total wanker. Anyway, Gavin ran back to check on the dog, then carried him ten kilometers to the vet. Spent all his allowance on vet bills. That's Gavin."

Teary eyed, I'm at a loss for words.

"Explains a lot doesn't it?" he asks, playing with his almost empty glass

All I can do is a nod in response.

James drains his glass. "When he first told me about you, I didn't think it was going to go anywhere."

I bring my glass to my lips and pause, taken back by his honesty. "Oh," I respond.

"Brooke had been on the junkie train for almost two years at that point, and he blamed himself. She was gone a long time before she was really gone, if you know what I mean. I was sure he was going to punish himself for her demise for years. I didn't think he would allow himself to be happy. Now that I know you, I can see it. You're perfect for him. It's seriously fucked up the way that you met, but I'm glad you managed to find each other, despite what brought you together."

A lump forms in my throat. "Fucked up doesn't even begin to describe it. When I stop and think about it sometimes, I feel guilty. Like we both should have mourned longer. But for me, and I think for Gavin as well, I mourned the loss of life, but the love died years before."

He looks at his watch. "If I keep you much longer, my best friend will think that I really have tried to run off with his girl. Come on, I'll walk you back to Gavin's office."

We stroll back to Gavin's building. James is silly drunk and jokes the whole walk back. He has no problem publicly humiliating himself for a laugh. We walk arm and arm, possibly because he's trying to be charming, possibly so he doesn't fall. I'm so happy Gavin brought James into my life. We spot Gavin coming out of the building.

James taps me on the shoulder and says, "Get ready for this." He gets down on one knee and belts out "I'm a Believer" by the Monkees.

Gavin stops dead in his tracks and glares as James dances around while serenading me. He finishes off the song by kissing my hand while receiving applause from the small crowd around us.

I kiss his cheek. "She who will not be named doesn't deserve you and has no idea what she is missing."

Gavin walks over to us with an annoyed expression.

James wraps his arms around me, protectively. "Lily has decided she loves me, and we're running away together. Unless you can top that," James taunts.

I spin out of James's clutches. "Oh! Is this like *West Side Story*? Will there be a sing-and-dance off?" I jest. I look around. "Is there a flash mob hidden?"

Gavin retorts, "You both seem to have forgotten I've already won the girl." He grabs me and gives me one of his panty-drenching kisses that leave me breathless and dizzy.

"Fine, Gavin, you win this time. Next time, I expect you to pull out your moves. We both know you've got them. Have a good night, kids. I'm off to find the next woman worthy of a serenade," James bellows as he walks away.

When I break free from Gavin's kiss, I get lost in his stunning blue eyes.

"Hey," he says.

"Hey back."

"Want to get out of here?"

"I thought you'd never ask."

He takes me home and reminds me that he has already won the girl. Over and over and over again.

Chapter Twelve

Gavin and I never get a chance to talk about O or Max or Lorenzo. Mind-blowing sex can be *so* distracting. But we'll have plenty of time after Em leaves. In typical Em fashion, she'll be here for less than forty-eight hours. Just enough time to stir up some trouble and then hightail it out of here.

I'd hoped to talk to him this morning about what he and James talked about during their lunch. Hopefully, James convinced Gavin that O isn't sweet and innocent, but I never got a chance to ask. She wasn't worth spoiling mimosas and orgasms. Breakfast of champions.

Then poor Gavin had to put himself together and tackle a full day of meetings. Downside of being CEO. I, on the other hand, doze for hours in his glorious bed, mentally replaying the last twelve hours.

Em's flight got in around six this morning. Her plan was to head to the Mandarin Oriental and nap, and then call me on her way over. She calls at noon from the cab. Before I even have a chance to drag myself out of bed, Willis calls to let me know I have a visitor. She's pounding on the front door before I make it out of the bedroom.

I throw open the door and hug her. "How the hell did you make it here that fast? I was still in bed... Resting..."

"The hotel is like a block away. Resting my ass. You're all glowy and rocking some lovely sex hair. Someone got some." Em tosses her purse and coat on the table by the front door and gives me a final once-over.

I feel myself blush as I lead her into the living room. "This morning, and last night. Are you hungry? Thirsty? I need to grab something, I'm famished." I motion to the living room. "Hang out here, I'll be right back."

I go to the kitchen and quickly throw together a nosh platter of fruit and muffins and grab two bottles of water. When I get back to the living room, I place the platter down on the coffee table while Em fiddles with her phone.

"I ate at the hotel, but don't let me stop you. Don't eat too much though. We have reservations for lunch. Not that it matters. With all the action you're getting, I'm sure we need to keep up your strength."

I grab a handful of grapes and say, "The greatest thing

about it is all this cardio balances out my lack of self-control when it comes to food."

"I'd say I'm jealous, which I am, but you totally deserve some lovin'. Your five-year dry spell makes me shudder. You have some hot, sweaty sex credits built up. After you get some food in you you'll have to show me around this place. I'm actually impressed. You know how hard that is to do."

"I know, right? This place is amazing. I told you that you could totally stay here and not be disturbed by my screaming. All. Night. Long."

"Bitch. I said you had it coming; I didn't say you needed to rub it in. You're dating a super-hot former underwear model and having copious amounts of crazy monkey sex. I got it. I'm not, so I'm testy. You'll want to tread lightly." She plucks a muffin top off of a blueberry muffin and takes a bite.

"Going through a dry spell?"

"Just been too busy," she says, taking another bite. "Holy shit, this is the best muffin I've ever had. I can't eat anymore, or I'll devour the whole thing."

"Best muffins on the planet. I can't remember the place where Gavin gets them, but be sure to ask him. Wait till you try their chocolate chip. To die for," I say grabbing the bottom of the muffin that she discarded. "So, what has been keeping you so busy?"

"I've got a book coming out, so I've been traveling doing guest lectures and presentations at conferences. There's never any men at those things for me to play with. Just a bunch of straight-laced academics and economists. I'm sure some are closet sex fiends, but I'd rather not fish in that pond."

"Do I even want to know what your book is about?" I finish off my bottle of water, still a little dehydrated from my early morning mimosas.

"The simplified version is it's about the economic impact of rising consumer debt from a macroeconomic perspective. But don't you worry your pretty head about it. It's way over your head."

"You won't be offended if I don't read it?" I ask.

"Have you read any of my books?"

I wince and flash a guilty look. "Not really."

She shrugs. "Why would you? It ain't your bag, baby. Nothing to feel guilty about. Enough about my book. Tour time!"

I show her around, and I can tell she's in love with the flat. Em doesn't gush, but her compliments are about as good as Em gives. After the tour, Em is ready to get moving. She reluctantly waits while I shower. I come out casually dressed in jeans and an Irish fisherman sweater Gavin brought me back after a day trip to Cork, which she rejects. She spends the next hour going through my closest complaining about my limited options. After an hour of her tirade followed by my promises of shopping, she settles on an appropriate outfit and we head off for lunch.

Em only eats at the most trendy, extravagant places, so we head to Berners Tavern. It isn't too far away, but she has a car service for her trip, so it makes it easy.

The prices there are high enough that one entrée could feed a family of four for a month, but that's how Em rolls. I've given up fighting her.

We have drinks in the Punch Room while we wait for our table.

After our martinis come, she probes. "So clearly the sex is good. How's everything else?"

I shrug as I center my glass on the cocktail napkin. "It's alarmingly perfect. He's supportive and loving. He doesn't leave globs of toothpaste in the sink, and he rinses his dishes off before putting them in the dishwasher."

"He knows where the dishwasher is? I don't even know where my dishwasher is."

I roll my eyes and sigh. "I forgot I was talking to a pampered princess who needs a full-time staff to run her house."

She wags her finger at me. "Don't judge. Having staff is good for the economy. Think of all the jobs I create."

"If that is how you want to rationalize your laziness, go right ahead." I smirk and sip my drink. "I really couldn't ask for Gavin to be better. He's spent the last few weeks trying to woo me with uber-romantic dates. Like right out of a romance novel romantic. He gives me just the right amount of space. I wish I were laying down some of my own roots here, but I just haven't had the opportunity."

Em lets out a sigh that I can tell is full of judgment. She puts her drink down and turns toward me. With the way she is staring me down, I can feel a lecture coming on. "If you really think you can give this relationship a go, you have to try, but we both know you can't live here without having your own life. If you don't start creating a life of your own, you'll wither away, just like you did with Ash."

I put my drink down and match her stare. "I will never, *ever* be like I was with Ash. It's like I died and been reborn. I'll never throw away my identity like that again. I'm still writing and the blog's doing great. I know I need to work on nurturing my own interests, but I'm in a honeymoon stage. I love spending time with him. When I'm not with him, I'm enjoying writing and having some downtime. It's been a crazy few months, as you may recall. Peace and quiet is just as good for my soul right now."

She reaches over and squeezes my hand. "I hear you. I just don't want him locking you up and making you his sex slave. While that is hot, it isn't healthy."

Before I can respond, the hostess tells us that our table is ready and escorts us to a booth in the back of the restaurant. A server delivers another round of drinks and gives us a few minutes to decide on our orders. I start to look over the menu when she says, "What has Gavin been doing to help you get settled? Have you met his friends yet?"

"A few. I've met his closest friends, and I adore them. Between people he has known his whole life, people from his party/modeling days, and business associates, Gavin's probably friends with all of London."

She laughs, and takes another sip of her wine. "What

is it with you and dating the most popular kid in school? It's like every boyfriend you've had is Jake Ryan."

"*Gavin* is like Jake Ryan. Garrett Stone was like Zach Morris, hot and nothing but trouble. Innocent trouble. Ash was more like Robert Downey Jr. in *Less Than Zero*, a runaway, coked-up train waiting to derail. Anyway, Ash wanted to show me off like a damn trophy, but Gavin actually wants me to be part of his world. I know he wants to introduce me to more people, but we've spent most of our time working on us."

"Code for crazy monkey sex."

I tap my glass to hers. "Hells yeah it is!" I declare. "I know I need to make my own friends and connections. That's my goal moving forward."

"Make a game plan," she tells me. "One that doesn't include bikram yoga or painting, as we know how well those turned out. On a different note, I need your help. I just found out that the professor who invited me to guest lecture tomorrow is about to have a baby. As much as the concept disgusts me, I need to get a baby gift pronto, and since you're pseudo preggers, I figured who better to take me shopping."

"Em, I'm not really pregnant. I don't know where to go shopping. I guess we'll head over to Harrods. They have everything. You know the press will have a field day with this, right? Can't you get her a spa day or something?"

She smirks. "Nope."

"You're doing this to torture me, aren't you?" I know her too well. "Just last week you said you'd rather gouge your eyes out than go baby shopping."

"That was before I realized how much fun *Bump Watch* can be. I saw that one of you a few days ago, you definitely looked like you'd packed on a few. I saw bumpage."

I move my hand protectively to my stomach. "I found an all you can eat sushi place. That was sushi bloat, not baby bump!"

"At least they aren't calling you a whore. Let's celebrate that," she says, raising her glass in a toast.

We enjoy our exorbitantly priced but delectable lunch. On the way out of the restaurant, we spot a pregnant woman at another table. Em, having no shame, pulls up a chair and asks her for the name of a chic baby store.

Em directs the cab driver to Ilovegorgeous, apparently a posh favorite. Between the crazy London traffic and the fact that the store is clear across down, we lose the press.

I see why the ladies love it. The store is so cute, I think even Em, who's philosophically opposed to children, felt her biological clock ticking. We nab a bunch of adorable outfits and head out.

In the cab on the way back to Gavin's flat, Em thrusts her shopping bags at me. "Just shopping there made me feel like I've been infected with domestication. I need a night on the town. I'm on the VIP list at Villainy. They have these exclusive, private rooms, where all sorts of debaucherous things are known to happen. "

"Okay, should I invite Gavin or is this girls' night?" Gavin and I haven't been to a club together, but the man can dance, so it could actually be fun bringing him along.

Instead of answering me, she pulls out her phone.

"How's my British boyfriend?" she says into the phone.

I nudge her shoulder. "Who are you talking to?"

"Gavin," she whispers. "What? No, that was Lily," she says into the phone. "I need to dance the night away, and I hear you've got some moves. Can you gather some friends to join us? I have a hot American chick with me that you might fancy."

I love that she and Gavin are friendly enough that she can call and pester him. Em hated Ash, and that kept us apart for years. I never want that to happen again. Being together while I was in the hospital bonded them. They built a relationship that is independent of me.

"Well, from what I hear, you fancy her quite often," Em replies. "I've got reservations for a chef's table at Marcus tonight. It seats ten, so invite your hottest friends, and we can let them fight for my attention all night. After dinner, we'll head to the club."

She pauses, presumably while Gavin responds.

"Do I get a vote in any of this?" I ask.

She covers the mic and says, "No. If you don't like the plans, don't come. Gavin and I get along just fine without you." To him she says, "It's a date. Your friends better be *enfuego,* Gavin. Only those with a Fuck Me

Factor of ten. A nine if he's entertaining. See you at eight."

"Fuck Me Factor?" I ask after she hangs up.

"Yes. When I look at a guy and think, 'Fuck me now,' they get a ten. The scale goes down from there. Gavin and I played this game at the hospital while you were taking your extended nap."

I glare at her. "You played Fuck Me what with my boyfriend?"

"Settle down, firecracker. He pointed out men, and I ranked them. Only Drew ranked a ten."

"Ah, McDreamy. Love me some McDreamy." We stare off into the ether for a few, until I picture Gavin playing Fuck Me Factor with Em. "I can't see Gavin playing that with you."

"Oh, Gavin played all sorts of my games. He learned it was easier to just play than for me to harass him."

"That's true. A bored Emily is not a happy Emily. What did Max think about this game?"

She crosses her legs. "Max never played."

I'm dying to know more, but I know better than to push her. If she wanted to talk about it, she would. She's spiteful enough that if I push too hard, she'll just forget all about Max.

Em and I hit Harrods for appropriate club attire. She's made it clear she hates everything I own, despite the fact that she was the one to help me pack for this trip. I just let her pick something out for me. Em chooses a silver Versace bandage dress that even I will admit I look amazing in. I'm not sure why she doesn't keep it for herself. My date is a sure thing while she's interviewing candidates. Having said that, I'm more than happy to keep Gavin drooling all night.

Em settles on a red halter dress for herself. Every man who sees her will feel it in the trousers. She's a knockout.

We futz around Harrods for the next few hours. Em amasses a mountain of clothes for me to try on. I end up buying some of them, not enough to make her happy, but enough to get her off my case.

Gavin has to work later than expected, so he's going to leave straight from the office. That gives Em and I a chance to go to her hotel and primp. Em and I did this for four years in college, and I miss it. Since I have to share her the rest of the night, I'm thankful to have some alone time with her now.

Our reservations are for eight, but Em always prefers to make an entrance. After Gavin texts twice asking us where we are, Em deems it appropriate for us to get out of the limo.

Dressed to the nines, we walk in like we own the place. Anyone with a penis, even the gay ones, can't help but stare. I spot James, Liam, and Gavin seated with a few men and two women I don't know. The men are still picking their jaws up off the floor.

Gavin pulls out my chair and whispers, "It's a good thing I met you here. If I saw you in this dress at home, we never would have made it out of the bedroom. You look positively edible."

Liam gives me a hug hello, but I can see he's looking right through me. His eyes are fixed on Em. James walks over and rubs my stomach. Then he leans down to give it a kiss. He is such a brat.

While I roll my eyes, I hear the clicks of cameras capturing this endearing moment with my nonexistent baby. "James, I'm never going to get off bump watch if you keep this shit up."

He winks. "I know."

Bastard.

"Sorry to keep you waiting, boys," Em says, not sounding sorry at all. "So who is everyone?"

Liam practically pushes me out of the way to grab Em's hand to kiss it. "I'm Liam, otherwise known as the future love of your life. I hear you've been looking for me."

Em stares him down. "You practically knock over a pseudo-pregnant woman to get to me, and that's the best you can come up with? Liam, from the way Lily described you, I thought I was going to meet a real charmer. Such a disappointment."

"Burn!" James shouts far too loudly.

Half the restaurant turns and looks our way.

James reaches his hand out to Em. "I'm James, the better-looking, smarter, more sophisticated friend."

"I've heard about you. You're the one who really likes to push Gavin's buttons. I like you already," Em responds.

Gavin laughs. "The last thing I need is the two of you pairing up. Opposite ends of the table, you two. Now, Emily and Lily, let me introduce the rest of our guests."

Gavin introduces the two ladies, Poppy and Eliza, and the three boys, Heath, Basil and Percy. It looks like Gavin invited a group of models to join us for dinner. Em should be pleased.

Gavin explains that Percy and Poppy are brother and sister. Heath and Basil played rugby with him and Liam at university, and Gavin rowed crew with Percy and James. Eliza and Liam dated a lifetime ago but have remained friendly. Poppy and Heath also dated. Despite the fact that everyone says they get along, I sense some tension. Quite the incestuous circle, but they get along well. Sounds like they became a tight-knit group in college and have stayed close ever since.

Dinner's fabulous. The food's outstanding, and the conversation flows freely. Poppy and Eliza are a riot, and we become fast friends. Em's showered with attention. Gavin and I quietly place bets on who's the front runner. I manage to drag at least one embarrassing story about Gavin out of each of them. Em counters with embarrassing stories about me.

After dessert, the chef pops out to say hello to Em. He hugs her and looks at her as though he wants to throw her over his shoulder and take her back to his cave. He recognizes Percy, and the whole group chats about the restaurant.

"Em," I whisper. "How do you know the chef?"

She casually swirls the wine in her glass. "We had a thing a while back. Nothing major. We would connect when I came to town. He's married now though, so it's platonic."

"That look he gave you didn't look platonic," I reply.

Em's love life has always been a never-ending string of casual, hot encounters that are completely void of drama. I don't know how she does it. She lives the way she wants, always seems sexually satisfied, and is never bogged down by relationship theatrics. She's a walking billboard for casual sex.

"Just because he's married doesn't mean he is dead. The sex wasn't good enough to walk into that hornet's nest, though. We've stayed friendly, and that's all. Now let's get out of here." She kisses her former lover good-bye and orders the group to get moving.

The club is packed, and walking in is a huge undertaking. Between Em, Liam, and Gavin, they seem to know everyone there. Each step forward means another introduction and kiss hello, but the music's so loud that I can't hear anyone's name. I sure hope there won't be a quiz at the end of the night because I'll fail.

After an hour of being Gavin's arm candy, I'm bored and ready to sit down, but we still haven't made it to our table. I keep looking over my shoulder, hoping Em will steal me away. It's wonderful that Gavin wants to show me off to everyone he knows, but he knows everyone! My cheeks are killing me from fake smiling. I came here to dance, not network. If anyone is really that important, I'll see them again in a setting where I can actually have a conversation. So after meeting yet another person I can't hear, I leave Gavin to his endless stream of acquaintances and beeline it for the table.

When I kiss him good-bye, he glares at me.

Three bottles of champagne in ice buckets await us at our table. I'm so thirsty, I down two glasses. Em grabs me and drags me to the dance floor. I catch Gavin's eye to see if he wants to dance with us, and he scowls at me. Fine, let him be pissy. I came here to dance!

The DJ is great, and Em and I have a blast grinding it out on the dance floor. She's frisky tonight and in super sexy mode. I quickly follow suit. The rest of the group, sans Gavin and James, come down to dance with us. Liam's an amazing dancer, and Em and I practically molest him on the dance floor.

While all of the guys are vying for Em's attention, Liam seems to be the front runner. It may be because he keeps ordering rounds of shots for all of us as part of a drink or dare game. He and Em have paired up to concoct crazy dares for the rest of the group. Knowing Em, I know to stay far away from their game. Em and Liam come up with the dares, yet it never seems to be their turn. Separately, they're master manipulators; together, no one stands a chance.

Poor Eliza and Poppy have kissed random strangers, male and female, taken off articles of clothing, and danced on tables. Percy has dared to grab a woman's ass. He went up to introduce himself to her and never came back. After an hour or so, everyone's so drunk they need to sit down. I make a lap around the club to look for Gavin. With all the nooks and crannies to hide in, he could be anywhere.

I turn a dark corner and run into Gavin. "Hey, there you are. I've been—"

His lips crash into mine, and his hands aggressively roam over my body. I don't mind his rough exploration, but it strikes me as odd after the way he treated me earlier. Maybe he's missed me.

Breathless, he pulls away. "Not here."

Before I have the opportunity to ask him what he means, he grabs my hand and drags me down the corridor. At the end of the hall, he opens a door to a room with a window that looks over the dance floor. I don't recall seeing it when I was dancing, so I wonder if it's a two-way mirror.

Looking at the dance floor full of writhing bodies, I search for our friends. Before I can spot them, Gavin spins me around then pushes my back against the window. Brushing his thumb over my lip, he stares at me. He has the strangest expression, as though he's studying my face. I smile, trying to reassure him, but his critical look doesn't waver.

I push up onto my tip-toes and kiss him. At first he doesn't kiss me back, which catches me off guard. After a few gentle kisses and some coaxing from my tongue, he pushes my shoulders against the glass and devours my mouth. He takes my lip between his teeth, making my knees go weak. I groan as I push my hips into his. Any doubt I had that he wasn't into this dissipates when I feel his impressive bulge against my pelvis. His hand runs up my thigh, pushing up my dress.

I can't help but grin when he reaches my hip. *Surprise!*

He pulls away and walks to the other side of the room.

He drops his head and runs his fingers through his hair. "Where the fuck are your knickers?" he growls.

I look at him, confused. This isn't the reaction I expected at all. "I'm not wearing any," I say, trying to sound as playful as possible.

His head snaps toward me. "Where the fuck did they go?"

I have no idea what to make of his behavior. Most guys would be ecstatic if their girlfriend went commando, but he's rubbing his temple the way he does when he has a stress headache. Maybe he's developing a migraine from how much he's had to drink and the thumping music in the club?

I cross the room and stand in front of him, trying to read his face. To comfort him, I put my hand on his waist, but he flinches. I pull my hand away. Whatever's got him riled up is messing with his head. Gavin never recoils from my touch. Desperate to fix whatever went wrong, I hope flirting will bring him back to the moment.

"I thought the dress looked better without panties," I say with a smile. I slowly drag my hands up my inner thighs, the hem of my dress rising as my hands travel north. "What do you think? Do you think this dress is better without panties?"

He glares at me. He's either extremely turned on or furious, but I can't tell which. I bite my lip in anticipation of his response.

He growls, then pushes me up against the wall. Opening myself to him, I wrap my leg around his waist.

I reach for his belt buckle, but he grabs my wrist and pins it to the wall. With his free hand, he undoes his belt and pushes his pants and boxers to the floor.

He trails his fingers from my knee to my core. I tip my head back and moan when his fingers dip into my wetness. He pulls his hand back and smells his fingers before he pushes them into my mouth. Typically I hate tasting myself, but with how temperamental he's being, I go along with it. I suck his fingers as though they were his cock.

"Taste like you?" he asks.

Uncertain of how to respond, I close my eyes and suck harder.

Seconds later, he plunges into me. His fingers fall from my mouth when I moan.

I look into his eyes, trying to make a connection, but his eyes are dark. He drives his cock into me with fury. The physical pleasure is amazing, but emotionally, the action feels cold, detached. I want to push him away and find out what the hell is going on when he reaches between us and rubs my clit. Reason for the bad mood be damned—this feels too good to stop.

My hand is still pinned to the wall. I put my other arm on his shoulder to steady myself as he relentlessly pounds into me. I dig my fingernails in as my orgasm approaches. "Oh, fuck!"

My cries incite him, driving him to go faster, harder. He leans his head against the wall as he comes. Out of breath, he pulls out, shooting cum all over me.

He pulls up his pants. After buckling his belt, he kisses me hard.

"You're mine. You'd best remember that," he says in an angry, almost threatening tone, then walks out the door.

Breathless, I stare at the door in disbelief. What the fuck just happened?

I survey the room for napkins but come up empty. I leave the room to look for Gavin or the bathroom, whichever comes first. I duck into the ladies' room, which thankfully has no line, and replay what just happened in my head while I clean up. Nothing about that felt right. Well, it felt amazing—it just didn't *feel* right.

After washing my hands, I leave the bathroom and make my way back to the club. As soon as I walk under the black light, it's obvious Gavin left his mark on me. The stains on my dress light up like a Christmas tree, leaving no doubt that I'm splattered with semen. Embarrassed, I rush to the coat check and grab my jacket. I need to get out of here.

Once my jacket is buttoned up, I walk through the VIP section to find Gavin so we can go home. I don't see Gavin anywhere, but I run into Em on the dance floor.

"What's with the coat?" she asks. "It's a million degrees in here."

I unbutton and open my jacket wide enough for only her to see.

She covers her mouth with her hand. "Someone got

busy."

"Yeah, well, now it's time for this someone to go home and stain treat. Can you help me find Gavin?"

She links her arm through mine. "Gladly. I need to ream him out about senselessly destroying couture! He better have a damn good dry cleaner."

We walk all the way around the club twice without finding him. We're about to recheck the VIP section when we spot James yelling at someone, but from this angle, we can't tell who. His face is beet red, and his fists are clenched, though. Em and I walk over to check on him.

"I've put up with a lot over the years, but you've gone too far this time. We're over."

James's body is still blocking my view of the person he's talking to, but I can tell this conversation doesn't warrant an audience.

I pull on Em's arm. "Let's give him some space."

"Hell no," she says. "That's O."

I stand on my tip-toes to get a better look. I see black hair, but that could be anyone. "How do you know? You've never met her."

She rolls her eyes. "That bitch hacked your email. You think I didn't look her up?"

Fair point. I tug on Em's arm again, trying to get her to leave.

James shouts, "He's my best friend, and you were dry

humping him against the wall!"

I freeze. "Liam?" It has to be Liam. There's no way Gavin would do that to me. Not with her. Not after what we just did.

Em shakes her head. "He's been with me the whole night. I'm going to kill this bitch."

Before I have a chance to respond, Em walks over to James and wraps her arms around his neck. "James, darling, where have you been?" She turns his face so she can kiss his lips.

I'm not sure who looks more surprised, O or James.

"Just who in the hell are you?" O screeches.

Em bats her eyes at him, then looks at O. "You must be the O I've heard so much about. So much trouble caused by such an insignificant creature. For all the drama you stir up, I was expecting a real stunner, but you're so ordinary. Really, James, I can't believe you've been jerked around by this inconsequential nothing."

"Oh, please. Another wretched American who thinks she can swoop in and nab herself a British gent. Pathetic. James, tell me you're not falling for this," O replies.

Em snuggles into James's arms and flashes O a condescending smile. "Olivia, I eat wannabe mean girls like you for breakfast. You've spent your life whoring around, and now you're nothing but a cum depository. At one point, you may have had James wrapped around your pinkie, but that time is done. As you can see, his fingers are needed elsewhere. If you ever come near

James or Gavin again, I will personally destroy you."

"Who the hell do you think you are?" O shouts.

Em tips her head back and releases a sinister laugh. "Oh, I'm your worst nightmare, bitch." Em grabs her phone and types away.

Seconds later, O's phone blows up with notifications.

"Check your phone," Em says. "I just tweeted that you're sick with food poisoning and everyone should wish you well. Notice who's responding? Society people. Business people. Athletes. Movie stars. I know everyone. Today it's just food poisoning; tomorrow it could be anything. Syphilis? Embezzling? Kiddie porn? I can be very creative. Stay the fuck away from my friends, or I will end you."

Notifications come from O's phone non-stop. "Was this supposed to intimidate me?" she says, holding up her noisy phone. "Who cares if you have lots of Twitter followers? I could just as easily switch the game around on you. Let's get one thing straight. James loves me. He's been in love with me since he was fourteen, and he'll love me til the end of his days. And as far as Gav—"

Em grabs James and kisses him as if he's going off to war. When they finally break apart, Em looks at O. "Oh, are you still here? How creepy! Just watching us make out. Well, if that's what you're into." She smirks and pushes James up against the wall, knocking O over.

When they don't stop to see if she's okay, O storms off in a fury.

"The coast is clear, guys," I announce when she is

gone.

"Emily, that was the most stonking thing I've ever witnessed," James says. "I thought she was going to combust she was so angry. How did you get so many people to respond on Twitter?"

She wipes lipstick off James's mouth. "I wasn't lying. I know everyone, everywhere. Destroying her would be child's play. She'd never get a job, date, or friend by the time I was done with her."

I hate to spoil their happy moment, but I need answers. "Who was she with?"

James looks at me. "Lily..."

"Who, James? Who was she with?"

He looks down and shakes his head. I know the answer by the look of devastation on his face.

"Em, I need out of here." I make a mad dash through the club.

As I get to the exit, James grabs my arm. He's red-faced and breathless. "Crikey, you're fast!" He rests his hands on his knees while he catches his breath. "Look, it may not be what it looks like. I went to find a friend in one of the back rooms, and I walked in on them. All their clothes were on, but she was all over him, and I didn't stay long enough to get a better read on the situation."

I tilt my head. "It sounds pretty obvious what was going on."

Em hugs James. "Please tell everyone we left."

James grabs my elbow. "I'm going to head out as well. For what it's worth, I want to believe Gavin wouldn't do that."

I shrug. "But he did, didn't he?"

James nods, and breaks my heart.

Em puts her arm around me and guides me through the exit. The valet hails a cab for us. As the cab pulls away, I look back, part of me hoping Gavin will rush out of the club with an explanation. As the building disappears from view, so does my hope that this is just a terrible misunderstanding.

The rest of the ride is a blur. Em doesn't ask, and I don't offer. I'm not ready to talk yet.

Once we're in her suite, she hands me a pair of pajamas. "Take a long shower. I'll order us a bottle of wine, and then you can tell me what happened."

During my shower, I try to piece together the evening. Dinner was fabulous, then everything went to shit at the club. He ignored me, then fucked me against the wall, and now this crap with O. Nothing makes sense. After I get out of the shower, Em hands me a glass of wine. I relay the events of the night to Em, and she's just as dumbfounded as I am.

"We're missing something," she says. "I know for a fact Gavin despises her. I was there when he found out she hacked your email. There's no way he would do anything with that twat."

I pull my knees to my chest. "But what about what James walked in on? How do you explain that?"

She takes a sip of wine. "James said she was all over him, not vice versa. I'm guessing James walked in on her throwing herself at Gavin. I'd bet my bottom dollar it's that simple."

I shake my head. "How many times did we have conversations like this about Ash? Rationalizing his behavior, finding excuses and plausible explanations, when the simple truth was always staring us in the face. The only thing that is 'that simple' is that I seem to be attracted to lying, cheating scumbags."

She puts down her wine glass and scoots closer to me on the sofa. "This is different, because Gavin is not Ash. He would never hurt you this way."

Feeling defeated, I slouch forward. "I wish I could believe you, but I can't. I don't know what to believe."

She takes my untouched wine. "You need to go to bed."

I nod and drag my feet to one of the bedrooms.

I'm exhausted, but I can't fall asleep. I keep looking at my phone, hoping he'll call or text. But the damn thing remains silent. I even turn it off and on, just in case it froze up. Around three, I lose my patience with waiting. I grab my purse and coat from the chair by the door and close the door quietly, hoping I don't wake up Em. After walking through the deserted lobby, I find the doorman watching *Googlebox*, a show I've become shamelessly addicted to. After commenting on the episode he's watching, I ask him to hail me a cab.

The doorman hails a cab. The hotel is less than three blocks from Gavin's, so even in the pouring rain, it takes us no time to get there. To shield myself from the rain, I pull my coat over my head and run to the building.

Just my luck. The door's locked, and the night doorman's nowhere to be found. I ring the bell and pound on the door, but it's in vain. I have to let my coat fall back to dig through my clutch for the key. Between the pulverizing rain and the heavy wind, the overhang does nothing to protect me, making it hard to see inside my small purse. I finally find the key and unlock the door. Shivering, I rush to the elevator.

My teeth are chattering by the time I enter Gavin's apartment. He's sitting on the sofa in the dark. The street lights provide enough light for me to see that he's drinking.

"I was wondering if you were going to show up," he says in a voice that sends chills up my spine. I've never heard him so angry.

Trying to stay warm, I wrap my arms around myself. "I went to Em's hotel."

He tips back his glass. "Em's, huh? You sure about that?"

Not knowing what to make of him right now, I stay where I am. "What the hell is that supposed to mean? Where else would I have gone?"

He shrugs. "I don't know. You tell me."

Anger warms my body as I storm to him. "Why don't you stop speaking in code and tell me what the hell is going on. What happened tonight?"

He looks me in the eyes and laughs. "I was just about to ask you the same thing. What happened tonight, Lily? I'm dying to know."

Fucking drunk asshole! I run my fingers through my sopping wet hair. "Enough with the god damn riddles! What the *fuck* are you talking about?"

He puts his empty glass on the table and stands. He looks me in the eyes. "I can't do this. I won't."

"Do what?" I scream.

"This." He points between us. "I won't do it." He turns and walks out the door.

When I hear the lock click into place, I scream and throw his glass at the door. As it shatters, I collapse on the sofa and sob.

Chapter Thirteen

I used to think my active imagination was my best asset. It makes me a hell of a writer, but this morning, I wish I could remove whatever part of the brain stores the imagination. An imaginationtomy. The last few hours have been pure torture while I thought about all the places he could be. Whose bed is he sleeping in? Or worse, not sleeping in.

I have a love/hate relationship with that door. On one hand, I so desperately want it to open and for him to walk through it so we can talk this out. On the other hand, I'm so angry with him, I'm not sure I'm ready to see him. If I'm being honest, I'm petrified of what he might say. Em's convinced this whole bit with O is some big misunderstanding, but something in my gut tells me there's more going on. He wouldn't have behaved that way if O had simply made a pass at him. I just don't know anymore.

The rain stops as the sun peeks over the horizon. Since he left without a bag, he'll likely come back before work, and I don't want to be here if he does. I change into jeans and a sweater, then pack my bags and return to Em's hotel. I'm not sure what I'm going to do next, but I know it's better to bring all my stuff so I have options.

When I arrive at her room, Em's getting ready for the day. She looks at my luggage. "What the hell happened?" She points at my closed bedroom door. "I thought you were still in there, sleeping."

Leaving my bag by the door, I follow her into her room. I sit on the edge of the tub and tell her about my cryptic conversation with Gavin while she puts on her makeup.

She looks in the mirror while applying eyeliner. "This whole situation is FUBAR. I have no idea what was going through his head. That's so unlike him. If I had to guess, he was just whiskey pissed."

"I'm too tired to decipher your Emisms. Translation please."

She puts the eyeliner back in her bag, then digs around for her mascara. "You know, drunk and angry beyond reason. Probably over something stupid and irrational that doesn't amount to anything once the drunken stupor has vanished. I know it doesn't feel like it now, but I think this'll work itself out."

"You're supposed to be on my side," I say, irritated.

"I am on your side. I'm protecting you from yourself." She puts the mascara wand to her lashes. "I'm pissed at him for hurting you, but as bad as it looks, I just don't think he would ever cheat on you. I believe there's an explanation, and I don't want to see you lose faith in him or your relationship before you hear all the facts."

"Still sounds like you're on his side," I sneer.

She looks at her watch. "Crap. I wish we could talk about this longer, but I've got to go. My lecture starts at eight thirty, and I can only imagine how long it'll take me to get there. Love London. Hate London traffic." She zips up her makeup bag and motions for me to follow her. "I've got the room until four, but I've left instructions that I'll pay for the week if you want it. I think this drama will expire by midnight though. Stay here for the day, let the dust settle. If I know Gavin the way I think I do, he'll be on his hands and knees before sundown. Either groveling for your forgiveness or—"

I hold up my hand. "I get the picture, but I wouldn't hold my breath. You didn't see him before he stormed out. I've never seen him so dark. This isn't going to have a quick fix." If I even want to fix it.

She tosses a few remaining odds and ends into her suitcase. "Have faith."

I roll my eyes. "You're one of the most cynical people I know. Isn't it a tad hypocritical for you to tell me to have faith?"

"You're right. There are few things in this world I have faith in, and you, my dear, are one of them. I have hope for you."

After she zips up her suitcase, I give her a hug. "Thanks, Em. For everything."

"Anything for you." She pulls away and frowns. "Just change this sweater. Where did you find this? I know I didn't pack it for you."

"I bought it here." I look down at my brown crewneck sweater. "What's wrong with it?"

"You can't pull off earth tones! Have I taught you nothing?" She looks me up and down. "The boots work, though." Her phone rings, and she looks at the caller ID. "That's my driver. I've really got to go." She gives me one last kiss on the cheek before running out the door.

After closing the heavy drapes in the bedroom, I pull off my boots and jeans and climb back into bed. Hopefully after a long nap, I'll find some of Em's faith. Seconds after I close my eyes, my phone rings. Both relieved and hurt that it's not Gavin's ringtone, I answer the phone and hear,

"Is this Lily?"

I don't recognize the number or the voice. "Who's this?" I ask as I drop back onto my pillow.

"We haven't met. This is Sabrina, Max's girlfriend."

Girlfriend? Needing to be more alert for this conversation, I sit up and lean against the headboard. "I was under the impression you were broken up," I say with probably more attitude than I should.

"We're on a break," she replies flatly.

I can't help but roll my eyes. "Okay, whatever." My memory is Max collecting his belongings off her front lawn when she threw him out. In what world is that 'on a break'?

"I'm still mad at him, but I know in the long run we'll end up together," she says. "Not that I owe you any explanation."

"So what can I help you with? It must be ridiculously early there, so I'm guessing this is important." I'm having a bad day already, and if her attitude keeps up, this may not end well.

"I got a message from Max."

I bring my hand to my chest as I let out a huge sigh of relief. "Oh, thank God. He's back?"

"No, he's not back. We have a special Facebook account he uses to send me messages when he's under. He hasn't used it in months, since long before we started our break."

"That's actually a clever idea. So what did he say?"

"The profile is for a stripper named Candy Biggins."

I roll my eyes. "Of course it is. That's so Max. That perv." I pick up a note pad on the night stand and scribble the name down.

"I know, right? He normally just makes some crass comment about her rack or something. When he comments, I know that he's okay. Last night, he said, 'Great show, but it isn't the same without Lily. She's hot stuff, buttercup.' Buttercup is our key word for trouble. Something serious is going on. He wouldn't have reached out otherwise. I'm worried."

The fear in her voice is evident, and it turns my mouth dry as dust. I look around the suite for a bottle of water. "Sabrina, how much do you know about this case?"

"Nothing. We hadn't really spoken in weeks. What do *you* know?"

"What he posted, was it out of character? What do you think he was trying to tell you?" I ask, ignoring her question.

"I don't know if he's trying to warn you about something or if it's an SOS. It doesn't make sense. Tell me what you know," she says in a no-nonsense tone. I'm starting to think this call is less about sharing information and more of an interrogation.

I find two unopened bottles next to Em's bed. I gulp down half of a bottle, but it does nothing to improve the dust bowl in my mouth. "Did you call the FBI?"

"No, they don't know about our secret way of communicating. They'd have his hide if they did." She clucks her tongue. "I'm sick of this being a one-sided conversation. Are you going to tell me what you know or not?" She sounds pissed, but I don't really care.

"I can't, but I promise you I'll do something to fix it."

Her tone changes as she switches tactics. I guess this is her good cop shtick. "Lily, you know I'm a cop, right? You can tell me anything. If Max is in trouble, you need to let the professionals handle this. If you do something on your own, you could get the both of you killed."

I return to my bed and pull up the covers. "Sabrina, I would tell you if I could, but I can't."

"I'm losing my mind here, Lily. I love him. I've always loved him. There's never been a doubt in my mind that we'll get back together. I can't just sit here knowing that something is wrong," she pleads.

I fiddle with my cross while I think about what to say to her. "Max had you reach out to me for a reason. If you can't trust me, trust him. I promise I'll fix this." I hang up on her.

Max would never reach out to Sabrina unless it was an emergency and he had no other options. I've got to get him out. Carlos knows where he is, but my only connection to Carlos is Lorenzo. Both men are impossible to reach.

I walk to the living room to get my laptop. After finding my briefcase, I return to the bedroom and power up the computer. Google doesn't produce very much on Lorenzo, which shocks the hell out of me. The man runs an organized crime organization, and he's like a ghost. The only thing I find is a newspaper article from ten years ago with a picture of him and a priest in front of a church in Manhattan that had been burnt down and rebuilt.

Then it hits me—I know exactly how to find him. It's too early to call the States, but if I catch a plane this morning, I may have answers by dinner time. My bag's already packed and there's a flight that leaves in three hours. There's no reason not to go.

I look at my phone. Do I call? After the way he walked out on me, I don't think he deserves a call. He should be groveling to get me to even consider accepting his apology.

I scroll through my contacts until I find his name. My thumb hovers over the call button. Calling would be the right thing to do, but I can't do it. I did nothing wrong, I shouldn't have to make the first move. When he calls me, I'll explain. If he doesn't call, then I guess I have my answer. The ball's in his court.

Now I have to decide what to do with my luggage. I have no idea where this trip could take me, and I'm not sure I want to be saddled with all this baggage. But I don't want to leave it in London either. If Gavin and I don't work things out, do I really want to fly all the way back here to collect my luggage? I'm sure Gavin would ship it to me, but I'd rather avoid that awkward situation all together.

Assuming the hotel provided Em with her driver, I call the concierge. I fib and say Em left two bags behind. She assures me she'll have the bags delivered to Em before her flight tonight. I send off a quick text letting Em know her driver will have a few things I need her to bring back to the States for me. She's teaching all day, so she won't get the text until I'm already in the air, thus saving me from a lecture. I'll call her tomorrow and explain.

I make it to Heathrow in time for my flight. After I board the crowded flight, I close my eyes. I hope I know what I'm doing.

******

New York in December is bitter cold. I never understood how so many people walk everywhere in this city. With the wind chill, it has to be below twenty degrees.

I rub my hands together and bounce while I wait for a cab. After being beaten out for a cab three times, it occurs to me that I better toughen up if I have any hope of being successful today.

I tell the driver to head to Hell's Kitchen while I turn on my cell phone to get the address.

I hope coming here is the right move. Hopping on a plane without confirmation that I'm barking up the right tree is a big risk.

Once I find the address, the driver tells me we have at least forty minutes before we get there, plenty of time to call head. But I don't. The element of surprise is the only thing I have going for me.

We cruise down the Van Wyck Expressway, and Manhattan comes into view. I love New York. I don't think I could live here, but I love to visit. I'd hoped to come here with Gavin one day. I think we'd have a ball. Considering I haven't heard a word from him since he walked out, the likelihood of future vacations is diminishing by the second.

The cab pulls up to an old five-story apartment building. Of course it's a walk up and I have to go to the top floor. When I get to apartment 512, I take a deep breath and knock.

When the door opens, I say, "Hey, Darlene. I need your help."

Chapter Fourteen

While Darlene typically looks confused, right now she looks really flabbergasted. "Lily, you're about the last person I would've expected to see at my door. Come in, please."

As I cross the threshold, my former mother-in-law gives me a tight squeeze. I hug her back, wishing this were just a social call. In the last five years, I've spoken to her twice. Once to tell her that Ash died and again to ask her to betray a mob boss. I'm winning daughter-in-law of the year, all right.

Her apartment is small but homey. The furniture is worn and practically threadbare but clean. I don't see a speck of dust anywhere. She doesn't have much, but she clearly does her best to take care of what she has.

With the exception of the short time she was married to Franklin, she's lived here her entire life. A rent-controlled apartment that has been in her family for seventy years—I can't imagine how low her rent must be. She motions for me to sit on the sofa. "Can I take your coat?" she asks.

As I sit, one of the sofa's buttons pops off and springs across the room. "Oh goodness. I thought I'd fixed that," she says, embarrassed. She bends to pick up the button and tucks it in her pocket. "Your coat?" she asks sheepishly.

"No, thanks. I can't stay long. So sorry about your couch. I drop in unannounced, then start trashing the joint," I joke, trying to ease the tension.

She waves me off. "Don't be silly, honey. Sewing it up will give me something to do later. The Lord knows, I have a shortage of things to keep me busy." She sits on the sofa next to me. I can't say how surprised I am to see you. Can I get you something to drink?"

I cross my legs and fold my hands in my lap. "No, thank you. I'm sorry to just drop in on you like this, but I'm in serious trouble and I think you may be the only person who can help me," I say. "I need to find Lorenzo Grimaldi, and I'm hoping you know how to get in touch with him."

She looks down and fiddles with the hem of her sweater. "Lorenzo? How do you know him, honey?" She's trying to look casual, but I see fear in her eyes. Her posture has changed, and I can almost see her shrinking before my eyes.

"How well do you know Lorenzo, Darlene?" I ask

"I know enough," she says with a tremble. "This is a tight-knit community. Lorenzo has always been like everyone's grandfather. He doesn't miss a baptism or first communion, wedding or funeral. He plays hopscotch with all the kids. Such a gentle old man, but we all know enough about him not to ask questions."

She continues to look down, avoiding my gaze. "I wouldn't change that policy," I reply. "All I can tell you is that Ashton left me in some very big trouble that I'm doing my best to get out of, but I need to find Lorenzo. Do you know how I can find him?"

She walks to the window and is quiet for about five minutes. I know better than to push her, but I wish I could read her mind.

"Frankie always blurred the lines between right and wrong, but he managed to keep it balanced," she says. "My son never learned that skill. I heard stories over the years about what he was into. When he died, I was devastated but not really surprised. I hoped that it would end there. I'm sorry you were dragged into it. Are you sure you need Lorenzo? If I tell you where he is and he doesn't want you to find him, you know what that will mean for me, don't you?"

I nod, even though she can't see me. "He isn't expecting me, but I don't think he'll be upset to see me. Well, not after I explain, anyway. And he'd never hurt you. You're an innocent in all of this. Even more than I am. But I won't tell him who told me."

She laughs as she walks to the door. "He'll know. He gets espresso every day at the bakery across the street from the school at three thirty. He likes to watch the kids leave school. You should hurry if you want to catch him."

I follow her, kiss her cheek, then clasp her hands in mine. "Thank you, Darlene."

"Come back and see me after this is resolved. I'd love to see you out from under this dark cloud. You've had enough darkness in your life. Time for some sunshine." She smiles as she opens the door for me to leave.

I haul ass to the bakery. It's so damn cold, but I don't have time to wait for a cab. It's already almost three, and I don't want to miss him. He isn't there when I arrive, so I find a table facing the door. Hopefully I won't give him a heart attack when he sees me. He's eighty-four, and something tells me I'm the last person he expects to find sitting here.

I call Em, but I get voice mail. She's probably on her flight to Boston. I leave her a voice mail thanking her for bringing my bags home and promise to explain more later.

I hang up just as Lorenzo walks in. He looks so sweet bundled up in his wool car coat and plaid scarf. I can see why people see him as the grandfather of the neighborhood. He doesn't look like a mobster, but I suppose that's how he's pulled it off for so long.

He hasn't looked at me, but I know he saw me. Even at his age, he doesn't miss a beat. A waiter comes to his table and Lorenzo whispers something to him.

The waiter approaches me and says, "The gentleman has invited you to join his table."

Always with the pomp and circumstance. He can't just wave me over. It has to be a production.

As I walk to his table, I vet scenarios in my brain, trying to decide the best way to play this. No matter what, it'll all come down to how he feels about me showing up. I hope he's in a good mood.

I pull out the chair on the opposite side of his table and sit. "Fancy meeting you here," I say with a smile. "I was in the neighborhood and heard this place has great espresso."

He stirs his espresso with the tiny spoon. "Is that so? You just happened to be in the neighborhood?"

I rest my elbow on the table and prop my head up with my hand on my chin. "A problem landed in my lap this morning, and I realized that I needed to come to New York to solve it."

"Oh?" he says, sipping his drink.

I point to the door with my thumb. "Would you fancy taking a walk on this blustery December day?"

He returns his cup to its saucer. "Fancy? You've been in London for too long. My car is coming around. We'll go for a ride."

I cock my head to the side. "Do I get to wear the bag this time? I sure hope you've washed it since the last time," I say, intending to be funny. Judging from the daggers coming at me from across the table, he isn't amused. I put my hands up. "Just kidding. A little humor to lighten the mood."

"Save the comedy for the professionals."

"I need to—"

He bangs his hand on the table.

"I'm sure whatever you need to discuss can be done elsewhere."

It seems I'm not playing by the rules.

Lorenzo's Mercedes pulls up to the curb. When we get to the car, Big Al steps out to open the door for us.

"This is about the last thing I was expecting to happen today," he says as I approach.

I pat him on the back before entering the car. "Hello to you too, Al."

After we sit and the car gets moving, Lorenzo says, "This is not our arrangement."

"Yes, I realize that. There are extenuating circumstances, and you didn't leave me much choice. Had you given me a phone number, email, or carrier pigeon, I wouldn't have to drop by unannounced."

He looks out the window, ignoring my remark. "You're resourceful. I'll give you that."

"If this is the first time you've picked up on that, you haven't been paying attention."

He laughs. "How I've missed your arrogance. Tell me, what's so dire that you had to break every rule I have?"

I tap my fingers on the armrest. "Max used some back channels to reach out to me. He's in danger, and I need to get him out. The FBI won't pull him, so I need you to tell me where he is."

He stares at me blankly. "That's asinine, you realize that."

"When has that stopped me before?" I ask. "I need to get him out, or this will end poorly for him, for me, possibly for Carlos. Tell me where he is, and I'll figure something out."

The car pulls up to the Waldorf Astoria. Al opens my door and extends his hand to help me out.

"Get a room. I'll call you," he orders.

Big Al leans forward and roughly grabs my hand. "Time's up, sweetheart."

When I'm on my feet, I pull my hand away. "Al, you really know how to make a girl feel special. For future reference, I prefer the Plaza," I say before I sulk off into the hotel. I'm not sure what I was expecting, but I feel like I have completely wasted my time.

Irritated, I register for a room. Between the flight and this room, I'm going to have to write ten articles just to break even. "Day of" accommodations in New York come with a high luxury tax. Max owes me big time.

It's almost midnight in London, and my phone hasn't made a peep. We wouldn't be us if we didn't have a bout of radio silence.

The room is nothing special, especially for the price, but it has a shower, and that's all I need right now. I turn the temperature to almost scalding and try to sear the day away. Gavin and I may be over, Max is in danger, Lorenzo is irritated with me, and I just blew three month's pay on this impromptu trip. This won't go down in history as one of my finer days.

An hour later, I decide I should leave some hot water for the rest of the hotel. The last time I engaged Carlos and his crew, I was kidnapped and didn't eat or sleep for days. Climbing into bed and getting some sleep is probably a smart plan. It's not even seven thirty, but it's dark outside and I'm still on London time. Just as I drift off to sleep, my phone rings.

"Where the hell are you?" Gavin shouts before I can even say hello.

"Um—"

"'Um?' You leave me and fly to New York and all you have to say is, 'Um?'"

I sit up against the headboard, trying to wake myself up. "How do you know where I am?"

"That's beside the point, Lily, and you know it. You owe me an explanation."

I pull the phone away from my ear and glare at it. "I don't owe you anything. You walked out on me."

"I needed a few hours to sober up and get my head on straight. That's a far cry from packing up and moving to another bloody continent! Were you even going to clue me in that you left, or was I just supposed to sit here wondering if you might grace me with your presence?"

"I'm just playing by your rules. You can't *do this*, remember?"

He releases a frustrated sigh. "I don't even know what to say to you right now."

"Good. The feeling is mutual." My phone beeps, letting me know that the call was dropped. Bastard. I bury my head in my pillow and scream.

My phone rings again. I push talk and bark, "What?"

"What's your problem?" a strange voice asks.

"Who is this?" I snap.

"It's Al. Lorenzo says to be ready by eleven thirty. A car will come get you."

"Where am I going?"

He laughs. "Don't you know better than to ask questions like that? You opened this can of worms. Hope you're happy with how it turns out."

This day just gets better and better.

****

After hours of fuming and cursing Gavin, O, Ash, and all the others I could think of to curse, my adrenaline is pumping. By the time eleven thirty rolls around, I'm ready for whatever Lorenzo is about to throw at me. I pity the guy who tries anything with me tonight.

Big Al is waiting for me by the cab stand. "You look like a lady on a mission."

"I am. Care to tell me where my mission is?"

"Nice try, sister. You get points for perseverance though." He laughs as I get in the backseat.

My bravado carries me along for twenty minutes, but then it falters. I have no idea where I'm going or what to expect when I get there. I've pissed off one mob boss by asking him to put me in touch with another, breaking the criminal code of conduct. Probably not the smartest move. My night may end with me being fitted for a concrete coffin.

As we drive over the Tappen Zee Bridge, the reality of the situation sets in. I'm not wearing the bag. That either means they trust me, or Al's driving me to my execution. I know Lorenzo's been looking out for me, but I also know that if I've become a liability, he'll have no choice but to eliminate me. My protection cannot supersede his own.

Despite how angry I am at Gavin, I wish I'd tried to talk to him before I went on this half-cocked adventure. In a typical situation, the onus should be on him to mend what's broken between us. It's his erratic behavior that got us here. But this isn't a typical situation. As I walk into the lion's den, I wish I had closure, even if I had to be the one to make the first move. I wish I knew what the hell happened that night. All our drama aside, I scared out of my mind and I miss him. I can't shake the feeling that I've botched things up between us, but I can't bring myself to call him.

Al merges onto the New York State Thruway. Looks like we're going to upstate New York. My phone plays "I'm Too Sexy" by Right Said Fred. I don't recognize the number. Who the hell programmed that? I hate this song.

"Hello?"

"Hey, Honey Bunny, what're you wearing?"

Al has the heat cranked up, and I'm starting to sweat. I shrug out of my coat. "Honey Bunny? Really, Liam?"

"Have you forgotten our rendition of the *Pulp Fiction* dance scene at the club? You weren't that hammered at the club, were you?"

"I recall, Pumpkin." I look at my watch. "You're up very late, or maybe you're just up really early. Either way, it must be important for you call me in the wee hours."

"I'm always up this early. Got to get my run in before practice," he replies. I forgot he's a rugby player. "You need to get that sexy ass on the next flight home, Honey Bunny."

I lean my head against the cold window. "I can't," I reply. "I'm dealing with a crisis that needs my immediate attention. Plus, I'm not sure I have a reason to go back to London."

"A reason? I'll give you a reason. Your boyfriend that adores you. You are the best damn thing that has ever happened to him, and I won't stand by and let you throw it all away over some stupid kerfuffle."

"Do you know the story?" I ask. "I can't get a damn word out of him. I have no clue what's going on!"

"I don't know all the details, HB. I don't need to. You

two need to sort this out. I repeat: Get your ass on a plane."

"Liam, this is really a conversation I should be having with him. Everything Gavin's done from the second we stepped into that club has been shady. He's got a lot to account for, but he's not talking," I shout, waving my hands wildly.

Big Al looks over his shoulder. "Everything okay back there? You're getting pretty animated."

"Keep your eyes on the road," I snap. "And turn the heat down, I'm melting back here."

Al hums the *Wicked Witch of the West* theme song. What an asshat! After digging around in my purse, I find a pack of gum and throw it at the back of his head.

Liam clears his throat. "You still with me HB?"

"Yes, I'm still here," I reply. "Like I said, I'm in the middle of something."

"I know Gavin's acting like a wanker. These moody streaks are his one major flaw. They come out of nowhere, but leave just as fast. You, however, packed up and flew across an ocean. Abandonment loses to moody every time. He was gutted when I talked to him earlier, he's sure you're gone for good. Pretty reasonable assumption, if you ask me. He and James had a row; Gavin tried to kill him. In all the years we've known each other, none of us has raised a fist in anger. *Something's rotten in the state of Denmark*. You need to come home and sort this shit out before I lose both of my best mates."

I smirk. "Shakespeare? I never know what's going to come out of your mouth."

"I was a theater major, my dear. And it isn't about what comes out of my mouth, but what I can do with it. Care to find out?"

"Let me get this straight. You call me to come back to London for your best friend and then offer me oral sex?"

"The way I see it, if Gavin and James kill each other over whatever is going on, I want first dibs. Just making my case now."

"If I stay away from London, you boys will go back to the way you were. It's better I'm gone."

He gasps. "You need to come back to London because it's where you belong and you bloody well know it," he says.

"I'm not sure I do know that. He said he couldn't do this anymore. I'm not sure anything is waiting for me in London but heartache." I pull my cross back and forth along my necklace while I debate if I really want to ask the questions that are burning my brain. Am I ready for the answers? "Do you think he slept with her?"

"Ha! He'd be more likely to ask for a blow job from a viper. Well, now that I think about it, getting one from O would be getting a blow job from a viper. Scratch that. My point is, Gavin would never cheat on you, and he would never sleep with O. Get that out of your head right now. You need to come home, before this gets more out of control than it already is."

I want to tell him that the reason I left has nothing to do with Gavin or what happened that night, but there's no way for me to do that without him asking questions I can't answer. "Like I said, Liam, I can't come back right now. And, unless he can carry on an actual conversation with me, he can piss off."

"He fucked up, but you left the country without even saying a word. That's cold, my dear. Get home," he says before hanging up.

I'm not sure what to make of that conversation. Gavin's talked to Liam about it, but won't talk to me? Liam claims Gavin's panicked I'm gone, but he's the one who walked out. Al's phone rings, and I'm reminded that my relationship drama has to take the backseat to the matter at hand. I have to push Gavin out of my mind.

Trying to clear my mind, I lean back and close my eyes. Sleep takes me quickly.

Al slams on the brakes, jarring me awake. "Rise and shine. You have a date to keep."

Chapter Fifteen

Groggy from my nap and emotional roller coaster, I drag myself out of the car. The ice cold air stings my exposed skin while I button my coat, and wrap my scarf around my neck tightly. We're parked in a grassy field in the middle of nowhere. There's no moon tonight and the sky is filled with clouds, so without the light from the car, I wouldn't be able to see a thing. I wonder if there's a gangster's guide to clandestine meeting locations. How the hell do they find these places?

Al hands me a flashlight. "Go down that path a ways. You'll see him."

As retribution for the witch reference earlier, I flash the light in his eyes. "How far is 'a ways'?" I really don't want to be wandering all night.

He knocks the light away. "Walk down the path. If you ain't seen him yet, you ain't gone far enough. Got it?"

"Al, you missed your calling as a tour guide," I say, rolling my eyes. It's now or never, so I head down the path.

The path leads me down a hill to a lake, and I make out Carlos sitting on a bench on the dock.

After rolling my neck and shaking the tension out of my shoulders, I take a deep breath and walk to the bench. "What is it with you and lakes in the middle of the night?"

"Look around. Do you see anyone?" he asks with a smile.

The metal bench is freezing. Even with my knee length, down filled jacket I can still feel the icy metal on the backs of my thighs. My whole body shivers, but I try my best to hide it. "No, because no sane person comes out here at this time of night. This place is like a scene out of a bad horror movie."

"If you're afraid of the boogey man, Lily, you shouldn't request a sit down with him," he says with a laugh.

"Touché." I smirk. A drug dealer with a sense of humor. At least he keeps it interesting. "On that note," I continue, "let's get down to business before something climbs out of that lake and tries to eat us. I had nothing to do with Max pursuing a case against your organization. I hear through the coconut telegraph not everyone sees it that way and my life and his may be in danger because of this misconception. I would like to rectify that and go back to me putting all this crap behind me."

"Just how to do you think you can do that? I suspect you've made efforts that have failed, or we wouldn't be sitting here."

I can hear the doubt in his voice. I need to ease his discomfort, but it's hard to sound convincing when my teeth are chattering.

"You're going to tell me where he is, and I'm going to get him and bring him home."

The words aren't out of my mouth before he laughs. "Do you have a death wish?"

"I already have a bounty on my head; why not pull out all the stops? If they kill me, I want to go out on my terms. Sitting around waiting for the next Charlie is not a choice. I'd rather walk into the lion's den than be stalked prey."

He stops laughing, but he still has a smile. "You could teach some of my guys a thing or two, you know."

"I'll set up a weekend retreat after all this gets cleared up. Give them all some tips on how to be awesome. In order to do that, I need to get off the damn chopping block. Tell me where he is. I'll put on a disguise, casually run into him somewhere, and get him out. I guarantee you we'll be in a different time zone before anyone notices he's missing."

"If you get caught, you'll both be dead and no one will ever find your body. That's not a guess; that's a certainty. I can't protect you there," he warns.

I rub my gloved hands over my arms, trying to keep the blood flowing. “Yeah, I've heard your children are fighting amongst themselves.”

He shrugs. “Power struggles are a part of life,” Carlos responds.

“I went to an elite boarding school, and I was in a sorority. There was always a mean girl in control and twenty girls dying to take her place as queen bee. They may not have had guns, but they may have been crueler than all your men put together. I understand power struggles.”

He laughs and shakes his head. “If things were different, I would introduce you to my daughter. You and she would get along well.”

“Sounds like you have your hands full,” I reply. “Look, Carlos, I know I can do this. Just tell me where he is. I'll get him out. I'll have to tell him some things, but not enough to betray you. I made a promise of confidentiality to you. No one at the FBI knows a thing about you or our relationship. I have and will continue to keep that promise. But, keeping Max there is dangerous for everyone involved, so to keep all our asses out of the fire, I might have to spill the beans.”

Carlos won't look at me. He walks to the shore of the lake. He tries to skip a stone, but there's a layer of ice forming on the surface of the lake. It's too dark to see, but I hear it scrape the ice as it slides along the surface. Still not understanding why this decision creates so much conflict for him, I decide to do what I do best: push. I walk over and throw rocks too.

“You're good at that,” he says.

"I grew up in a small town, across the street from a lake. Fishing, skipping stones, I can do it all. Although, ice stone skipping is a first for me" I get a small smile from him. "Tell me why this is such a hard decision. I know you don't owe me an explanation, but maybe if we talk it out..."

"We have a code of silence. I've brought you in too much already, and my judgment has been called into question. You should have been eliminated. That's... standard operating procedure. But I knew you wanted nothing more than to run as far away from us as you could, and I didn't expect you to resurface as a problem."

"If you had eliminated me, I promise Max going under cover would be the least of your organization's concerns. Between Max, Greene, and Sully, the FBI would have been out for blood. I can't even imagine what Gavin would have done." I try to maintain my cool. It isn't every day you're reminded how expendable you are. "You made the choice with the least risk. Anyone who can't see that is an idiot. What am I saying? They gave Ash five million dollars. We aren't talking about the sharpest knives in the drawer."

"Most people asking favors don't throw insults around. Especially to me," he spits at me.

Dropping the stone in my hand, I put my hands on my hips and look him square in the eyes. "Am I wrong?"

We stare at each other for a few moments.

He breaks our stare and shakes his head.

He mutters, "The balls on this girl. What's your plan?

Let's start there."

"You need to tell me where he is before I can create a plan to get him out."

He takes a deep breath. "He's in Tucson."

"What?" How the hell does this come back to Tucson? "Where in Tucson?"

He picks up a rock and flings it. "They operate out of a club called Seven Spades."

Cock-sucker-mother-fucker. It always has to come back to Ash, doesn't it?

Anger boils within me, but I can't lose my temper. I turn and walk down the shore, throwing a few more stones. Carlos is kind enough to give me space to pull myself together, but I know he won't be patient for long.

"You understand that Max would have found them at Seven Spades regardless of my involvement. It would have been all over Ash's file. He was digging for a connection, and that's an easy one to make," I say through gritted teeth.

"Yes, *I* understand that. There are others who aren't sophisticated enough to make that connection."

I shake my head in disgust. "So it started back then? While we were in school?"

"Yes."

Ash was always into something, but I never dreamt it went back that far.

"We lived at that damn bar. I always assumed it was because his fraternity brother managed it. That, and their bathroom was always clean and they had a velvet couch that was the best place to lie down after too many shots."

Ash's problems didn't start in DC; they started right under my nose in college. When I could have gotten out. How the hell was I so damn blind? When we were in DC and I saw the changes in him, I turned a blind eye to them. He wasn't hiding from me, I was choosing to ignore it. I felt superior because I thought it was on my terms, not his. When we were in school, I thought he was harmless. Flashy, arrogant, and always looking for excitement, but benign. How did I miss how deep the trouble he was in was, even then? I thought I was smarter than that, but instead I'm a freaking cliché.

No time for a pity party. "If he's at Seven Spades, I know just how to get him out. I need a bit of time for planning, but I know how to do it. Good-bye, Carlos." I walk back toward the path

"Don't you think we should discuss your plan?" he shouts.

I turn around to face him. "Does it matter? If I fail, I'm dead. You wouldn't have told me where he is if you didn't think I could do it."

I hear him laugh as I trek back up to the car.

"Come on, Al," I say. "I've got a plane to catch."

Chapter Sixteen

I've seen enough spy movies to know that when dealing with bad guys, it's always better to be inconspicuous. Flying into Tucson may raise red flags, so I fly to Vegas. Not only would no one expect that, but I need help from an old friend.

During the long drive to the airport, I'm fixated on the clock. It's morning in London, and I wonder what Gavin is doing. He hasn't called. Calling him would either ease my pain or break my heart, and I can't take that risk. I need a clear head for what I'm about to do.

When we arrive at the Buffalo airport, I'm floored. I knew we drove a ways, but I didn't realize how far. I catch a seven a.m. non-stop to McCarren. Before we take off, I text a friend I haven't spoken to in years, hoping she can help me out. Isn't that what sorority sisters are for?

Sleep takes over as soon as the plane takes off. It may be the last sleep I get for a few days, so I treasure every minute of it.

Stepping off the plane, I'm reminded of what a zoo Vegas is. Before I even get off the jetway, I hear the annoying ping of slot machines. People getting off their planes are full of excitement and hope. People boarding planes look as if they've been rode hard and put away wet. Such is Vegas.

I text my sorority sister and ask her to meet me at departures. That's an old airport trick I learned from Ash. I spot a shiny red Mercedes convertible, and I know I've found my ride.

A stunning redhead jumps out of the car. Her hair wasn't always red, but I'd know her anywhere.

She runs to me with open arms as soon as we make eye contact. When she reaches me, she hugs me so tight, I can barely breathe. "Hey, Britt. Thanks for coming to get me."

"Anything for you, doll. You tell me you need help only I can provide, I'm there for you." She releases me and nods in the direction of her car. "Now get in and tell me what the hell is going on."

Brittany was in my pledge class. We weren't really into the whole sorority thing but were doing it anyway. Britt because her parents made her, and me because I thought it was a wise move. She was a ballet major from a strong Southern family that expected her to carry on the family name with pride. To say they were shaken up when she dropped out of school, eloped to Vegas, and became a showgirl is an understatement. Britt was disowned but never looked back. She's now making a killing starring in a show on the strip, *Scandalous*. Her last show I saw was jaw-droppingly sexy.

"I have to go back to Tucson, and I need to be incognito. Can you use your showgirl magic to make me over? I need to be there by ten, so we have about six hours."

She throws the car in gear and pulls away from the curb. "Suga, that's more than enough time."

"One more thing. Can I borrow your car?"

She laughs and rolls her eyes. "Anything else?"

I shrug. "Just the makeover and slut-wear."

"You've come to the right place," she says with a smile. She pats my legs. I can't help but notice the ice that adorns each of her fingers. She looks like she robbed a jewelry store.

I assumed we would go to her house, but she takes me to the hotel she works at instead. As we walk through the casino, I flash back to hazy memories of gambling, dancing till dawn, and out of control parties. They were good times, what college was supposed to be about. But as I sort through the haze and remember the drama that comes with inebriated teenagers with money to burn and no appreciation for the consequences of their actions, I get a sour taste in my mouth. Living in the fast lane isn't necessarily a good time. It's just fast.

Britt takes me through the dressing room to her office. The sign on the door says "Executive Producer."

"Wow, Britt, you've certainly worked your way up in the world."

"Come on, now. You know I'm more than just tits and ass," she says with a wink. "Now, before I get started, do you trust me?"

"Why do you think I'm here? I trust you with my life." If she only knew how true that statement is.

"Okay, let's get started."

Three hours later, I'm made up and ready to go. If only Tucson were down the street. "Britt, I've got a six-hour drive. I'll have sweated off all this makeup by then. No one can know I'm there. I can't use my credit cards or stop by someone's house. What should I do?"

She hands me her keys and her wallet. "I made you a reservation at the Arizona Inn. Drive down, check in, and take a quick nap. Don't shower, just touch up the makeup. Even you can manage to do it, I promise. If you need help, call me. I expect to see you back here tomorrow, or I'm sending someone to get you. You feel me?"

She knows. She doesn't know what, why, or how, but she knows.

"How..." I start to ask but trail off. It doesn't matter.

"Honey, I could smell the deep shit on you when you walked off the plane. Whatever you've gotten yourself into, you're too good for it. Get down there, fix whatever needs fixin', and get the hell out. Go back to that fine man you've got in London."

"You've seen, huh?"

"Oh yeah. You look great for being knocked up." She laughs. "Oh, one more thing." She hands me a cell phone. "Give me yours."

I dig in my pocket for my phone, then hand it to her. "Why?"

She rolls her eyes. "If I need to explain that you can be tracked by your cell phone, then you have no business doing whatever it is you're doing. This is a burner cell. I'm the only one who has the number, and my number is programmed into it. I'm turning yours off. As far as Big Brother is concerned, you've gone dark."

She walks to her supply closet and rummages around for a moment. She turns back toward me, then hands me a small box. "Colored contacts. Those pretty green eyes can now be baby blue. They sting like a bitch, so don't put them in until the last possible minute. You'll tear up, so fix your eye make-up afterward." She slaps my ass. "Now, get."

I hug her and whisper, "Thank you."

I haven't spoken to her in over five years, and she dropped everything to help me. This clearly isn't her first time dancing with the dark side of life. One day, I'll find a way to repay her. If I don't end up buried in the desert, that is.

******

I'd forgotten how beautiful Arizona is. I wouldn't be

back here unless my life depended on it, but it sure is beautiful. It's an easy drive from Vegas. Once I get over the Hoover Dam and past Kingman, AZ, it's pretty much flat and straight. Britt's Mercedes drives like a dream. I can feel lead in my foot, and as I drive, I see the cops still use the same places for their speed traps. I know where I can go ninety mph and where I need to keep it at the limit. The drive gives me plenty of time to get lost in my thoughts. Being back stirs up ghosts I wish I could forget and makes me long for Gavin.

Once I hit Phoenix, butterflies creep into my stomach. What I'm about to do is crazy, but so is this whole situation. Sometimes the only way to fight crazy is with crazy. The butterflies turn to panic when I see the first signs for Tucson. I was well known here. What if someone recognizes me? If Ash was dealing with these guys, they clearly know who I am. What if Britt's makeover isn't good enough? What the hell have I gotten myself into?

It's crazy how much Tucson has changed in just five years. Britt picked a great hotel for me to lounge in. It's a high-end hotel that usually hosts academics and wealthy parents—not the type of place a drug dealer would think to look. Especially since I'm checking in as Brittany Hills.

I'm sure the room is lovely, but I don't even look around. I get into bed and close my eyes. I don't fall asleep, but I try to pull myself together. At nine, I get into my costume. The contacts are a pain in the ass to get in, but after a million tries I get them in and they don't pop right out. Brittany knows what she's doing. I look in the mirror and gain some confidence; I may be able to pull this off. Hell, Max may not even recognize me.

I now have long, thick black hair that goes all the way down to my ass. My green eyes are now piercing blue. They remind me of Gavin's. The clothes take the cake though. I'm wearing skintight leather pants and five-inch stilettos; no man will be looking at my face. Brittany provided me with a free boob job, at least for the night. The silicone bra lifts take my Cs to at least D's. The skimpy tank top she gave me accents my man-made cleavage. The way she taught me to do my eye makeup really changes my look.

I take one last look in the mirror. It's a damn good disguise. I've been completely transformed. It reminds me of a costume party where we went as Charlie's Angels. But this ain't no costume party. Looking the part is only half the challenge. I need to pull this off flawlessly.

Ten thirty. Party time.

I hop in the Mercedes and drive downtown. I'm hoping to get to the bar before Max does in case someone recognizes me. The staff has probably changed in the last five years, except for the manager, Todd. Todd was Ash's fraternity brother and frequent partner in crime. Knowing what I know now, those crimes were probably far more substantial than I ever realized. If he spots me, I'm done for.

After finding some street parking out front, I check the mirror one last time. It's now or never. Channeling my inner bad girl, I strut into the club. It's still early, so there aren't too many people there yet. The bartender is new, and I watch his eyes rake over me. I want to punch him in the throat when he asks my breasts what I would like to drink. I shouldn't be mad since that's exactly the reaction I was hoping for, but I'm a woman. Sometimes I get pissed when men do exactly what I set them up to do. Fortunately, my irritation adds to my bad girl image.

The bartender takes his time making my drink, giving me a chance to scan the bar. No sign of Max, but I spot Todd right away. He glances at me and devours me with his eyes. Game on.

Todd crosses the bar and says to the bartender, "Put whatever she's having on my tab, Scott."

I smile. "Thanks, but I can buy my own drinks."

He steps back and looks confused. "Do I know you?"

Fuck. "Nope. I'm in from Vegas for the weekend. First time here."

"There's something about you. I feel like we've met before."

Fuck. Fuck. Fuckity fuck. I never stopped to think that he could recognize my voice.

Time to call an audible. "Nope. Can't say we've met. Want to show me around?"

He gets a wicked look on his face. "I'd love to." He puts his hand on the small of my back and leads me through the bar. When we pass into a back room with slightly better light he says, "Has anyone ever told you that you're a dead ringer for Brooke Livingston?"

I hadn't thought about it when I checked myself out in the mirror, but I suppose I do sort of look like her. A point I can agonize about if I make it out of here alive. Right now, I need to keep my head in the game.

The bar has two stories. Five years ago, there were cameras everywhere except in the backroom upstairs and in his office. He was known to take guests in there for the VIP tour of his dick.

Staying true to himself, he takes me around, and we end up in the back room. He pulls me in close to dance. He dances so close I feel like we're dry humping. My skin crawls, but I need to get him comfortable.

I rub my body against his and whisper, "Todd, you're going to pretend I don't know you and you don't know me. In exchange, I'm going to give you a gift. After you close tonight, scrub this place down and make sure there's nothing you wouldn't want your mother to see. Forget I was ever here. Do you understand?" I turn his face to look me square in the eyes. "Do you understand?"

He looks at me with confusion.

Before he says anything, I add, "This is a once-in-a-lifetime stay-out-of-jail-free card. You and I both know if this place burns down, your South American friends will let you burn with it."

He looks at me with confusion in his eyes. "Who *are* you?"

"If you haven't figured it out, I'm not going to tell you. If your few remaining brain cells start to work and you piece it together, keep it to yourself. So to go over it again. You don't know me. I don't know you. Clean house. Got it?"

He nods.

"Good." I smack his ass and walk out of the room. Hopefully I just scared him into thinking he has an inside tip that will behoove him to keep his mouth shut.

By the time I get downstairs, I see the bar has filled in. Lots of twenty-something college teeny boppers are full of alcohol and low on inhibition. The bar is the best place to scope the crowd, and I'm lucky enough to grab one of the last open stools. Scott, the bartender, pours me another drink. I have no intention of drinking it, but it gives me something to play with while I wait.

It takes me a while, but I spot a group of familiar faces at a table in the back. Memories of me dancing the night away while Ash hung out with "his boys" flood my brain. They were guys I never knew well, and had no interest in knowing, but I still saw them several times a week. Damn, I was oblivious.

Todd isn't my only concern anymore. I've got to pray that group has seen enough tail come and go that they won't remember me. Standing at the bar is too dangerous. They could lock in on me and stare until it jogs their memories. Looks like it's time to dance.

Hitting the dance floor gives me cover while I keep an eye on the crowd. After forty-five minutes, Max enters the back of the club. Casting my eyes on him, I can breathe a little easier. He's safe. At least for the moment.

He looks good. His hair's a little longer and full of

product, trying to pull off a California preppy look. It's not him, but he wears it well. I've been so worried about him, I haven't paid attention to how much I miss him. Max was my rock throughout all of the Not-Charlie drama. That time together bonded us in a way that can never be replicated. Without him in my life, there's something missing. A void even my relationship with Gavin can't fill. Gavin's amazing, but he doesn't share my strange addiction to reality TV shows about Alaskan fishermen and gold miners. If Gavin and I are really over, I'm going to need Max to put me back together.

He makes his way through the crowd, stopping to greet all of Ash's old cronies. He'll head to the bar at some point, so I casually leave the dance floor. Knowing Max the way I do, I lean up against the bar seductively, leaving my ass on display.

"If I had a dime every time I saw an ass that stunning, I'd have ten cents. Really, sweetheart, it's a work of art." The Boston accent is gone, but the voice is the same. "I'm Joey, and you are?"

I turn to face him. "Hiya, Joey. Just call me Slugger."

From the way he continues to assault my ass with his eyes, I can tell it's not registering. I try not to be offended that he doesn't recognize my voice. "Slugger, huh? That's an interesting name."

"It's a nickname. My old roommate gave it to me when I almost took his head off with a baseball bat."

Max's eyes go wide, and he steps back, looking me up and down. He waves to the bartender. "Hey, Scott, I need some shots over here. Tequila, *por favor*."

He turns back toward me, looking casual. "That's one hell of a get up, Slugger. You need to wear leather pants more often. *Dayam*, you've got an ass that won't quit. And that rack! I'm sure there's a story there. I don't care how they got there as long as I can stare at them."

Scott brings over our shots.

I raise my glass. "Here's to my ass saving yours."

Max takes the shot but gives me the evil eye.

"I'm not sure how to play this, Slugger. I'm not playing the type of game you show up uninvited to. You catch my drift?"

I suppose it was naïve of me to think he was going to jump for joy that I've come to his rescue, but I expected him to at least look happy to see me. "Candy Biggins told me you were looking for me. So here I am. I've got this all worked out, and you're just going to follow my lead. Sound good, *Joey*?"

"Candy grossly misunderstood the message, but I'm listening," Max replies.

I'm not sure what he means by that, but if Sabrina gave me the wrong message, it's a little late now. "You and I are going to hit it off. We're going to make it seem like we're so hot for each other that we need to take this party elsewhere. Then we're going to get into my car, drive away, and never look back. Got it? So pretend you're into me."

"That's not hard to do, babe," he says, leaning in to me.

"Lay it on me," I say. "Give me your best pick-up line. Let's see the goods."

He reaches into his back pocket, then throws a condom on the bar. Looks like Max getting lucky is standard operating procedure. This will work out perfectly.

"Oh, baby. Just because I'm wasted doesn't mean this condom should be. A good condom is a terrible thing to waste."

I can't keep a straight face. "Oh, that's bad, Joey. Real bad."

He leans in and whispers, "They've all been watching you but don't worry. They'll never figure out who you are. Hell, I might not have known who you are in that get-up. Now laugh like I just said something funny."

I giggle and bat my eyelashes. I lean back into him. "Do you frequently leave with girls? Make sure you play your typical game. Don't do anything out of character." He may not realize it, but he's been burned. I'm sure these guys are just waiting for the perfect opportunity to take him out. One misstep and we could both end up dead.

He smiles and laughs as if I just said something clever. He leans back, trying to get a better view of my ass before giving it a good squeeze. "Don't worry about it. With the vibe you're throwing, no one will think twice about me leaving with you. I may have to fight off a few guys first, but no one will question it."

We order another round of drinks and find a small table in the back, in sight of the cartel boys that Max has been infiltrating They're close enough that they can watch us, but far enough that they can't make out our conversation. I may not know these boys well, but I do know them. Max and I'll have plenty to talk about on the drive back to Vegas.

I can feel them watching us, so I want to put on a good show. I become hyper aware of my body language. I turn to him, leaning forward so he has my attention and so he can stare at my cleavage. My legs are pressed up against his and my hands are constantly touching him.

"Tick, tock, Joey. We have a short time to pull this off. Last call is in an hour. Whisper sweet nothings in my ear."

He leans in and recites his football picks for this Sunday. I smile and giggle and touch his arm when he gets closer.

After ten minutes of football banter, I say, "We have to kiss. They aren't going to buy it unless we're all over each other. So in a few minutes, you're going to kiss me. The kiss will get carried away, and we'll both pull back. Okay?"

He rolls his eyes. "Just make it look good."

We fake flirt back and forth for a few more minutes. We name the best and worst things about Tucson. His favorites all seem to be strip clubs.

When I tell him one of my sorority sisters is married to the owner of two of them, he whispers, "Now you tell me. We could have moved this party there!"

I give him a dirty look. "Gee, I really should've factored a farewell lap dance into my plans. How insensitive of me."

Out of nowhere, he kisses me. My first response is to push him away, but I catch myself before I do. To pull this off, we need to be convincing, which means I need to give Max the kiss of his life.

I can't help but think of Gavin. Whatever our relationship status may be, kissing Max feels wrong. Kissing Max in general is wrong. It's like kissing my brother. He sticks his tongue in my mouth and I have to concentrate on continuing the kiss without gagging.

Throwing up on him would be devastating. On second thought, no one would think twice about a quick getaway if we were both covered in puke. Disgusting, but thinking about anything other than the fact that we're kissing has helped me keep it together.

When I finally pull away, Max blushes.

"Damn, Slugger, you've been holding out on me."

Oh, fuck no. Don't say that, Max, please don't say that.

Another round of drinks comes, saving me from the awkward moment. "Did we order these?"

"No, sweet cheeks, they're from the table over there." The waitress points at the dreaded table.

"We'd better go and say something." Max sighs as he stands.

I grab his arm by his elbow. "They know me. Or at

least they used to."

He holds his other hand out to help me from my seat. "Trust me, they won't know you like this. Just smile and flirt. What's your name tonight, Slugger?"

I take his hand and he pulls me up to his chest. "Brittany."

"You are *so* not a Brittany." He squeezes my ass. "Let's get this over with."

Max takes me over and introduces me to the guys. They all look a bit more weathered than when I saw them last. All the drinking, drugs, and hot desert sun isn't good for the skin. It's hard to believe Ash's loser friends wield enough power to issue my death warrant. I take the threat seriously, but when I think about how these guys gave *Ash* five million dollars and expected they would get it back, they seem more pathetic than intimidating. Apparently it doesn't take a genius to move up the ranks in a cartel.

After another round of drinks, the guys at the table stand up, their eyes fixed on the door. I turn my head to see what they're looking at. My eyes go wide, then I quickly turn back around. "We have to get out of here," I whisper in Max's ear. "The guy that just came in, Rafe. We knew each other well, had a bunch of classes together. He'll know my voice."

Max looks at me like I'm overreacting. "You haven't seen him in five years. There's no way he'll recognize you."

"He was at Ash's funeral. I spent over an hour talking to him."

Max nods. "Go to the bathroom. I'll say my goodbyes, then we'll get out of here."

On my way back from the bathroom, I find Max and Rafael in the middle of a heated conversation at the end of the hall. I duck behind a corner until they finish. Max walks down the narrow hallway toward me, but Rafe doesn't leave. His eyes are glued on Max's back.

I push Max against the wall and kiss him with all I have. I rub against him as though he's on fire and only my body can put out the flame. With each clash of our tongues or his hand on my ass, I am creeped out, but the show must go on.

As I push against him, I feel a little poke. I break our kiss and lay small kisses on his neck until I reach his ear. "Do you seriously have a fucking erection now?"

He grabs my shoulders and spins me so that I'm up against the wall. "Wasn't that the goal?"

I break the kiss. I look at him, trying to read if he's joking. He's usually such a smart ass, but it almost sounds like he's serious. Maybe the lack of accent is throwing me off. He smirks, then pulls me back to him for one last tongue-twirling kiss.

When we separate, he takes my hand and leads me back through the club. He high fives one of the guys at the table. "I'm out," he says with a wink. We hold hands till we get to the car.

I get in, lock the doors, and look at Max. "Holy shit, that worked. I was sure Rafe was on to you."

"Slugger, we have to get out of Tucson before we can

say that. He knows something's up, but he hasn't pieced together what yet. Get moving."

I put the car in gear and pull onto Congress Street. "Do you have anything you need to get before we leave town? Anything incriminating?"

"Lily, this isn't my first rodeo. I'm smart enough not to leave loose ends. Now drive the car."

I weave through Tucson's small downtown area until we hit I-10. Neither of us says a word for the first twenty minutes. As the city lights disappear on the horizon and we realize we're safely out of the city, Max looks at me.

He points his thumb behind us. "That back there was a suicide mission we somehow escaped from. Rafael's the one that called the hit out on you. He's running the whole Southwest operation, and moving up the ranks quickly. He's convinced you know more than you let on and that Ash has more shit hidden somewhere. You could have gotten us both killed by coming here!" he shouts. "How did you even find me?"

I tap my thumbs on the steering wheel. "It's a long story."

"Then start talking. *Now*."

Chapter Seventeen

I tap my thumbs on the steering wheel as I drive. "I need to know that I'm talking to Max my best friend, not Max the agent. Can you promise me that?"

"They're one and the same, slugger," he says firmly.

"If I can talk to Max my friend, then I can tell you the whole story. Max the agent will get the sanitized version. You make the call." I trust that he'll be honest with me. If he can't keep my secrets, he'll tell me.

When he doesn't reply, I say, "Why don't we start with you? Why did you reach out to Sabrina?"

"I heard rumblings about you. I think there's a hit out on you. I reported it, but as this is a DEA case, they just want to know where the drugs are. I was told that they didn't find the threat credible. She was supposed to protect you, not let you go *Charlie's Angels* on me."

"Yeah, dude, there was a hit on me because my roommate decided to try to infiltrate the cartel to defend my honor. You were made a while ago. They were just waiting to take you out."

"How do you know this, Lily?" he demands.

I grip the steering wheel so tight my fingernails dig into my palm. "I had this handled Max. I was finally in the clear, then you had to go and get involved," I say, ignoring his question. "Now they want to kill you and me. Of course they won't go after you because it'll bring too much attention, but I have a huge target on my back. Again."

He reaches over the center console and touches my arm. "I need to know how you know all of this," he says softly.

I take my eyes off the road for a moment and catch his eyes. "I can't. You just have to trust me."

He shakes his head. "No can do, Slugger. You need to tell me more. This may end here for you, but I have people to report to. There are a dozen policies and procedures that we just completely disregarded. Ignoring protocol can fuck up an entire investigation and I have to answer for that. My job's on the line. You owe me more."

"I can't give you more. I'm sorry."

He bangs his fist on the dashboard. "Damn it, Lily. That's not going to fly."

Knowing that we are at an impasse, I say nothing and allow silence to overtake the car. We're both tired, wired and too emotional to have this discussion. I'd rather sit in uncomfortable silence than fight for the next five and a half hours. I'm guessing Max feels the same ways since he doesn't say a word until I blow past the exit to Sky Harbor Airport.

He points to the exit as we drive by it. "Ah, Slugger, don't we need to catch a plane?"

"Flying out of Vegas. I have to return the car and the costume. Plus it's safer. Don't worry, it's a smooth drive."

"When was the last time you slept?" he asks.

I shrug. "More than a nap? Christ, I can't recall." I left London two days ago, but it feels like a month.

He taps my elbow. "Pull over, let me drive."

When we drive past the 101 Freeway, I see something my body simply can't resist. In-N-Out Burger. I exit the freeway and pull into the drive-thru, but the bastards are closed! Hungry and tired, I pop out the contacts and curl up on the passenger seat. I'm asleep before Max gets back on the highway.

I wake up as we cross over the Hoover Dam. "Hey," Max says. "Good nap?"

"Much needed one. I've gone from London to New York City, to Buffalo, to Vegas, to Tucson and now back again. I need a bucket of eye make-up remover, a long shower, and an actual meal."

"I bet you are eager to get out of those pants," he

teases. He reaches over and pats my thigh. "I'm not ready for you to be out of those pants, but I bet you are."

I punch him in the arm. "Jackass."

He rubs his bicep. "I forgot how hard you punch." He looks me up and down. "Were you trying to look like Gavin's junkie ex, or was that just a coincidence?"

I punch him again. "Touchy, touchy," he says while rubbing his arm.

We're both quiet until we pass a string of billboards advertising various casinos on The Strip. "I'm guessing once we get situated we're going to part ways. I think we should talk about what happened in Tucson before we split up."

I look away, focusing on the landscape. "I told you, I'm not telling you more than I already have."

"Not that part. The other part. What happened while we were there."

I look at him, hoping not to find anything other than friendship in his eyes. "We did what we had to do to get out of there alive."

"Between us, Lily." He points his finger back and forth between us. "You're telling me you didn't feel anything?"

Urg. I do not want to go here. I'd rather spill my guts and risk Carlos's wrath than discuss kissing Max. "You're my best friend, and I adore you, but I love Gavin."

"Yeah, I get that. But this has nothing to do with Gavin. This is about you and me and what went on there. Our lives are too tangled to ignore it. We're not leaving this car until we talk about it."

I hate it when he puts on his agent pants. He can be so condescending. How can I tell him that kissing him was one of the most revolting things I have ever done? That I feel sick and wrong, and I desperately want to bleach my mouth.

His hand is resting on the gear shift. I place mine over his and intertwine our fingers. "Max, it was just two people doing a job. It was no different than any other task." I know he's had to fake relationships while undercover before. There's no way he's thrown by our pretend attraction. Sure we kissed, but when we were living together, we'd done intimate things and he never showed signs he was interested in being more than friends. I've cuddled with him, slept in his bed. He's seen me in my underwear and never given me a second glance. A bad kiss shouldn't have changed that.

He brings my hand to his lips, and places a gentle kiss on the top of my hand. "There was heat. We can't ignore that."

Oh crap. Apparently a bad kiss can change everything. I pull my hand away. "Yeah, Max, it's called Arizona. Of course it was hot," I say, trying to deflect.

He shakes his head and quietly laughs. "That was bad, Slugger."

All of a sudden the leather pants feel too tight, and my tank top feels too low. I adjust my clothes as much as I can, but it doesn't make me less exposed.

"I'm assuming you and Gavin are on the outs. There's no way he'd go along with this," he says.

"He doesn't know I'm here," I say quietly, looking away.

He cups his ear and leans toward me. "Excuse me? I must have misheard you. I thought you said he doesn't know."

"Yup, that would be what I said." I brace myself for a lecture.

He puts both hands on the steering wheel, griping so hard his knuckles are white. "Wow, I'm not sure who I'm more nervous about, the cartel or the big bad Brit. Thanks, Slugger. Remind me again why you're here. I thought you said it was to help me, but after this little escapade, I'll probably lose my job and it'll be a toss-up who gets to me first. The cartel or your boyfriend. "

"He may not be my boyfriend anymore," I reply. Why did I just say that? Having a boyfriend is my fast pass out of this conversation. But I'm an idiot and have now opened the door to a discussion about Max and I becoming more. If there's a pile of shit around, I always manage to step in it.

I look at him out of the corner of my eye. He looks giddy. "When did that happen?" he asks, trying to sound concerned, but failing miserably.

"We had a big blow up, then I got the call from Sabrina and hopped on the first flight. We really haven't spoken since."

He taps his thumb on the steering wheel. "So you're

not officially broken up?"

I shrug. "Honestly, I have no idea what we are."

He smirks. "Interesting."

I turn up the radio hoping to end this conversation. *Waking Up in Vegas* blares through the speakers. Max laughs, then says, "It's a sign. We should get married." It's official. God has it out for me.

I lean my head against the window and close my eyes.

I open my eyes just as we approach the city. Dawn over Vegas is an interesting sight. The clean light of day on the blinking lights of the casinos is just odd, making the City of Sin look rather out of place. Like wearing last night's party clothes, smeared makeup, and torn stockings at seven a.m. while everyone else is dressed and ready for work. The Strip in the morning is the physical representation of the walk of shame.

I call Brittany, who is shockingly up at this hour. Perhaps she still hasn't gone to bed. Who am I to judge? She gives me directions to her house, and Max and I head right over. With any luck I can be back in London today.

Brittany's house is in Green Valley, an upscale part of town I'm not familiar with. Pulling up to her house, I see being a showgirl can pay off. Her house is huge! There are a bunch of cars in the driveway, but I seriously doubt she's hosting brunch. I'm guessing the party is still going on from last night. After parking, I jump out of the car. I cannot wait to get out of this costume and shower, but I need to clear things up with Max first.

"Let's clear the air before we go in," I say. "I want to leave all of this in Tucson, so get it out now."

He folds his arms across his chest and plants his feet. Everything about his posture is telling me he is not going to budge. "I need to know more about what you know. I have to tell something to the FBI."

I mimic his movements, making it clear I'm not budging either. "Tell them your cover was blown, and leave me out of the story altogether. Tell them you had an opportunity to get out safely, and took it. It's the truth. You don't need to know anything else," I reply firmly.

"Fine, I'll see if I can make that work. But I'm not hopeful. You're going to have to find a way to meet me halfway here." He exhales loudly, and soon his shoulders soften and he lets his arms fall to his sides. "We need to talk about what happened between us, though."

I avoid his gaze and focus on a crack in the driveway. "Nothing happened between us. It was acting."

He steps toward me. "I don't think so. There's more there."

I look up and meet his gaze. "No, there's not."

Before I have a chance to say anything else, he grabs me and kisses me.

I push him back, and wipe my mouth with the back of my hand. "Max! What. The. Fuck?"

He looks crushed. "I- I- I'm sorry," he stammers. "I

had to know."

"Boston, what the hell are you doing here?"

"Em?" Max and I say in unison. Oh, this day just gets weirder and weirder.

Em's hands are on her hips and she looks ready to pounce. "Who the hell is this hooker?"

"Max, what the hell are you doing here?" That's the last voice on the planet I expected to hear. I turn to face Gavin.

When his eyes meet mine, his jaw drops. "Lily?" He looks at Max and growls.

Before any of us have a chance to speak, Gavin throws a left cross and drops Max to the ground.

"That's gonna leave a mark," Em deadpans. She walks back toward the house shouting, "Britt, we're gonna need some ice out here."

I bend down to see if Max is okay. Knocked out, but probably okay. "Jesus, Oxford. What was that?" I ask, still in shock.

He glares at me. "Yes, Lily. What was that?"

I let out a long sigh. "We have a lot to talk about. Can we take care of Max first and get into this later?" I examine Max, trying to avoid the anger radiating from Gavin. "I hope you didn't break his jaw."

He grabs my arm and jerks me up harshly, causing me to crash into his chest. "Max can piss off. Why were you kissing him? And what the fuck are you wearing?" he asks motioning to my costume.

I pull my arm back. "It's a long story I would be happy to tell you if you stop punching people and let me get a word in edgewise," I bark at him.

He folds his arms over his chest. "Does this story explain why you left me without a bloody word?" he sneers.

I try to match his glare, but once I see the pain in his baby blues, I turn away. It hurts too much to see him this upset.

Brittany's husband, Phil, comes out, looks at all of us, and laughs. "I love my life. Never a dull moment." He whistles, and two mammoth guys come out and carry Max inside. "Come on in, everyone. Looks like you have some issues to sort out."

We enter the foyer of their spectacular home, and Brittany gives me a hug. "You played the part well, my lovely. Come on, let's get you out of character. Emily, you keep that handsome man settled down. I have way too much crystal in this house to tolerate a brawl when that one wakes up," she says pointing at Max.

"Sugar Cube, no fair. I don't want to be on babysitting duty. Let's remember who has seniority here," Em says. Em was Brittany's big sister in our sorority, and she loves to pull rank.

Brittany grits her teeth. "You know I hate it when you call me that. And in case you didn't get the memo, I am queen bee here. Stay, supervise, protect my breakables while I bring our Lil here back to her naturally beautiful self."

Em huffs and puffs but does what she's told. "Whatever you say, Sugar Cube."

Ah, sorority sisters. Get them together, and we all become eighteen again.

Brittany takes me to a guest bathroom and helps me out of the wig and cap. More importantly, she helps me out of the leather pants. They may look sexy, but they practically need to be cut off. They might as well be a chastity belt. Picturing trying to take them off in the throes of passion sends me into a giggle fit.

Britt looks at me like I lost it. "Oh, suga', you need a nap. How long have you been running like this?"

"Two days, maybe three. It all blurs together." I've been going balls to the wall for days. I'm going to crash at some point.

After a long shower, I finally feel back to normal, but I can't seem to make myself leave the bathroom. Gavin is just down the hall, and I'm too petrified to talk to him. He's here, so that has to mean something. I need to know the truth about what happened that night, but I'm not sure I'm ready to hear it. I've replayed that night over and over in my head, and while I don't question what James saw, I just can't see Gavin as a cheater. Certainly not with O. But even if I set the O thing aside, his mood that night was completely out of line. Just thinking of the cold look in his eye before he left gives me chills.

Brittany knocks on the door. "Quit hiding, baby cakes. Time to face the firing squad."

I groan. When I don't come out a minute later, she

says, "I do have the key to this door. I'll give it to that sexy man in my living room if you don't come out on your own. I have a strict no pussy policy in this house. That goes for whores trying to sleep with my husband, and cowards hiding out. Time to face the music."

Reluctantly, I open the door, and Em pushes past Brittany and hugs me. "What the hell's going on? You left Gavin? For Max?"

"No! Of course not. It's really complicated, but there's nothing going on between me and Max."

From the look on her face I can tell she doesn't believe me. "That's not what it looked like."

"Trust me. Max may actually be deluding himself into thinking there's something, but I can promise you there's nothing. Less than nothing. He's just a friend. You know that. I'd never come between you two."

She stares at me indignantly. "There is no me and Max."

I roll my eyes. "Whatever you say."

I pick up my costume off the floor, fold it and place it on the counter. Em points at it. "Is this crazy trip why you made me lug your crap back to Boston?"

I nod. "It's a long story, but coming here was a necessity. Thanks for bringing them back for me. You saved me a humiliating call to Gavin to beg him to ship it to me."

"I know things got seriously messed up that night, but I think you jumped the gun a little bit. I've spent the last day with that man, and I think he'd move heaven and earth to get you back to him."

I lean against the wall. "How did you get dragged into this anyway?"

"Gavin saw that you bought a ticket to Vegas, and he called me to see if I knew what was going on. I didn't have a clue, but I had a feeling if you were taking a random last-minute trip to Vegas, you might get in touch with Britt. I called her, Gavin and I flew out and here we are. Enough hiding in the bathroom."

She grabs me by the elbow and drags me down the hallway into the kitchen where everyone, minus Max, is having breakfast. Em turns to Brittany. "Sugar Cube, let's grab some breakfast cocktails so you can tell me everything you've been up to while these two hash it out."

"No need. Lily and I are leaving," Gavin says.

"You are?" Em asks.

"Yes." He walks over to Brittany and gives her a hug. "It was a pleasure to meet you. I'm so sorry to drop in on you and leave. You've been a smashing host. If we're still here later tonight, we'll come see the show. I'm sure it's brilliant. Please ring us if you come to London. We would love to spend more time with you." He walks over to Phil, shakes his hand and thanks him for his hospitality. He comes back over to Em and hugs her. "I'm sure you can manage from here?"

"Yeah, I'll get Boston sorted out once he comes to. Lily, call me."

"All right. We're off then," Gavin says, grabbing my hand.

"Do I get a vote in all this?" I ask, feeling like a child being handled.

Em, Brittany, and Gavin shout, "No."

Gavin practically drags me out the door. Brit and Em shout, "Love you, Lil!"

Traitors.

Chapter Eighteen

Gavin opens the passenger door of a long, black Bentley. As I slowly walk down the driveway, I can't help but notice how handsome he looks. He's wearing jeans, which he never wears. I wish he would, because no ass has ever looked better in a pair of jeans. What does me in are the dark aviator sunglasses and the sexy scruff along his jaw. The whole package is so damn sexy, I almost forget we're at odds with each other. But as I approach the car, I notice his clenched fist, ramrod straight posture, and the firm set of his jaw, and it all comes back to me. I have one angry Brit on my hands.

As I step into the car, I notice his glasses slide down the bridge of his nose. Instinctively, I find his eyes. I have to look away the moment I do. Eyes are the window to the soul, and Gavin is in a very dark place. I can't say I blame him—he did just see Max kiss me. If it had been me instead of James seeing Gavin and O kiss at the club, my reaction would have been nothing short of a nuclear meltdown. But I know there's more behind Gavin's bad mood than Max. We have so many issues to address, I don't even know where to begin.

Once I'm in my seat, he slams the door. I open my mouth to say something when he gets in the car, but I quickly change my mind. With so many issues on the table, I need to think about how to approach this. The tension in the car is stifling. He doesn't say a word—possibly because his jaw is locked so tight, he's grinding his teeth. I hate being the passenger when someone is angry driving. He's not out of control or reckless, just faster than normal and a bit heavier on the brake. Each bump and turn feels like a message about how angry he is.

I'm familiar enough with Vegas to know we're headed back toward the Strip, or maybe the airport. I'm curious, but I refuse to be the first one to speak. After a few minutes, we pull up to Mandalay Bay. While this is an amazing hotel, it isn't Gavin's taste, so what the hell are we doing here? He drives around a bit, and I see it—the Four Seasons sign. I forgot the Four Seasons takes up the top four floors of the Mandalay Bay.

He opens my car door and grabs my hand. I try to pull my hand away, but he squeezes tighter. Not so hard that it hurts, but firm enough to let me know he's not letting me go anywhere. Does he think I'm going to make a break for it? When we step into the empty elevator, I pull away again, needing a little space. The torrent of anger flowing through him sucks up all the oxygen around him. I'm suffocating from his fury. I try to step aside and put some distance between us, but he pulls me back. I tense as he puts his arm around me, bringing me into his chest.

He takes a deep breath. "Please don't. For the last forty-eight hours, my mind has gone to the darkest recesses of my imagination. Wondering where you were. If you're safe. If I'll ever see you again. Just allow me a few moments with you next to me, so my heart can finally start beating again."

I breathe him in. As angry at him and confused by him as I am, I've missed him over the last few days. I know once those elevator doors open, he'll let me go, and we'll have to sort through our mess. Feelings are bound to be hurt, and painful things will be said. The question is, where will Gavin and I be when the dust settles?

We take the elevator to the thirty-ninth floor, then he opens the door to yet another breathtaking suite. The room has floor-to-ceiling windows that look over the Strip. At night, the view'll be phenomenal. If we haven't killed each other by then, that is.

I should be impressed, but I'm not. The room is adorned with fresh-cut flowers and a bottle of champagne on ice. Yes, the suite is opulent, and under different circumstances, it would be romantic. But under the current conditions, I feel as though I'm in an interrogation room. This is far nicer than my interrogation room at the police station, but I'm still trapped.

After stepping into the room, my protective instincts take over, and I look around for the best spot to have this conversation. With how angry he is, I know I need space. When Ash and I fought, he always got me into a corner and intimidated me until I backed down. Gavin isn't Ash, but his anger is so intense. I'll never allow myself to be bullied like that again.

The furnishings in the room remind me of my grandmother's formal living room: beautiful, but not designed to ever be sat on. It's clear the intention is to make spending time in the room as unappealing as possible so the guests will get back to the casino. I choose a stiff armchair and hope for a short conversation. If not, my back may need a massage afterward.

He sits in the chair across the coffee table from me. "When was the last time you slept? Ate?"

"I slept a bit in the car. Ate?" I tap my fingers on the arm of the chair while I try to remember. "I'm not exactly sure. London, maybe? Some pretzels on the plane. I stopped at In-N-Out in Phoenix, but they were closed."

He gestures toward the bedroom. "Why don't you take a kip? Or order some food?"

I cross my legs. "Sleep can wait. We need to talk first. Should we start with you kissing O or Max kissing me?"

"You need to eat." He walks across the room, picks up the room service menu, and hands it to me. "I never kissed O. She made a pass at me, and I threw her across the room."

I snort while I flip through the menu. "I'd have paid to see that. Not the kissing part, but the throwing her across the room part." I put the menu down and look at him. "Why did she kiss you? Was this before or after you fucked me against the wall?"

He sighs and runs his fingers through his hair. "I owe you an explanation about that night. I planned on giving it to you when I got home that night, but you'd packed your things and run away with Max."

I tilt my head and smile sardonically. "I didn't run away with Max, but I'd love to hear that explanation."

"And I want to know why Max had his tongue down your throat," he says through gritted teeth.

This conversation is going nowhere fast.

"We're going in circles. We're both pissed and want answers, but we're not going to get them by arguing about who has the bigger axe to grind. Can we just start with the night at the club and chronologically go from there?"

"You left me, and I find you kissing Max, and you just want to be let off the hook?"

"You left me first! You 'can't do this,' remember? I'm happy to tell you everything that happened after I left." I cross my arms. "But since you left first, you go first."

"I didn't leave you," he snaps. He picks the menu off the coffee table and hands it to me. "Order first, then we'll start."

I roll my eyes as I take the menu. "Just get me a cheeseburger, fries, and a chocolate shake."

He pulls his phone out of his pocket and texts in my

order.

I point at the chair. "Start talking. What the hell happened at the club? One second we're having a ball at dinner, then we step into the club and you pull a Dr. Jekyll and Mr. Hyde."

He runs his fingers through his hair as he sits. "I'm not proud of my behavior that night. I'd had way too much to drink at dinner, then when we got to the club, people kept ordering me shots. I was out of my head drunk."

"I've seen you drunk dozens of times, but never like that. 'I was drunk' isn't going to cut it."

"Just let me get this out, all right? Like I said, I'm not proud. It might take me a moment." I nod, and he continues. "I hadn't been to a club in some time... since Brooke. If I'm being honest, I was feeling some déjà vu."

My jaw drops. "Are you comparing me to *her?*" Brooke's memory plagues me enough as it is. Knowing he's scrutinizing my behavior to see how I match up makes it ten times worse. I know it's only natural—I certainly contrast him and Ash at times—but I don't want to know about it.

He glares at me, probably impatient that I've interrupted again.

"Sorry, go on," I say.

"We hadn't been married that long, a year or so maybe. Things were fine, or so I thought. One night, we went to a club. When we arrived, I was sucked into the crowd, just like I was that night with you. A bunch of people I really couldn't care less about all wanted to do a shot and rub elbows. She made it clear she was bored, kept looking over her shoulder for someone better to talk to. After a while, she disappeared. I found her later on the dance floor, practically shagging some bloke. I got jealous, and she became hysterical. Told me I was being ridiculous, trying to smother her. She disappeared. I figured she found some friends and was blowing off steam. When I was ready to leave, I searched the club for her. I found her in a back room, high as a kite, half naked, and freshly fucked. By two different men. I'd love to say that was the first and only time that sort of thing happened, but it became a pattern."

I push the flowers to the other side of the coffee table and sit on the edge in front of him. "That's horrible. I'm sorry Brooke did that to you, but you seriously didn't think—"

He holds up his hand. "As I said, I was positively plastered and wasn't thinking clearly. The way you bolted from me, it stirred up memories. I tried to shake it off and focus on having a good time. I ran into some friends from secondary school, including O. They had one of the back rooms reserved, and we downed a bunch of shots. My memory's a bit hazy, but I'm fairly certain it was absinthe, which in and of itself is always a mistake. Absinthe makes me crazy. On top of how much else I'd been drinking, it was a miracle I was still standing."

"So that's your excuse. You were drunk and kissed O?"

"It's not that simple. Like I said, I had a bunch of bad

memories floating around in my head. O started pushing buttons, and I sort of went down an emotional rabbit hole."

God, I despise that woman. "What does that mean exactly?"

"From the room I was in, I had a perfect view of you on the dance floor."

A perfect view of Em and I practically molesting every guy we danced with. It was all harmless fun, but now I feel like a fool. Ash never cared who I danced with or how risqué I danced. Quite the opposite—the hotter I danced, the more it turned him on. It never occurred to me that Gavin would be hurt by it. I'm such an idiot. Ashamed, I bite my lip and look away. "Oh."

"O was in my ear, telling me how you were just like Brooke, how you'd end up breaking my heart and making a fool out of me, just like Brooke did. Then she told me she loved me, that she'd always loved me. That now that I was free of Brooke, it was our time to be together. She said you were down there cheating on me anyway, so it was the perfect time to cut you loose and run to her. She threw herself at me. I pushed her off me and stormed out."

He runs his fingers through his hair and shakes his head. "I came down to find you, and you were all over James. I watched you, and my blood boiled. I know he's my best mate and I didn't really have anything to worry about, but O's words were ringing in my mind, and I was petrified of losing you. Once you left the dance floor, I followed you. I... I needed to make you mine."

The wild club sex makes more sense now. It was actually pretty hot, but his behavior had been all over the place. Now I understand the trail of cum. I still think it was gross, but I understand. "So you marked your territory."

His eyes meet mine. "I told you I wasn't proud. I was drunk and in a dark place, and I let my imagination get the best of me. My behavior followed suit. Then I heard you went home with James, and I lost my mind."

"What? I didn't go home with James! We left at the same time, but I went to Em's."

"I know that now, but at the time, I was convinced you were shagging my best friend. I took a cab home to wait for you and drank half a bottle of scotch while I watched the door, feeling more angry and humiliated with each passing second. When you came home, it was clear you'd showered and changed. I thought the worst. You wanted to talk, but I just couldn't. I needed to sober up and get my head on straight first. If I'm being honest, I was a coward. I couldn't bear to hear you say you were leaving me."

"And then I left."

I know none of this is my fault, but I feel bad for not even calling him before I left. Gavin always seems so together that it's jarring to see him vulnerable and uncertain. In the past, when he spoke about Brooke, he seemed so resolved, as though he'd come to terms with everything that had happened. I thought he'd made peace with it, but clearly, I was wrong. She really did a number on him.

Everything about Gavin oozes confidence and

security, but there're cracks in his shell of perfection. He has insecurities and fears just like the rest of us mere mortals. I'm relieved to learn he has a dark side. While his endless optimism can be comforting, it can be equally annoying. This moody-broody side tells me there are depths to Gavin I have yet to see, but based on how this experience went, I'm not sure I need to see them again any time soon.

"In the sober light of day, I realized I was being absurd," he says. "I came home and found you'd moved out. I drove to James's and pounded on his door, demanding to see you."

"Oh, no." Based on how hurt James had been at the club, I can only imagine how well that went.

He nods, looking disappointed in himself. "Yup. It was a disaster. I accused my best friend of sleeping with my girl. He accused me of going after O. It got ugly. We both got a few good shots in before Liam pulled us apart."

There's a knock at the door. I gesture for Gavin to stay while I get it. A gentleman carries a silver tray into the room and places it on the dining room table. I pat my pockets and realize I don't have any money for a tip.

Gavin pulls out his wallet and slips the guy some cash. "Is there something for me to sign?"

"The bill has already been added to the room, sir. Enjoy," he says with a smile before leaving.

I open the lid and see a familiar white cup with red palm trees. "You got me In-N-Out!"

"Perks of staying here. They'll get you anything your heart desires." He motions to my burger. "Eat up before it gets cold."

I sit at the table, and Gavin sits across from me.

"Thank you for explaining about that night at the club. No matter how many times I went through the night in my head, I couldn't piece together what had happened to make things turn sideways. I wish that you'd had more faith in me," I say as I unwrap my burger.

"It's not like that. I know I behaved poorly, but it wasn't a commentary about my feelings toward you. I was beyond blotto. A dark mood got the better of me, and I behaved like a prick. That's all it was. *One bad night*. Each and every day I work hard to show you the depth of my faith and trust in you. Please don't throw all of that away because I fucked up one night. One night does not define me or us."

I slap the bottom of the Heinz bottle, trying and failing to get the ketchup to come out. "It's going to take me a little while to sort through that one night. I hear what you're saying, but what it sounds like you're really saying is, 'I didn't trust you, but trust me now that I really trust you.' I have to try not to be offended that you equated me with your junkie late wife. And that you allowed Skanky McCumbucket to worm her way into your brain, the maggot that she is. I hear you, Gavin, but it'll take me a little while to believe you."

He takes the bottle. "If you hit the 57 on the side of the bottle, the ketchup comes right out." He taps the side three times, and ketchup slides out.

I drag a French fry through the ketchup. "That's some

trick. There's another one of your tricks I'm curious about—how'd you know I was in New York?"

Gavin sits in the chair next to me. "Sabrina called me, told me all about Max. She thought you might run off and do something stupid, like track him down and try to pull him out. I panicked. I tried to track your phone, but it was turned off, so I watched your credit cards."

I throw my fry on the wrapper. "What the fuck! Who the hell do you think you are? You have no right to invade my privacy!"

"Do you recall being kidnapped twice—no, three times? While under FBI protection, no less. Has it slipped your mind that you've made enemies with a Mexican drug cartel? My company develops technology that can track down terrorists in the most isolated corners of the globe. Do you really think I wouldn't use every resource at my fingertips to find you?"

"This time, I hadn't been kidnapped—I left." As soon as the words come out of my mouth, I realize how foolish I sound. That won't go down as the most effective comeback in history, but it's the best I've got. I point at him and scowl. "Don't think just because you have noble rationale that it excuses your Big Brother tactics."

His face softens, and the sharp edge to his voice fades. "Why didn't you ring me? How could you just get on a flight without talking to me? Did you think about how I would feel? We could have come up with a plan together. Something less dangerous than..." He furrows his brow. "What did you do exactly? How'd you find him?"

I take a sip of my shake, trying to look as casual as possible. "I asked Lorenzo to get me a meeting with Carlos, then I begged Carlos to tell me how to find Max. He told me. I made a pit stop in Vegas for a makeover, then drove to Tucson to get Max."

His eyes go wide. "Bloody hell, Lily, you're mad. Certifiably mad! You could've been killed!"

I roll my eyes. "I was fine."

He looks down and runs his fingers through his hair. "Do you know what these men are like?"

"Of course I do. I'm not an idiot," I snap.

"Really? If they had caught you, what do you think they would have done to you?"

"I lived through Charlie, remember? I know exactly what they would have done to me."

"Just last month, they captured a blogger who wrote about crime in Mexico. She never once blamed it on the cartel, but they still took offense. They tied her up, gang raped her daily, and emailed videos of it to her father. For fifty-seven days—one day for each blog post—that's what her father woke up to. When they finally decided to kill her, they dropped her in a tub of lye. They scooped up the goo and mailed it to her parents, along with a DVD of her death."

I cover my food, the sight of it making me ill. "Oh my God."

"Six months ago, they captured the girlfriend of a wealthy business man. They gave him thirty days to pay them three million dollars. They tied her up in a dirty basement and beat her, raped her. He paid the money, but he didn't get her back. The cartel sold her to some sick bastard who likes to torture women before fucking them. By the time Interpol tracked her down, she was dead. I'm worth thirty times what that bloke's worth. What do you think they would have done to you? They know you're with me, even if you don't. You'd be an excellent acquisition for them."

I cover my ears. "Stop! Just stop!"

He crouches in front of me and pulls my hands away. "No, you need to hear this! Do you know what it would have done to me if something had happened to you? Especially with the way we left things? I wouldn't recover. You need to think about that the next time you run off to play hero! It would decimate me if they ever got their hands on you."

Tears stream down my cheeks as I scream, "Max's cover was blown! He was a sitting duck. I had to get him out of there. If he died because of me, it would decimate *me*!"

He lets go of my hands and steps back. "That's what it's always about, isn't it? You needing to live your life the way it suits you. Never about us or the life we're building together. It's all about you. I guess that's the difference between us. I see us as a partnership, and you still see us as separate entities."

I jump out of my seat. "I had no idea if we were even together! You had just walked out on me!"

"I have one bloody bad night and you think I'd throw it all away? Do you honestly think I'd end our relationship like that?"

"What was I supposed to think?"

His face turns red as he throws his hands in the air. "You're supposed to think that I love you! You're supposed to know that I'd never let you go without a fight. You're supposed to understand that I can't imagine my life without you. It's inconceivable to me that after all we've been through, you still don't get it!"

I don't hear Gavin raise his voice very often, and the depth and tenor of it rattles me. With clenched fists, he storms into the living room and looks out the window. From the way his shoulder blades rise and fall, I can tell he's fuming. Somehow I've become the bad guy.

With his back toward me, he says, "We have one fight, and you accept our relationship is over. Without giving it a second thought, you pack up and leave. You were willing to throw us away so easily."

I lean back in my chair and replay the conversation in my head. I just lived it, and I still feel as if I need a map to follow all the twists and turns that discussion took. He's not wrong. I make decisions about my life and don't always take into consideration how it will impact our relationship. I never paused to think about how he would feel about my plan to save Max. It never even occurred to me that he could or would want to help me.

I'm independent and always have been. A natural byproduct of losing my parents so young, I suppose. It was one of the reasons why Ash and I worked. He lived his life, and I lived mine. I needed nothing from him, wanted nothing from him, which was perfect for him, because he had nothing to give me. When I saw people in relationships where their lives were intertwined, bound by codependence, I'd think how lucky I was not to be tied down.

Looking back on it now... god, I was a fool. I wasn't autonomous—I was just alone. Ash didn't respect my independence. He took advantage of the fact that it never occurred to me that I deserved better. Gavin wants it all, and I'm not sure I can give it to him. I'm not sure I know how to be what he wants.

I cross the room and lean against the window next to Gavin. "I'm sorry. I've never had anyone I could ask for help, so it never occurs to me that it's even an option. I've never had to worry about how my actions affected anyone, because there's never been anyone who cared enough about me to let my actions affect them."

"Well, you do now," he snaps. "The question is, do you want someone to care about you? Do you want to share your life with someone?" He rakes his fingers through his hair. "Maybe you don't. Maybe you prefer to be on your own."

His eyes meet mine, looking for assurances, but he closes his eyes and looks away. Apparently he didn't find what he was looking for. I'm blowing this, and I have no idea how to fix it. I don't know how to give him what he wants.

"I hate this feeling," I say quietly. "You're ten feet away, but it still feels like there's an ocean between us."

"Welcome to my world. You always feel just out of reach." He turns from me and walks to the sofa.

"It's not intentional, I swear," I say as I follow him.

"I believe you, but the 'I don't know any better' excuse only goes so far. At some point, you need to make the choice to let me in. Not because you'll hurt me if you don't, but because you want me there."

I crawl into his lap, then lean my head against his chest. His arm curls around me, holding me close. I pull his hand to my chest, covering my heart. "I want you here."

His heart pounds in my ear. The rhythm is hypnotically soothing. After all the drama and chaos of the last few days, being in his arms feels so good. My body relaxes into his, and I feel all the tension start to fade as I close my eyes. The peace is temporary, though. Until Gavin and I work through this, the angst will still fester under the surface.

"I love you, and I want this to work more than anything. I promise I'll try harder," I say.

"And Max?"

I wince. "I was hoping you'd forgotten about that."

"I don't expect I'll forget seeing my mate kissing my girlfriend any time soon," he growls.

"Max had a moment of temporary insanity. I promise once the adrenaline high comes down and he takes a nap, he'll realize he was just caught up in the moment."

"I helped him out with the nap part. Hopefully the pain he feels every time he blinks will remind him to keep his hands to himself."

"I don't think that'll be a problem." I shudder and gag. "Kissing him was just wrong. But then again, kissing anyone but you is wrong."

He kisses my forehead. "Best you remember that."

I smile at him. "As shocked as I was that you knocked him out, I have to admit, that was kinda hot. The whole caveman thing."

He raises an eyebrow. "Oh yeah?"

"The club sex was hot too. I wish it were motivated by different reasons, but at the time, I thought it was hot. Broody and possessive looks good on you."

He lifts me out of his lap, then nods toward the dining room. "Go finish eating. You're going to need your energy." He winks, then walks to the bedroom.

"Where are you going?" I ask.

"Shower," he calls over his shoulder.

Hmm, cold burger or Gavin? Not even a competition.

Chapter Nineteen

"What were we fighting about again?" I ask, out of breath. After rolling around the sheets for hours and seeing stars four—no, make that five times—we've come up for air.

"I can't recall, but I never want to have another row with you," he says, smiling. "I can't bear to be away from you for that long again."

"No more oceans between us," I promise.

He lets out a quiet laugh. "Yes, luv. No more oceans between us."

Gavin pulls me closer and kisses me. Our kiss deepens, and despite feeling sore, I'm eager for him again. Our tender moment is disrupted by a loud knock on the door and shouting from the hallway.

"Urg, what now?" Gavin groans as he gets up and puts on pants. "Stay here."

My libido is disappointed, but my slightly overused girly parts are relieved by the interruption. In Gavin's absence, I try to doze. That goal is cut short when Em storms into the room. "You need to get the hell up and referee out here!"

Max. I search for my clothes, but I'm fairly certain they, along with the complimentary robes, are strewn about the living room. One of the few things I learned in college was how to make a fantastic toga, so a minute later, I storm into the living room in my sexy sheet dress. Em is separating Max and Gavin.

I use my fingers to whistle. "Enough, children. Someone want to tell me what's going on?"

"Nice toga," Em says with a smile. Things must not be *that* bad if she can stop for compliments.

"Thank you. Max, what are you doing here?"

Gavin looks hurt that I chose to hear Max out, and he stomps off to look out the window.

"I needed to clear things up with you," Max says. He grabs my hand and looks deeply into my eyes. "Lily, I don't love you."

I let out a deep laugh. "Yeah, I could've told you that."

He gently takes my elbow and drags me to the sofa. "I took the job in Tucson after I heard some horrible chatter about what the cartel had planned for you. That bastard who kidnapped you may not have been theirs, but Rafael had something worse cooking. I needed to get in there and take the fuckers down."

I throw my arms around him. "I love that you love me that much," I whisper.

He gently pushes me back. "Just let me finish, okay?" I nod, and he continues. "You were all I thought about while I was working. When you showed up, I think everything got jumbled. I get really into character when I'm on the job, and sometimes it can be hard separating what's real and what's not. I think I just got caught up in the moment. You and me, we're tight, but we're not right for each other. Not in that way. I'm sorry I let the lines blur."

That's a relief. I don't have enough friends to lose one to unrequited love. "The whole experience was so emotionally charged. It's understandable that we got caught up in the moment." By "we", I mean him, but I'll take some of the heat if it means I can get out of this awkward conversation.

"But you have to admit, we were fucking hot together. I mean, that kiss," he says with a huge smile. "I kept delaying our exit because I wanted a little bit more."

Damn it, Max, you don't know how to quit when you're ahead.

Gavin growls from across the room. He looks at Em. "You don't have a problem with this?"

She scoffs. "One, I have no reason to have a problem with this. I don't have a horse in this race."

Gavin and I roll our eyes. I know she's just putting on a show. Em couldn't possibly let someone think she has real feelings for them.

She counts on her fingers. "And two, Lily is a spectacular kisser. No arguments from me there."

Oh no, she didn't!

"*Emily Harrington!*"

"Oh, I must hear about this," Max says, practically bouncing up and down. "Are there pictures? Video? How often does this happen?"

Dear lord, he's like a kid on Christmas.

"Yes, Em. Do tell us all about how good a kisser Lily is," Gavin chimes in.

I seriously doubt he's thinking about Em and me kissing, but I can guarantee he loves making me squirm.

"Oh, my lips are sealed. I don't kiss and tell," Em replies with a wink.

"Subject change, please," I beg. "Max, you don't love me, so can we be friends again? Gavin, can you and Max be civil now?"

"G-man, really, I'm so sorry. I don't know what I was thinking," Max says.

Max extends his hand as a sign of peace, but Gavin folds his arms across his chest, showing no sign of accepting the olive branch.

"I'll get over it. I'm still bloody pissed at you, but I'll get over it," Gavin relents.

Max shoves his hand into his pocket, trying to recover from Gavin's rebuff. "You did knock my ass out. That has to get us closer to even."

Gavin's face turns hard. "Not even close. Best you remember that." Gavin walks to the bar, pulls out a bottle of scotch and pours a finger's worth. "Anyone else?"

"Hit me," Max says.

Gavin flips over another glass and pours. "Don't tempt me."

Max holds up his hands. "Just a joke, man. I remember you used to have a sense of humor."

He hands Max his drink. "What happens now? Do you go back to DC? " he asks, ignoring Max's comment. His tone's still curt. I can't tell if he's asking because he genuinely wants to know what's going on with his friend, or if he's trying to figure out how fast he can get Max and me in different time zones.

Max eyes Gavin while he sips his drink. I suspect he's thinking the same thing I am. "I'll go back and tell them I was made and needed to make a quick escape. They probably have enough to go in and make arrests."

I should have accepted that drink. "Max, that could be very bad for me. You realize that, right?"

"No, I don't. You won't explain it to me, so how can I know?" Max slams his drink on the table.

In less than three seconds, my friend who was all apologies and love morphs into the hardened agent who's still very much pissed at me. The instant change makes me wonder if his apology was genuine or if it was just a way for him to get me talking to him without Gavin knocking him on his ass. I know how seriously Max takes his job. He wouldn't hesitate to manipulate me if it helped him get his collar.

"Cool it, Max," Gavin warns.

"I don't know what you expect me to do! I'm an FBI agent; they're bad guys. I'm supposed to put them away. Did you really think you were going to pull me out and I would turn a blind eye to everything I know? They put drugs on the streets, Lily. I know for a fact they sell to children. I saw a fourteen-year-old junkie who they've now wrangled into prostitution to pay for her habit. They need to be brought down. How do you not get this?" He's shouting, and his face is red with anger.

"I don't know," I scream. "I don't know what the answer is!"

Am I buried so deep in this that I've lost sight of who's a villain and who's a hero? Am I so worried about my self-preservation that I can justify leaving drug dealers on the streets? What the hell has happened to me? I thought I'd saved myself when I made my deal with Carlos, but all I did was sell my soul to the devil.

Max continues. "Lily, I don't know what the fuck is going on, but you need to come clean now. This game you're playing is dangerous, and you're out of your league. You could've gotten us both killed last night.

Who knows how many more lives you've put in danger. How many other lives do you have to risk before you put your ego aside, huh, Lil?"

His words cut like a knife. Not because they're harsh, but because they're one hundred percent true. How could I let things get so out of control? How could I have been so naïve that I thought I'd handled the cartel? The lines between right and wrong have become so blurred. I've justified my actions because my life is on the line, but was there a better way? I've had tunnel vision this whole time, convinced that my approach was right and ignoring all other possible options. I've put so many at risk because I rationalized that my way was the right way. Guilt overtakes me as I reach my breaking point. Sobs erupt out of me; I couldn't contain them if I tried.

Gavin and Max start screaming at each other.

Em steps between them. "Max, you crossed a line. I don't know what's going on here either, but this isn't the way to handle it." Em orders, "Let's go. Now."

"I'm not leaving until she fills me in," Max says, standing his ground.

My sobs are wild and uncontrollable. I couldn't respond even if I had something to say. Gavin picks me up and smoothes back my hair. I lean my head against his chest. He carries me to the bedroom and slams the door.

Max is still yelling about answers, but my weeping drowns him out. Gavin cradles me in his arms, whispering soothing words, and lets me get it out. I needed this release, and he recognizes that. Through the door, I can hear Em coaxing Max out the door. From the crashing and banging I hear, he's literally kicking and screaming.

Once the tears stop, I feel hollowed out and void of emotion. I'm raw, and the nerve endings are just under the surface. One scratch, and the wounds will open again. I've exhausted all my energy, but I can't sleep. Gavin keeps holding me in our big bed overlooking the Strip, stroking my hair. Listening to his heartbeat keeps me from thinking about anything. Eventually, it lulls me to sleep.

I wake up with Gavin still wrapped around me. Poor Gavin hasn't moved in hours. He's going to have a massive case of pins and needles when he wakes up. I try to untangle myself from him, hoping he'll fall into a more natural position, but he grabs me and pulls me back to him.

"You can't be comfortable," I whisper.

"I don't care. I haven't slept with you for far too long. I want you right here next to me. Anything else is unacceptable," he says in a groggy voice. Sleepy Gavin is so damn sexy.

I nuzzle against him, soaking him in. The feel of his stubble on my cheek. The contours of his toned arms as they wrap around me. His intoxicating scent. Every detail about him draws me in, allowing me to finally feel safe.

He trails his finger lazily along my outer thigh. "I've never had this before, where I needed someone. Sleeping together was about proximity and convenience, but with you… I *need* to be close to you. When I lose my connection with you, I become fragmented. Nothing in my life works right, and there's a void inside me. But when I hold you, the pain dulls, and my heart soars. I feel whole."

I'm high off his words. His confidence is alluring. He's a man who knows what he wants and isn't afraid to take it. So damn sexy.

I curl into him and kiss his neck. "I love you, Gavin."

My stomach releases a growl that could wake the dead.

He runs his hands over my stomach. "It sounds as though I'm neglecting you. Time to order room service."

I wipe the sleep out of my eyes. "You did make me abandon my burger yesterday after I was only a few bites in. Other than that, I can't recall the last thing I ate."

He hands me the room service menu and waits while I pick something. After I settle on chocolate chip pancakes with scrambled eggs, he places our order.

"I know it's only been a few days, but it's clearly taken its toll on you," he says. "When I saw you at Brittany's, you stopped me dead in my tracks."

I nudge his shoulder. "That was because I was in costume and didn't look anything like myself."

He pulls me back down so we are lying on the bed facing each other. "No, I knew it was you instantly. Lily, I would recognize you anywhere no matter how elaborate your costume was. You look gaunt, hollowed out even. Between the dark circles under your eyes and how pale you've become, I'm worried, luv. You need a break from all of this. I want to take you away."

I gesture at the room around us. "Notice the hotel room? We are away."

"Don't be cheeky. I mean completely out of reach, where we can unplug and focus on relaxing. An island paradise with no mobiles, no villains, and most importantly, no clothes. I know just the place. Please, let's go." He takes my hands. "Let's go today. I'll book a flight, and we can leave all this behind."

"That sounds wonderful and I think we should do that, but not today. Christmas is just a few days away, and I haven't celebrated Christmas in... I can't remember how long. Ash wasn't interested in anything but the presents, and Em is philosophically against holidays. Before that, I was at boarding school. I haven't been able to get a tree and decorate it since my parents were alive. I'd love nothing more than to actually celebrate Christmas this year. Can we do that?"

Gavin gets up and walks to the living room. He grabs his bag and pulls out his laptop. "I think that's brilliant. I'm sure we can catch a flight to DC this morning."

Distracted by the view of his perfect ass, I almost miss what he's said. "DC? No, Gavin, not DC. Take me home."

I'm a coward. I should be able to say what I feel, but the words won't form on my tongue. Words turn a beautiful concept such as us living together, and pours cement shoes on its' feet, throws it in the Thames and tells it to swim. The carcinogenic rays of reality have a way of turning everything good in my life to carnage. What I have with Gavin is precious, I'm not about to tarnish it with things like commitments that have no hope of being honored, and naïve expectations of forever. I just want to bask in the beauty of now, so I ambiguously tap dance around the subject and pray my eyes convey my offer.

I think he knows what I'm saying. Thankfully, it seems to be enough for him right now. He sits on the bed next to me and kisses the top of my head. "What do you think about going to the country house? That's where my family always celebrated Christmas. Liam and James will be down that way visiting their families. I'm sure they would pop by."

I pull the sheet up around me. "Do you think James will come? After everything that happened?"

"James and I will mend this," he says as he powers up his laptop. "I actually think inviting him for Christmas will be a good olive branch."

I kiss his shoulder and lean back against the headboard while he searches for flights. "Sounds like it's a good thing we're home going then. Do you know what you're going to do about O? After what happened at the club and with James, I think you need to address it."

He pauses his search but doesn't look at me. "I've taken care of it," he says in a curt tone then resumes his search.

"What does that mean?"

He sighs, then closes the laptop. “She came by my flat, and we had a row. After everything that was said, I don’t think she’ll be a problem moving forward.”

Interesting how I’m just now hearing about this. “You need to give me more than that.”

“You didn’t give me much more when you discussed what transpired between you and Max. You told me I didn’t have to worry about it, and I believed you.”

“Yeah, after you knocked his ass out! You can hardly compare the two.” A thought pops in my mind, and I smile sweetly. “Unless you’re saying that I have permission to take a swing at O. I’d love to bust up her perfect little nose.”

Gavin resumes his search for flights. “Her father paid good money for that nose. And her cheek bones, and her chin, if I remember correctly.”

I kick him in the ass. “You’re deflecting. What happened?”

He takes the computer off his lap and sets it on the nightstand. “You have to remember, we’ve known each other our whole lives. Our row wasn’t about one thing, it was about a million things. Rubbish was dredged up from twenty-five years of friendship. Even if I dictated it back to you word for word, it probably wouldn’t make sense to you. Hell, I’m not sure it made sense to me at the time. I did see an ugly side to her that repulsed me. The bottom line is I can’t forgive the ways she’s tried to sabotage our relationship. No matter what excuse she has, I can’t look past it. So we’re done. Or I’m done at least. Shouldn’t that suffice?”

No, it doesn't suffice! After all she's done, she deserves to be strung up from the rafters and have her fingernails ripped out. Not that I can say that to him. "Fine. I guess I can live with that." I point at him. "I promise you, she's not going away. When she comes back, you'd better be ready to deal with it."

He kisses my forehead. "Olivia can do whatever she wants. As of this moment, her antics will have no impact on us. Now, can I please get back to getting us a flight home?"

I gesture to his computer. "Carry on." I tap my fingers on the bed while I think of my own unresolved issues. "What do you think I should do about Max?"

"I think you need to tell him everything. Lorenzo, Carlos, everything."

I shake my head. "I can't do that. I heard what he said earlier, and I'm not protecting them—I'm protecting him. If I tell him everything, he'll go after Zo and Carlos. That'll get us all killed. I need to keep him on a leash, or it'll spiral out of control."

He slams his laptop closed. "It already is out of control! This is bigger than you are. You can't keep fighting this on your own!"

Offended, I glare at him. "I think I've done pretty well on my own. I'm still here, aren't I?"

Gavin throws his hands up in frustration. "By the grace of God! You run off with this hare-brained plan, completely defenseless. You're fighting a dragon with a chopstick! It's asinine!"

"This isn't about me," I snap. "It's about your need to be the hero. Your ego's bruised because I refuse to be your damsel in distress. Sorry, but I'm not wired that way!"

He jumps up, recoiling from my words. A look of disgust flashes across his face. "How dare you!" He runs his fingers through his hair. "This conversation needs to stop before we say things we'll regret." He storms out of the room, slamming the door.

Unable to just lie around, I stomp to the bathroom and turn on the shower. I replay our conversation over and over in my mind. Why can't he just let me handle my own problems? If he'd put his ego aside for just a moment, I think he'd actually be proud of what I've done. I sure as hell am! If he can't see that I'm strong enough to fight my own battles, he'll never respect me. If there's no respect, we're doomed.

The shampoo bottle slips through my hands.

If there's no respect, we're doomed. I'm demanding he respect me, but have I been respectful of him?

The bottle lands on my big toe, causing me to jump back. I slip on the slick tile and fall through the glass shower door. Tiny shards of glass fall all around me as I hit the marble floor. Gavin bursts through the door. He scans the room in disbelief.

"You insulted my fighting skills, so I thought I'd show you by taking on the shower door. Impressed yet?"

This gets a small laugh from him as he carefully extricates me from the glass. "Always so damn cheeky."

Less than ten minutes later, the hotel has people in the room to clean the mess. As it turns out, the rubber stopper on the bottom of the door was damaged, thus impacting the integrity of the tempered glass. The whole stubbing my toe and falling bit didn't help, but the door could have shattered at any moment. Gavin's livid. I think he's taking all of his frustration with me out on the poor hotel manager. Something tells me, by the time this is all said and done, I'll have a lifetime of free stays at the Four Seasons.

The best part of being in a Vegas casino: concierge doctor. A very cute doctor was in the room within minutes to pick out all the tiny pieces of glass in my skin. Considering how big the shower door was, I got very lucky. Only two stitches needed. While the doctor diligently looked me over, I couldn't help wondering how someone gets stuck with his gig. I'm guessing serious gambling debt.

Once I'm deemed glass free, the manager moves Gavin and me to the suite down the hall. The door clicks as the manager leaves, and Gavin and I are left alone. The shower door fiasco only prolonged the inevitable.

"I let you save me from the shower door. That has to count for something, right?" I say, trying to break the ice.

His eyes are fixed on the floor, as though the answer is written in the carpet design. "The fact you think my intentions are derived from some narcissistic need to be a hero slays me." His fist goes to his chest, as though he's trying to rub away the pain I've caused. He looks me square in the eye. "All I want is you safe. I love you, and the thought of you in danger is more than I can handle. So in that respect, I suppose it is selfish. I want you alive so that I can wake up to you every morning and kiss you good night every night. That isn't about my ego, that's about how profoundly I love you. What have I ever done that's led you to believe otherwise?"

"I don't know," I whisper. "I suppose it's easier to blame you than it is to acknowledge my own role in this. I need to be free of Ash, and all I can see are the roadblocks in my way of that freedom."

His eyes narrow. "That's how you see me? As a roadblock?" He staggers backward a few steps before hitting the sofa. He sits and lets his head fall in his hands.

I wipe the tears from my eyes. "In my mind, I needed to clean up this mess myself. It's my punishment for marrying Ash. My penance."

He laughs. "Catholics! I'll never understand it."

In dire need of a tissue, I walk to the bathroom. "Watch it, Oxford. I can poke fun at my Catholic crazy, but you can't." After washing my face and blowing my nose, I return to the living room. "I promise I'll try. That's all I can do. You need to be patient because I'm going to screw up. We're trying to rewire something that's been ingrained in me for almost fifteen years. It won't be easy, but I promise I'll try. I'll even come clean with Max."

He kisses me. "All I can ask is that you try. I'll help you. Just don't shut me out. I'm not trying to dominate you. I just want to protect you."

I nudge his shoulder. "You want to be my super hero. Just be honest," I tease.

"Not everyone can pull off that look. Tights and a cape are hard for a man to wear and still look manly," he jokes back. "I love you. Your safety and happiness are crucial for my existence. I'll stop at nothing to give you the world because you deserve nothing less. You can't fault me for that."

"Fucking-A, Gavin. I'm supposed to be the wordsmith in this relationship. I can't hold a damn candle to you," I say, fighting back tears. "You missed your calling as a poet or romance novelist or something."

"I've found my calling, and you're right here."

Chapter Twenty

After finally getting off the emotional roller coaster of the past few days, make-up sex is definitely called for, but I don't have it in me. I never thought I would be too emotionally drained to orgasm, but I am. While I feel like Gavin and I are in a better place, I can still feel the gravity of everything else weighing on me. It's time to get the hell out of Vegas.

After booking the nine o'clock flight to London, Gavin calls Max to set up a time for us to meet before we leave. I can't leave the country without clearing the air. Once plans are in the works, Gavin drags me downstairs to get something to eat. He wants fancy, and I just want to plop myself in front of the sundae bar at the all you can eat buffet. Nothing cures emotional exhaustion like bottomless brownie sundaes.

Gavin wins, however, and he ends up taking me to Hubert Keller's restaurant. The prices are far fancier than my mood, but they have a "little plates" menu. I'm a sucker for getting to try bites of lots of different things. The same concept could have been accomplished at the buffet for a lot less money, but Gavin insists I won't regret it.

He orders so much food, we need to move to a larger table to have room for it all. The meal is amazing. I may have been too tired for sex, but clearly not too tired for a foodgasm. My only regret is that I'm not wearing yoga pants. It's going to be a long flight home with my pants this tight!

Since we have a few hours before we can see Max, I insist we sit at a few tables. How can we go to Vegas and not gamble at least a little?

Of course the brat beats me at blackjack. I know Vegas has systems in place to stop card counting, but if anyone could beat that system, it would be Gavin and his damn memory. We both do well at craps thanks to my stellar rolls.

When my streak breaks, I notice we need to leave soon to meet Max, so I drag Gavin toward the cashier. On the way, we pass a roulette wheel.

"Come on, Lil. Let's let it ride. We'll put it all on black," Gavin says.

"No, never black. Always play red," I insist.

"Black."

"Red."

"Black," he says throwing all his chips on the table.

I put my chips on red, and we watch the wheel spin. "Oh, it's on, Oxford. It. Is. On."

"You won't be saying that when I win, luv," he taunts.

"Oh yeah? Let's make it interesting."

"I'm listening."

"Loser has to... get a tattoo of the winner's flag." As soon as I say it, I regret it. What am I thinking?

"You're done for. I can't wait to see the Union Jack on you." He leans in and whispers, "My cock is getting hard thinking about where we're going to put it." He pulls me in closer as if I needed evidence that he's telling the truth.

One of us walks away with a lot more money in his pocket, and one of us is fearing a trip to the tattoo parlor. Despite my loss and impending tattoo doom, I'm having the best time. I forgot how much fun we have when we aren't dealing with crazy stalkers or drug cartels. It reminds me that I never want to let him go.

The valet brings our rental car up, and we hop on LVB to meet Max.

"Seriously, where do you find a Bentley as a rental car?" I ask.

"It's a hire car, luv. If I tell you, how will I impress you? Some secrets must be kept secret."

"Let me guess... You call the Four Seasons, tell them what you want, and they find it for you?"

He smirks but doesn't respond.

"Yeah, that's what I thought," I say, rolling my eyes. "Where are we meeting Max?"

"I'm not sure. He just sent me the address. Max insisted on picking."

"Oh Lord," I groan.

"Yes?" Gavin replies.

I punch him hard enough to give him a dead arm.

"I told you, I'm never calling you that. Get over yourself."

"You called me God plenty of times last night. Why is Lord so difficult?"

"Shut it, Oxford." My cheeks flush with the memory. "As I was saying, you can never leave it to Max to pick the place. We could be going to a strip club or a Chuck E. Cheese."

"Maybe it's a tattoo parlor. Seems like a perfect time for you to pay up, don't you think, luv?"

"Shut it. I'll make good on that bet when I'm good and ready. Not today."

"We'll see, luv. We'll see." His tone clearly says he doubts my follow-through. "We only have a little over two hours before we have to leave for the airport. Wherever he has chosen can't be that bad. Think of it as an adventure."

"It always is with Max. If it's karaoke, I'm not singing. That wasn't part of the deal," I insist.

We pull up to Frankie's Tiki Room. I won't have to sing, no screaming children, and no one will be getting naked. So far so good.

We head inside, and it's just what I would expect in a Polynesian-themed bar. Dark, tiki torches, and big drinks with umbrellas. Max and Em are waiting by the door.

Em grabs Gavin. "Let's leave these two alone. You and I are going to head down the street to a bar that doesn't make me feel like I've stepped back in time to a frat party."

"No way, Em. They can go off on their own, but I'm not leaving. Suck it up and have a Mai Tai." He takes her elbow and leads her off into the dark depths of the bar.

Max looks at me. "I usually choose places like this while I'm on the job. Dark, people tend to mind their own business. You ever go to Kon Tiki in Tucson? Did all my secret meetings there." His voice is cold and distant. Professional.

I'm not sure what to expect from this meeting. A few drinks may do us both some good.

I nod my head "The place where the drinks come in a fish bowl? It's a popular spot to start on twenty-first birthdays. Which is stupid because after one scorpion, most people are either passed out or ready to puke."

"Come on," he says, putting his arm around my shoulder to lead me to a table.

Our server comes to the table to take our order. We

both order a Thursten Howell. How can we not?

Max has avoided my gaze since I arrived. Knowing he isn't going to make this any easier on me, I just start. I tell him every detail—probably more than he needs. He doesn't say a word; he just twirls his straw in his drink.

When I finish, I say, "Max, say something. Please. Anything."

"Slugger, what I really need to know, more than anything, is how I can get a hold of some photographic proof of this kiss with Em. Video? Anything? Can we have a repeat performance? Since she told me, I can't sleep. I can't eat. I can't do anything but think about it. I need something. Anything. You're killing me."

I'm dumbfounded. "That's all you have to say? I just tell you my deepest, darkest secrets, and you want to know about me kissing Em?"

The server drops off our drinks. I'm not sure what's in it, but it's damn good.

"The other stuff is... whatever. It is what it is. I get why you kept it a secret. I'm pissed you didn't trust me. I let you into my life, into my home, and you still couldn't trust me but I'll get over it. I think you're getting that secrets are dumb and can get you and everyone you love killed. No need to dwell on it. I've got to figure out where to go next that will put the bad guys behind bars and keep you safe. Safe and hopefully kissing Em." He claps his hands and then rubs them together with an evil grin on his face. "So how do we make that happen?"

I take a big sip of my drink. "Max, I'm going to break your heart, but Em and I have never kissed."

He chokes as he gasps. "The lies you tell, woman! Say it ain't so!"

"Em and I figured out that if there's ever a tense situation with a group of men, we can start discussing two girls kissing, and it'll usually be a big enough distraction to escape whatever's going on. That line has gotten us out of more sticky situations than I can remember. It got you and Gavin to stop fighting."

"I hate you. I hate both of you. That was cruel and unusual punishment," he says. "I think you owe me that kiss as retribution for my pain and suffering."

"We fake kissed once. We can show you that," I suggest. "It's easy; you tilt your head and make sure your lips are near the other person's mouth. If everyone is pretty drunk or not looking too closely, you can get away with it."

He covers his ears. "Stop. Just stop. You're ruining it for me. I've been thinking and dreaming about this, and you've crushed me. I can't think of kissing ever again."

"Speaking of kissing, are we okay?" I ask, not sure I want to hear the answer.

"Us? What?" The look on his face tells me he's connecting the dots. "Oh yeah, we're fine. It was not enough sleep, too much tequila, and way too much adrenaline. Hazard of the job. It doesn't matter since I'm never speaking to you again unless you and Em kiss and make up."

"Em and I don't need to make up. We're totally fine."

He slams his hand on the table. "Damn it!" he shouts

as he storms off to the bar.

I go find Gavin and Em and call them over to our table. Max returns with four Three Rum Scums, and I know I'll sleep well on the plane. Whenever Bacardi 151 is involved, it's "good night Lily."

The four of us have one last drink (or maybe three or four) before Gavin and I leave. Em and Max are staying one more day as they both detest red-eyes. My guess is there's more to their decisions than that, but I know better than to ask. Gavin and Max seem to have put their issues behind them. I think we can all be friends, but I don't think Gavin will ever be okay with me living with Max again. Not that I see that happening anytime soon.

Gavin calls the Four Seasons, and they send someone to drive us to the airport and return the rental. The poor kid who has to chauffeur us has the patience of a saint. Happy Drunk Gavin, as opposed to Moody Drunk Gavin, is hilarious but a lot to handle.

Thankfully the Vegas airport is used to inebriated passengers. Gavin always stands out no matter where we are, but I don't think we're making asses of ourselves.

Our flight is delayed due to high winds. We've drunk quite a bit and then stopped. We aren't sobering up as much as getting tired and cranky. We can either ride it out and hope neither of us loses it before we get on the plane, or we can keep drinking. The McCarren airport commemorative cup is hard to resist, so we go with option B.

There's no place in the world more interesting to

people-watch than Vegas, especially at the airport. Gavin keeps me entertained with his non-stop commentary. His favorite game is to pick out someone and come up with their Vegas story. Like the guy in the rumpled suit. Gavin says he came to Vegas to surprise his wife who was here on a conference only to find she's cheating on him with a stripper named Pat—gender ambiguous. He really should be a writer because his imagination, especially his drunken imagination, is creative and hilarious. Knowing Gavin, if he tried, he would have a best seller on his hands.

I look around while he finds his next story victim. "Lots of brides and grooms. Have you noticed that?"

"It's Vegas," he says. "Lots of people come here to get married. Not us, though."

I laugh at his drunken observation. "No. Last time I checked, we didn't get married."

"We won't get married in Vegas," he says, slurring his words a bit.

"I can't imagine we will." I chuckle.

"Nope. Our wedding is going to be amazeballs."

"Amazeballs? I didn't know you even knew that word. Have you been reading my romance novels?" Oh, he's in rare form tonight! We've never talked about it, but I don't think marriage is in the forecast for us. Been there, done that. I'm sure Drunk Gavin is just creating another story.

"We spent some time with Brittany's showgirls before you arrived." He holds his finger to his lips. "Shhh, don't tell Lily."

I almost spit out my drink. I manage to swallow and wipe my mouth with the back of my hand. "Don't worry, Oxford. Your secret's safe with me."

"Amazeballs, I tell you. Not sure where yet, still plotting that out. But I know it will be..."

I'm not sure if he lost his train of thought or if he's about to pass out.

"Amazeballs?"

He smiles and points at me. "Yes! Exactly. It'll be the best wedding ever. Know why?"

"Why?"

"Because I'll be marrying you." He kisses my forehead, then leans back into the chair and closes his eyes.

"Twenty bucks says you won't remember this conversation by the time we land."

"Maybe not, but that won't make it any less true."

His response is a bit more serious than I expected. A voice in my head screams, "Abort. Abort! Move directly to an emergency exit!" I don't want to talk about marriage. I can't even say out loud that I'll move in with him. Talking about marriage, even in this drunken state, is stupid and a recipe for disaster. He'll get hurt, I'll get hurt. I'd be an idiot to continue this conversation.

"You've actually thought about us getting married?" I'm such a glutton for punishment.

"Of course. Just because you're afraid to talk about it doesn't mean I'm not thinking about it. You're not there yet, though."

"No. No, we're not." Phew. Landmine averted.

"Not yet. Soon, I think. Maybe after New Years'," He says.

KABOOM!

My jaw drops. I know I should say something, anything, but as a landmine just exploded in my brain, I can't seem to find the words.

"Oh, they're calling our plane. Let's go," he says nonchalantly, as though he hasn't just dropped an atomic bomb in my brain. He kisses my cheek, grabs my hand, and pulls me toward the gate as if everything is hunky dory.

When will I learn to just keep my mouth shut? Why do I open cans of worms? I hate worms! Worms are gross and stupid and icky. When we reach our seats, I down my champagne as well as Gavin's, and ask for two refills before take-off. At this point, I don't care if he remembers this conversation as long as I can forget it.

Chapter Twenty-One

The flight is long and restless. I fall asleep, but am plagued by dreams of weddings and hit men. At one point, I'm walking down the aisle toward Gavin, and Ash jumps up from behind the altar with a machine gun to take out all the guests *Scarface* style. But when he shoots someone, they don't die—they turn into a pile of cocaine.

Instead of addressing the fact that he's shooting people at my wedding, I scream at him, "Ash, preppy boys from Potomac shouldn't ever try to pull off a Cuban accent. You're too WASP-y to pull that off. You sound like a tool!"

I'm sure that dream is riddled with complex psychobabble, but I'm too jet lagged to figure it out right now.

Between the long flight and the time difference, I'm so turned around I'm not sure which way is up. The altitude's caused me to swell. Everything from my pants to even my shoes feels too tight. To top it all off, I have a throbbing headache. To say I'm cranky is an understatement. Gavin slept the whole flight, is chipper, and looks perfect. I really hate him sometimes.

The cab ride perks me up. I've only been gone a few days, but I didn't realize how much I missed London. Returning to Gavin's flat feels like coming home. Looking around as we get settled, I'm hit with a dozen memories of Gavin and me. Nothing earthmoving, but lovely all the same. Gavin and I cooking dinner, the way he steals the crust of my pizza, him scolding me not to leave my shoes by the door. Being here with him is spectacular not because of the opulence or the mind-blowingly romantic dates, but because of the million sweet nothings that take place every day. The intimate moments which fortify my deep connection to him. I know I love him, but it isn't until this moment that I realize the place he has taken in my heart, my soul, and my life.

After unpacking, I gaze over the bed that has become home to me. I soak it in until he comes up behind me and wraps his arms around me.

"Where are you, luv?"

"Oh, I'm right here, I promise." I lean back into his embrace.

"Good," he says, squeezing me tighter. "I went a little mad while you were gone. Don't do that to me again. Ever."

"I won't." The moment is calming and serene. For once, I feel Zen.

"I was thinking..."

"Oh, dear. That's when all the trouble starts," I tease.

"Shut it," he mocks me.

"Get your own lines."

"Anyroad. My visit to the US reminded me how nutty you Yanks are about holiday decorations. I was going to have Mason decorate the country house, but I thought, with this being your first official Christmas in over a decade, you might want to pick out your own decorations. I don't know how much is left in the shops, and I'm sure it won't be as gaudy as what you would have found in the US, but why don't we go and see what's there?"

I spin around in his arms and beam at him. "Can we get a tree?"

"I figured we would cut one down when we get to the country house tomorrow."

"What about a twelve-foot inflatable Frosty the Snowman that waves and sings Christmas carols?"

"Luv," he groans. "I want this to be special for you. I want you to have everything you could possibly desire. Except that."

"But I need one." I pout. A look of pain washes over his face before I decide to put him out of his misery. "Just kidding, Oxford. Have you ever known me to be so ostentatious? Let's start simple. I just want a tree and some ornaments and maybe some garland."

"Mistletoe. We need lots and lots of mistletoe," he says with a smile.

"Like I need more motivation to kiss you! It takes all my self-restraint to not attack you every time I'm near you." To prove it, I kiss him. It starts soft and sweet and becomes a tango of lips and tongues and lust. Hot damn, this man can kiss me breathless.

He pulls away first. "I would love to see where this could go, but we may want to run to the shops before they close. It's four days before Christmas; there may not be anything left."

"Fine." I pout and stomp my foot like a disgruntled teenager.

"I want this to be perfect for you. You deserve to have a happy Christmas. There will always be time for kissing."

"It's a merry Christmas."

"You're in England, and it's a Happy Christmas." He hands me my coat. "No time for arguing, let's go," he insists.

Thank goodness he has a Range Rover. We hit Harrods, Selfridges, and the Christmas Shoppe for ornaments, "bits and bobs," and other decorations. We find more than I expected, and everything we buy is sweet and tasteful. My only over-the-top purchase is a life-sized polar bear from Selfridges that I name Harvey. I couldn't help myself. Who doesn't need a life-sized polar bear? Gavin put forth a good fight against

Harvey, but after some passionate snogging in the fitting room, I was able to get him to see it my way.

When I was a child, my mother and I searched each year for the perfect ornament that represented that year in our lives. A ballerina for when I got my first set of pointe shoes, a Jeep when my father surprised my mom with a Jeep Cherokee to replace our old beat-up station wagon. Gavin and I only have today, but I search and search for the perfect ornament. The stores are fairly picked clean. It was silly for me to expect to find the perfect ornament. What could I possibly get that would symbolize the year I've had? I don't think Hallmark makes a drug cartel ornament series.

The crowds are over the top and the lines are lengthy, but it all disappears for me. All I can see is Gavin. Making these choices together, blending our images of the holiday, creating memories which are uniquely us is so simple, but heavenly.

After we've hit every store with a Christmas tree in the window and the Range Rover is filled to the brim with bags (and a bear strapped to the roof), we go back to Gavin's flat.

******

The drive to the country house is a little over two hours long. I'm still failing English geography, so I'm not really sure where we are in relation to London. All of the shires, woods, and hams confuse me. It sure is beautiful, though.

I'm not sure what I expected, but the country house is more than I can wrap my head around. This isn't a house; it's freaking *Downton Abbey*. People don't live in places like this! They pay money to tour them to see how people lived during the Golden Ages.

"You grew up *here*?" Blown away doesn't begin to cover how I feel.

"Pick up your jaw. It's just a house. It's been in my family for six generations, and it's drafty and costs a fortune to maintain. I grew up at boarding schools. This was just where I came to visit on holiday."

"At least we won't have trouble making room for Harvey," I tease.

I can see that Gavin's uncomfortable. Gavin detests having his wealth highlighted, so I try my best to pretend that Cinderella's castle is just any other boring house.

Before we even have the opportunity to get out of the car, a large man and rotund woman come running out the door.

Gavin runs toward the woman. "Hazel! It's so good to see you."

"Gavin, it's been too long!" she says before slapping him on the backside. "How have you had Lily here all this time without bringing her here? You were raised better than that, young man."

"Ouch, Hazel. That hurt. Okay, come meet Lily." He grabs my hand and brings me over. "Hazel, it is my honor to introduce you to Lily Clark. Lily, this is Hazel.

Hazel was my nanny, and she's married to Mason here. Mason keeps this place running."

Hazel is so sweet looking. She's five feet tall if she's lucky, and soft all around. Mason must be six foot six, and he looks extremely fit for his age. I'm guessing they're both over fifty. I know these two people mean the world to Gavin, and for all intents and purposes, they're the only family he has left.

Hazel and Mason give me the introductory tour, telling me everything I never needed to know about its architecture and design. After an hour, we've barely covered half the house. Mixed in are plenty of embarrassing Gavin-growing-up stories, like when he was four and would only pee in the potted plants or when he broke his left arm trying to surf down the stairs on a serving tray. I hear Gavin groan with each story, but the dirty looks Hazel shoots him tells me he knows better than to interrupt.

"We're short on time, so let's get decorating," Hazel cheers. "First we need a tree. Gavin, hop to it."

He kisses her cheek and grabs my hand. "Let's go pick a tree."

When we're out of earshot, I say, "Gavin the lumberjack. It's kinda hot. Can you wear flannel?"

"I don't own flannel, but I'll buy some if you promise to keep looking at me like that," he says with a wink.

Gavin directs me to the ATV in the garage. He drives like a mad man, and if I didn't know better, I'd think he was trying to throw me off. The sparkle in his eye and mischievous grin tell me he's probably just regressing to his twelve- year-old self.

It takes us over an hour to decide on a tree as it seems we both used to chop down trees for Christmas and we have different opinions about what the tree should look like. I eventually give in, not because he is right but because my hands are frozen and I think my toes may fall off. I'm thankful we have the ATV and don't have to drag the tree back.

I was right. Lumberjack Gavin is crazy hot. The way his back looks while he swings the axe... The fact that I'm the luckiest girl on the planet is not lost on me.

While we were out, Hazel and Mason brought down decorations from storage. Gavin tries to protest—because he wants this to be all about starting fresh—but I think it's sweet to use some of the things from when his parents were alive. Beyond that, we need them. This place is a huge!

After dinner, Gavin hurries off to do a video conference. His company connects soldiers with their families during the holidays, and he likes to be hands-on with the project. I get to hear more Gavin-growing-up stories from Hazel and Mason while he's busy.

Mason takes some wreaths and garland outside to begin decorating the windows and doors, leaving Hazel and me to make the gingerbread houses. "You're quite good for him," Hazel declares. "I wasn't sure what I would think of you, what with the way the two of you met and how fast your relationship has developed. I thought he was just jumping into someone else's bed to forget all about Brooke. But watching the two of you together is lovely. I can see why he's so smitten."

"How we met was rather unorthodox. We've been moving so fast my head feels like it is spinning," I say.

"It's nice to see him happy. Brooke was horrible for him. A bad match from the start that drained the light from his eyes."

Unsure of what I can or should say, I just keep working on my gingerbread house.

"They were married in name more than actually having a traditional marriage, as I'm sure you know," Hazel continues.

From her tone, I'm guessing Hazel's itching to dish some dirt. I won't start a Brooke bashing session—I don't know anything about her to bash—but I won't stop someone from starting one either.

"Gavin thought when he married her, it would be just like the tabloids said it would be —a dream. She was a little too perfect, though. That's how I knew she was fake."

"Some could say that Gavin is a little too perfect as well," I point out.

Hazel huffs. "Gavin doesn't have to try. Brooke was always trying. It must have been exhausting keeping up all her facades. She had so many walls, Gavin could never get close. She always kept him at a polite distance so they could live their separate lives. I understand that sort of relationship is commonplace in Hollywood, but I wanted more for Gavin."

Déjà vu makes me ill. Gavin not only likes to play the hero, but he likes his damsels jaded, with impenetrable walls around their hearts. Looks like I actually do have some things in common with Brooke. I hate that I'm part of his pattern, and I hate myself for putting him through the same crap he fought for years.

"His parents put him in boarding school when he was just a wee lad," she continues. "He had me, but he never had a home with a mum and a pop that acted like a family. When he married Brooke, he hoped that was what he was going to get, and it never happened. He told me once, when Brooke was at her worst and I begged him to leave her, he said, 'I don't deserve a nuclear family. This is the life I was bred for. I can't hope for a happy wife and a minivan full of footballers. It isn't in the cards for me.' He always saw his wealth as a curse."

I put my frosting knife down. "Poor Gavin," I say. Looks like I'm not the only one paying penance.

"Can you give him that, Lily?" she asks.

I rearrange the gumdrops on the gingerbread house, racking my brain to find the right thing to say. "I grew up like that. White picket fence, a dog. We had a station wagon instead of a minivan, though. I had two parents who loved each other more than life itself. The only thing they loved more was me. It was so long ago, I sometimes wonder if it was all a dream. I hope I can have that again one day, but I'm so broken, I don't know if that's possible. I love Gavin. I know with all my heart I don't want to be with anyone else. As far as tomorrow and tomorrow's tomorrow, I can't make promises. Life throws too many curveballs. I'll never intentionally hurt him. I can't see myself leaving him, but life is too unpredictable for promises."

She clasps my hand. "Oh, dear, you're not broken. You've just had a heaping lot of the hard part of life. Don't push people away because of it, or you'll miss out on all the good parts."

My cell phone rings, snapping us out of the moment. While I answer, I wipe away the tears that have welled in my eyes.

"Hey, Em, what's shakin'?"

"I'm coming to visit," she says with fake enthusiasm.

I pop a marshmallow in my mouth. "Great. When? Another lecture?"

"I'll be there Christmas day. No lecture. I just need to get out of town."

Anticipating this is going to be an in-depth conversation, I motion to Hazel that I'm going to take the call outside. Thankfully, there's a door to the backyard off the kitchen. I'd probably get lost if I went through the house.

To call this a backyard doesn't do it justice. Gavin owns all the land in sight and then some. Acres and acres of rolling hills sprinkled with sheep, a duck pond, tennis courts. There are paths that wind all around the property, but it's been too cold to venture out.

From what Mason's told me, when Gavin's family was alive, the grounds were far more elaborate, with a topiary maze and lavish rose gardens. Gavin never uses the house to entertain, so Mason has scaled back dramatically. Personally, I think it's beautiful as is.

As soon as I step out the door, Hazel comes running

after me with my jacket in her hand. "You'll catch your death out here if you're not careful."

I tuck my phone under my chin, while I pull my jacket on. "Thank you," I say as she scurries back inside.

Once I'm zipped up, I say, "I'm surprised you aren't going someplace tropical with other beautiful people who avoid the holiday. Why do I feel there's a story here, Em?"

She's silent, and I clear my throat. "Don't offer me bullshit. I'll see right through it."

"Fine." She sighs. "Max asked me to come with him to see his family on Christmas. I told him I don't celebrate holidays, but he wouldn't back down. Then he got all emotional and asked questions I don't answer. Instead of shutting him down, I told him you needed me and I was coming to see you."

Too cold to stand in one place, I walk down the path that I think leads to the front of the house. "So you're flying to London on Christmas Eve so you can avoid talking about your relationship with Max. Do I have that right?"

"Max and I don't have a relationship," she insists.

"Bullshit! You and Max have *something* going on. Maybe you're friends, maybe you're more—I don't know. But it is something, and it is real. Come to London if you want, I'd love to have you here, but don't kid yourself about why you're coming."

"I don't do holidays, especially big family holidays with families I don't know. You know that, and you've always respected that. He can't. But that has nothing to do with why I'm coming to see you. You better than anyone know I have no problem telling him no. I don't need to flee the country to avoid him."

The wind picks up, so I pull my hood up and dig into my pocket for my gloves. "You won't go to his family event, but you'll come to mine? You should be warned, I'm going all out. Tree, dinner, presents, party. I don't care if you get shitfaced on eggnog all day, but the holiday is being celebrated."

"Fine, I can tolerate that as long as there is copious amounts of alcohol, I do what I want, go where I want, and see whomever I want. Those are my rules. If Boston can't deal, then that's on him."

"So you're saying that you are seeing Max?"

"Lily, end of. Seriously!"

"Okay, okay. Whatever you say. We're at the country house. Call Gavin to find out where it is, because I have no clue. The crew you met when you were here last is going to be here on Christmas. Get this—this place has its own bowling alley! We're going to drink, bowl, and I'm insisting on a Yankee swap."

She groans. "Is this the good kind of Yankee swap where everyone brings booze or the lame kind where I end up with a chia pet?"

"I told everyone it's a grown-up swap."

"Ooh, naughty Yankee swap is so much fun! Maybe I'll get a vibrator!"

"Liam is coordinating it, so if I had to guess, it'll be

very naughty. Gavin lives way out in the middle of nowhere, so you may have to stay here. I doubt there's a five-star hotel nearby. But this place is bigger than the White House, so I think you can manage."

"I'll stay for a day or two and then head back to London."

"I can't wait to see you," I say. This is shaping up to be an interesting holiday.

"One more thing before you hang up," she says. "Do you remember Ash's fraternity brother, Todd Masters? He ran that techno club Ash used to drag you to all the time."

I stop in my tracks. "Yeah, what about him?"

"He died. Sounds like the club burned down one night. He was trapped inside. All the boys in the house are going back to Tucson for the funeral."

Maybe it's a coincidence. Clubs burn down all the time. Faulty wiring. Bad pyrotechnics. The place is full of alcohol, for Christ's sake. One cigarette left burning, and the whole place could go up in flames. Just because he died under questionable circumstances doesn't mean the cartel killed him. It doesn't mean I got him killed.

Maybe if I tell myself that enough I'll actually believe it.

"Uh, Em. I've got to run. Text me your flight info."

I dial Max's number, but it goes straight to voice mail. We haven't spoken since Vegas. That has to be a good sign. He has to know about Todd. If he thought it had anything to do with the cartel, he'd let me know. Wouldn't he?

I shove my phone in my back pocket, and realize I have no idea where I am. The house is no longer in sight. Freezing, I run as fast as I can back the way I came.

When I open the door to the kitchen, I find Hazel in the kitchen finishing our gingerbread house. "Look at you! You're an icicle. Let's make you some tea." She puts the kettle on, then wraps me in a blanket. While I defrost, she tells me more stories about Gavin and his parents. Once the kettle whistles, she makes me a cuppa with extra sugar, and puts out a platter of teacakes. Typically, I hate tea, but there's something comforting and soothing having tea with Hazel. I can see how Gavin managed to grow up warm and compassionate, even if his parents weren't.

It's long after midnight by the time Gavin comes out of his office. His hair looks like he's been pulling at it all day, and there are bags under his eyes. He looks exhausted. "Long day?" I ask.

Hazel gets up from the sofa. "You work too hard." She gives him a hug. "I'm off to bed. You should be too."

Gavin sits next to me, then kisses my temple. "Sorry I neglected you, luv. I had to put out a dozen fires burning back at the office, and there's been some snags with the Christmas project."

I look through the cabinets until I find a bottle of scotch. "You have a company to run, Oxford, I get it. You've been chasing me around the world, so it's only natural you have stuff to catch up on. Hazel and I have been doing just fine without you. Oh, and Em is coming for Christmas."

"Coming to see Liam?" he asks.

I hand him the glass, then rub his shoulders. He's all knots. "Running away from Max. I wouldn't be surprised if Liam being here isn't an added bonus though."

His chin falls to his chest, giving me better access to rub his neck. "I have to run back to London tomorrow morning for a meeting. Let's go to bed, yeah?"

I walk up the stairs and he says, "Where're you going?"

I point upstairs. "I assume one of the gazillion bedrooms upstairs."

He looks at me, confused. "Why would we do that? Upstairs is haunted."

"*What?*" I run down the stairs and hide behind him.

He shrugs. "The place is over three hundred years old. Of course it's haunted."

I look over his shoulder at the stairwell, petrified I'm going to see Casper float by. "Tell me you're joking."

He puts his arm around me and chuckles. "Don't fret, luv. They're friendly ghosts."

My jaw drops and I shake my head. "You brought me to a haunted house." I look at my watch. "If we leave now, we can be back in London by what two? Three?"

He laughs. "We're not leaving. But I have a surprise." He threads his fingers through mine. "Come on. If you hate it, I'll drive you back to London."

He leads me through the maze of the house, then opens a set of double doors which lead to the solarium. Shivers run up my body as I step on the slate floor of the all glass room. The floor is so cold, it feels like I'm walking on ice.

"Is your surprise frostbite? 'Cause I'm already losing feeling in my toes."

"Don't be cheeky. Do you trust me?"

"You take me to a haunted house and now bring me to a walk in freezer. Should I trust you?"

"Yes. Now lie down and it'll be worth it, I promise." He motions to the makeshift bed, made of an air mattress and a mountain of pillows.

I lie down on the air mattress and pull the blankets up to my chin. He turns out the lights, and the glass ceiling is illuminated by the brilliant sky. He climbs into the bed and wraps his arm around me. "Most of the time, the cloud cover is so thick, you can't see the stars." Being this far into the country, the stars are brighter than street lights. There isn't a cloud in the sky, providing us with a view of the heavens which rivals that of the planetarium.

"I know it's cold, but I brought the warmest blankets we have, and I set up space heaters," he says. "Plus I have it on good authority that I'm good at keeping you warm. What do you say? Stay and look at the stars or go back to London?"

I snuggle close and kiss his cheek. "We can stay. As long as you protect me from the ghosts."

He kisses my temple. "You're such a mug."

"What does that mean?"

He chuckles. "It definitely doesn't mean you're gullible."

I elbow him in the ribs. "You're an ass!"

He pulls me back to his side. "But you love me."

"Yeah, I guess I do." I lean my head against his chest and close my eyes. "The air mattress is going to do a number on your back."

He runs his thumb along my jaw. "It's worth it to see that look on your face. Your breath hitches a little, then your eyes get big and your smile gets bright."

"No one's ever done things like this for me before. All these romantic gestures... it blows my mind. You make me feel like the most special girl in the world."

He gently kisses my lips. "Because you are."

The sparkle in his eyes makes me want to believe him. "I bet you say that to all the girls."

He turns his head and closes his eyes. "Are you ever going to believe how much I love you? I wish I could make you understand. Since you've come into my life, I've come alive for the first time. The air's cleaner, the sun's brighter. It's like every sense, every nerve ending, every molecule in my body is vivified. Everything before you was dull and muted, and now my life is a box of Crayolas. The big one with more colors than I thought possible. My life is bold and vibrant, all because of you."

I had that box when I was nine. Every shade of every color I could possibly imagine, with silly names that they had to stretch to come up with a 25th word for orange. That box was a rainbow, not only of color, but of possibility. I could create anything, and it was a glorious feeling. Gavin feels that way about me.

He holds me tight and kisses me so intensely he almost touches my soul.

I learn some valuable lessons tonight. One, crayons are the most romantic creation on the face of the planet. Two, air mattresses are designed for sleeping only. Other activities result in popping said air mattresses and falling quickly to the floor with a thud. Three, falling on a slate floor hurts like hell. Four, sometimes sex is so earth-shatteringly good, it's worth it even when you have a bruised tailbone that hurts like hell.

Chapter Twenty-Two

Genius strikes at the most random times. I've been stressing about what to get Gavin for Christmas because he has everything and if he ever wants something, he just buys it. Just after I fall asleep in the solarium, I wake up to some creepy sound that old houses make. While trying to fall back asleep, I come up with a brilliant Christmas present. I just hope I can pull it together in time.

Careful not to wake Gavin, I slip out of bed in search of my phone. If anyone can pull this together, it's Em. It's late in the U.S., but I know she'll be awake. She tells me she's on it, but I'll have to be flexible. A couple hours later, I get a text with an address and a time. It's in London, so I'll have to hitch a ride with Gavin.

After he wakes up, I tell him I left my birth control back at the flat and need to get back to take it right away. After all our activity last night, he can't argue with that.

With traffic, it takes us close to three hours to get back to London, leaving me just enough time to get ready for my appointment. Before rushing off to the office, Gavin tells me he wants to be on the road to the country house by five. I'll be cutting it close, but I'm sure it will work out. It's not like he'll leave without me!

My trusty cab driver, Lionel, is waiting for me at the curb after a quick primping session. After fighting traffic across town, we pull up to a sweet little cottage in a lovely neighborhood in a part of London I've never been to.

Making my way up the walk, I get cold feet. I turn around to bolt, but Lionel's already left. I pull out my phone to call him when the door opens, and a tall woman with red, curly hair waves me in. She's wearing leggings and a T-shirt. Her relaxed demeanor puts me at ease.

"Hey, I'm Josie," she says when she shakes my hand. "Welcome to my studio. Come on in."

She takes my coat and purse and hangs them in the coat closet. She motions for me to sit down in one of the two arm chairs. She prepared tea and pours us both a cup.

"How do you know Emily?"

I add honey to my tea and blow on it to cool it down. "We were college roommates. You?"

"We run in similar circles. I was in Paris working, and Em was at a few wrap parties. That woman knows everyone."

Josie offers me a plate of cookies and crackers, but I'm too nervous to eat. "She sure does. Thank you for squeezing me in."

"I'm not much into holidays, so this really is perfect timing for me. Tell me, what are we doing today?"

Deep breath. "My boyfriend and I had a bet that I lost. Loser is supposed to get a tattoo of the winner's flag on their ass. I was drunk; it was a stupid, stupid bet. There is no way I'm actually going to get a tattoo of the British flag on my ass, so I thought maybe we could take some photos of me in these." I hold up a pair of Union Jack boy shorts. "I thought it might make one hell of a Christmas present."

A wide grin spreads across her face and she starts bouncing on the balls of her feet like a kid in a toy store. "Oh, darling, we're going to have so much fun. I'm glad you came without makeup. I'll touch you up a little, but I think this will be better *au natural*. Go get changed."

While she sets up the lighting, I get into my skimpy boy shorts.

When I get out of the restroom, Josie holds a bottle of tequila. "Em said this may help."

"It's always time for tequila!"

I take three shots before moving over to the vanity. I offer one to Josie, but she politely declines. "I'm not the one in my skivvies, dearie."

Josie puts a little bit of powder, mascara, and gloss on me. "Let's get started, shall we?"

She walks me down the hall into one of her shooting rooms. There is a white drop cloth coming down from the ceiling and tons of lights. She puts on her "sexy playlist", starting with *Pony* by Ginuwine. It's hard not to feel sexy with that song playing. She turns on a fan to give me that windblown look, but all I feel are goose bumps spreading across my skin. "Don't worry," she tells me. "Those won't show up. Except the nips. I'll keep those all pebbly. Taunting Gavin. Too bad I can't make the photo paper lickable."

I swallow hard, feeling exposed and rethinking my plan. Maybe a gift certificate to IKEA would make a good Christmas gift for Gavin?

She puts her arm around my shoulder. "Just kidding. All your bits will be covered up. I find that creating an image that sparks the imagination is far more seductive than one that just lets it all hang out there." Once I start breathing again, she says, "Come on. Let's get started."

She tells me to center myself in the middle of the white drop cloth. "Look sexy," she orders, which makes me burst out in giggles. She pulls the camera down from her face. "We're going for sexy, not silly," which only makes me laugh harder.

"Ass up! Tighten those abs! Chin down! Pout those lips!" Josie barks at me like a drill sergeant. She poses me in awkward positions that show off my body without exposing my breasts. "Put this arm here. Keep that arm there. Twist this leg to the right and hold it," she tells me. Like holding it is the easiest thing to do.

This is why models do yoga. Not so they can stay toned and whatnot (clearly that is what Photoshop is for), but so they can stay in these seemingly natural positions that're anything but natural. More than a few times, I fall on my ass.

"Sultry. Steamy. Sexy. This is the look we want. You want him to see these pictures and have the urge to mount you, not pick you up and kiss your boo-boo. Find your inner sex kitten and let her out!" All of this encouragement was meant to get me in the mood, but it just made me laugh harder. Which made her laugh harder. More than once we had to stop and pull ourselves together.

After falling on my ass again, she says "Let's mix it up a little. Do you trust me?"

"Well, you've taken pictures of me in my underwear for an hour now. I'd say I trust you."

She pours another round of shots. "Good. Now strip."

"Totally nude?" I gasp. "I'm going to need a few more shots then."

"Don't worry, you'll be covered up in the pictures. No nip slips or beaver shots. It'll be clear you're naked, but it will be tasteful."

"Ah, tasteful porn." I laugh. "These had better not show up on the internet. I'm supposed to be pregnant."

She walks over to adjust the lighting. "What are you talking about? Nude pics when you're pregnant are all the rage." She stops in her tracks. "OMG, that's you? I thought you looked familiar. You're not really pregnant, are you?"

"Nope," I say, downing another shot. "But the tabloids love to weave their tales."

She holds up the bottle of tequila. "Phew. I was worried there for a second."

"Are you drinking with me this time?" I ask.

She pours two shots. "Why the hell not? I've been staring at your ass all afternoon, I think we are old friends by now. "Here's to the paparazzi and your fake pregnancy."

We take another hour of photos before she pulls out a real British flag and hands it to me.

I look at her skeptically. "I hope it isn't disrespectful for me to be rolling around naked in the flag."

"He'll love it, I promise," she says.

After shooting a million more shots, she says, "Okay, I've got more than enough to sell to the tabloids. I'm going to make a fortune."

My heart drops, and all the oxygen sucks out of my body.

She holds her hands up. "Kidding," she says. "Just kidding. You've got to lighten up! I don't care if I'm homeless and destitute, I wouldn't sell a thing to them."

My heart starts to beat again. "That was cold, Josie. Cold and cruel."

"I'm a bint, what can I say? Go get dressed. I think your cab will be here any minute."

I look at the clock for the first time since we got here. Damn that went fast! I rush to the rest room to change.

Once I'm dressed, I find Josie on her computer downloading the images. When she notices me behind her she turns off her monitor. "No peeking! I'll go through these tonight and email you the proofs. Once you pick, I'll get them printed and put them in a portfolio. It will look smashing. My mum and dad live out by where you're staying, so I can drop it off to you tomorrow."

"That's so fast! How is that possible?"

"I own a print shop. We're closed for the holiday, so I have total access without having to worry about all those pesky customers." She winks.

"Thank you so much, Josie. Gavin is going to love them. I hope!"

She hands me my coat and purse. "If he doesn't love these, he's either gay or dead."

I kiss her cheek. "Thank you. How much do I owe you?"

"I can't take your money. This was too much fun. Promise you'll come visit me when you're back in town. You bring the tequila next time."

"You're on!" I say as I walk out the door. Closing the door, I pray I didn't just make a colossal mistake. If these pictures come out terrible, I'm without a gift. If she sells them to someone, I'll forever be humiliated.

I make it back to the flat just before Gavin, giving me

time to throw a few things into a bag to fulfill my cover story. Gavin spends the whole drive to the country house on the phone, addressing problems with his project. I love how much he cares about bringing soldiers home to see their families for the holidays. Tomorrow is a big day for the project;—hundreds of soldiers are flying home for a forty-eight-hour leave funded by Gavin's company. With so many moving parts to the project, each one seems to have a hiccup.

While he works, I get emails from Josie. The pictures are amazing. Despite the giggle fits and uncomfortable poses, she made me look sexy. It looks so natural even though it was anything but. They're tasteful, artistic. I don't feel like I'm looking at tawdry porn, but it sure is naughty. If they make him say "naughty" over and over, I'll be in heaven. On the pictures with the green back drop, she superimposed the Union Jack in the background. I'm amazed. It's not a tattoo, but I think he will like these better.

When we pull in the driveway, I have a chance to take in the estate. The decorations make it look spectacular. Even though this place is something out of a movie, the decorations make it look homey and festive.

"Mason did a great job, but it feels naked," I tease. "It really needs a mechanical Santa and reindeer sleigh covered in blinking neon lights. Without that, it doesn't say 'Merry Christmas' to me."

"That's because it's 'Happy Christmas.' There will be nothing with neon on my house," he insists.

I know he's pretty sure I'm kidding, but a part of him wonders if I'm not. He doesn't say "our house," which makes me take pause. He always calls the flat "our house." Maybe it's because this is his family estate, or maybe he just doesn't want me to think I have free rein to put pink flamingos in his flower beds. There's always the third possibility. That he meant nothing by it at all and I'm blowing it out of proportion. It certainly wouldn't be the first time.

We spend the rest of the night decorating the tree. I love all the ornaments we bought, especially the red double decker buses, red phone booths, and Big Ben. We have a violent screaming match over tinsel. I've never had a tree without it, and he's adamantly opposed to finding it everywhere in the house for years to come. Fortunately, our screaming match turns into passion. Lamps are knocked over, furniture is pushed around, and curtains are pulled out of the wall. You know sex is hot when you end up with rug burn and you need to call a handyman.

After we're wiped out from our tour of sexual destruction, we go back to the solarium for another night under the stars. It's cold and the floor is hard, but the view is to die for.

Chapter Twenty-Three

Gavin is called back to London to deal with some last minute problems. I'd like to go with him to meet some of the soldiers and their families, but Josie is on her way over with the pictures. I'm anxious to see them without worrying about Gavin walking in.

"What the hell, woman! You didn't tell me you live in a castle," Josie says when I greet her at the door.

"This isn't my house; it's my boyfriend's. It's ridiculous, I know. I'm still getting used to it myself."

"Well, show me around, then I'll show you what I brought."

I now understand why people have staff in houses like this. Twice, Hazel had to come find us because I got lost and kept walking in circles. Yes, this place is *that* big. Gavin needs to install "You are Here" directories. Or perhaps hand out maps at the door like at Disney World.

After my horribly guided tour, I put together a platter of munchies while she goes to her car to get the prints "Close your eyes," she instructs when she returns. "No peeking until I tell you." I hear her moving about, and she finally says, "Okay, open them."

The album is leather bound with a cover designed like the British flag. As I flip through the pages, the pictures blow my mind. She did a blend of black-and-white and color. The shots range from playful to sexy and seductive. I'm never seen fully naked, but there's enough shown to spark the imagination. This is way better than a tattoo.

"Oh my god, Josie. These are unbelievable. It's hard to believe that's me!"

She pats my arm. "Believe it. You're one sexy wench."

I feel a blush cross my cheeks. "Please. I've seen your work. You shoot supermodels. You've seen my ass. I have dimples, and not the good kind."

She rolls her eyes and laughs. "I'm not going to dignify that with a response."

I reach over and give her a hug. "Thank you. This is really so much better than I could have imagined."

"I'm so glad you like it. I stayed up all night putting it together."

"Josie! You didn't have to do that. Please, let me pay you for this!" I say.

She waves me off. "Not a chance. I had too much fun. I've been doing so much commercial work lately, it was therapeutic to do something real. I have one more thing to show you. Don't freak out until you've thought about it."

With a warning like that, I'm already freaking out. She walks behind the sofa and brings out a 4'x4' package. She unwraps the brown paper to reveal a blow up of one of the black and whites. The flag has fallen out of the shot, so all I can see is me. Between the angle of the shot and the way my body is arched, all that can be seen is the lens traveling down my abs and thighs. No one would know it's me, but I'm not sure I'd want this put up on a wall. Where would he even hang something like this?

She takes a sip of her tea. "Just think about it," she begs. "If you don't want to keep it, give it back, and I'll put it up. I could sell it and make a killing."

"You will do no such thing! Just let me think about it, okay?"

"Please. If I wanted to make some serious cash, I'd sell the story about how your twins are in danger because of your reckless tequila drinking."

I shake my head. "I should introduce you to my friend James. I swear he's conspiring with the tabloids to perpetuate this silly farce."

Josie picks up a cookie. "Is he fit?" she asks before taking a bite.

"Um, I'm not sure if he works out."

She wipes the crumbs from her lips. "Silly American. Fit means sexy. Like your boyfriend's fit."

"You Brits and your damn slang. Would it kill you to have just said sexy? Yes, James is totally hot. He's crazy smart and a total prankster."

"Well, well, well. I'm going away on holiday. But when I return I think you will have to introduce me," she says. "Speaking of holiday, I have to dash."

I show her out and kiss her goodbye.

Gavin's bogged down in London and may not get back until late. It isn't the Christmas Eve I was dreaming about, but the cause is worth it. Hazel and I run into town for some last minute shopping. When we return, she and Mason leave to visit their family, leaving me in this big, creepy house completely alone.

This is my thirteenth Christmas without my parents. It never gets easier. Even though my memories of them dim a little bit each year, I still ache for them. Growing up, my house was the neighborhood party house, celebrating everything from the Fourth of July to Valentine's Day. Mom was an outstanding cook, and all it took to pack our house with people was a rumor she was making a feast. Every Christmas Eve, I swear half the town showed up. As a child, I thought people were desperate for my mom's apple pie, but the adult in me thinks they were probably just trying to get tipsy before midnight mass.

Feeling nostalgic, I decide to cook. I don't do that very often, at least not without a visit from the fire department. I need to feel closer to my family so I make my mother's beef stew. It's heaven in a bowl and next to impossible to screw up. The longer it cooks, the better it gets. With Gavin's ETA up in the air, it's ideal for tonight.

After wrapping the rest of the presents, I build a fire and curl up with my Kindle. Next thing I know, I'm woken up by my phone.

"I'm so sorry, luv," Gavin says. "There was an accident on the motorway. I'm in dead stopped traffic."

"Too bad. I've been reading steamy romance novels all night. I'm all revved up with nowhere to go," I tease.

"You minx. I could be hours from home!"

"Want to guess what I'm wearing?" I look down at Gavin's beat-up Oxford sweatshirt and a pair his sweatpants from high school that I found in a closet. They're huge on me, so I had to roll the top over a few times. "I'll give you a hint. It's very sexy."

"You realize this is torture, don't you?"

"You know what's torture? Sitting here in this red, lace nightie all by myself. The lace is so sheer, anyone could walk right in and see every, single part of me."

"Lil," he says with a husky voice.

"I should go put a robe on and cover myself up, but I'm so hot. I've got the fire roaring. How is it where you are? Is your fire roaring?"

"Oh, God Lily.

"You have to stop or I'm going to smash up my car." I can hear the hunger in his voice. When he gets like that, he's insatiable. If I want him to make it back in one piece, I'd better cool it.

Since it's going to be a long night, I get up and throw another log on the fire. "Okay. I'll stop. I need you to get home safe."

He audibly exhales. "Working on it, luv. Working on it," he grumbles. "Hey, I've never asked you. Do you open presents on Christmas Eve or Christmas morning?"

Nice subject change, Oxford. "Christmas morning. Doesn't everyone?" I desperately want to say something about him opening me as his present, but I refrain.

"We always did on Christmas Eve," he answers.

I roll my eyes. "I didn't realize Santa made a priority delivery run for the obscenely wealthy."

"My parents never did the whole Father Christmas thing."

I'm gobsmacked. "*What*? You never believed in Santa Claus?"

"I think it was far too whimsical for my parents. Plus, it takes some commitment to keep up the myth and mystery. They never had that in them. Mason and Hazel did the shopping for presents."

I walk to the bar and pour a glass of wine. "Gavin, that's just heartbreaking. I believed in Santa till I was almost eleven. The only reason I stopped was because my parents sat me down to tell me the truth after I got teased by all my classmates. I was devastated and wouldn't leave my room for a week. At one point, I tried to get on a bus to Canada. I was going to hitchhike to the North Pole to prove them wrong."

He laughs. "This coming from the 'I'll believe it when I see it' girl? Luv, that may be the most adorable thing I've ever heard."

I know he's trying to poke fun, but he's right. I have no idea how to respond. I was such a naïve, trusting girl, and I've morphed into a jaded, hard woman who keeps everyone at arm's length.

"Shall we open presents tonight or tomorrow?" I ask to change the subject.

"At this rate, I won't get there until New Year's, so it won't make much difference."

"Don't be silly! Just tell me where you hid my present, and I'll open it tomorrow morning. It's important to keep with tradition," I tease. I walk over to the desk and start looking in the drawers.

"Stop snooping. Your present is with me, so you're out of luck, luv."

"Fine," I growl, abandoning my search. "Hurry up then. I made dinner!"

"You? Made dinner?"

"Yup," I say, walking to the kitchen to stir the stew. "Try not to sound too shocked."

"Just so you know, there's a fire extinguisher right

next to the stove. The emergency number in England is 999. When the kitchen catches fire, call 999 right away, as the fire brigade is a ways away."

"Ha. Ha. Ha. I won't burn down your house."

"Try to remember it's been around for six generations. It's an albatross to me sometimes, but I'm not sure I want to torch the place."

I walk back to the study and curl up on the sofa. "Have some faith. Anyway, the ghosts won't let me burn it down if I tried," I insist.

"Too right! Oh, traffic is moving. Maybe there is hope for me to deliver your presents tonight after all."

"I'm going to get back to my book then. I'm in the middle of a steamy scene where he's ... delivering his package."

"You naughty, naughty girl. You've given me lots to think about for the rest of my drive. Cheers."

****

"Wake up, luv," Gavin coos in my ear.

I'm so warm and comfortable, I don't want to open my eyes. Gavin is wrapped around me, and I feel the hot lick from the flames in the fireplace. The warmth draws me back to sleep while Gavin's kisses on my neck urge me into consciousness.

He looks down at my pajamas. "Funny, I pictured your outfit quite differently during our conversation."

Damn, I meant to change but must have fallen asleep. I give him a shy smile and shrug. I try to think of a witty comeback. Something sexy and provocative, but my brain is still asleep. "I ... changed?"

He kisses that spot behind my ear that sends jolts to my core. "While I do find it sexy when you wear my clothes, do you know what I think looks sexiest on you?"

"What?" I whisper.

"Nothing at all." In one swift moment, he pulls my sweatshirt over my head, and pushes my sweatpants down. After my clothes have been removed, his hand clutches my neck possessively, almost too rough. The way he's holding my neck forces me to look at him. "You were a very naughty girl, Lily. Teasing me like that whilst I was driving."

I bite my lip. "I'd say I'll never do it again, but then I'd be lying."

He picks me up aggressively, throwing me over his shoulder. Gavin's never shy in the bedroom, but the way he manhandles me, it's almost barbaric. I'll have to remember to push his buttons more often. He carries me down the hall to the billiards room and places me on the edge of the pool table. Digging his fingers into my hips, he abruptly flips me over.

He runs his hands over my backside, occasionally dipping his fingers between my thighs. Not far enough to touch anything but close enough to drive me crazy with need. "Thanks to you, I drove over one hundred kilometers with a raging hard on. All I could think about was how I was going to fuck you when I got home. I could barely keep my eyes on the road."

"What'd you come up with?" I ask.

"Driving with a hard on is dangerous." He slaps my ass, the sound echoing against the stone walls of the room. I jerk, not because it hurt, but rather because it shocked me. Gavin doesn't strike me as a spanker, but I should know better than to assume anything with him. This man never ceases to surprise me. He gently rubs the spot where he'd slapped.

He bends over me, his erection grinding into my ass. After sweeping my hair to one side, he whispers in my ear. "You have no idea how hard it was, driving—"

I interrupt him. "How hard was it?"

"Naughty girl." He slaps again, harder this time. That one had to have left a mark. While he rubs away the sting he says, "I almost had to pull over and release myself. That's how hard my cocks was. But I wanted to save it for you."

I defiantly look over my shoulder at him. "So are you going to talk my ear off all night, or are you going to give it to me?" Maybe that wasn't the right answer. Seeing this side of Gavin is so sexy, and I want to play along. But it seems even my dirty talk makes me sound like a snarky bitch.

Slap. "Always so fucking cheeky." This time he doesn't rub away the sting. I hear his belt unbuckle and the soft swoosh of his pants falling to the floor. Without warning, he slams into me. I tilt my head back and moan.

He has one hand on my hip and the other on my shoulder, his fingers digging so hard into my skin they're bound to leave a mark. With the depths he's reaching inside me, the pleasure is well worth the pain.

My forearms are resting on the edge of the pool table. The felt is chafing my wrists with each powerful thrust. It burns, but I don't want him to stop.

He finally starts to hit the money spot, and tingles begin in my toes, promising an orgasm. "Ah," I moan. "Don't stop."

Suddenly, he pulls out. Panting, I wait a moment, preparing for him to slam into me again. But he doesn't. *What the hell?* I'm about to ask him if everything is okay, when he flips me over. Now that I'm facing him, I try to read his expression to anticipate what's going to happen next, but he gives nothing way.

"Are you punishing me by not allowing me to come?" I ask.

He harshly pushes me, causing me to fall back on the table. Gavin being Gavin, he puts a hand out to make sure I don't hit my head. He may be playing the bad boy role at the moment, but he can't hide who he is at heart.

Once I'm lying down, he hooks both of my knees and pulls, so that my knees are bent and my ass is at the edge of the table. "This is for me, not you," he says before diving between my legs. He swirls his tongue around my clit. I start to moan, but last time I did that he pulled away, so I stop myself and I bite my lip.

He's taking his time. Slowly licking and sucking, as though I'm a delicacy he's trying to savor. I gasp as he slides two fingers inside me. The more attention he gives my body, the more I ache to come. Desperate for more, I grind my pelvis against his tongue, creating the frenzied friction I crave. Unable to hold it in, I moan in ecstasy.

The son of a bitch pulls away again.

I open my eyes and see him sitting on his heels with a Cheshire grin. He wipes his mouth with the back of his hand. "I told you it was for me, not you."

"Oh yeah?" I reply as I slide my hand down my stomach to my wet core. I'm so worked up it only takes a few seconds before I scream with my release. I open my eyes as my body comes down from the high. I flash him a shit eating grin. "That was for me, not you."

He jumps up from his crouched position, and places one hand on either side of my shoulders, hovering over me. His hard cock brushes against my thigh. I came seconds ago, but I'm already yearning for more. "You may have enjoyed that, but trust me, I enjoyed every second as well."

Lowering his head, he takes my nipple into his mouth. My body is still sensitive from my orgasm. Each lick sends a shockwave through my body. He teases me by running his dick along my thigh. I push my pelvis toward him, but he pulls away.

I close my eyes, struggling to find the patience for this game. Just as I take a deep breath, he grabs my hips and pushes them back on the table. "Watching you make yourself come is one of the sexiest things I've ever seen," he says. "But not as sexy as when you come undone all over my cock." I gasp as he plunges into me.

I close my eyes and let my head fall to the side. "Open your eyes," he says as he grabs my chin so that I'm looking at him. "I want to watch you come."

He sure is putting those abs to work. He pounds into me so hard I worry he's going to break the damn table. He changes his angle, now hitting my g spot. I keep my eyes fixed on his as the wave builds. My whole body tenses, followed by the euphoric release.

Spurred on by my orgasm, Gavin picks up speed. I can tell by the devious gleam in his eyes that he wants to push me to another orgasm, but I know I don't have it in me. I squeeze my core with every ounce of energy I have. He gasps as he drops his head back. "You're gripping my dick like a vice. You're going to make me come"

"Eyes on me, Oxford."

His eyes meet mine as he finds his release. Breathless, he collapses on top of me. "Who knew I could get traffic to work in my favor?" I say with a chuckle.

He pushes up from the pool table and gives me a quick kiss. "One thing England has in abundance is traffic. Perhaps we'll have to play this game more often."

His stomach growls. "Maybe after I feed you," I reply.

"Yes, I'm curious about this meal that you cooked. I can't tell you how thrilled I was to drive up and see the house still standing."

I poke him in the stomach. "Shut it."

He stands, then collects our clothes from the floor while I run to the bathroom to clean up. While I'm washing my hands, he opens the bathroom door to deliver my sweats. Once I'm dressed, I meet him in the kitchen where he's dishing out bowls of stew. I pour two glasses of wine while he brings the bowls to the table.

I pick up my spoon and dig in. The first bite is heaven. Just like my mother's. I notice out of the corner of my eye, Gavin watching me carefully. "Go ahead, try some. It won't kill you."

He takes a bite, and a look of disbelief comes over his face. "This is pretty good," he says.

"Don't look so surprised."

He pauses mid-bite. "The oven caught fire when you tried to make Cumberland pie. Not to mention –"

I hold my hand up. "I'm well aware of my culinary failures. But this," I say pointing to my bowl with my spoon. "This, I make well. So, tell me about today."

"It was stressful, but one thousand seven hundred and forty-three soldiers are home for the holiday."

I lean over and kiss his temple. "You're a good man, Gavin Edwards. Don't ever let anyone tell you otherwise."

"I'm not sure my employees would say that. About twenty of them were there with me until the last soldier boarded the last plane. They gave up time with their families to make sure the day went off without a hitch."

"If I had to guess, they were there because they wanted to be there, not just because it's their job. Your enthusiasm is inspiring."

"And I pay bloody well," he says before taking a bite.

The rest of dinner is spent with him filling me in on the details. He spent part of the day at Heathrow waiting with families for their soldier's flights to arrive. I love how his eyes sparkle when he talks about the families he met, and the touching moment when the soldier walks into baggage claim and finds the family waiting there. Apparently someone wanted to make a documentary of it, but Gavin refused. He felt those moments should be kept private.

After we clean up the dishes, we climb back into our makeshift bed. Once the lights are out and we're both quiet, he opens up about his time in the military. He doesn't talk about it often, so I'm touched he feels comfortable opening up to me.

His stories keep me captivated till dawn.

"Sun's coming up," I say as I see it creeping over the horizon.

"Hmmm," he moans, possibly half asleep.

"We have people coming over, and we need to get cooking. You're the least toxic in the kitchen."

He responds with soft snores.

Looks like it's me and the turkey. God help us all.

Chapter Twenty-Four

Fuck. Fuck. Fuck. Why didn't I ever learn to cook? One of the many downsides of losing my mother young is I never learned how to cook things like a turkey. I have a cookbook, but it's completely useless! Stuffed vs. unstuffed. Did I brine? What the hell is brine? I just need to know how many minutes per pound and at what temperature, but the damn cookbook is American, and my turkey is in grams and the oven is in Celsius. Fuck the damn metric system!

Hazel's gone, and Gavin is probably as useless as I am. My computer and iPad are both in the solarium where my very tired boyfriend is sleeping. However, I spy Gavin's briefcase in the front hall. Digging around in it for his iPad, I find a little box. A little robin's-egg-blue box. His briefcase slips from my hands as I stare at the little box of impending doom.

NO. NO. NO. NO. NO. NO. I have a turkey to cook and a kitchen to try to not burn down. I can't think about little blue boxes. My cell phone ringing in the distance makes me jump and throw the box across the room as if it's a venomous snake. Ignoring my phone, I crawl around searching for the box so I can return it to its hiding place, hopefully for a very long time. I give great consideration to "misplacing" the box. No box means no ring. No ring means no proposal. No proposal means not having to think about things that suck the oxygen out of my lungs. Instead, I grab the iPad and walk away, trying to pretend I never saw that box and that I won't have to have a marriage conversation soon. Denial is beautiful.

The iPad and I figure out a plan for the turkey, and I stick it in the oven. I make the sign of the cross in front of the oven, praying not to burn down the house or give us all salmonella. My phone won't stop ringing, so I have to go on a treasure hunt to try to find it. In a house with so much stone and marble, sounds echo off the walls, making it hard to figure out exactly where my phone is. Eventually I find it in the library.

"Where the hell have you been?" Em screams.

"Sorry, I lost my phone, and hide-and-seek is next to impossible in this house. Once you get here, you'll understand. It's bigger than Sacred Heart was."

"Hmmm." She's trying to sound bored, but I know she's curious. "I'll be there soon, I think. The GPS says less than an hour."

"See you soon."

Over an hour and a half later, Em arrives. When I open the door, she says, "It's a fucking castle, Lily. You didn't tell me it was a castle." Her driver brings in her bags and sets them by the door.

She hands him a tip. He tips his hat and closes the door as he leaves. I glare at her. "You couldn't have rented a car? You made the poor man work on Christmas?"

"Don't look at me like that," she replies. "That man now has five hundred more bucks in his pocket to spend on Christmas. That's how the economy works." She hands me her coat. "Now, show me the loo. That drive from the airport is a bitch."

While she freshens up, I put together some nosh food and pour some juice.

"When's everyone coming?" she asks, munching on a croissant.

"Between four and five, I think. We wanted everyone to be able to see their families. They do Christmas dinner here early, like around one. So I just told people to swing on by when they were done. Liam said he doesn't know when he can get here. His parents host a big gathering with"

"I've heard," she says. "Eight brothers and sisters and their spouses and kids and in-laws. *He* was smart enough to say that he wouldn't invite me because he knew it would make me miserable."

"You've been talking to Liam?" I can't keep up with

her love life!

"Don't start, Lily. I talk to lots of people. You said he was organizing the Yankee Swap, so we discussed it. As you know, Liam's fun. I enjoy spending time with him, but there's nothing more to it. Stop reading into it." She walks over to the fridge and starts rummaging around. "Do you have any champagne to go with this juice? I'll even take some vodka if you have some chilled."

"I have no idea, but you can check. You'll be drinking on your own, though. I'm still waking up. Too early for me to start drinking. If I start now, I'll be asleep before everyone gets here."

She shrugs. "Yeah, you're probably right." A devilish look crosses her face. "Stay here. I have something for you." She runs back to her bags in the entrance. When she returns she hands me a box wrapped in black wrapping paper.

"What is this? You don't *do* presents." I shake the box but can't tell what it is.

"No, I don't. But I had this brilliant idea and had to get it. As you can tell by the wrapping, this is not a holiday gift."

I tear the wrapping off and laugh hysterically. "What the hell is this, Em?" It's a package of five dolls that look creepily like Gavin.

She looks at me like I'm crazy. "What do you mean? It's the Gavin Doll collection. There's Tux Gavin, G. I. Gavin, Alpha CEO Gavin, Sexually Frustrated Gavin, notice the short running shorts, and Club Gavin. If you push the button on the back it goes 'unce unce unce.'"

I try to say "What the fuck," but I'm laughing too hard to formulate the words.

"You always describe Gavin like he's a Ken doll, and I have a friend in the doll biz. Open it up. I made sure he's anatomically correct."

My jaw drops. "You didn't!" I tear open the package.

She pulls out Sexually Frustrated Gavin and lowers his pants. "Since I don't have first-hand experience, I had to guess on the dimensions. I tried to be generous. Was I right?"

Blush scorches my cheeks.

"What?" she asks. "Bigger?"

I smirk. "Yeah, bigger. Much bigger."

She stares at the now naked Gavin doll. "Damn."

I grab the doll from her. "Stop ogling my boyfriend."

She dresses the doll and puts it back in the box. "Well, I've seen Gavin's goodies, let's see yours. Show me your porn."

"My *what*?"

"The pictures Josie took. I'm dying to see them."

I give her a dirty look. "The pictures aren't porn. They're tasteful."

"Bitch, you're naked. It's porn. Now gimme before your British beefcake wakes up!"

I clean up our plates and put them in the dishwasher,

and lead her to the library. "The pictures aren't the only thing I have for him."

She sits on the sofa and crosses her legs. "Oh?"

I nod. "I submitted my application for a visa. To stay here."

"Well, well, well. Look at you. Pretty bold move for you, Lily," she says. "London looks good on you. I'm proud of you."

I throw another log on the fire, then stab the logs below with the poker. "Don't speak to soon. I just found a pretty blue box in Gavin's briefcase."

"Ahhh, and now you're searching for the eject button. Don't be a tool, Lil. You have a freaking fairy tale going on here. Look around. Don't throw it away because you have commitment issues."

I sit opposite her and bring my knees to my chest. "I don't have commitment issues," I insist. "I have marriage issues. This is going so fast; I don't want to ruin it by moving even faster. I was ready to make a big step—not marriage, but a big step. Now I'm totally freaked out and rethinking everything."

"Why? Why would you rethink everything? We both know you came to your decision after a ridiculous amount of angst and worry. You came to the right decision for you. Don't back out because you're scared. If it makes you feel any better, I doubt it's a ring. At least not 'the' ring. No way Gavin would make that move without clearing it with me first." She looks at me as though I'm being unreasonable. "While we're sharing news, Max has been suspended."

My jaw drops. "What? When? Why?"

"Putting that journalism degree to good use, I see," she teases.

I lightly punch her in the shoulder. "Bitch, fill me in. Why didn't he call me?"

"He got back to DC and put in his report. The higher-ups are pissed, and he's suspended pending an investigation."

Damn it, this is my fault. "I've got to call him."

She holds her hands up. "Don't, Lily. He needs time," she says. "He's frustrated and really confused. If you talk to him now, you'll both say things you'll regret."

He blames me. She doesn't have to say it. It's my fault, me and my dumb-ass plan.

"Come on now, show me that porn," she orders.

******

Hours later, Gavin strolls into the library. As he walks in, I put my fingers to my lips, then point to Em, who's passed out after looking at the pictures. I cover Em with a blanket and motion for him to follow me to the hallway.

"Merry Christmas, sleepy head." I point up at the mistletoe we're standing under.

He pulls me into his arms and kisses me breathless.

"Happy Christmas, luv. How's the turkey?"

"Oh, crap!" I sprint to the kitchen and find it still in one piece. The oven, however, does not appear to have ever been turned on. It's set for the right temperature, but I apparently needed to press start.

I open the over door. Gavin and I look at the raw turkey, then at each other. "Who wants Chinese?" I say with a guilty grin.

Two hours later, James arrives, and he and Gavin take a walk around the property. One perk about being in such a big house is all the windows to spy from. Em and I run from room to room, following Gavin and James. Em makes up dialogue to match their facial expressions. According to her "lip reading"; they watched *Magic Mike* recently and think they need to open a chain of male strip clubs. The conversation gets heated at times, which Em declares is over who is the better dancer: Channing Tatum or Joe Manganiello. It's a tough call; I can see why they almost come to blows over it. But when the boys come back to the house, they're laughing.

"Clear the air?" I ask Gavin.

"As much as we can. There're still some rough edges, but nothing we'll sacrifice our friendship for." He kisses my temple.

Moments later, Basil, Eliza, Percy, and Poppy arrive. Heath and Liam aren't far behind. They were kind enough to pick up Chinese on the way over.

"Chinese? Why are we doing Chinese?" Percy asks.

I unpack the take-out bags and place the containers on the center of the table. "I ruined dinner," I admit. "Why was I cooking anyway, Perc? You're the big-time fancy chef. I apparently can't even turn the oven on. We're in luck the guys found a place that was open."

"Chinese is always open on Christmas. It's possibly their biggest sales day of the year. New Years, I'm cooking," Percy promises.

We eat ourselves into an MSG-induced coma. The boys find a *Dr. Who* marathon, and we all become transfixed. I've never watched it before, but it's just what the doctor ordered after my dumpling indulgence.

Liam's the first one to get antsy, and he motivates us all to go to the bowling alley in the basement. At least once a year, they get together for a "bowling death match," as Liam describes it. Since we're all highly competitive, this has the makings of a brutal night. We're playing for pride, but Em decides we must make it a drinking game. Two shots for gutter balls. When someone gets a strike, everyone else drinks. Five hours and seven games later, all of our arms are worn out and no one is sober enough to keep score without a calculator. Liam and Em were the high scorers, but the rest of us are sure something shady went on there. Those two together are nothing but trouble.

Eliza begs for a food break, so we all head upstairs and heat up leftovers. Heath and I arm wrestle for the last of the dumplings, which I win —because I kick him in the shins.

"You've got to come out here," Liam calls as we clean up the dinner dishes.

"Where is he?" I ask.

"He must be outside. He was grabbing something from his car," Em replies.

As it turns out, while we were in the basement, it snowed close to four inches. As the whole group stands on the front stoop admiring the snow, Liam pelts us with snowballs. Bedlam ensues. This isn't your Christmas movie snowball fight that ends with everyone making snow angles. It's a knockdown, drag-out, take-no-prisoners snowball fight. Alliances are formed, but betrayal is common. Every person is out for themselves, and no one's opposed to playing dirty. I feign getting something in my eye to create a distraction for Liam and James, then my partners-in-crime turn on me twenty minutes later, carrying me into a snow pile. Basil has a black eye from one of Em's snowballs, and Poppy may have sprained her ankle. We're frozen, battered, and weary. It was spectacular.

After hot showers and pajamas, we drink hot chocolate and Irish coffee for the Yankee swap. Liam explains that we all take numbers and pick a wrapped gift in order of the number selected. We can either keep our gift or swap it out for an already opened gift. I get number one which means that I open the first gift, but I get to wait to the very end to decide if I want to swap.

The gifts are hilarious and random. I'm used to swaps with twenty dollar limits. Liam didn't place a limit, and these guys went all out. Two different sets of vibrator packages that must have cost a small fortune are opened. I'm fairly confident Liam and Em either teamed up to buy those, or they're just that in sync. Either way, it's frightening. They pick as a team and split the booty, looking pretty cozy on the sofa. Cozy enough to make me wonder if they'll be keeping to the room assignments tonight.

A set of top-of-the-line cookware with a gift certificate to Percy's restaurant, a gift basket of four bottles of top-shelf scotch, a certificate for a tattoo of any size, color, or location, and a full spa package are just a few of the gifts. The Snugglie I bought doesn't quite hold a candle. Thankfully Gavin's weekend at any Four Seasons makes up for it. The only gift that tops mine is a twelve-foot inflatable Frosty. *Thank you, Em.*

After all the gifts are opened, I have to decide if I want to keep the complete set of *James Bond* on Blu-Ray or if I want to trade.

"Get the vibrators," Em shouts.

"If you take one of those, I will be mortally wounded," Gavin responds.

"Oh, lighten up, Gavin," Liam says. "Toys keep it interesting!"

"If you need toys to keep it interesting, that's your call," Gavin retorts, slurring his words. "Last I checked, I'm a man, and I don't need to play with toys. I don't need something with batteries to keep Lily... interested. All I need is hard work, dedication, and commitment to excellence."

"Mate, wasn't that our primary school motto?" James asks, causing the three very drunk boys to laugh hysterically.

"A strong, proper education you had there, Gavin," Eliza jokes.

Before I have a chance to decide on my gift, Gavin

picks me up and says, "Good night all. Time for me to make things interesting. Happy Christmas!"

He practically sprints to the solarium and kicks the door closed. The windows in the solarium were fogged up until dawn. No batteries required.

Chapter Twenty-Five

No one rolled out of bed until late in the afternoon. Occasionally a faint buzzing, followed by giggles and quiet moans, could be heard through the halls. I know those giggles well, so my only question is if Em is alone with her array of vibrators or if she has the company of a handsome rugby player. I know better than to ask.

We're all sore and varying degrees of hung-over. Too many hours of bowling and drinking followed by a snowball version of *Call of Duty* left us walking wounded. Poppy, Eliza, and I are the most functional of the group, so we run to the market. Percy cooks a traditional full English breakfast of sausage, bacon, eggs, beans, mushrooms, tomatoes, and something called black pudding. Heath and Percy had a heated debate about whether the pudding is really English or Scottish. I've never seen people get that passionate over pudding. Whichever country it's from, I stay clear of it. It looks disgusting and I think it's made with blood.

Most of the gang needs to return to London. Some for work, others for family or Boxing Day obligations. This leaves me, Gavin, Em, and Liam at the country house. I think James wanted to stay, but with whatever's happening with Liam and Em, I think he felt like a fifth wheel.

Once he's packed up, we meet him in the foyer.

"Do you have to go?" I ask him.

He puts his arm around me. "It's for the best. I've got to fly to Vienna tomorrow, and then I'm meeting my family in Paris for New Year's Eve. Better if I go home and sleep in my own bed. This place always gives me the creeps. I'm quite convinced it's haunted."

"Me too!" I say. "All those creepy noises, and I swear, my phone keeps getting moved."

"Perhaps the ghosts of Edwards' past are trying to tell you something," he teases. "You're on Gavin's plan now. Maybe they're worried you're eating up all of his data minutes."

I lean my head on his shoulder. "You crack me up."

He kisses the top of my head. "That's what I'm here for. Comic relief." He lets me go, then picks up his bag. "I really have to get going."

"Okay, but before you go... Not to bring us back to a sore subject, but are you and Gavin okay?"

He adjusts his bag on his shoulder. "Yes, I think we worked through it."

I cringe. "I heard the gist. Sounds like Gavin lost it."

He shrugs. "He went too far, but in his defense, you had left him without a word and he was trying to sort it all out. He was convinced you cheated on him and then fled. He couldn't come up with any other reason you would just pick up and leave like that."

"Gah! I wish people would stop saying that like I abandoned him!" I'm sick of justifying myself.

He holds his hands up. "Settle down. Let's not open old wounds, shall we? My point is, he was a total wreck when you left, so I cut him some slack. If someone I loved the way he loves you disappeared like that, I'd go mad too."

Not knowing what to say, I give him another hug.

He opens the front door and motions for me to go first. "Just because I understand it doesn't mean I'm going to make it easy on him, though. Tormenting him is so much fun," James says with a smirk.

While James is putting his bag in his car, Liam and Em come out the front door. "We're leaving too," Liam shouts as he and Em walk toward his BMW.

"'We'?" I respond.

"Yup, Em and I are heading back to London," he replies.

I point at Em. "Oh you are, are you? Heading back to London?"

Em rolls her eyes. "I need room service, housekeeping, and a masseuse on call. You know that, Lil." She hugs me goodbye, gets in Liam's car, and rolls down the window. "I'll be back in a little over two weeks for Gavin's gala. Wait till you see the dress I got!" She whispers, "Give him the present we both know you're thinking about not giving him. He deserves to know how much you care about him. He's dying for some sign that you're in this as much as he is and you aren't going to bolt across the pond the second this gets tough. Don't fuck it up."

"Did he say anything to you?" I ask.

She puts her seatbelt on. "He said enough," she says.

Why does anyone think speaking cryptically is helpful?

"What does that mean?" I ask.

"It means pull your head out of your ass." She motions for me to move my hand, then pushes the button to roll up the window. I guess that's all she's going to give me. The woman is like a freaking vault. I plaster a big, fake smile on my face and flip her off. "Love you," I mouth.

Liam walks over and puts his arm around me. "Truth is, Honey Bunny, Gavin kicked us out. Seems he wants you all to himself. Can't say I blame him, but with you being my ex-wife, it sure makes me crazy." He winks. "I still can't get over you being with anyone but me."

I bring my hands to my chest, covering my heart. "You're getting back at me by shacking up with my best friend. Oh, Liam, I thought we were passed the point of hurting each other for sport." I lean into him and fake sob.

He pats my head. "There, there, Honey Bunny. I know I've ruined you for all other men, but you'll just have to get used to that," he shouts loud enough to draw Gavin from the house.

James laughs hysterically in the background.

"Bloody hell, if it isn't one of you trying to steal my girl, it's the other. Both of you get the hell out of here!"

Gavin yells.

I hug Liam. "In all seriousness, do you know what you're doing with her? I see some spark in your eyes, and I'm worried. She isn't that kind of girl. I know she's honest about her level of commitment, but many guys think she'll change or they'll be different. She doesn't do relationships. She doesn't do emotions. If you don't know that going in, she'll break you."

He looks me in the eyes. "Em and I are one of the same. You don't have to worry about me."

I wish I believed him.

"Better get this one inside before I take her with me," Liam threatens. "Too late!"

He picks me up and runs around the driveway. Liam keeps taunting Gavin, listing off the number of debaucherous things he'll do to me. I can't see Gavin, but I hear him growling. Liam is tackled, and we fall into the snow.

Gavin picks me up, kisses my temple, and carries me inside without even saying good-bye. "Sorry, luv. I had to stake my claim." He kisses me deeply. "It was smashing having them here for Christmas. This will go down as one of my most favorite holidays. Having said that, I'm thrilled they're gone and I can have you all to myself."

I kiss him back, giving him everything I've got in hopes we can avoid talking about presents a little longer. This time with him is blissful. If he pulls out a ring, our happy holiday will be tainted with conversations about commitment. I'll ruin everything. My only option is to distract him with sex. It'll be a tough job, but totally worth it.

"I like having you all to myself, Mr. Edwards. I was just thinking it's time to make some new memories in this place. Time to go christen some rooms." With the amount of rooms in this place, we could be busy for a month!

****

My plan keeps him distracted until just before midnight. After seven rooms and more positions than I can count, I'm sure we've both overdosed on orgasms. I can barely move or formulate complete sentences.

Gavin stands up and puts on a pair of boxers. "I can't wait any longer. I must give you your presents. Stay here, luv. I'll go grab them."

"Hold up, I want to give you mine first." I stand up and look for my clothes, but realize they're still in the dining room, where this sex parade started. Gavin hands me my robe.

"Thanks," I say as I put it on.

"I moved our bags up to the master bedroom. Sleeping under the stars has been great, but even though we replaced the air mattress we popped with a better one, I know your back is still sore. We did a number on you that first night."

I smile at the memory. "So worth it, though. Okay, let's meet in the master bedroom then."

I think back to all the rooms we've been in. Each room was huge and had its own bathroom. "Wait," I shout before he leaves the room.

"Yeah?"

"Which one's the master?"

"Remember the room with the big mirror?" he asks with a smirk.

I blush. "How could I not?"

"That's the master. See you in a minute." He runs out of the room.

I run to my secret hiding place and grab the box with the photos and stare at the other wrapped box. Looking at it, knowing what's in there and what it means, paralyzes me. I don't regret the choice to apply for my visa, but if I give it to him, it might open the door to other conversations. The photos will result in orgasms; the visa could result in tears. I'll choose orgasms over tears any day of the week and twice on Sunday. I grab the photos and shove the other box back in its hiding place.

We meet back in the master bedroom and I see that he has two boxes, perfectly wrapped. No sign of the blue box of terror. Could I have completely misread the situation?

"I want to go first," I insist. "I'll start by saying, shopping for you is impossible. There's nothing you need, and anything you want, you just get for yourself. You definitely don't have this, though." I raise my eyebrows suggestively. "I know I'm supposed to get a tattoo, but we both know I'm never going to do that. I thought this made a fair compromise."

He shakes the box and turns it over a few times. "Trying to figure it out?" I ask.

He nods with a chuckle. "It isn't often someone can

surprise me, but I have to say, I have no idea what's in here."

"Well, open it and see. The suspense is killing me!"

He opens the box and sees the album cover in the design of the British flag.

"You bought me something with Union Jack. It's not a tattoo on your ass, but I like it already."

"Keep going, it gets better."

I wish I had pictures of him as he turns the pages. His eyes get wide. His jaw falls slack, a flush covers his cheeks, and he seems breathless. He looks at each page carefully, as though he is savoring each image. The silence is awkward for me, but watching his reactions makes it worth it.

After looking at the last picture, he swallows and closes the album.

"So what do you say? Am I off the hook for the tattoo?"

"Bloody hell, Lily. I—" For once, Gavin Edwards is actually speechless.

"Cat got your tongue?" I say seductively.

He walks over to an end table and places the book down gently, as if it's fragile. He stares at me with an intensity that makes my body shiver, and he stalks back to bed, never breaking eye contact.

"Best. Present. Ever."

He attacks me with a kiss. My robe disappears, and within seconds, he's plunging deep inside me. His eyes roll back and he lets out a quiet moan, like a heroin addict who just got a long-awaited fix. Despite the fact we've been having sex all afternoon, he looks as if he's starving for me. He pounds into me as though he's on a mission, all his energy committed to burying himself inside me. Our connection's powerful and fierce, the action almost violent in its intensity. We have had sex countless times but never like this. I'm consumed by his passion and desire, every part of my body coming alive. After we reach our climax, we lay tangled up in each other, breathless and slick with sweat.

"Holy hell, Gavin. That was... there aren't words for what that was. I've never seen you like that. Not that I'm complaining."

He brushes a piece of hair out of my eyes. "Those pictures... Oh my God, Lily, those pictures. You're Aphrodite. A temptress with seduction beyond description. All I could think about was how this insanely sexy creature was mine. I'm the lucky bastard who knows how soft your skin is, who knows what it's like to make you quiver, who knows the ecstasy that it is to be inside you."

I smile. "I'm glad you liked them. I'll have to remember this for the future."

"Oh, yes." He smirks. "I'm curious, who was your photographer? While I'm grateful for his work, I need to know who to kill. The fact that a man is walking around after seeing you like that... No, no, no. I can't permit that."

I stroke his cheek. "Jealous Gavin is very sexy. He is a she. Em's friend, Josie, took the pictures and processed the prints. You're the only person with a penis who has seen them."

He lets out a deep sigh. "That's good. I'm too euphoric to kill someone right now. My turn. Your present puts mine to shame, but I hope you enjoy them. The first one, Hazel helped me put together." He hands me the first box. As I unwrap, he continues, "I was chatting with a friend a few weeks back. He was taking his girl home to meet his parents, and the whole weekend they were together was filled with stories of him growing up. I think you know more about me than anyone who walks the earth, but I realized that, other than stories from Liam and James, you won't have one of those weekends. So I asked Hazel to help me put this together."

I tear open the wrapping and find an album. Great minds think alike, it seems. However, if Hazel helped put this together, I'm guessing I won't find scandalous pictures of Gavin. I open it up to find I'm wrong. The first page is full of naked pictures. Baby pictures, that is.

He pats next to him on the bed. "Come here and cuddle up, luv. This's a photo documentary of my life. The good, the bad, and the ugly."

He spends the next four hours going through each picture, telling me the stories that have made him the man he is. From when he knocked out his two front teeth playing cricket, to Sunday dinners with his grandparents, to the day he was accepted at Oxford. There are plenty of adorable pictures of Liam and James. They were cute kids, and it's sweet to see how they grew up together. I adore seeing these three sexy men with missing front teeth, gangly and awkward. My favorite is one of them after a soccer game. They're covered in mud from head to toe, bloody and bruised, thrusting a trophy above their heads. They look so damn happy.

Dawn is breaking when we finish the last page. The album ends right as he enters the military. A wise place to end, since Brooke comes into the picture soon after he leaves the service, and I don't need to see that. "Gavin, this was the best present ever. Really. My present was all smut and sizzle. This gift... You gave me you."

"I'm pretty sure you gave yourself to me too, luv. Don't knock smut and sizzle." He kisses me on the temple. "I'm glad you liked it."

"I loved it. Can I open the other box now?"

"Of course. This one's from my studio."

I open the perfectly wrapped box, and gasp. "It's perfect." I hold up the glass ball Christmas tree ornament that has an American Flag melding with a British flag.

"I know we couldn't find the perfect Christmas ornament, so I tried to make one," he says as I stare at the glass ball. "First time I tried something like this, but I hope you like it."

I gently place it back in the box, then kiss him. "Thank you! It's perfect. How on earth did you make this?"

"A little blown glass," he says casually. "It took me a while to get it right. I know you wanted something to remind you of this year. But with so much that has happened this year, I wanted to focus on the best parts. Where you and I met, and our adventures together began."

I roll my eyes. "Of course. You know how to blow glass. Who doesn't know how to blow glass?"

He picks it up and holds it to the light. "Look carefully. If you hold it in the right light, you can see a Ben and Jerry's logo in the background."

I look carefully and catch a hint of it when the light catches it the right way. "Damn, you're good Oxford."

He smirks. "I know. One more!"

Crap. "Tomorrow? Or later today, I guess. I'm so tired, I can barely keep my eyes open." Big fat lie. "I think it's almost eight in the morning. Way past my bedtime."

His face falls. "It'll only take a second. Please. I'm really excited about this one. When I saw it, I knew it had to be yours."

I force a yawn. "Please, Gavin, please let's just do this later," I beg. I don't think I'm masking my anxiety well. I've downshifted from jubilantly happy to panicked in less than ten seconds. My hairline is soaked with sweat, and I can't seem to catch my breath.

He takes my hand. "What's going on, luv? Talk to me." He looks me in the eyes, searching for an answer that I know he won't want to hear.

I smile. "Nothing, Oxford. I'm just really tired. I think the day's catching up to me."

"Okay, luv. Why don't you rest? I'll save this one for another time." He pulls me close and settles us back into bed. "Get some sleep, luv. Maybe when you wake up you'll be ready to talk. I love you, but if you think I'm buying this story, you're sadly mistaken."

"Gavin..." I'm not sure what to say. He's seen through my transparent, pathetic attempt to deflect, and I don't have a good excuse that won't hurt him.

"Shhhh, just sleep." He kisses my forehead and hugs me tight.

******

Gavin doesn't bring up his present again, nor does he push me to talk about it. The next few days are spent casually enjoying each other, both in and out of the bedroom. We walk around quaint little towns and find old pubs with fabulous stories. My favorite is Canterbury. The town is impeccably decorated for the holidays, and the cathedral there is one of the most spectacular buildings I have ever seen.

He drives me to Cornwall, and we walk on the beach. It's freezing but lovely. He takes me to the Old Coastguard for the best roasted chicken I've ever had, complete with a breathtaking view. I'd never thought about England having beaches. Stupid, since it's an island, but I never thought of it as a beach place. We drive up and down the coast and see the same names of towns on Cape Cod, which makes me laugh and reminisce about my childhood. Gavin promises to bring me back when the temperatures are above freezing.

My cheeks hurt by the end of the day. More smiles than I can count and endless laughter. It wouldn't be us if there wasn't a little bit of competition. Who can fly their kite higher, who can find the biggest shell. It's all in good fun and quintessentially us. I forget about rings and marriage, cartels and suspended agents. It's just the two of us, and it's heaven.

We're supposed to return to London for New Years. Percy and Poppy are throwing a party to show off Percy's new flat in Lewisham. At the last minute, Gavin changes his mind, and we return to his flat. We order pizza, which takes four hours before it's delivered. By the time it arrives, we've gone through three bottles of champagne. Right before midnight, Gavin makes some sort of spiked, hot apple cider concoction. We grab blankets and bundle up on the terrace to watch the fireworks.

After the fireworks, he refills our mugs, then joins me back on the terrace. I'm entertained by the masses of drunken fools wandering around on the sidewalk. He pulls me away from my live reality show, brings me back to the lounge chairs.

"Luv, I haven't brought this up in days because I didn't want to upset you. Honestly, I wanted you to come to me to talk about why you were so upset Christmas night. I haven't asked, and you haven't offered. As I think about where I was this time last year, I never in a million years could have dreamt up how a year could change my life. After the past four months, I couldn't imagine being happier, freer, or more in love. When I saw this, I had to get it for you. It spoke to me."

I've had too much champagne to lodge a protest. Before what he's saying sinks in, he's offering me that little blue box. Too late to run now.

"Open it," he insists.

"Gavin—"

"Just open it, Lily."

The smile never fades from his eyes, and my heart starts to break. If I open this and tell him no, that smile will disappear. We'll disappear.

He chuckles. "It won't bite."

I slowly unwrap the box, trying to delay as long as possible. It's a tiny box, so it doesn't allow me much time to procrastinate. The wrapping paper falls to the ground, and Gavin takes the box. As he opens it, the box makes that creak as the hinge bends back.

"You have to open your eyes, luv. And please, breathe."

I open my eyes and look down. It's beautiful. Stunningly beautiful and sparkly.

"It's the Celtic symbol for fate. I thought it was appropriate for us." He put the necklace bearing the diamond-encrusted pendant on my neck. "You've always said that a crazy twist of fate brought us together, so when I saw this, I thought of you."

"Gavin, it's so beautiful and so perfect."

"So do you want to tell me what all the panic was about? You didn't think it was a ring, did you?" He shakes his head and smiles. "Silly girl. Don't you know I know you better than that?"

I bury my head in my hands to hide my embarrassment. "Gavin, I'm an idiot with a massive head case problem."

"I know," he says. "I love you anyway."

"Can you wait right here? There's something I need to get for you." I run inside and find my second present for Gavin buried in my bag. When I return, I say, "I've been afraid to give this to you. I was afraid it would open doors to conversations I'm afraid of having."

"Just because it's scary doesn't mean it will end poorly," he says. "I love you, and you love me. It's that simple. We can face anything as long as we do it together. Never hide something from me out of fear. I'll never leave you because you were honest. I promise."

I hand him the box, and he unwraps it quickly.

When he opens the box, he sifts through tissue paper and looks confused. "I don't understand."

"I applied for a visa. So I can stay in London."

He puts the papers down and hugs me. "You were afraid if you gave this to me, it would be a slippery slope?"

I nod against his shoulder. "I'm an idiot, I know. It isn't logical, but it scared me. I was sure you would ask for more than I can give and that this bubble would burst. I can't even say the M-word without wanting to vomit."

He pulls away and furrows his brow. "Do you doubt us?"

The hurt in his eyes makes this excruciating. I want to say the words he wants to hear, the words that will ease the anguish, but I can't. Lies may put a smile on his face today, but will just end up breaking his heart down the road. All I can do is be honest, even if the truth hurts. "No, of course not. I wouldn't apply to stay here longer if I did. I have faith in us; it's life I'm afraid of. I refuse to make promises I can't keep. How can I promise forever if I don't know what'll happen tomorrow?"

"None of us know what will happen tomorrow. If I've learned anything from my relationship with Brooke, it's that marriage isn't a promise of happily ever after. Marriage is a promise to not give up, to be there night and day, perish or prosper. It's a promise that you'll never, ever, *ever* have to face something alone. You and I both got married for all the wrong reasons and expected all the wrong outcomes. I don't know about you, but I'll never make that mistake again. But, I certainly hope the fact that I tried and failed once doesn't mean that I'm barred from trying again.

Especially, when I know deep down in the depths of my soul that I' have found the right person."

I'm in awe of his hope and optimism. I can't buy into it, but god damn, I'm in awe of it. I wipe the tears from my eyes. " Your words always steal my breath. But they also scare me to death. You have so much faith, so much confidence. You've figured it all out, and I'm still struggling to figure out which way is up."

He tips my chin so I have to look at him. "That's just it, luv. You're trying so hard to figure it all out, and you can't. It's not possible. You're looking for answers that you'll never find. There's no guarantees. There's no certainties. Life and love are big risks. All I know with absolute certainty is that I love you. I have faith everything else will fall into place.

I'm not going to ask you to marry me when the word makes you break out in a cold sweat. The fact that you're willing to stay here with me and see where we go is a huge step for you. I appreciate how hard that is for you and the risk you're taking. I don't want you to think for one moment that I don't treasure the gift you've given me. I do. I just hope that one day you won't be afraid of forever."

"I love you, Gavin. I can promise you that."

"That's all I need, luv." He holds me close and kisses me gently on the top of my head.

I take a sip of my now cold cider, then put it on the end table. "Since we're wrestling our demons here, I figure we might as well face them all," I say. "A few weeks ago, when the papers announced I was pregnant, do you remember calling me?"

"Yes," he says with a twinge of irritation. Leave it to me to take a sweet moment and turn it sour.

I pull my knees to my chest, creating a barrier between us. "You sounded furious that I might be pregnant."

His shoulders soften. "I apologize for that. There was a lot going on at my office, and my PR department had a conniption over the 'news.' I didn't mean to take out my frustration on you."

"What if I were?" I ask quietly.

His eyes widen. "Pregnant?"

"Yes. We've never talked about that. I'm on the pill, but it's only ninety-nine percent effective. One in a hundred times, anything could happen. We've had sex way more than one hundred times. Hell, we may have had sex one hundred times this week!"

"I'm good, but I'm not that good," he teases.

I nudge his shoulder. "I'm serious. We've never talked about it. Odd since the rest of England is planning the birth of our child, but somehow we've never discussed it."

"I hear that Harvey is in the running for the most preferred name if he's a boy," he says, deflecting.

"Why do you think I named our polar bear Harvey?"

"I see."

"Gavin, you're avoiding the question. You're the one who's so gung ho for forever. Shouldn't we at least make sure we want the same things?" If we don't, then we can get out now before we get any more invested.

"Do you want children?"

I shrug. "I don't know. I'm not sure I'd make a very

good mother. But I do want to know if it happens, I can come home and talk to you about it without getting growled at."

"Oh, Lily," he says, squeezing me tight. "I would never—"

I cluck my tongue. "But you did," I say with more of an edge than I should. "If I were pregnant, I would have been petrified. Would I have hidden it from you? No. Would I have wanted to get official results before talking to you about it? Maybe. I don't know. That story could have been true."

He lowers his head while he rakes his fingers through his hair. "And I've apologized for that. It was a stressful day and I didn't respond well." He looks up and finds my eyes. "I'm not perfect, Lil. I'm not always going to say or do the right thing, but that doesn't change the fact that I love you and want to be there for you. Just promise me if you even suspect that something is going on in your life, a baby or a drug cartel with a bounty on your head, please, for the love of God, talk to me. You don't need confirmation first. You don't need to get your head on straight first. Let me help you. We're in this together, no matter what it is. You just have to let me in."

"I'll try," I reply, knowing I may not be capable of keeping my word. I don't even know where to begin.

He cups my cheeks and looks into my eyes. "You're not alone," he says. "You'll never be alone."

Chapter Twenty-Six

As perfect as New Year's Eve was, New Year's day is one calamity after another. I'm woken by something dripping on my forehead. A faulty pipe leaked and flooded the bedroom. The carpet, and bedding are all ruined, not to mention the whole wall needs to come down to fix the pipe. Instead of spending the day with friends, Gavin and I are stuck home with the plumber.

Gavin's swamped with work. Not only is the gala coming up, but apparently he's acquiring a new company. It sounds like he's going to be working sixteen to twenty hour days, and I shouldn't expect to see much of him. He called Audrey, his decorator, and set up a meeting, but made it clear he needs me to manage it from here on out.

The next morning, she drops by with fabric samples. After Willis sends her up, I open the door. She looks confused. She steps back and double checks the apartment number. "I'm sorry, I must have the wrong flat. I'm looking for Olivia, Gavin Edwards' girlfriend. Are they on this floor?"

O's like a cockroach. No matter what I do, I can't get rid of her. "Right apartment, wrong girlfriend." I hold out my hand. "I'm Lily."

Audrey drops the sample book, and covers her mouth. "How embarrassing. I'm so sorry. Olivia was my contact during the remodel. She oversaw the whole project. Well, until the last week or two anyway." She shakes her head. "You probably don't want to hear about that. I'm sorry. I'm making an ass of myself."

I pick up her book and gesture for her to come in. "Don't worry about it," I say hiding my irritation. "O was acting as his assistant at that time. Getting him coffee, picking up his dry cleaning, that sort of thing. I'm sure she was lending a hand while he was in the US with me."

She walks in and takes off her coat and rests it on the back of the sofa. "Oh. For some reason I thought she was his girlfriend. Maybe I was confused since she had a key, and he trusted her to make decisions when he couldn't be reached."

I wouldn't put it past O to tell people she and Gavin are together. "Honest mistake," I say trying to be polite. I point to the hallway that leads to the bedroom. "Why don't you inspect the damage, then we can get started."

Once we are able to move past the awkward introduction, Audrey and I work together well. We quickly pick new bedding, carpet and paint colors. Presuming the contractors show up on time, the room should be good as new by the beginning of next week.

After she leaves, I pack up and head to a meeting with

Poppy to discuss the gala. The most complicated thing I've ever planned is a sorority party, which is the easiest thing to throw together. One trip to Party City and the liquor store, and poof, you've got a party. Gavin's event is really a week-long schmooze fest for all the rich and beautiful people. It's filled with teas, cocktail parties, outings, and it concludes with a black-tie gala.

When I offered to help, I thought I'd be hanging balloons or showing people where the restrooms are. Oh, no. Poppy, the despot event coordinator, rules with an iron fist and will not accept anything but one hundred percent focus and dedication. I thought I'd signed up to help, but what I really did was enslave myself. For the next three weeks, I'm her bitch.

Poppy puts me in charge of finalization duty since I have an "all-access pass" to Gavin. Somehow it's my job to get Gavin to sign off on the things she either can't get him to agree to or is afraid to talk to him about. Most of the time, he has more questions or needs more options, and it becomes my responsibility to come up with solutions. With how busy he is, finalization is not an easy job. We barely see each other, and when we do see each other, I'm pestering him about seating arrangements or color schemes. Giving up sex to talk swag bags is simply unreasonable!

During our discussion last night, Gavin told me he didn't like the programs, so I have to work with the graphic designer to come up with new options. I spend five hours trapped in an office with a guy who seems to be averse to showering, but I think I've got it the way Gavin wants. I've never valued fresh air as much in my whole life as when I open the doors to that office and escape the toxic stench.

My jubilation is cut short when I see Gavin and Skanky McCumbucket coming out of a hotel.

His arm is around her, and he's whispering something into her ear which makes her stop and look at him. I know that look. She's lost in those hypnotic sapphires. He keeps talking to her and holding her hand! O tries to walk away, but he pulls her back into a tight embrace. What the hell! They break apart, and they're holding hands again. Smiles turn into laughter as he leads her *back* into the hotel.

How can this be happening? Is he really doing this to me again? How could I just stand here and watch it?

In Vegas, he had me utterly convinced that she was out of his life. That he wanted nothing to do with her. I believed every single word out of his mouth. Have they really been carrying on this whole time under my nose? I toggle through my memories. Audrey thinking O was his girlfriend. All the nights he came home late, phone calls he needed to take in the other room. Christmas Eve, when he was "stuck in traffic." Was it all lies?

He's always teasing me about being gullible. Maybe I am.

I'm frozen. My legs are unwilling to continue my walk to the Tube. I want to follow them. Maybe there's an innocent explanation for all of this. Deep down, I know the only thing waiting for me if I follow them is heartache. I shouldn't step foot in that hotel.

I'm such a masochist.

They have a head start, and I lose them in the lobby. They aren't in the restaurant or in the bar. I check the schedule of meetings in the conference rooms, and unless they've become orthopedic surgeons studying the latest techniques in bone setting, I don't think they're there. After I'm done with him, he may need an orthopedic surgeon!

I stop at the front desk and feed the young desk clerk a line about trying to find my boss who will fire me if I don't give him the files in my hand. Sadly, the guy is a boy scout who simply refuses to release any guest information regardless of how hard I come on to him. He tells me I'm more than welcome to wait for my boss in the lobby. At first that seems like a fantastic idea. I'll wait and catch them when they come down from their afternoon delight. Three hours and six glasses of wine later, humiliation and indignity drive me into a cab. I may have had some motivation from the bartender, but I can't be too sure.

Where do I go? Gavin has proven he'll monitor my credit cards to track me down if I go MIA. All of my friends here are tied to Gavin and O, and I can't drag them into it. Part of me wants to go back to the flat to see when he'll drag his ass home and hear his pathetic excuse. But the thought of him coming into the bed we share smelling like her makes me vomit. Thank God we're at a red light and I can easily open the door. The last thing I need is a cab-cleaning charge. Six glasses of wine on an empty stomach wasn't a good idea. Then again, neither was shacking up with a lying, cheating bastard.

After my stomach has been relieved of everything I've ever eaten, I lay back and close my eyes. With my head a little clearer, my sadness switches to fury. Why am I worrying about what I'm going to do? He's the one who's in the wrong. He's the one who owes me an explanation. Hiding from him allows him to escape.

"Oh, hell no! He does *not* get off that easy!" Oops. That was supposed to be internal.

"I beg your pardon, miss?"

Crap, I've scared the cab driver.

"Sorry, just losing my mind back here. Don't mind me." I've already retched in front of him. Why try to save face? "Please just get me to Knightsbridge."

"It's my pleasure, dearie."

When I get back to the flat, I shower off the stench of wine and dirty cab, and wait in the white room for him. The serenity of this room keeps me from grabbing a butcher's knife while I wait. I wouldn't use it on him, but it would scare the piss out of him!

Around midnight, he strolls in, but he doesn't see me. He looks exhausted. I guess a long day of fucking will do that do you.

"I wouldn't have thought you'd cheat on me, but never in a million years did I think you would cheat on the Four Seasons. The Ritz, Gavin? Really?"

He sets his briefcase down, then walks toward me. "It's not what you think."

I jump off the couch and step away from him. "Isn't that what every scumbag who gets caught says? 'I know you caught me in the act, but it isn't what you think. I fell with my penis out, and her vagina just happened to break my fall.' Tell me, if what I saw today outside the Ritz was not you and O having an affair, then what was it?"

He holds his hands up as he takes slow steps closer to me. With each step he takes toward me, I take one back. "Olivia is going through something, and she needed me. There was nothing remotely inappropriate going on. Just one family friend helping out another."

He's just a few feet in front of me and my back is against the wall. His blue eyes meet mine, pleading for forgiveness. Knowing he was looking at her all afternoon makes me nauseous. I push off the wall and cross the room. "Family friend, huh?" I reply, not hiding my disgust or sarcasm. "After all the headache and heartache she's caused! To our relationship! To your relationship with James! To your company! You promised me she was out of your life for good. How am I supposed to believe a word you say?"

He sits down, leaning his back against the wall. "I'm sure what you saw was confusing, but how can you possibly think I would ever be interested in O? You know what I think of her." He bangs his fist against the wall. "You and I had a knee trembler this morning, right here against this fucking wall. After our mind-blowing sex, why would I even think about another woman?"

My memory flashes back to this morning and that very lovely wall, which quite possibly has a few cracks in it now. Gavin was cutting strawberries. He fed me one, which I received seductively. Then... No! Out, sexy thoughts! Out! But I've already given him the opportunity to take control of the conversation.

He stands and walks toward me again. "I love you and only you," he says. "I did not and never will have any sort of a relationship with Olivia, but there is something I have to tell you. I should have told you ages ago, but I hate thinking about it, let alone talking about it. Can you listen?" His eyes are bright and gentle. For a lying, cheating bastard, he looks like he may be telling the truth.

I nod. "Yeah, fine. I'll listen." I sit on the chair furthest from him.

He walks to the bar and pours two glasses of scotch.

When he hands me one, I decline. "I drank six glasses

of wine at the Ritz waiting for you to come down. I'm not sure I need another."

He puts the drink on the table next to me. "You're going to need it." He downs his glass and walks back to the bar to refill it. Instead of one finger, he pours about four.

I hate scotch, and he knows it. Giving me alcohol is his "In case of emergency, break glass and pour down Lily's throat" move. If he's telling me to drink, this must be intense.

He sits on the sofa across from me. After a few long sips, he speaks. "Olivia had a sister named Daphney. I was fifteen when she died. Right before I walked out on my parents. In fact, her death probably was the catalyst to me leaving."

James had mentioned something about Daphney, but I know nothing about her.

Gavin takes another sip. "O's family and mine were always close, but Daphney was special. She was a dancer, just like my mother. She became the daughter my mother never had, practically living at my house for periods of time in her life. My mother was a cold, unfeeling woman, but she had a soft spot for Daphney. We all did."

He toys with the glass in his hand, the ice clinking as the cubes bounce off each other. "She really had it all. She was beautiful, brilliant, and so talented. Recruited to dance with some of the best companies in Paris. She always had the highest marks in school, and everyone adored her. Everyone except her parents.

"They pushed her so hard, and her best was never enough for them. They always found something to criticize. Her dancing, her school work, her weight. The girl couldn't have weighed five stone, and they still pushed her. They demanded she take on more activities, harder auditions, tougher classes. She used to say her childhood was a series of one epic failure after another. It was heartbreaking, because from an outsider's point of view, Daphney was golden.

"The older she got, the worse it became. Once she was of age, her parents wanted her to throw away the career that *they* had forced upon her and marry a proper gentleman. They arranged dates with men that could bolster their family's social status and blackmailed her into going. As much as Daphney hated them, she craved her parents' approval more, so she went."

He takes a deep breath and begins to pace. "One night, she showed up at my parents' house. Her dress was shredded, and her face was bruised and bloody. I think she hoped my mother would help her, but all my mother did was help her cover it up. She spent the night at my house, and right before dawn, she crawled into my bed, sobbing. She begged me to help her, but I was just a kid. I didn't know what to do any more than she did. Two weeks later, she was engaged."

I'm still not sure what this has to do with him and O and the hotel room, but he has me by the heartstrings. "Gavin, that's wretched. No wonder you left."

He shakes his head and scoffs. "I haven't even gotten to the bad part yet."

I swallow. "Oh."

"January twelfth, about a month later, once the bruises had healed, his parents decided to throw an engagement party. A big black-tie affair at the Ritz. About halfway through the party, Daphney disappeared. She was due to take more pictures, but she was nowhere to be found. Her mother sent me to look for her. I checked everywhere. After running out of places to look downstairs, I went to her room."

As Gavin sits back down, I notice his bottom lip tremble ever so slightly. He clears his throat and blinks a few times. "Her mother had given me a room key, so I let myself in. I found her in the tub. I think there was more blood than water in the tub by the time I found her. I called 999, but it was too late."

He sniffs and brushes a tear from his cheek.

I'm an ass. He wasn't having an affair with O; it was the anniversary of her sister's tragic death. I move next to him and onto the sofa. He looks down and turns his back to me slightly, probably trying to hide his tears. Wrapping my arms around him, I rest my chin on his shoulder and whisper, "I'm sorry," over and over.

He continues. "Despite the fact that her parents were never satisfied, they glorified Daphney in death. But the pressure they put on Daphney pales in comparison to their expectations of O. The difference is if O doesn't meet their standards, they don't put more pressure on her; they just shut her out. She doesn't exist if she doesn't make them happy.

"O is warped and twisted, but she grew up in the shadow of a ghost she could never compete with. She couldn't get love and attention from her family, so she sought it in all the wrong ways. She uses her beauty and brains as weapons. She's so jealous of others' happiness that she'll stop at nothing to tear it down so she doesn't have to witness it.

James was the only good thing in her life. The only pure thing that wasn't tainted by her games and vindictiveness. I always thought in the end, they would make it. I wanted that for her. I knew with James, she could be happy.

"I'm still pissed at O for what she has done, but when she called and said she checked into Daphney's room at the Ritz and she needed me, I *had* to go. O is in a low place right now and I couldn't risk history repeating itself." His eyes squeeze shut. "I couldn't live with myself if ..."

Running my fingers through his hair I say, "Of course. Of course you needed to be there."

"She wanted to know why. Over and over, she asked me why. Why didn't I get there a little bit earlier? Could I have saved her? Why didn't I get her help? Why didn't I save her? Bloody hell, they're the same damn questions I ask myself."

"Gavin, you were fifteen. A child. Her problems were too big for you to solve."

We talk in circles for hours until he tires and can no longer speak. The emotions and scotch overtake him, and he needs sleep. He has carried this burden with him for so long, and I won't be able to help him in one night. I get him to bed, and he falls asleep the second he hits the pillow. I'm up all night trying to process what all of this means.

I understand now that O will always be tied to him. No matter what she does, no matter how cruel or vindictive, he'll never let her go. He needs to save her. When Daphney died, my super hero was born. His need to save the world is buried in those memories of loss and misguided responsibility. My heart breaks for fifteen-year-old Gavin. My heart even breaks for O.

Chapter Twenty-Seven

Sometimes life brings you closer and pulls you apart at the same time. Gavin showed me a part of himself that he's kept buried. What he went through with Daphney's death is unspeakable. A teenager doesn't have the capacity to process that kind of trauma. His parents were part of the machine that drove her to her suicide, and then they martyred her after her death. Their deplorable behavior was the impetus for him cutting ties with his parents. He could no long look at them with love and respect. He lost a friend, his parents, and his innocence all in one tragic day.

Being estranged from his parents, he didn't have anyone to convince him it wasn't his fault, to protect him from the demons born from that kind of guilt. Years and maturity tell him that Daphney's depression and tragic choice wasn't something a fifteen-year-old could solve, yet her death is the cross he bears.

I'd felt as if I knew everything about him, but perhaps he doesn't fully understand how profoundly Daphney's death changed him. I understand him so much better now. Why he is the way that he is. Why he feels the need to protect and save everyone and everything. Hell, the man can't even let furniture die. Brooke cheated on him, demanded separate lives, and became a junkie, but he fought for her. He'll never give up on O, no matter what she does. I get it now. I'm not happy about it, but I get it.

Unlocking this piece of Gavin's past has brought me closer to him, yet he's slipping further and further away. O has stirred up the ghosts that haunt him, and with the events this week, he also has to face the memories of his fallen troops. Gavin has absorbed the responsibility of every death, every injury, the heartache of every man and woman he served with. His guilt is a yoke around his neck, and right now it's crippling him in a way I've never seen. What was he thinking scheduling this event at the same time as the anniversary of Daphney's death? He's like sand slipping through my fingers, and I have no idea how to help him.

His dark mood overtakes him. My once loving and attentive boyfriend is cold and distant. I ache for his wanton, come-hither stares. All I get now are vacant glances that send shivers up my spine. Since we met, I've basked in the glorious warmth of Gavin's attention. In the last week, he's built up walls that shut me out in the cold. Every effort I make is ill received. He won't talk to me. Hell, he won't even fight with me. If I say or do something that I know upsets him, he just looks at me with those distraught eyes. It kills me that he won't let me help him. I understand he gets into these moods. The best thing I can do for him is give him space until it passes. The question is, what kind of shape will I be in when it does?

With gala week approaching, I'm kept busy, and I couldn't be more thankful. Otherwise, the enormity of Gavin's withdrawal would kill me. When we're in public, he acts as though everything is fine. He's full of polite smiles and socially appropriate chit chat. But when we're alone, I can barely get two words from him. We haven't so much as held hands since that night. I'd say he's pushing me away, but to push, he'd have to actually make contact.

The only time I can get him to speak to me is Monday, hours before we have to be at our first gala-week reception. Gavin spent the day at the office, and he came home to "collect" me before dinner. He'd told me to be "appropriately dressed and ready to leave by six o'clock sharp."

Not wanting to disappoint him, I put all my effort into being the perfect date. I'm minutes away from finishing my makeup when I get a call from Greene.

"Hey, kid," he says. "To give you a heads up, Max got his pink slip today. He isn't handling it well."

I'm in complete shock. "What? How is that possible?"

"He appealed his suspension, and not only was the appeal denied, but they found cause to terminate him. His career is over."

"Greene, I—"

"Call him, Lily. He's too proud to call, but he needs you."

"Thank you," I say before I hang up.

I dial Max right away. We haven't really spoken since Vegas. I tried when I heard he was suspended, but he wouldn't take my calls.

"'Sup, slugger," he answers.

"Max..." I try to hold back my tears.

"Slugger. Huh, quite the appropriate name for you." He's drunk. His voice is husky, and there's a slight slur to his words. "You sure took a Louisville Slugger to my career, didn't you?"

"Max, I—"

"What? You didn't mean to? You're sorry? Well, fuck sorry. You destroyed my life. We slept under the same roof for how many months, and you lied to my face every single day! You played with fire with the worst type of criminals, and I'm the one who got burned."

"Max, please..." I don't know what I can say, but I want to make it better.

"I put my life on the line for you, and it was for nothing. For lies and deception. How am I repaid? They take my motherfucking badge. My badge, Lily. That meant everything to me, and now it's gone."

"Please, there must be something I can do. Someone I can talk to. I'll take all the blame. I'll tell them you didn't know. I can fix this, I know I can."

"Fix this? Fix this? You think you can fix it? Please, it was you trying to fix shit that got me in this mess in the first place. Stop trying to fix things because all you do is fuck it up. You're like poison. Just stay the fuck out of my life."

"Max!" I cry, but it's too late. He's hung up, and I'm a blubbering mess. I try calling back, but he sends my calls to voice mail. Ten minutes later, I receive a text.

Max: My shit's out of your apartment and now you're out of my life. Do me a favor and lose my number before you infect anything else.

Just as I read this, Gavin walks in.

"You're not bloody ready?" he snaps.

"No, Gavin. I'm not bloody ready," I snap back. "I just got a call from—"

"You're not in any shape to accompany me this evening," he says coldly. "I'll go alone. This event is too important to risk its success over you being too caught up in your own issues to be an adult." The walls shake when he slams the bedroom door as he leaves.

I've always said he's the wordsmith in the relationship. His words can melt my heart or cut me to the bone. The two most important men in my life have shut me out. My heart has shattered into a million pieces, and I'm left immobile on the cold marble floor. I'm too broken to cry. I just lay there, numb and emotionally hollow.

At some point, I hear someone come in the flat. It could be ten minutes or ten days; I've lost all sense of time.

"What a shame. That has got to be the sexiest underwear I've ever seen, and let me tell you, I've seen a lot of underwear." Liam crouches next to me on the floor. "You laying there in that get-up could be so hot, but it's totally ruined by the puffy eyes and sniffling. Damn, Honey Bunny, snot is not sexy. You really know how to kill the mood."

He hands me a tissue. "What are you doing here, Liam?" My throat is raw, and I sound as broken as I feel.

"Em called and asked me to check on you. She heard some shite went down with your old roommate, and said you're not answering your phone. When I didn't see you at the reception, she asked me to drop in on you."

I wipe my nose. "Thank God I have Em."

"Now, now, you've got me too, HB. You have Gavin. This week is hard for him; it is every year. He puts on a great show, but behind the scenes, he's in one of his moods. He can be a callous arse. It's not on purpose; it's just his way of dealing with this week. Once it's all said and done, he'll go back to being Mr. Perfect. Don't you worry." He wipes the hair out of my face. "I'm going to pick you up and carry you to the bed. I fully intend to cop a feel while I'm doing it, so be prepared."

Liam is always true to his word. He grabs both T and A while carrying me to the bed.

"HB! You thrust your ass into my hands! What are you thinking? This is a terrible time for you to come on to me," he teases.

"If you're trying to get a rise out of me, it ain't happening. I fully intend to be miserable the rest of the night."

"Something in here is getting a rise, that's for sure."

I crack a slight smile.

"Ah, there's my girl," he coos. "Come on now. Keep smiling for me, okay? This'll pass with Gavin. I don't know the deal with the other bloke, but Em said it was pretty bad. All I can say is fuck 'em." He plants a wet kiss on my cheek. "Who needs him when you've got me?" He lays me down on the bed and grabs the Oxford sweatshirt.

"Criminy, this thing is old. Can't believe it's still around. Gavin bought this when he was first accepted at Oxford, before his modeling money started coming in and he didn't have two shillings to his name."

I pull the sweatshirt over my head. "Maybe I'm just destined to be with Em for the rest of my life. She seems to be the only one who can be with me without suffering from Lily Rot."

"Two questions. Lily Rot? Is that like crotch rot? If so, maybe I should sit over there. I love you, but my love only goes so far."

That gets a full-blown laugh from me.

"Second. You and Em? Together? Is there video?"

Damn, not him too! "No comment. Thank you for putting me to bed. I'm thinking I should sleep in the spare room tonight."

"Stay here, Lily. You're hurting, and he should see that. Try to get some rest, though. You really do look like shite."

I kiss his cheek. "You always say the sweetest things. Good night, Liam."

"Later, Honey Bunny."

Sleep takes me some time after Liam leaves. I never hear Gavin come home, but when I wake up around dawn, he's in bed with me. I use the term "in bed" loosely. He's technically on the bed but as far away from me as possible. We might as well be on separate continents.

We don't discuss what happened on Monday night. For the rest of the week, he tells me when and where to show up, and I comply. Onlookers would have no idea anything is going on. We play the part impeccably.

The only good thing about the week is that I get to meet so many soldiers, veterans, and their families. Their stories and strength are awe-inspiring. Alex Baker, my cardiologist, is at almost every event, and since Gavin's busy schmoozing, Alex takes me around and introduces me to the men who served with him and Gavin. Gavin was a medic in Afghanistan, and I get to meet soldiers who are alive today because of Gavin. It makes my heart soar with pride.

There's nothing like watching the camaraderie between Gavin and people he served with. Practicing the art of stalking without being detected, I watch how happy and connected he is with them. His time in the military is another piece of him that has always been securely locked up. This week, it's out on display, and I couldn't be in more awe.

On Wednesday morning, we have a brunch to honor the fallen. Gavin puts up a brave front, but I feel him dying inside. He's still tormented by the day he lost his troops in a surprise attack. The event is a beautiful memorial, but it stirs up haunting memories that add to Gavin's guilt. Seeing him in so much pain is excruciating, especially because he won't let me comfort him.

Poppy has certainly outdone herself. Each day brings a different social gathering. Cocktails at the Royal Air Force Museum, brunch at the Imperial War Museum, dinner at that Old Royal Navel College. My favorite is the lunch at Churchill's War Room. Poppy wanted each location to be interesting and unique. Each location was to be more than a venue; it was to be an experience. The love of my life may not be speaking to me, but at least I get to see some cool stuff. I'm all about the consolation prize these days. A girl has to find a reason to schlep around in four-inch heels all night.

My salvation comes on Friday when Em arrives. She's meeting us at the dinner reception at Tower Bridge. Em's a social butterfly at events, but I insist she remain glued to my hip. I simply cannot fabricate a smile for another evening without some serious support. I'm half tempted to tell her to be Gavin's date so I can stay home and go to bed. That, however, would be relationship suicide. I hope once the stress of this week has passed, we can try to find each other again.

Gavin and I arrive and make one lap around the event. Like clockwork, as soon as we have politely greeted all the tables, he shrugs me off. So far, the week has brought in some serious cash, making all of this worth it.

Em arrives an hour late in typical Em style.

"You're supposed to be my social shield tonight. That's hard to do when you're not here," I say when I greet her.

"Whining like that will give you frown lines. Let's grab a drink and mingle."

Men circle around Em like sharks. She relishes the attention, and I'm thrilled the spotlight is off of me. She dominates the conversation so my brain can take a much-needed break. Around eleven, I take a leisurely trip to the restroom to escape the crowd. I get sidetracked and wander around the Tower for close to an hour.

On my way back to the bar, I come around a corner and see Gavin on the phone. He's pulling at his hair and pacing like he does when he's stressed. Not wanting another run in, I turn back the way I came. When I hear him speak, the stress in his voice stops me in my tracks. I shouldn't eavesdrop. That would be a terrible violation of his privacy. What kind of girlfriend does that?

This kind of girlfriend.

"Bloody hell, this is a clusterfuck," he barks. "What are we going to do?"

He pauses, assumedly to listen to the person on the other end.

"I can't bloody well tell her now. I've got too much going on this week, and we both know how she'll react. I can't deal with that right now."

Is he talking about me? Can't tell me what?

"I know how you feel about her right now, and I respect that. I can keep you away from each other. Em is here. She'll keep Lily busy while you and I figure out what we need to do. I'll send them shopping or something. I just need you to get here. The sooner you get here, the sooner I'll be able to breathe. This is crushing me."

I want to run away screaming, but I can't stop listening.

"Yes. I need you here. Now. I can't deal with this on my own. This whole mess has me tied up in bloody knots, and I can't afford that right now. This disaster has gone on long enough. I've respected Lily and her feelings, but it's time I take matters into my own hands."

That's enough. I don't want to hear any more. I don't want to know any more. I want to run away and not look back, but I can't. I did that before, and it blew up in my face. I know I only heard one half of a conversation, but I heard enough to know that something is about to go down. Whatever it is, I need to deal with it head on. No running and hiding. I refuse to be a coward again. Whatever is about to happen needs to happen so I can move on.

Desperately in need of air, I fight my way upstairs to the walkway. The Tower Bridge is just that—two towers connected by a bridge and a walkway. The view is spectacular. I fall a little bit more in love with London every day. Even now, with my life and my relationship in a state of confusion and uncertainty, I look out over this city and know there isn't anywhere else I want to be.

As this was an unexpected detour, I didn't bring my jacket. It's a cold night, but the January air feels good. The arctic shock saves me from falling down the "what if" rabbit hole. It's hard not to try to piece together what he was talking about.

"Don't jump," a sexy voice calls.

"You sure about that?" I ask with a flat tone.

"Don't even joke," Gavin replies.

"I just needed some air. It was getting a little intense down there."

He laughs quietly. "Intense is a fair way to describe this week. Are you ready to go?"

He has said more to me in the last five minutes than he has all week. I have no idea what that means, especially in light of what I overheard. But I'm staying true to my word. I'll face this head on, whatever this is.

"I'm ready whenever you are."

Chapter Twenty-Eight

Spa day. Regardless of all the crap going on in my life, while I'm at the spa, life is beautiful. Em and I are getting rubbed down, scrubbed, soaked, and polished before the gala tonight. My date and I may not be on speaking terms, but at least I'll look good.

Chatty Gavin went back into hibernation as soon as we got into the car last night. He hopped on his cell and worked late into the night. I went to bed alone and woke to an empty apartment. He left a note in the kitchen letting me know a limo would pick me up at the Four Seasons at seven and that I would meet him at the gala. Is that romance or what?

I'd hoped Em and I would go to the gala together, but Em, being Em, refuses to arrive until the event has been underway for at least an hour. If I could get away with that, I would. Hell, I'd skip the damn thing if it wasn't so important to Gavin. Logic and reason say I don't have to appease Gavin since he'll barely look at me, but I love him, and there's nothing I wouldn't do to fix us. Even if that means enduring another night of the cold shoulder. I'll tolerate this for one more night. Come tomorrow, all bets are off.

The fact that we aren't going together tells me I'll be on my own to socialize. When I bought my dress for this shindig, I did so thinking about my first major event on Gavin's arm. With the amount of press that will be there, I wanted to make sure I played the part of arm candy to a T. The dress is a striking red gown with a plunging neckline that shows off all kinds of cleavage while still being tasteful. In this dress, even I think I look jaw dropping. I may not be on his arm, but I'm damn well going to make him wish I were.

At the other events, everyone in attendance knew whose bed I was sleeping in. I received lots of attention, but it was all innocent. Tonight, over eight hundred people are on the guest list, the vast majority of them unaware of my relationship status. I won't balk if some attractive man pays me a little attention. In this dress, I'm bound to turn some heads, and if one of those heads isn't my boyfriend's, well... so be it.

Midafternoon, Gavin sends a curt text informing me that security has been amped up tonight and I need to arrive extra early. I arrive with an hour to spare, and find he wasn't kidding. There are security guards everywhere. My purse was searched and I had to be wanded and pat down before I was allowed to enter. I wonder how the upper crust of London's high society is going to feel about being frisked before entering. I can't fathom what sort of security risk would cause Gavin to go so overboard, but I'm sure he knows what he's doing.

Since there was no line, I'm in about an hour before the event starts. Once Poppy lays eyes on me, she sends me running all over, tying up last minute loose ends. They're annoying tasks, but it's wonderful to feel needed, wanted, and appreciated. I tell her so, and she snorts and mutters something about if I really understood that, things would be so different. Was that a dig about Gavin and me? I call her out on it, but she brushes me off.

Once all the I's are dotted and the Ts are crossed, I sneak away to the back bar and watch the room fill up. After a good dose of liquid courage, I decide it's time to get out there. I push my shoulders back, channel my inner super model, and strut across the room. I don't make it too far before I'm stopped by a handsome man who offers to buy me a drink. Lame, since its open bar, but I smile at him just the same. The way his eyes rake over my body is the confidence booster I need. I chat for a few minutes before excusing myself to work the room.

Gavin and I don't cross paths. I occasionally spot him from across the room as he schmoozes. God damn, he is so sexy in a tux—until he looks at me. I'm chatting with three men who are all solicitors, which I think is like a lawyer, when Gavin catches my eye. I see so much heat in his gaze until he observes the company I'm keeping. Then all that sexy fire gets hit with a polar vortex. Is he jealous? Angry? Bitter? Who the hell knows with him these days! I flash him a saccharine, Stepford-wife smile and mentally count down the hours until this stupid party is over. Until then, one point for me. Not that I'm keeping score.

Poppy observed what just happened between me and Gavin, and she commands me to go to the silent auction table and butter up the guests to bid higher. They did a great job of obtaining auction items that should draw in some major cash. They have a wall of soldiers' helmets that have been painted by a slew of famous artists as well as tons of trips and other once-in-a-lifetime experiences. I bid on private cooking classes with a very handsome yet unruly celebrity chef. The item I want most is private soccer lessons with a well-known British soccer star who looks oh so good in his undies. Sadly, it specifically states that the lessons must be for a child sixteen or under. Oh, I've never wanted to borrow a kid for the day more.

One item takes the cake. *An Evening of Romance and Seduction with International Rugby Star Liam Moynihan*. I was under the impression he had offered tickets to some of his games or something, but I should have known he would offer himself up on the auction block. I place a decent bid since he is my sorta, kinda, not really ex-husband. I can't help but notice the top bid came in from the internet. Kelly Klein. Funny, that was the name on Em's fake ID in college.

An hour in, the party is hopping. At least five hundred people are here already, tons of them famous celebrities. Gavin is laughing it up with the aforementioned soccer player. The benefit of not being on Gavin's arm is that I can quietly drool over him from afar without making an asshat out of myself by being unable to formulate words.

"Wipe the drool off your damn chin. You look ridiculous."

I turn around and hug Em. "Glad you could make it finally. You look beautiful." The black silk halter tuxedo dress looks amazing on her.

"Gavin is way hotter, you know. Not saying Soccer Boy isn't obscenely hot, but he's no Gavin. Go up and say hello. Just remember you've had a hotter man's penis in your mouth. You have no reason to be shy."

"Did you really just say that, or was that a hallucination?" Great, now I'm thinking about Gavin and the things we used to do all the time but haven't done in far too long. Now I'm an asshat, *and* I'm getting randy.

"Anyway, why are you here talking to me when you should be with your boyfriend talking to Soccer Boy?"

"I haven't spoken to Gavin yet tonight," I respond.

A waiter walks by with a tray of champagne. Em and I snatch his last two glasses. "Ah, I see. That's why he was dancing with that actress when I came in. Man, that boy can dance." She's trying to get under my skin, and its working.

I completely missed Gavin dancing, but I'd bet it was his response to those three men hanging on my every word. Now he's hanging out with Soccer Boy, probably because he knows I have a little crush on him. Fine, *little* may be an understatement. When Gavin plays, he plays to win.

"Just go talk to him, Lily. Enough is enough," Em says.

"Tomorrow," I reply. "When all of this is done, we'll fix us. I'm thinking of taking him to the country house. We need to get away, just the two of us."

"Good idea. To be honest, Lil, I'm over the drama between the two of you. You're perfect together, you love each other, and you know you can trust him. *Enough* already."

I take a sip of my champagne. "Damn, Em, tell me how you really feel."

"I always do. I'm also over broody Lily. Let's mingle. I

see just the guy to introduce you to that will make Gavin's blood boil."

Em drags me from group to group, introducing me to a variety of ridiculously hot men. I'm still not sure how I live here, sort of, yet she's the one who knows everyone. But that's Em. She and I make the rounds until I'm in desperate need of the loo.

After my nose is properly powdered, Em and I head back to the party. Around the corner come James, Heath, Basil, and Liam with smirks so big they scream trouble. I've seen that look on James once before, and I have a sneaking suspicion I know what's about to happen.

"Emily, how is it that you've been here for over an hour and you've managed to speak to every person in the building with a penis except for me?" Liam asks.

"That's not true. I haven't spoken to the rest of the boys yet either. Hello, boys." She plants big sloppy kisses on each of their cheeks before pushing past Liam toward the party. She looks over her shoulder. "The dance floor is calling my name, and I've got to find a partner. Come on, Lily."

"Did she just do that?" Liam asks James.

"I think she did, mate," James replies with a grin.

"You're in for it now, Emily. Last chance to come back here," Liam calls. "I'm warning you. If you don't turn around, I can't be held accountable for what happens next."

Em just keeps walking.

The boys all look at each other.

Liam belts out, "Why do you build me up, buttercup?"

All heads in the hallway turn to Liam. Em spins around and points at him. "Stop right there."

Liam opens his mouth and Em says, "Don't do it."

He smirks. "Have a drink with me and I'll stop. Otherwise, I have no problem serenading you in front of this whole party."

"He'll do it too," James chimes in. "Right, Lily? We're not afraid of a little public humiliation as long as we get the girl."

Liam waggles his eyebrows. "What do you say Emily?"

"You've got some balls, Moynihan. I'll give you that," Em states with a tone so flat, I can't tell if she's about to kiss him or kill him. "If you promise to never, ever, *ever* do that again, I'll let you escort me to the bar. I make no promises about the condition of your heart after we're done. Got it?"

Someone from the crowd screams, "Kiss him." The boys start chanting it, and soon the whole crowd is into it.

A rebel to peer pressure, she says, "If I did that, I'd have to charge you admission."

She takes Liam's hand, and they head off to the bar. She subtly leans into him as they walk, and I can see that she's fighting back a big smile. "Come on, you," James says, wrapping his arm around me. "You look far too stunning to not be twirled around on the dance floor."

James is one hell of a dancer. He spins me around for almost an hour. My legs feel like Jell-O, my cheeks hurt from smiling, and I haven't looked for Gavin once.

James is the most wonderful distraction—probably because I know he has no intentions other than making me smile. I spot a beautiful girl scoping him out, so I insist on giving my feet a break. I lead him off the dance floor and practically push him into her. I apologize for being so clumsy and then make myself scarce.

I watch them from afar, feeling proud of my matchmaking, until I see Em storm out of the room. I spot Liam at their table, looking devastated. God damn it. I warned him about her.

"You okay, Pumpkin?" I ask, wrapping my arms around him.

"I have no idea what just happened. I thought we were getting along smashingly, then she got a text and ran out. I tried to stop her, and she wouldn't even look at me. All she said was 'cocksucker-motherfucker.'"

Ash. What the hell is going on?

"I need to go find her. Something's up, but I'm sure it has nothing to do with you." I kiss his cheek and run out of the room looking for Em.

It takes me a while to track her down. When I do, she's kissing Max.

"What the fuck, Emily?" Liam shouts.

Damn, he followed me. This is going to get messy.

Looking perfectly calm, she takes a step away from Max. "Liam. I told you I needed to handle something."

"Oh, I'm something you need to *handle* now?" Max retorts.

"Can someone please tell me what the hell is going on here?" Realizing his volume has attracted attention,

Liam lowers his voice. "Who the hell is this, Emily?"

Max looks at Liam and then looks back at Em. Max is very good at reading people and situations, and his face falls. "Yeah, *Emily*, who the hell am I?"

"Liam, this is not the time or place, and this is none of your business. Go back to the party. Now," she orders looking Liam square in the eye. Despite the fact Em never promises commitment or monogamy, boys are always surprised when they find out that they are just a number on Em's long list of suitors.

I look between Max and Liam. I can see the anger spreading over both of them. It's like watching two trains driving full throttle right at each other. I wish I could do something to stop the impending disaster. They've both played Em's game and lost.

Liam walks to Em and turns her toward him. "Fine, you want me to leave, I'll leave. After this." He plants a massive kiss on her and lets her go. "I'm leaving, but don't expect me to come back. Consider this closure." He turns on his heel and storms down the hallway.

A crowd has formed. Trying to minimize the impact of the scene, I pull Em and Max down a side hallway. The moment we leave, the crowd breaks up.

I watched Max's face while Liam kissed her. He looked crushed. He glares at Em, hatred oozing out of him. "I was warned you'd chew me up and spit me out. I just didn't expect it like this. I've lost my job, my best friend, and my house, but none of them hurt as much as this did," Max says through gritted teeth.

When Em gets caught, she turns cold and distant. She pushes her shoulders back, and strengthens her stance. Between her beauty and demeanor, she appears untouchable. There's an icy chill to her voice." I'm sorry you're hurt, but I've been nothing but honest. I don't do relationships. You knew that. You showed up at an event unannounced. Did you really think I wouldn't have a date?"

Max tips his head back and laughs. From the sound of his laugh, I can tell he's ready to snap. "You're a selfish bitch, Em. You hide behind your *honesty* so that you can have your cake and eat it too. You think your 'boundaries' give you carte blanche to fuck with people's minds. As much as I want to pulverize that guy, whoever he is, I can't even be mad at him. He's just some poor sap you suckered into falling for you so you could throw his heart back in his face. Be honest, Em. You love it when guys fall in love with you. You just don't want to love anyone back."

A casual onlooker would think Max's words bounced off Em as if she were Teflon. I, an Em expert, can see he has cut her deep. The way she's digging her nails into her hand. The fact that she hasn't taken a breath since he started speaking. Max doesn't mess around when he's hurt, and though Em may not show it, he has wounded her.

Emily takes a deep breath. "Max, I'm sorry you aren't mature enough to handle this kind of relationship. I don't fuck with anyone's mind. I'm direct, honest, and I always stick to my word. You were a fun fuck, and that's all it ever was and ever will be. If you deluded yourself into believing it was something more, that's your problem, not mine. Time to go back to the kiddie pool. You aren't man enough to swim with the big boys." Before he has a chance to respond, she storms away.

"Max?" I reach out to him, but he shrugs me off.

"Save it. I want to speak to you even less than I want to speak to her." He turns his back to me and walks off.

Considering the night is imploding, I make my way to the closest bar. Martini in hand, I begin my search for Em. The room is jam-packed and it's hard to navigate through the crowd. When I make my way to the edge of the dance floor, I spot Gavin dancing with O.

This night just gets better and better. Her family bought a table, so I knew she was going to be here and Gavin would have to be polite. I didn't realize being civil equates to dancing so close a piece of paper wouldn't fit between them.

Her obvious flirtation is obnoxious. Every time she laughs, she tips her head back, exposing her neck. She casually runs her fingers through his hair or along his jaw. It's disgusting, and he's letting her get away with it.

Unable to watch any longer, I walk away from the dance floor and resume my search for Em. The song ends and the MC calls for everyone's attention. I turn to the stage just as he asks Gavin to say a few words. He takes a step toward the stage when O pulls on his elbow. He stops and turns to face her. Standing on her tip-toes, she goes to kiss him! Thankfully, Gavin catches on and turns his head at the last second. She has to settle for a kiss on the cheek.

Fuming, I slink to the back of the room. I might draw more attention to the situation by leaving, so I stay in the room and try to look like I'm paying attention. Internally, I plot all the ways I'd love to destroy O. It's not entirely her fault, though. She may hang all over him, but Gavin doesn't seem to do anything to stop it.

Having edited eight drafts of the speech, I could recite the damn thing word for word. A brief explanation about the foundation and all the amazing programming made possible by the funds generated tonight. Gratitude to all the big donors and contributors, while paying special attention to guests of honor. He sounds so charming, as though he isn't a mixed-signal-sending, royal prick.

"Last, but certainly not least," he says, going off script. "I would like to thank my lovely girlfriend. Lily, could you come up here."

This was certainly not part of the plan, but I go with it and make my way to the stage. He offers me his hand to help me up the stairs to the stage. Once on the stage, he kisses my hand and leads me to the center. "This evening would not be possible without your endless support and dedication." He turns to the audience. "It's possible I may have been a bit of a cad these past few weeks." The audience laughs.

I smile at him as I try to read his face. I can't image he brought me up just to thank me. Perhaps he's trying to get on my good side after he let O molest him.

"Get those checkbooks ready, because the silent auction ends in twenty minutes. Thank you again for coming and enjoy the rest of the evening." He puts the microphone in the stand, then kisses me breathless. An appropriate kiss for a public event, but still enough to get my heart going.

The audience whistles, cheers and clinks their glasses. When he pulls away, I play to the audience by fanning myself. I get a few laughs, then people go back to their conversations and dancing. I can't help but notice O storm out of the room, tripping on her gown as she weaves through the crowd.

He puts his hand on the small of my back and leads me off the stage. "What was that?" I ask when we are a safe distance from the microphone.

He whispers in my ear. "I couldn't let O get away with

that. I needed to publicly show her and everyone else that you're mine."

He pulls away, then kisses me on the cheek. "I have to get back. I'll find you later." He flashes a smile at me that warms me from the inside out.

I'm about to continue my search for Em, when Poppy grabs me by the arm and drags me to the silent auction table, to help with the last minute bids. She keeps me busy for the next hour and a half while I help her wrap up the auction.

Around one a.m. the party is finally winding down. I spot Liam by the bar. I'm going to need some help getting him out of here.

My first call is to James.

I tap my fingers on the table while it rings, praying he can help me. "Hey, can you come to the back bar and help me get Liam out of here?" I ask.

"Can't, darling. I'm already in for the night," he replies.

I look down at my watch. "So early?"

"I was needed," he says with a quiet voice.

"Oh, James. You didn't chase after her."

"She needs me," he says. His voice sounds desperate, and maybe a little ashamed.

Liam gets louder and more belligerent, screaming at the bartender about cheating whores. "James, I've got to take care of Liam. Please take care of yourself."

As I walk to the bar, I see Liam's been joined by Max. "Well, aren't you two the odd couple?"

He points back and forth between himself and Max. "This is the Emily Harrington Sucks after party," Liam slurs. "You can be our third member, Honey Bunny. I won't even charge you the membership fee, since you're my wife and all."

I sit next to him at the bar. He leans his head on my shoulder. "Ex-wife, pumpkin," I reply. "In case you've forgotten, you're still at the *actual* party. After parties occur after you've left. Speaking of leaving, let's get you two in a car. Come on, up, up."

"I'm not going with you," Max huffs. "I still hate you."

I know he's drunk and has plenty of reason to be angry with me, but it still stings to hear the rage in his voice. He really does despise me. Regardless, I need to get him out of here. "Fine, you can continue to hate me on your way to wherever you're staying. Which is where?" I ask.

"Gavin and I never got that far. I was told to get on a plane, so I got on a plane. I got changed when I got here. My bags are... somewhere." His eyes glaze.

Liam is falling asleep on the bar.

I don't know where Liam lives or how to get him inside his place, so I make a decision.

"Okay, new plan. Everyone is going to Gavin's. Let's go. I've got a car waiting."

Two of the bartenders are kind enough to help me get the boys outside and into the limo. I ask the driver to wait while I run in and find Em.

She's by the front bar, talking to my favorite British actor. Too tired and emotionally overwhelmed to be intimidated by him, I interrupt them and pull Em aside.

"I've got Thing 1 and Thing 2 in my car. I found them drinking together."

"See, I bring people together," she cheers.

"Yeah, you're a real peach that way. You want to tell me what happened tonight?"

"I cleared up my dance cart." She smirks before tipping back her glass of champagne. "Now I have plenty of free time to explore that yummy piece of British ass over there." She motions to the blond actor.

I can't believe she's not remotely bothered by what happened between her and the boys. I fold my arms across my chest. "Is that how you're going to play it?"

She rolls her eyes and sets her empty glass on the table next to us. "I'm not like you. I don't want to play house. The thought of being tied down to one man gives me hives. They knew my rules, but both of them thought I'd change. Their heartache is on them, not me."

I look at her with disbelief. "I know you desperately want to believe that, but deep down you know it's a crock of shit. You push men away so they don't get the chance to hurt you."

"Don't make me out to be the bad girl." She kisses me on the cheek. "I'm going to get back to Jax over there."

"You know that isn't his real name, right?" I say.

She looks over her shoulder as she walks away. "Shh, don't ruin the fantasy."

Before leaving, I quickly look for Gavin. Poppy says he's buried trying to close out the party. I send him a text letting him know I'm headed home with house guests, then hop in the car with the bosom buddies. I get them home, tuxes off and in bed without anyone puking. Quite the accomplishment after the night I've had.

Excited that the dark cloud over us might finally pass, I decide to wait up for Gavin. After a long shower, I throw on sweats, make a fire, and curl up with my Kindle on the sofa. Two sentences in, I fall asleep.

Chapter Twenty-Nine

Sometime in the middle of the night Gavin collects me from the sofa. I rest my head against his chest. My hair sticks to his skin, still damp from the shower. I take a deep breath and inhale his scent. So clean and masculine. It makes me want to wrap my arms around him and never let go.

He lays me on the bed, then scoots in behind me, wrapping his arms around my stomach. I thread my fingers through his, pulling him even closer. He's restless, shifting and adjusting, trying to find a comfortable position. "This isn't going to work."

That's not how this is supposed to go. The gala ends, Mr. Moody Broody goes away, and my sexy, loving boyfriend returns. That was the deal. Wearing only boxer briefs that highlight his abdominal glory, he definitely has the sexy part down, but the frown and furrowed eyebrows have got to go. My eyes narrow. “What’s not going to work?”

He tugs at my sweatshirt. “I need this off. I need all of it off. After the week we’ve had, I just need to be close to you. I need to feel you.”

I pull my sweats off and toss them on the floor. I lie down with my back facing him. He lies on his side behind me. I expect him to pull his body next to mine, but he doesn’t. He’s a good foot away. I look over my shoulder and see his eyes raking over my body. There’s a hunger in his eyes that sends chills up my body. I reach to pull the sheet over me. He gently grabs my wrist. “Just let me look at you.”

With a feather light touch, he runs his forefinger along my side from my ribs to my waist. His breath hitches. “I don’t think I told you how ravishing you look tonight.”

I smirk. “It was all the dress.”

He leans forward and kisses my neck. “Yes, you looked positively stunning at the gala. That dress was pure sin. But I was referring to now. In this moment, you look ravishing.”

He plants soft, sensual kisses from my stomach to my hip bone. “This is one of my favorite parts of you. This line that goes from the curvature of your hips to the swell of your breasts.” He runs his tongue along the contours of my body, making me squirm with anticipation.

Each touch of his tongue to my skin stokes the fire burning within me. We have so much to talk about, so much to work out between us. But at this moment, I can only think of his hand that’s creeping up my thigh.

"Your legs are torture to look at. So toned and smooth. They go on forever. Every time I look at them, all I can think of is the paradise waiting for me when I reach the top." He shifts his body behind me, so that he can kiss my thighs. "I love how soft your skin is," he says before kissing a spot halfway up my thigh. "Do you know what I love even more?"

My breath hitches as he kisses the top of my thigh. I can feel his breath on my core. "What?" I say, challenging him.

"The way you taste." I tip my head back and moan as he runs his tongue along my pussy. One deliciously slow lick after another. As good as it feels, I know it can feel so much better. Desperate for more, I grind against his tongue. He moans. The vibrations make me quiver. I squeeze my thighs, keeping his head in just the right place. Spurred on by my greed, he swirls his tongue around my clit, bringing me right to the edge.

He lightly blows, sending shockwaves throughout my body. "I know I have a lot to apologize for," he says. "Do you mind if we skip ahead to the make-up sex?"

Breathless, I look at him and see his chin glistening from my juices. "Seems like cheating," I say.

He blows again, and I scream. "Sure is," he says. "I promise I'll make it worth your while." He dives back down, and pulls my clit between his teeth. The tingles start in my toes, then blast through my body. All the tension releases in one euphoric wave.

Before I can catch my breath, he flips me onto my stomach. "I hope you're not in the mood for soft and sweet because I haven't been inside you in weeks. I don't have it in me to be gentle." He slams his cock into me.

I gasp as he fills me. He's right. It has been too long. "Soft and sweet is overrated."

He plunges deep into me again, and I scream. "Glad you see it my way," he says.

He reaches his hand between my thighs and rubs my clit while he thrusts into me.

"Oh Gavin," I moan. "Don't stop. Don't fucking stop."

The sensations overpower me. He's so deep inside me, hitting all the right places. The buildup is so intense, I don't think I can take it. I brush his hand away from my clit. "I can't. I can't come again."

He pins my hand behind my back. "You can and you will." He resumes rubbing and fucking. Every muscle in my body tenses. I'm wound so tight it hurts. Unrelenting, Gavin pushes deeper inside me and I come undone. He comes immediately after me and we collapse in a heap on the bed. Panting and satisfied, we lie tangled together until we fall asleep.

We both stir a few hours later.

"You awake?" he asks.

I sit up and reach for my water glass on the nightstand. "Sort of."

He takes the glass from me and takes a sip. "We should talk."

I return the glass to the table, then wipe the sleep from my eyes.. "This week sucked. In fact, the past few weeks have sucked. You shut me out, and I hated it. Don't ever do that to me again."

He cups my cheek and kisses me. "I was an ass. An ill-tempered, self-absorbed ass. I promise it'll never happen again." He looks away and sighs. "This whole week was a cock up."

I raise an eyebrow. "If my memory serves, this was the first time your cock was up all week."

He shakes his head and laughs. "I promise you it was up plenty of times, I just never had time to do anything about it."

I pull the sheet up around me. "Maybe if you had made the time, you wouldn't have been such an ass."

He laughs. "If only you'd said that to me before, the week wouldn't have turned into such a blunder. It was completely my fault. I fucked up. The gala's always hard for me, but this year was so much worse. The event gets bigger and bigger each year, which is always added stress. Plus it opens up old wounds for me. Factor all that in along with everything else going on in our lives. I overloaded and emotionally shut down. It was the only way I could get through it all without falling to pieces. I'm surprised you didn't tell me to go to hell and run for the hills."

His hair is sticking up in every direction. I run my fingers through it, trying to tame it. "Oh, I thought about it," I say with a laugh. "Several times. But my dress for last night was so kick ass, I couldn't let it go to waste."

"You were the most stunning woman there. I've never seen you look so sexy and sophisticated. If I had come near you, I don't think I could have stopped myself from throwing you over my shoulder and hauling you to the nearest flat surface so I could have my wicked way with you. Table, wall, dance floor. I would have lost all restraint."

"Would that have been such a bad thing?" I ask,

playing coy. I lean forward to kiss him, when the doorbell rings. I look at the clock on the bedside table. "It's so early. Who the hell is at our door?"

The bell rings again. I groan as I pick my sweats up off the floor. "I'll go."

"No, luv, you can stay in bed," Gavin protests.

I look at the now dried mess on his crotch. "You're in need of another shower. I'll be back in a second." I throw my sweats on. "It's probably a neighbor out of tea or something."

As I make my way to the door, I see Liam in the kitchen looking like death warmed over.

"Just stay right there, Liam. Don't answer the door or anything," I tease. In the shape he's in, I'm shocked he made it to the kitchen.

I open the door to find the new door guy.

"Sorry to bother you so early, Ms. Clark. I have a package for you. It's marked urgent."

"For me?" Who's sending me something?

He hands me the envelope with handwriting I'd recognize anywhere. Lorenzo.

Lily,

There's been an uprising in the cartel. The new leadership is cleaning house. Carlos believes you're on their target list. Stay under lock and key until you hear from me.

For once, stay out of trouble. The cartel is out for blood, and they will stop at nothing to get it.

I've included supplies for your go-bag. I suggest you pack one.

Be safe. I will be in touch.

LG

Fuck me.

I look inside the envelope and there are fake IDs, passports, credit cards. "Gavin!"

Liam covers his ears. "Honey Bunny, enough with the yelling."

I ignore him as I run back to the bedroom. On the way, I stop in Max's room and shake him.

"Max, you need to get up. Please." I'm panicked, and I need all the help I can get.

He pulls the covers over his head. "Fuck you, Slugger. I'm hung-over, and I hate you. Leave me the fuck alone."

"I don't care if you hate me. Get your ass up. I just got a letter that the cartel is after me."

"Why the hell do you think I'm here? It's certainly not to see you. Or the sights. Or you. Wait." He pokes his head out from under the comforter. "Letter? What letter?"

"Get up, and I'll show it to you." I jump off the bed and make my way to the door.

He calls out to me. "Lily, wait. I have to tell you what's going on. Just give me a second to put pants on."

"Fine, meet me on the terrace. Something tells me I'll want some fresh air for this conversation." I first stop by the bedroom. Gavin's in the shower.

"Who was it?" he asks.

"Lorenzo."

He drops the soap. "What?"

"Not him him. A letter from him." I grab my toothbrush and quickly brush my teeth.

"You, Max and I need to talk," he says. "There've been some developments that I haven't had a chance to tell you about."

I rinse off my toothbrush and put it back in the holder. "I woke Max up."

He turns the shower off. I hand him a fresh towel from the cabinet. "Go talk to Max. You two need to sort things out."

I openly gawk at him while he dries off. "I'm surprised you two are so chummy now. In Vegas, you couldn't wait for him to go back to DC and out of my life."

He kisses me. "I'm not worried about you leaving me for Max. He has his hands full with Emily, so I don't foresee any further kisses coming from him. Plus, how can I ask you to be tolerant of O, if I can't be tolerant of Max."

I wipe a dab of shaving cream off his chin. "You're so mature it's disgusting."

He slaps my ass. "Go talk to him. I'll be out in a bit."

Max is waiting on the terrace. I wrap myself in a blanket and head out.

He hands me a steaming white mug. "Irish hot

chocolate. Try it; you'll like it. Even if you don't, in twenty minutes, you'll appreciate it. Lord knows I need a little hair of the dog right now."

I take a sip, and it's shockingly good. Not what I expected, but good. "What's in this?"

"Hot chocolate, Guinness, Bailey's, and Jameson."

"So much liquor this early in the morning, things must be bad," I reply, taking another sip.

"Actually, I just want to get you drunk enough that you won't do something stupid, like try to take them on all by yourself." He moves from the chair to the spot next to me on the two seat sofa. "I haven't forgiven you; I just want in on this blanket action. It's fucking cold out here."

I unwrap the blanket and lay it over our laps. "Talk, Max."

"The FBI and DEA were about to take down the cartel. Between my investigation and others, they had enough to take down their American organization. We had an inside source feeding them intel. The set up was perfect. All the big fish were going to go down."

My mind goes to Carlos. I wonder which side of this he's on. I take a sip of my drink and nod for him to continue.

"There's a leak," Max continues. "No idea who or from which agency, but there's a leak. The bastards were tipped off, and they cleaned house before the raid. There were shootouts in a few locations, and a lot of good agents went down. It was a fucking catastrophe. I should tell you. Todd Masters was killed, along with a few other people tied to the organization that could rat them out."

I sigh. "I heard from Em. I tried to call you, but you weren't really talking to me then."

He scoffs. "If I'd told you what was going on, you probably would have hopped on a plane to Mexico and tried to infiltrate the cartel all on your own. I had my hands full with the leak, I didn't need to manage you too."

I want to argue with him. Prove to him that I'm not some loose cannon that needs to be wrangled in, but now isn't the time. A bunch of dedicated agents lost their lives trying to break this cartel down. Defending my relevance in this fight is petty. "Please tell me something positive happened during the raid. Did you glean any information? Make any arrests?"

"We captured one of their guys. They had him in interrogation for days. The only thing he said was 'get ready for the show'.

"What the hell does that mean?"

"Things are about to get bloody."

My hands tremble, so I put my cup on the table and tuck my hands under the blanket.

"Two days later, we received word that some politicians they paid off didn't live up to expectations. They threw Molotov cocktails at power stations, knocking out power in eleven towns. In the middle of the night, they kidnapped the children of the politicians."

I gasp. "That's horrible."

"The boys were returned when the politicians paid them off. The girls... the girls'll probably never be seen again. These bastards are big into human trafficking."

Just the thought of what those poor girls are going through makes me gag.

"As soon as I saw things were heating up, I called Gavin."

The picture becomes clear. "Hence all the security last night."

He nods then takes a sip. "Gavin wanted to cancel or at least keep you home. I didn't think we needed to go that far. While I'm not entirely convinced you are in danger, we need to start working together to keep you safe. These guys are on a mission to prove their dominance. You're a loose end that got away. That's unacceptable in their book."

I shake my head. "I'm no one. Why the hell would they waste time on me?"

He taps my forehead. "You have to think like they do. Your boyfriend is this hot-shot defense contractor and your roommate is an FBI agent.... Former FBI agent. Killing you would catch lots of press and would give them tons of cred. "

I squeeze his leg. "I'm sorry about your job."

He waves me off. "It wasn't entirely your fault. You didn't fucking help, but it's not all on you. Whoever's working with the cartel inside the Bureau pushed to get me out. It fucking sucks, but with the leak and other shady shit going down inside the Bureau, I'll be more effective working in the private sector."

The pain in his eyes is so clear. Max lives and breathes being a FBI agent. To be betrayed by them must break his heart.

He continues. "Gavin's got all the resources we need

to keep you safe, and I can do some more snooping under the radar. Gavin's company can get away with way more shit than I ever could as an agent. While we sort this shit out, you need to lay low. Do you hear me? I can't do what needs to be done if I'm distracted by you sneaking off to play dragon slayer."

"You make it sound like I just randomly decided to square off with the devil. I was backed into a corner and had no other choice," I say.

"You *saw* no other choice. It wasn't that you didn't have options, you just couldn't' see them. There's a difference," he states. "Either way, just stay in the fucking house and do what you're told. For once. Please."

Before I have the chance to answer, he stands. "Don't know about you, but I need a refill. You're going to love this one. Hot chocolate, tequila, Kahlua, and Grand Marnier."

I laugh. "Jesus, Max. You're pretty serious about keeping me incapacitated."

A few minutes later, Gavin comes out with my refill. "If the law enforcement thing doesn't work out, Max can switch gears and become a bartender. This is brilliant." He joins me on the sofa and pulls me close.

I take a sip and put it back down. It's good but strong.

"Are you okay, luv?"

"I'm sloshed before noon. I'm not sure that qualifies as okay."

He threads his fingers in mine. "How are you feeling about everything Max told you?"

"I'm petrified. I just don't get it. I'm not that interesting. You'd think they'd have bigger enemies to go after."

He sighs and speaks with a quiet, somber tone. "You damaged their reputation. Your story has gotten out. You got away, you pulverized one of their men, and you snuck into their turf and snatched someone they were about to make a play for. You keep making them look bad, and they can't handle that. They think you snitched on them, and they cannot tolerate betrayal. Going after you will set precedent."

"Criminal psychology a hobby of yours?" I ask.

He tucks a lock of hair behind my ear. "This is part of my job. I help people fight bad guys, so I have to understand how the bad guys work."

I fiddle with my cross. "I keep forgetting about that. You don't talk about your job too often. Conceptually, I know what you do, but I really have no freaking clue. I always thought it was more communication technology. Walkie-talkies and whatnot. "

He laughs. "It's more complicated than that. We do make communication products. Very fancy walkie-talkies. We have a whole division that develops medical products to be used in the field. The bulk of what I do is top secret, so I can't discuss it. Just know that there's no one on this planet who can keep you safer than I can." He kisses the tip of my nose. "You just have to let me."

I wink. "My own personal James Bond, huh? You do look mighty fine in a tux, Mr. Edwards."

"I'm being serious, luv. This situation is a colossal clusterfuck. It has gotten completely out of control, and you won't be able to dodge it alone. We have to hit this head on, and that makes it way out of your league. Promise me you'll let Max and I take care of things. I know you don't like anyone else running the show, but you have to let go. If not for you, then for me. I'll never recover if something happens to you. So for my sanity and your safety, please do as we ask."

Between the spiked hot chocolate and the heavy conversation, I don't have the strength to fight him. I hate being a sitting duck. If someone's coming for me, I'd rather fight them head on. But that is a conversation for another time.

"We need to get Liam out of here," Gavin says when I don't argue. "It isn't safe here. With all the press you've been getting, our address is public knowledge. In a few days, I want to move you to the country house. The property records are in the name of the estate. Even if someone comes looking for you, it'll take some time before they figure out I have property there. I'm installing additional security, and as soon as they're ready, I want you out of here."

I snort. "Another wonderful upside of being on baby watch."

"In some ways, it's another level of protection. It's hard to get to you through a gaggle of photographers," he replies.

I laugh. "I can see one of the paparazzo taking out a hit man just because they think he's trying to steal the better shot. Those guys are vicious. The cartel better watch out!"

"Sad but true," Gavin replies. "Do you think Em can help get Liam home?"

I shake my head. "I don't think Liam or Max will be speaking to Em anytime soon."

He sips his hot chocolate. "Do I even want to know what happened with them last night?" he asks.

I shrug. "Typical Em. Making everyone fall for her but remaining perpetually unattached."

"Ah," he says. "I thought she and Liam were different. I thought there might be something real there."

"With Em, you can never tell. I'll call James. It's the perfect excuse for me to check on him without being too obvious."

He narrows his eyes. "Why would you need to check on him? What else did I miss?"

"He went home with O," I answer.

Gavin shakes his head. "I love James as a brother, but I'll never be able to save him from himself. Liam's a big boy; he can get home on his own. I'll go kick him in the arse and get him in a cab." He kisses me on the forehead. "I'm going to go check in with Max."

I grab his elbow. "Hey, Lorenzo gave me a bunch of stuff for my go-bag. What the hell's a go-bag?"

"A bag with everything you'd need to flee. Money, identification, passport, important documents. When you leave with a go-bag you don't plan on returning."

I run my cross along my necklace. "Do I need one?"

"I've heard of worse ideas."

Max and Gavin stay squirreled away all day, plotting and keeping me drunk enough that I can't contribute. I throw in a few suggestions like, "Let's just nuke the fuckers," and "What if we dress up as ninjas and kill them all in their sleep?" Nothing productive, but they'd make excellent ideas for a movie. By sundown, I've been drinking all day and fall fast asleep. With the amount and crazy mix of liquor I've had, I could sleep for a week.

****

"Lily, wake up," Gavin whispers. "Come on, something important is going on. I know you may still be knackered, but you have to get up."

I cover my eyes to block out the light. "Urg, what time is it?" I groan.

"Two thirty in the afternoon," he replies.

"What day is it?"

"Monday. You've been asleep for almost a full day."

"Holy crap." I jump up. "Wait! Did Max drug me to make sure I don't interfere? I'll kill him."

He laughs. "No, luv. You were just really blitzed and over-tired. But there's a major situation we need to discuss."

"Okay, okay. I'm up," I reply. "What's going on?"

Gavin looks tense, like he's dreading this conversation. Gavin doesn't dread anything, so that furrowed brow makes me very nervous.

He takes a deep breath. "Lily, do you have a child?"

I rub my eyes. "What? No, Gavin, I don't have a child. Don't you think you would know if I have a child?"

"I know you don't currently have a child, but did you

ever have a child?" he asks.

The worry in his eyes breaks my heart. He really thinks I would keep something this monumental from him.

"Oxford, I've never, ever been pregnant. Never even had a scare. What is all this about?"

He drops his head back and releases a deep sigh, I'm guessing of relief. I'm pretty sure I hear him mumble, "Oh thank heavens," but I can't be sure.

He grabs me by the neck and pulls me in for a fiery kiss. "Greene called. Your condo was broken into and trashed. There was a note that said they were going to find your son."

"My son?" I can't imagine who they're talking about. Gavin rattles off some more information about the damage to my condo, but I'm not really listening.

It isn't until later, while I'm brushing my teeth, that it clicks.

"Gavin! I shout.

He runs into the bathroom. "Luv?"

I put my toothbrush back on the charger. "Did they say my kid or Ash's kid?"

"I don't know. Why?" he asks.

"Ash had a kid with that stripper, Crystal. I mean, we don't have a DNA test, but the kid looks just like him. I don't know what happened to him after she died. That's the only thing I can think of."

"That's an idea. I'm going back to the office to see Max. I'll keep you posted." He kisses me and runs off.

I hope I'm wrong and that they haven't drug that poor boy into it. He's already been through so much. He lost his mother and his good-for-nothing sperm donor of a father. Guilt wells up inside me. How have I not thought about him? When I saw his picture at Crystal's apartment, I knew what Charlie had done to her and that the boy was probably all alone. I should have done something. I've taken on all of Ash's debts and responsibilities except for the most important one. So many innocent lives are at risk because of Ash, and as much as I want to, I can't blame it all on him. I've done a masterful job of endangering the lives of everyone around me because I was sure I could take care of this on my own.

I spend the rest of the afternoon sulking and brooding. I'm making brownies, a much needed accompaniment for my pity party, when my phone plays "I Think I Love You" by the Partridge Family.

"Hello, James," I answer "I've been worried."

"Lily, I'm stuck, and I don't know what to do."

I can hear the agony in his voice.

I put the pan in the oven, and set the timer. "Start from the beginning. What's wrong?"

"I've been with O since Saturday. When she's lost it like this in the past, it just takes her a few hours to snap back. But not this time. I can't get her to eat or sleep. All she talks about is how she has to get Gavin and get rid of you. Half the time she doesn't make any sense; she just rants and raves endless nonsense. Seriously, Lily, I'm worried. She's gone completely mad. What if she hurts herself... or someone else? The way she talks about going after you..."

I sit at the table while I process what he's telling me.

"Jesus," I say quietly. "With Daphney's history, it's something we need to consider. Have you spoken to her parents?"

"Her parents left for holiday after the gala. I can't reach them. I'm scared to leave her alone. I don't know what to do." He's quietly sobbing.

"You need to call her doctor. Sounds like she needs a sedative and maybe some antidepressants or something. I'll talk to Gavin; maybe he has some ideas. You need to get some rest too. Does she have any other friends or family who can stay with her?"

He clears his throat. "Her cousin's on her way over. I have a business trip tomorrow, so I need to go home and pack. I'm just scared."

My heart breaks for him. "James, I can't imagine what you must be feeling. It sounds like the situation has gotten out of hand. Please call her doctor," I say.

"I'll call him right now."

"I wish I could help you more, but if I get involved it will probably agitate her more. Keep me posted."

"Of course," he says as he clicks off.

Gah! I feel as if we're stuck in this cyclone of catastrophe. Everyone and everything in my life is an unstable disaster. I pray to God something lets up, and soon!

Chapter Thirty

Max and Gavin don't get home until after midnight, and they plan on being back in the office before sunrise. Even though I slept for almost a full day, I'm exhausted. Excessive drama drains all the life out of you. My life has been pure chaos for over a week, and my nerves, brain, and heart just can't keep up.

Max is still trying to locate Crystal's son. He found out that the kid went into foster care after Crystal's death, but that's as far as he's gotten. Everyone agrees that the boy is most likely who the cartel was talking about. If they think he's my kid, he could be in real danger.

I talk to Gavin about O, and he promises to reach out to her parents and family in the morning. I know I shouldn't waste a moment's thought on her, but I can't leave this all on James. My biggest fear is that she'll try to kill herself to get Gavin's attention. Her sister will forever be in Gavin's heart because of her suicide, and I wouldn't put it past O to give it a try. She loves herself way too much to actually harm herself, but she's batshit crazy enough to make it look convincing.

After our short chat about O, I'm out like a light. When I come to the next morning, Max and Gavin are gone. Gavin left a note telling me to pack and be ready to leave for the country house this afternoon. I'm going there indefinitely, so I pack up everything. When I applied for my visa, I hired movers to go to my condo, pack up the rest of my clothes, and ship them to me. I still don't have very much, but I might as well take it all.

I'm deep in Gavin's closet when I hear a noise. "Gavin? You home?" I call out.

It's barely noon, so I can't imagine he's back already. Maybe this time he'll ask if my parents are really dead. Or if I have a long-lost evil twin. Everything else in my life feels as though it's from a melodramatic soap opera, so who knows what'll pop up next.

More crashes come from down the hall.

"Oxford, I'm not cleaning up whatever mess you're making." Gavin doesn't really make messes. Oh, I bet it is Max.

I storm out of the closest and into the hall. "Maxwell McCarthy, you had better not—"

The distinct sound of a gun being cocked catches my attention. "Hello, Lily."

I turn around. "Olivia. How did you get into my house?" My eyes are focused on the gun in her hands, but I can't help but notice the changes in her appearance. When James said was planning on coming after me, I didn't expect this.

"*Gavin's house*!" Waving the gun around she says, "None of this is yours. This isn't your life; this is *my* life. You've just hijacked it. I'm here to take it back." She steps toward me, glass crunching beneath her feet. It appears she threw all the framed pictures of Gavin and me on the floor.

"You went blonde, huh? And either you've hijacked my dry cleaning, or you've been trolling through my online shopping receipts. I really wouldn't put either past you. Is that part of taking your life back, because it seems like you're just trying to steal mine." I should know better than to be a snarky bitch to someone holding a gun. But every single time it happens, I just can't seem to help myself.

Chapter Thirty-One

Gavin

Traffic's jammed up again. I'm not sure why it still surprises me. It's raining cats and dogs, so of course traffic'll be a bitch. I waste so much bloody time stopped on the motorway. With all the different directions I'm being pulled these days, I don't have the time to spare. Perhaps it's time to break down and hire a driver.

I finally arrive at the SIS Building thirty minutes late, but nothing ever starts on time at the Secret Intelligence Service. After going through security, I'm escorted to a briefing room, where I'm told to wait. Typical.

My mobile rings whilst I'm waiting. Olivia's cousin? What could she want? Over the last few days, I've gone back and forth with her and James, but there's nothing I can do to help O this time. They need to sort it out themselves. "Eleanor, this is not a good time. Can I ring you back?"

"No! O's missing."

Bloody fantastic. More theatrics, courtesy of Olivia. "Slow down, and tell me what's going on."

She takes a few deep breaths. "She said she was taking a kip. She hasn't been sleeping, so I thought a long sleep would be good for her. I went upstairs to see if she wanted lunch and she was gone. The doorman said she pulled her car out hours ago! I've rung her mobile, but I just get her voice mail. I'm worried, Gavin. She isn't well. She shouldn't be driving."

I run my fingers through my hair. "Eleanor, I empathize, but I'm not sure what I can do. I'm heading into a meeting."

"What if she does something? She's not stable. She reminds me of Daphney before..."

The gentlemen I'm meeting with come into the room.

I lower my voice and say, "I pray she doesn't. I have to jump off, my meeting is starting. Keep me posted, please."

Icing on the bloody cake.

SIS is buying a piece of counterintelligence technology from us, but they're making us jump through hoops. After years of working with them, I'm used to their process, but today, I don't have the patience for it. I would have delegated this meeting, but I need to check in with a friend at SIS, so it made sense for me to come in person.

Leo's in charge of Latin America and has been keeping his ear to the ground for all things cartel-related. He sent me a text this morning about losing two in the murder of crows. I'm sure if I thought about it, I could decipher his meaning, but I'm just too damn tired for cloak-and-dagger bullshit.

Max and I have been burning the candle at both ends trying to get a handle on Lily's... situation. The civil war within the cartel makes it difficult for us to figure out who's on which side, who's a threat, and who could be an asset. Between Max's and my connections, we're making some headway, but every time we think we get a handle on things, they start killing each other. After each showdown, we have to start all over again.

As soon as the meeting wraps, I head up to Leo Goldstein's office. I've caught him in the middle of a late breakfast. Leo looks as though he's been in the espionage game too long: rumpled clothes, thinning hair, pudgy around the middle, and deep creases on his face from too many years of stress, bad diet, and all night stakeouts. He may not look like much, but he knows every in and out of every organized crime syndicate from Mexico to Argentina.

"I lost my secret decoder ring, so I have no idea what your message meant." I sit on the chair in front of his desk. "Enlighten me."

He puts down his bagel and wipes the cream cheese from his chin. "I'm glad you came by." He gets up and closes the door. "Your boys made some major waves yesterday."

"They're not my boys, but go on."

He sits back down. "That target list you showed me?"

Max and some of the others on his task force had put

together a list of potential targets. As soon as he brought me into the loop, I took the list to Leo.

"Yes?" I reply.

"They're all dead. All of them hit within the last forty-eight hours, and each death more brutal than the last." Leo shifts some papers on his desk until he finds a pad. "Carlos Sanchez was found hanging from a bridge. He'd been beaten, all his teeth were gone, and they skinned him. Alive."

I swallow hard. It sounds as if they're going after high-level targets in Mexico, but I can't imagine they'd come after Lily.

"Here's another interesting fact. No one else will make this connection, but Lorenzo Grimaldi was killed yesterday."

My jaw drops as I break out into a sweat. "What?"

"He was in some tiny Italian restaurant for a party for some kid in the neighborhood that just made his confirmation. They sealed the exits and torched the place. Ninety-some people died. You need to get your girl into hiding, and keep her there until the dust settles. At the rate they're killing each other, they'll all be dead in a couple months and she'll be in the clear."

I jump out of my seat. "I have to go."

He shouts as I leave his office, "Let me know if I can do anything to help!"

I dial Max as I run to my car. "Max, you have to get to Lily. We need to get her to the safe house now."

"One of your guys is driving me to your place now. Did you get my messages?"

I pull into traffic, driving like a bat out of hell. "Max, you have to listen to me. The cartel is coming for her!"

"What? This isn't about the cartel. Your security company called. Your fire alarm went off. Fire department's on its way."

I tap my thumbs on the steering wheel whilst I wait at a traffic light. "Have you spoken to Lily? Did she get out safely?"

"Her phone goes straight to voice mail."

"Get there," I scream before ending the call.

I'm twenty minutes from home in normal traffic. Too bloody long. I plow through red lights and go the wrong way on two one-way streets, praying I don't kill anyone. If a traffic officer catches me, so be it. I'll lead him back to the flat. Max and I could use the help.

I arrive at the flat in fifteen minutes, a record for sure. Fire engines line the street. I don't bother parking; I just leave the Rover on the street. Willis opens the door for me.

"Have you seen Lily? Did she get out?" I ask.

He shakes his head. "No, sir. I haven't seen her."

The lift is blocked by firefighters, so I take the stairs two at a time.

When I get to my floor, my heart stops. Smoke burns my eyes and lungs. The stench makes me gag.

"Lily!" I run through the door. I'm only a few steps into my flat when Max tries to push me out the door.

"No, man. Don't go in there. You don't need to see that," Max says.

Isaac, the head of security for my company, grabs my arms and pulls me into the hall.

I pull free of Isaac's grip and shove Max as hard as I can, but he doesn't budge. "Get the fuck out of my way! I need to get to her!"

Isaac moves to block the doorway.

Max gets in my face. "She's gone, Gavin. I'm telling you as your friend, you *don't* want go in there."

I drop my shoulder to ram him, but he and Isaac push me back against the wall. "I need to see her!"

Max puts his hands on my shoulders, pushing me into the wall. "There's not enough of her left to see."

The air is sucked out of my lungs as I drop to my knees.

He sits next to me on the floor. "I'm sorry, man. I'm so fucking sorry."

"I'm sorry, Edwards." Isaac crouches in front of me. "The fire chief said we can stay, but we have to stay out of the flat and out of their way."

I notice both of their shoulders slump forward. They think I've given up. I jump to my feet. Isaac reaches out to stop me, but I smash my knee into his chin, making him fall back. I run into the flat.

The smell is far worse inside my flat than it was in the hallway. I have to fight back the urge to vomit.

Once I step into the living room, all I see is red. Red splattered everywhere. The sofa, the carpet, the walls. I step forward, and something crunches beneath my foot. I step back and look down to see what I've stepped on.

Oh dear, God! A ... finger. I've stepped on a finger. I look around the floor. Fingers are scattered over the blood soaked floor.

A police officer pushes me out of the room, screaming about preserving the evidence. I stumble into the kitchen, and I see her. She's nailed to the wall, like Christ on the cross. Her body is charred, almost unrecognizable. Smoke looms around her as her body continues to smolder.

"Lily," I scream. I run to her. "We need to get her down! Someone, please, get her down!"

Max and Isaac grab my arms and drag me out of the room. "She's gone, Gavin!" Max screams. "She's gone! You have to let her go!"

I fall to a heap on the floor. Max and Isaac lift me by the arms and carry me to the hall.

Time stands still. People bustle around me, but I'm frozen. Not thinking, not feeling. My heart may be beating, but my life has come to a halt. I let Lily down. I promised to protect her, and I failed. Now she's gone.

I try to imagine what her last moments were like. Ghastly images flitter through my mind. The pain she must have endured. Every thought that comes into my head makes me want to scream, to break something, to kill someone. *How could I let this happen?*

The lift dings, and a man in medical scrubs steps out. A fireman and police officer meet him at my door.

The fireman hands the man a clipboard. "We have to be careful with this one. The body's in bad shape. She was alive when the bastard set her on fire, the sprinklers went off and the water compromised the evidence—"

Torturous screaming drowns them out. They turn and stare at me. The police officer steps toward me. He's talking, but I can't hear him over the screaming. Max pushes past the officer and looks at me with a frantic expression. He shakes me hard, and the screaming stops.

"Man, they need us to get out of here." He pulls me to my feet. "Let's let them do their job."

Their job? Finding her killer? They won't have a chance to do their job. I'll hunt those bastards like the animals they are. There won't be a place on Earth they can hide. Every second of pain they put her through will come back to them a thousand fold. They'll pray for the depths of hell by the time I'm done with them.

They're all going to burn.

Read the gripping conclusion to Lily and Gavin's story in

When Fates Align

Available now!

Dear Reader,

I imagine you hate me right about now. It's okay, you can admit it. I highly encourage you to reach out and vent. You've been kind enough to join me on this wild ride, the least I can do is hold your hand when things take a turbulent detour! I'm anxious to hear what you think, so feel free to let me have it!

Email: Isabellerichards8@gmail.com

Facebook group: Isabelle's Book Belles

Facebook: www.Facebook.com/isabellerichards-author

Twitter @88IsabelleR

Mailing list: http://eepurl.com/bcfzP1

I can't thank you enough for coming with me on this adventure and I look forward to hearing from you!

Acknowledgements

When I write, I get a one track mind. In every song I hear, I can somehow link it to the characters. When I walk through the grocery store, I think, *what would they have for dinner?* When someone tells me about their day, I often respond, "That's nice, but back to my book."

I'm not quite that bad but close. Since I dive into a book bubble, I have so many people to thank for the endless support, countless brainstorming sessions, and the number of times I've been talked off of the ledge.

To Karin, my friend and sister, without you Lily would still be called "Female Character". You've been such a support system through this crazy journey and I'm so happy we did it together.

Kimberly, thank you for sharing a brain with me! Words cannot express how much I love and appreciate you. You kick me in the ass when I need it, keep me motivated, and help me stay focused amid my sea of chaos. Facebook may drive me crazy, but I'll always be thankful because it brought us together. I'd be lost without you.

Cassie, you're a hell of an editor and you've helped me come so far. You treat my characters with such love and respect. I know when I send you my words, they are in good hands. I'm constantly learning from you!

Paige Randall. How I miss our Friday afternoon brainstorming sessions. You've been with me every step of the way, and I'm so lucky to have you. Your hatred for the semi-colon has changed me forever!

Kari, what can I say? You're such a beautiful person, and emit rays of sunshine and happiness with each person you connect with. But the grace of God, I'm lucky enough to be one of those people.

Jesey, I'll never be able to express how much your friendship means to me. Even though we only know each other virtually, you've become one of my dearest friends. And in my darkest times, you always let me know you were there.

Keri, the fact that after all these years, we're still friends and books have been yet another way for us to stay connected makes me ecstatic. I am so thankful you're willing to read my work and I know that you give it the critical eye I need. Being able to trust in that honesty is such a rare occurrence, and I'm so lucky I can trust you. And you are the writing block master!

To all of the bloggers that have read my work and supported me, THANK YOU!! I know the pressures you are all under, and I respect how much time, effort and energy it takes to keep a blog rolling. I'm so appreciative that you've taken the time to read and promote my work. Special love goes out to my Schmexy Girls Jen, Trish and Jesey, Fiction Fan Girls, Jaime and Dena, all of the girls at One Click Addicts, and all the ByoB girls!

Thank you to my family who has been so patient and understanding through this entire journey.

One last final note... I've gotten several reviews that my story is complicated with so much going on. It's an indisputable fact. Friends ask me all the time: "Where do you come up with this stuff?" I do an absurd amount of research, but I genuinely must give my mother the credit. Mom and I have bonded over Lifetime movies for as long as I can remember. Movies full of plot twists, non-stop drama, and plenty of bad guys lurking in the shadows. It's now how my brain works!

That time with my mother has been precious to me, and I know I'd never be where I am without her. She raised me to believe that there is nothing I can't do, and I believe that to my core. So when thought about writing a book, I knew I could do it. That confidence (and at times craziness) is thanks to my mom. Love you, Mom!

And special love to Dad who tolerated years of watching "the man hater channel."

Thank you so much for reading Lily and Gavin's story. Stay tuned for book 3!

Made in the USA
Charleston, SC
22 October 2015